MW01259185

Flood Summer

FLOOD SUMMER

A Novel

TRENTON LEE STEWART

SOUTHERN METHODIST UNIVERSITY PRESS
Dallas

This novel is a work of fiction. Names, characters, places, and incidents are either the product of the author's imagination or are used fictitiously.

Copyright © 2005 by Trenton Lee Stewart
First edition, 2005
All rights reserved

Requests for permission to reproduce material from this work should be sent to:
Rights and Permissions
Southern Methodist University Press
PO Box 750415
Dallas, Texas 75275-0415

Cover art: "Rain—Exit 106" by Warren Criswell

Jacket and text design by Teresa W. Wingfield

LIBRARY OF CONGRESS CATALOGING-IN-PUBLICATION DATA

Stewart, Trenton Lee.
Flood summer : a novel / by Trenton Lee Stewart.—1st ed.
p. cm.
ISBN 0-87074-505-0 (acid-free paper)
1. Floods—Fiction. 2. Trailers—Fiction. 3. Arkansas—Fiction. 4. Failure (Psychology)—Fiction. I. Title.

PS3619.T535F58 2005
813'.6—dc22 2005050013

Printed in the United States of America on acid-free paper

10 9 8 7 6 5 4 3 2 1

For my parents

Acknowledgments

I wish to thank my parents, Jerry and Sandi Stewart, for their unflagging faith and support; my wife, Sarah Beth Estes, and my friends Mark Barr, Todd Kimm, and Lisa Taggart, for their thoughtful and valuable comments on early drafts; and my editor, Kathryn Lang, for her green lights and checkmarks.

Prologue

Summer nights are best. Black pavement giving up the ghost of a summer day, the highway night warm and heavy as sleep. Between trouble and trouble there is always the highway.

Along the roadside, reflecting markers flash past. At first Marie counts them; then, drowsily, she forgets. The window is down, and there is nothing for her but the strong warm wind, tangling her hair, wearing away her thoughts. It holds her in a warm, rushing silence. Outside under the headlights the road is short. The yellow dashes slide into view and slide away. Now and then she is caught off guard by a sudden impenetrable darkness of trees where she thought the highway lay, by the body-pull of a deep curve, finding herself leaning against the passenger door as the car holds the center. She remembers only as afterthought the elbow-jointed arrows of yellow highway signs they have passed. She is dreamy and can't guess the road.

Beside her, her mother grips the wheel, slumped into another long night's drive, relaxed by habit, apparently unthinking. Her newly blond hair has lost its haphazard part in the rush of air from the open windows. A cigarette hangs from her lips, its red glow brightening and dulling slightly as she breathes. In the dark cab of the car there is only this pulse of red and a faint green luminescence from the dash. Occasionally her left hand reaches up, and she flicks the ashes into the stream of air at the window, places the cigarette between her lips again. When it is finished she will let the wind take it, and in the outside mirror Marie will catch a glimpse, a small shower of red sparks on the dark road behind them.

The radio is on, but quietly because her mother thinks Marie is sleeping, or should be sleeping, and the wind carries the strains of music over Marie's head, melodies faint and thin and distant as sleigh bells in a story, the deep sleepy voice of a late-night disc jockey coming to her in snatches; he's talking to her but she can't make out what he says, can't wake herself up to listen. He intones parts of phrases and dedicates a song, the words faint and warm and senseless as they slip by above her.

The dashboard cigarette lighter pops out with a click. Glowing red circles pass their color to the end of her mother's new cigarette, fade to orange, disappear into the dash again. Her mother shifts slightly; she sits differently when she has a cigarette, her elbow propped in the open window, her chin a little higher and to the side. Her eyes flick to Marie and return to the road. She sighs unconsciously, settles into her new position. Doesn't even check her watch. They're making good time.

Marie finds herself slipping away.

Somewhere in the darkness lies an invisible, stagnant lake, and as they pass it an insect slaps against the windshield like a fat raindrop, smearing. Another hits with the same quiet thud, then another, then more and more, an uneven heavy spattering.

"It's a bug storm," Marie murmurs.

"Shit," her mother says, fiddling with the windshield wiper knobs, triggering streams onto the glass. The wipers leave a fan-shaped sheen of insect. They groan and shudder and pause, groan and shudder and pause. After a minute she switches them off. The glass, speckled and streaked, looks like a half-erased and inscrutable map.

Marie watches and listens from a distance, down under the warm cover of wind. The faraway music scratches, pauses, and resumes as her mother changes stations. Now the radio has picked up the sounds of a woozy steel guitar, wobbly legged and sleepy and drunk. It eases itself sleepily onto the wind. One song eases into another. Through half-closed eyes Marie glimpses a flash of red at the top of the windshield, reflecting the road behind them, tumbling cigarette sparks on the dark drowsing highway.

Part 1

Chapter 1

It was still coming down. The ditches were running like creeks. Abe plowed the center of the road, his truck fenders sending up arcs of spray. At his trailer, where he'd packed a small bag and left extra food in the hubcap—sliding it back under the porch so his cats could eat out of the rain—he had looked across the pasture to see Simmons's cows standing flank-deep in mud. Last month Simmons's old barn had finally gone over with the help of a tractor, but the new barn wasn't finished yet—there'd been too much rain. Now his cattle were planted in the muck, living in a swamp and no help for it.

Abe cut through the neighborhood behind town. Lockers Creek, Arkansas, was a small, wooded place, more of a highway village than a town, a motley scatter of ranch houses and low-slung brick homes, clapboard and aluminum-sided duplexes, the occasional new trailer with a porch and latticework. In some yards thick patches of crab grass lay under standing water, country seaweed, still alive and stubbornly green. Rusted shed roofs sagged under the weight of a month's rain, sweetgum balls bobbing in the roofwater like tiny spiked mines. Most people had accepted that there was nothing to be done but look out at the mess through streaming windows; still, during a recent afternoon lull a few optimistic old women had put flowers in their tire planters. In the waning light Abe could just make out the flowers, floating now like lilies in a frog pond.

He turned onto Main Street and got caught at the traffic light. He was just shaking loose of a bad mood, and he considered running it, but someone was sure to see him. The townfolk were funny about the new light, having paid good money for it. So he waited and looked around. Sandbags were banked all along Main Street: small-town businessmen with no trust in the weather and no patience for umbrellas had been stacking their storefronts in their shirtsleeves, their slacks rolled up over mudboots. In the rainy evening the abandoned strip had an oddly fortified look, like some shell-haunted city in a war zone. Ridgeway's Grocery, where Abe's mother worked, had a sign in the window that said "Rainwater for sale, cheap." Across the street the post office flagpole stood barren of its American flag, which hadn't flown for forty days because of rain and threat of rain.

He tried to remember the last time he'd checked his mail. He ought to go by next week. The postmistress would tell people he was avoiding his bills.

The light turned from red to nothing; the green bulb was out and nobody would change it in the rain. Abe went on past the grocery store and turned onto the highway, passing the boarded-up Dairy Shack and the Phillips 66 and Purdue's used car lot and Emma's Café, until finally he was clear of the town and eastbound for the Saline County line.

His truck tires sizzled on the wet asphalt. The windshield wipers rocked ceaselessly. From time to time he glanced offroad, with a subtle and indeterminate longing, to where the land fell away into the pine woods. He was too susceptible, he thought, to the forbidding and lonesome feel of them. It made him want to be with someone, although he'd be hard pressed to say who. He and some nameless woman driving together in the rainy twilight, with the deep woods out there and that lonesome good feeling he hadn't had in ages, like something's about to happen.

He tried the radio, but in this weather, in these woods, the radio was hopeless.

Just before Owensville, coming into the hard curve there, his headlights caught something in the trees. A flash, silver and quick. He pulled over and peered out into the woods. A flat plane of gray water spread over the ground, dimpling under the rain and the dripping trees, lapping against the trunks. The woods had been flooded for weeks, the runoff from the Ouachita Mountains lifting countless creeks. Although Abe had finally grown used to the sight of all that water, he'd never seen a fish flip out there before, and he marveled at the thought. As a boy he had played down among those trees and later would ride his horses there, over that broad forested land between the Ouachita foothills. In the spring, when it was warm and damp, you could ride down from a piney ridge and feel the cool coming off the creeks. Now you couldn't tell creek from land; now fish were threading their way through the trees.

He pulled back onto the highway and in minutes was through Owensville and Crows, towns even tinier than Lockers Creek, and had downshifted his way up the muddy woods road to Jim Townsend's house.

The porch light seemed strangely naked, with not even the bugs out to flutter it up. The tin roof gutters murmured and droned, leaking like faucets at their bolted seams. Through the kitchen window he saw Jackie bent over a recipe, thumbing a loose strand of gray hair behind her ear. She was in most respects a plain woman, small of stature, with unremarkable features, but she had been a dancer as a girl and still had that lovely dancer's way of bending with a straight back. A certain efficient grace. As a boy Abe had thought he loved her, would somehow grow up to marry his friend's mother.

He tapped the window. She turned and saw him under the porch light, smiling at her through the spray of leaking gutter water that splashed up from the railing. She smiled back, somewhat mournfully, and beckoned him inside. Abe hesitated at the door a long moment, getting drenched.

In the living room an argument had started up. Repeat and Kylie were on their knees over a spread map, shouting at each other, drawing their fingers along disparate highway routes with the insistence of men tracing their own lifelines. Behind them the television blared the evening news. Roberto, ever blithe, was the only one watching it. He sat in the recliner with his arms folded across his barrel chest, ignoring the others, brown pug-face intent on the screen. He nodded as Abe slicked back his hair and wiped his shoes on the sodden mat.

"Pitt," he said, by way of greeting.

Repeat climbed to his feet, saying, "Pitt, talk some sense into this idiot," his voice cracking at the end. Repeat had a perpetual splinter in his voice, the result of a blow to the throat his father had given him when he was a boy. If he spoke loudly, the effect was worse; you sometimes had to infer his meaning.

"Just a minute," Abe said.

He went into the kitchen, where Jackie was sliding a pan into the oven with that same straight-backed bend. He stood still in the doorway, hoping he wasn't dripping. He often felt cloddish around her. And he knew what kind of mood she'd be in tonight, with Jim leaving.

"Hey," he said.

She looked over her shoulder at him, her cheeks flushed and brow shining. It was hot and close in the kitchen. "Mr. Pittenger," she said. "How are you?"

"Pretty good, Miss Jones."

"Oh, Lord," she said. "Don't you dare call me that."

"Sorry."

She shut the oven door, its spring hinge creaking, and dusted her hands with two officious claps. "No, don't be sorry. It just surprised me coming from you. I mean, you never called me Mrs. Townsend when my name was Mrs. Townsend, so why should you call me Miss Jones?"

"Did I call you Miss Jones?"

"Yes, you did. You know you did."

"Well, I'm sorry."

"Oh, Abe, I know, I'm just saying is all." She patted his cheek. Her hand was still flour-powdery and smelled like chocolate. "Don't you worry," she said. "I'm just feeling kind of crazy tonight. I mean, it's good. I need to get used to it someday, right? But you of all people have got to keep calling me Jackie. Somebody has to."

"Well, we need to fix that gutter of yours when it stops raining, Jackie."

"That'll be the day. Doesn't seem like it ever will."

"Weatherman says it's supposed to clear up by Tuesday."

"Oh sure, the weatherman says," she said, a little distractedly. She was checking her recipe. Abe got ready. These days, whenever her mind wandered, it came back angry.

Sure enough, after a moment she reached and set the oven timer with an irritated jerk of her hand. "At least *you* get to ride down there with him," she said, out of nowhere. "Not everybody can just pick up and go to Florida."

"No, ma'am," he said quietly. He knew she would feel bad for saying that. "Are those your seven-layer cookies?"

"Mm-hm. They ought to be ready in time to send them off with you. They don't take long once you get them in the oven." She turned away to wash her hands, but not before he saw that wounded look on her face. He waited, but she kept her back to him.

"So. Jim in his room?"

"He's on the phone with that . . . with his *father*. I guess he wanted to ask the best way down there. Abe, promise me y'all will be careful. You won't do dumb boy stuff?"

"We won't," he said. He waited, but she didn't turn.

"I better go calm these guys down before they tear up your house," he said.

Kylie was still on his knees at the map. Roberto and Repeat were watching clips of a fight on the news, Repeat shadowing the moves as he watched. He looked like something of a boxer himself, his strong back and shoulders prominent beneath his tight yellow T-shirt. The only faltering thing about Repeat was his voice. Though not a big man, he was hard and fast and certain of everything. He'd just finished his fifth year on a track scholarship. He and Kylie had only got back into town the week before, down for the summer from the university in Fayetteville.

"Take a look at this map, Pitt," Kylie said from the floor.

"I don't want any part of it. I don't care how we get there as long as we get there."

"Just look," Kylie insisted. He stared up with those wandering, bulbous eyes of his, eyes that made you feel disoriented if you weren't used to them. "Let me show you what I'm saying." He gestured irritatedly at Repeat. "He won't listen to common sense, and now he's pretending to ignore me."

"All right, what have you got?"

He stood behind Kylie and watched without interest. Repeat was not pretending to ignore him, Abe knew. Repeat didn't pretend anything, and anyway they had all learned the trick of shutting Kylie out. Abe was doing it right now. He wasn't listening but wondering instead what it would be like without Jim in town, wondering too about Jim's lapse in judgment, telephoning his father with Jackie here on this of all nights; and in another part of his mind he was noticing how from this angle you had a perfect view of Kylie's bald spot, which normally you didn't see on account of his height. Noticing also that Kylie had applied some kind of tanning cream to that little circle of scalp, or maybe it was brown shoe polish, in an effort to trick the eye.

"You see my point?" Kylie said.

"Looks good to me."

"Well, tell *him* that!"

"Y'all keep it down," he said, heading down the hall. "Jackie's got enough on her mind without you giving her a headache."

Kylie spluttered and thumped the map. The television volume went up.

He found Jim sitting on his bed in shorts and a T-shirt, reading. It was like any other time Abe came to find him. Now, though, the bed was stripped clean of sheets and pillows, and except for the phone sitting on the mattress beside him, the room was utterly barren. Jim looked up from his paperback.

"Hey," he said. "You're here."

"Been here. What are you doing? I thought you were on the phone with your dad."

"He wasn't home. His little trollop said she'd have him call if he got back in a few minutes." He checked his watch. "I don't think it's gonna happen."

Jim sat up and looked around at his empty room, maybe hoping to muster some nostalgia. The walls had once been papered with newspaper clippings, outdated calendars, photographs, and post cards. Now they were bare, and hundreds of nail and tack holes swirled wildly across the white plaster like the photographic negative of a galaxy. At the sight of them, the last thirty days of work kicked awake in Abe's head. Despite his silent promise that he would never do such a thing again, he had gone back to work for his father hanging sheetrock and blowing ceilings—if only until the rain let up and he could get back on roofs. Looking at Jim's pocked, scarred walls, he felt an unwanted urge to tape and hang, to board them over and spackle them smooth.

Jim had quit looking around. He wore a look of amused resignation, as if he'd hoped for more but couldn't have said what, and thought it was kind of funny he'd hoped at all.

"They done fighting yet?" he said. "Seems quieter in there now."

"More or less."

"They're already getting on my nerves, Abe."

"Well, you better enjoy it while you can."

Jim stood up and stretched. In the empty room his slight build seemed even smaller. His mustache was well-trimmed as usual, but a heavy gray shadow of stubble spread over his cheeks. He'd risen before dawn to have breakfast with Jackie, who drove into Hot Springs each morning to St. Joseph's Hospital, where she worked as a nurse. Jim's coarse brown hair, combed back with water at the start of the day, now stuck up in a mass, almost as if he had teased it. He looked out the curtainless window at the muddy yard, at the rain falling steadily on the patch of ground illuminated by the porch light.

"It's gonna be a long night," he said.

Originally it had been Abe's idea to drive down to Tallahassee with Jim, taking a bus back up to Arkansas. Then Repeat got wind of it and suggested they all go together, a send-off trip and a chance to get out of the rain. It was more the latter than the former, and everybody knew it. Repeat and the others liked Jim well enough, but he was Abe's friend, not theirs. Jim had always been a private sort. Even as kids they had all figured him for college and never to be seen again. But then Jackie was such a wreck after his father left, Jim stuck around to shore her up. Stuck around three years, working a desk job he hated in Hot Springs, clerking for a couple of businessmen he was smarter than, until Jackie finally quit fighting the divorce and signed the papers. His sister had long since married and moved to California. Now Jim, too, was leaving, following the job his father had promised him and enrolling in the university down there.

"How is she?" he asked, jerking his head toward the kitchen.

Abe shrugged. "I guess you know better than I do."

"Yeah, well, that's how it's been." He took a last glance around the room. "Okay, listen, you get those dumbasses out of the house for a few minutes, and then I'll be out."

Abe had no trouble herding them to the cars; they were impatient to go. Especially Repeat, who kept saying two days in Florida weren't enough. He wanted to stay longer, but Kylie and Abe both had to be back Monday morning to work. Kylie worked summers at a Photo Stop in Little Rock. He used to work at the one in Hot Springs until they offered him a quarter raise if he switched locations. The drive was more than twice as long, which meant he lost money once you figured in gas; but he would be a temporary assistant manager, and so Kylie, being Kylie, accepted. Repeat, though, was not one to let work interfere with play—especially not others' work—and he'd pressed the issue until he was sure that Abe, at least, wasn't giving in.

One of the things Repeat didn't yield on was taking his car, despite its being too small for such a long trip. He had insisted, arguing that the Camaro was most suited for cruising the strips, and that anyway on the way down one of them would ride with Jim in his car, which was packed to the ceiling in back but had room in the passenger's seat.

He'd also insisted on bringing his stepfather's CB radios to keep them in touch on the drive, and as he took them out now and started hooking them up, Kylie hustled over and climbed into the Camaro, claiming squatter's rights in what he figured to be the party car. Repeat finished with the radio inside Jim's car, then stayed there. Kylie made a fuss about this, as he made a fuss about anything irregular, but it made sense in light of their running argument—they didn't need a full-on fight at the outset. So Abe and Roberto got into the Camaro, and they all waited damply and peevishly with their doors closed against the rain, until Jim charged out to them with a covered tray of cookies in his hand, and Abe saw Jackie standing with her arms crossed behind the screen door, shoulders hunched as if she were cold.

They drove out through mud onto asphalt, out of the hard rain into a fine sprinkle; east then south, drizzle blurring the harsh white lights of Benton, Butterfield, Malvern, Sheridan. They went complaining through Pine Bluff, where instead of filtering the chemical stench of the paper mill the rain seemed to percolate it. The lights were behind them long before the smell was. Then the smell was gone too, and it was just the drizzle and the darkness again. Night settled in full—they began to see more possums than traffic on the slick black roads. In the mist the sparse lights of Star City passed like a hazy, distant dream.

Kylie did most of the talking until Roberto interrupted to say, "Two hours of sunshine, man. Is all I want, just two hours. Just two hours for hitting the beach, and it'll be worth all this driving bullshit."

They looked at him. Roberto didn't talk much, maybe because of his English, maybe by natural inclination. When he did speak, you always stopped to look at him, the way you do when you spy a deer in your front yard.

Abe said, "Why not three?"

"I take three, man, but two is okay."

"We had sun for a minute tonight. Didn't you see it? We had us an actual sunset."

"No way I didn't see it. Jim, he told me about it. I was asleeping with the goddamn TV, I guess."

"I seen it," said Kylie. "Literally took me a minute to figure out what it was."

"It was a big red son of a bitch," Abe said, "all black around the edges like a blood blister."

"Like a what?"

"Like a *sangre . . . Como se dice* 'blister'? It was all dark around the edges, because of the clouds."

"Fine," Roberto said. "Like a nice blood thing."

"Blood blister."

"Blood blister. Fine. So why is every time it stop raining I asleeping on the goddamn couch? I swear when we get there I ain't asleeping one wink, man."

Kylie said, "Well, but the rain didn't stop, though. It was still raining. Did you see that, Pitt? That was the weird thing, with the rain still coming down like it was."

Abe had seen it. He had dropped by his parents' house for supper, something he seldom did anymore despite his mother's entreaties, and afterward he'd stood in his old room, holding the filmy curtain aside with his elbow and staring out at the improbable red sun beyond the trees. In the driveway, rain drummed on his truck. The sky was dark gray and heavy. But there was the sun, a red stain in the gloom like the deep blood-dark in undercooked meat.

He'd stood looking at it, trying without luck to remember the sailor's adage his father had taught him, and considered braving the rain to climb the hill and watch the sun set again, as he had sometimes done as a boy. But it didn't really set. It simply disappeared behind a distant mass of dark clouds, and the trees across the road grew indistinct, fuzzy with the dusk and drizzle. His focus shifted to the neighbors' yard, to the abandoned mud-spattered plastic balls and bicycles the kids had brought out, full of hope, when the rain stopped for a few hours. Then to the side yard, where rainstruck dogwood blossoms lay in pink and white circles around the muddy base of their trunks. And going to the other window he saw his father's tool shed—from which Abe, as an adult, was no longer prohibited but which he still avoided—with its new, precarious tilt. A foundation built on sand, he thought, with a certain mean satisfaction, though he knew every backyard shed in town was built on sand, more or less.

His ghostly reflection in the window was scowling. He was annoyed with himself. The sun had made him hopeful, had got him thinking maybe the rain was over and he would have an excuse to stop working for his father. It was his own fault. He wasn't that hard up for money, but his father kept prodding him, and after a while he got to thinking it might not be so bad. As it turned out, nothing had changed. Every day they met at the work site, groggy and grim, and over a cup of coffee they would take a quick look at their previous day's work, then begin the new day's work in earnest, in discomfort, and in silence.

His father had always wanted Abe to work for him but was really only suited for working alone. He was irritable, sallow and silent, a hard drinker with teeth and fingertips irredeemably jaundiced from nicotine, who in spite of all headache and gut-pain and weariness rose every morning at dawn. In the evenings, after the supper dishes were cleared and he had a few drinks in him, he was more pleasant, would work around the house or help Abe's mother in the kitchen, then watch television until midnight with the sound turned low. But during the day he brooked no conversation, not even a radio, and Abe preferred any amount of roof-work back pain and sunburn to working with him.

His mother knocked on the open bedroom door and leaned against the doorframe. "Did you see that?" she said, lifting a half-smoked cigarette to her lips. He saw soap suds drying near her elbow. "Red sky at night, sailor's delight."

"I was just trying to think of that."

She exhaled smoke through her nostrils. A tall woman—almost as tall as Abe, if not so slender—his mother had brown hair teased and hairsprayed into bangs, just going gray in places, and a habitual slouch she had developed as a younger woman embarrassed by her height. Her eyes, very dark and slightly protruding, were like the glossy button eyes sewed on a doll, her face long and angular. Abe had got her face but not her eyes—his were blue and deep set like his father's—and he'd got her smile too, though you could never tell it, because she only smiled nervously, little quick flashes of teeth that were gone at once.

"Kind of put me in a good mood," she said. "Seeing the sun like that. I'm thinking about making a cake. You want a lemon cake?"

"I won't be here to eat it. You ought to make whatever kind you want."

"If I started it now, you might could have a piece before you left."

"I've got to go here in just a minute. Thanks, though."

"Well," she said. She shifted to lean against the other side of the doorframe. "How's Jackie taking it?"

"Who knows. What do you think?"

"I think it's got to hurt seeing your son go off to live with the man who left you. A man who said there was nothing worth saving except maybe the children."

"He's not going to live with him. He's moving into one of his dad's duplexes. Mr. Townsend's living with his girlfriend now."

"That's even worse."

"Well, you can't really blame Jim. Can't beat the rent, and it is Florida, after all."

"Florida ain't so great as they make it out to be."

"I guess I wouldn't know."

She was cupping her hand under her cigarette butt, looking thoughtful. Abe had an empty glass. He held it out to her. She smiled her quick smile and dropped the butt into the glass.

"We used to go when I was a girl," she said. "The ocean's nice. So *big*, like a great big . . . I don't know. Well, like a ocean, I guess; that's why they call it that. And the beach is pretty nice. But it's too crowded down there. I couldn't stand it, bumping into sweaty people every which way you turned."

"I guess I'll see," he said. He took her wrist and turned it gently to check her watch.

"You don't have to go just yet, do you?" she asked. It was almost a plea. Abe was about the only company she ever had.

He squeezed her arm, kissed her cheek. "I'd better get. Repeat's been champing at the bit all day. Thanks for dinner."

He went and leaned in through the living room doorway. His father sat in the recliner in front of the television, cradling a glass of whiskey. The room was dim except for the television. "Taking off, Dad," he said. "See you Monday."

His father twisted toward him in his chair. His cheeks were flushed and stubbled, his eyes rimmed with red. "Off to the redneck riviera, huh?" He reached for his back pocket. "Come here a minute."

"That's all right, Dad."

"Get on over here," he said, pulling out his wallet. "I ain't bestowing no fortune on your head, but you can take what little I offer you." He handed Abe a twenty dollar bill. "Y'all have some fun for me."

"Yes, sir. Thanks."

"You're gonna be tired come Monday morning."

"I'll be all right."

"I won't pay you for sleeping, you know."

"Don't worry about it."

"I ain't. I'm just telling you."

Abe waited, not knowing what to say to this. He knew what he wanted to say, but he didn't say it. His father leaned back into his chair and said, "Y'all have fun now."

"We'll sure try."

As he went to his truck he pictured himself tearing out of the gravel drive, swearing, trying to yank the steering wheel off. He saw it too clearly, enough to worry him. You must practice the art of quick forgetting, he told himself. This sounded like the instruction of a kung-fu guru, which almost made him smile. It calmed him down. He got in and backed quietly onto Merrill Road. Drove the two miles to his trailer, fed the cats, packed his bag, headed out. Artfully and quickly forgetting.

"You know what I think I saw while ago?" he said now. They had passed through Monticello, its lights a constellation in the rearview.

"Excuse me," Kylie said. "Someone was talking."

"What you see?" Roberto said.

"I think I saw a fish jump out in the woods."

"Yeah, I seen a couple too. They coming up out of the creeks. We gonna have to take a boat out there, maybe catch us some."

In Bastrop, Louisiana, Abe took the wheel in Jim's car, and Repeat went back to his Camaro. No sooner had Abe cranked the ignition than Jim settled back and opened a can of beer. He saluted the others with it as they pulled out of the parking lot. They saw Repeat frown and scramble for the radio.

"Where'd y'all get the beer?" he said.

"Found it," Jim replied, and snapped off the CB.

"How could Repeat not know you had an ice chest?"

"Kept it under the blanket. And it's got one of them plastic freeze-a-majiggies in it, so you don't hear the ice sloshing around. You want a swig?"

Abe took a pull and handed it back to Jim, who drank it down with unusual earnestness. "My dad finally called," he said, crushing the can. "Right after you went outside. I was in the bathroom, so I guess you know who answered the phone."

Abe winced. "Now why did she do that?"

"You got me."

"She all right?"

"Well, when I came out she was just standing there, all stiff, squeezing the phone with both hands like it might try to kill her. They talked for a minute and then she handed it over to me."

"And?"

"And that's it. She didn't say anything about it. She was upset but trying hard not to show it, you know."

"I know they don't ever talk."

"No. And I shouldn't ever have called him from the house, not tonight. Pretty damn stupid. I don't know what I was thinking." He sighed, reaching back for another beer. "You're gonna drive for a few hours at least, right?"

"I'll drive as long as you want."

"That's my boy."

They went for miles along a wooded stretch of highway, the wet road hissing under the tires. The rain was soft yet, but the wind grew blustery, the oak trees swaying and shuddering. Abe swerved now and then to avoid broken branches in the road, some of them dead wood but some still feathery with wet green leaves, the exposed sapwood gleaming like naked bone in the headlights.

"Just had them a storm, looks like."

Jim had been working the radio dial with no luck. He switched it off.

"You got your guitar back there?" Abe said. "Maybe you ought to break it out."

"Sorry. It's in the trunk."

"I can pull over."

"I couldn't play it anyway. It's full of underwear."

"It's what?"

"I took the strings off and packed it with underwear. One less bag to carry."

Abe grinned. "That ain't hardly natural, son."

"It needed new strings anyway," Jim said. "Wish I'd thought of it, though. A little traveling music would do us good."

"You're still planning to hook up with a band down there. You haven't changed your mind."

"I don't know. Maybe I will."

"No maybe to it. One of us has got to make it big."

"Don't put it all on me. What about you?"

"Fine, I'll make it big as a clumsy strummer. Clumsy strummers have a certain mystique."

"You could do more than strum if you'd ever practice. You've never practiced for shit."

"I used to practice, I just practiced strumming is all."

"Well, and you spent most of your time fooling with your horses," Jim said. When Abe didn't respond, he added, "Which, that was a good thing. I don't mean it was bad."

"I know," Abe said. He checked his rearview mirror, but the view was obscured by boxes. He checked the side mirrors. Jim watched him a while, finally shook his head. He slumped down into his seat, bony knees pressed against the glove compartment. He sipped his beer and sighed again. "We were gonna be rock stars," he said.

Abe laughed and glanced over. "We sure were."

"Country poets on the road. Rocking the Delta, rolling the hills. You remember that? Sex and checks and *guit*-tar necks."

"I guess there's still a chance," Abe said.

They went for some time in silence, only wipers and rain. They were used to driving together. As a teenager Abe had often ridden one of his horses out to Jim's house, following game trails and creek beds through the foothills, cutting across the highway and coming up the long dirt drive. It would take him an hour to ride out. Jim would be reading or playing guitar in his room, even on the most beautiful days, and if it was a weekend Jackie would be working in her garden alone—back then Mr. Townsend lived there but was seldom home—and would call out to him: "Thank God you're here. Kick that boy in the pants, will you? I swear I'm raising a grub worm." Abe would prod Jim out of the house, and Jim, stretching and gazing up at the sky, would suddenly seem to gain height and color. He'd take a deep breath of the clean pine air and break into a surprised grin. "My God," he'd say, "what was I doing inside?" He meant it, too. But he was always inside when Abe found him.

They would drive the back roads, looking for anything halfway interesting and sometimes finding it—an escaped band of cows grazing the ditch, delinquent boys burning a shed—and talk and talk. Talking was their natural state. Sometimes after hours of driving they'd stop to fill up at the Phillips 66, go inside to pay, and get back into the truck without ever having stopped talking. There was never nothing to talk about, as Jim liked to say, and never enough time. For most of one summer they'd gone round and round about God and death and love until Jim, disgusted, said, "Let's face it, we don't know jack about any of it," and Abe, feigning alarm, said, "But if we did know, could we even tell? Maybe we know but can't know about knowing it." So they went round and round about knowing, and in this way drove off the good afternoons. On the bad ones they stayed inside arguing about books, or Abe would show him poetry or stories he'd written, and Jim would offer brutal critiques, making liberal use of the word *execrable*, of which he was overly fond. The poetry—usually about some girl who'd disappointed Abe, or whom he'd disappointed—was almost always execrable, the stories flawed but good. Eventually Abe just quit writing poetry. They argued about that too, debated the merit of writing bad poetry rather than none at all. They made elaborate plans to become famous.

Thinking back on those days, Abe said, "I guess you're leaving just in time."

Jim sniffed, looked blinking at him, rolled his neck. "I think I was dreaming," he said after a moment.

"Dozed off?"

"Something about chickens," he said. "Chickens or pigeons."

"Go on back to sleep then."

"No, I want to hear this. Why am I leaving just in time?"

"A lame joke. I was going to say it looks like we've just this minute run out of things to talk about."

"Oh," Jim said. "Well, yes, that is lame."

They fell into silence again. These were likely the last hours they'd ever spend driving and talking together, they would miss all that talking, and neither of them felt like talking.

There was rain through Monroe and Tallulah and all the way to Ferriday, where they crossed the Mississippi River into Natchez. The bridge was longer than any Abe had ever been on; it hardly seemed like a bridge. The metal reflected an eerie blue overhead. Jim pressed his face against the window, staring up through the beams at the sky.

"You'll want to take a look at this," he said.

"What?"

"Stars."

The windshield wipers muttered against the glass. Abe turned them off. When they cleared the bridge they were driving on dry road. Above them a low ragged edge of cloud was dragging slowly from south to north. Beyond its fringes he saw a deep black sky powdered with stars.

"Oh, I love Mississippi," he said.

Behind them Repeat was flashing his headlights. Jim switched on the CB, and they heard Kylie's voice coming through: "—to pick up? The rain's gone! Do you see this shit, you dumb—"

Jim switched it off again.

They rolled their windows down and breathed the cool night air. There was a faint, tart odor in it, like split grapes. The road curved away from the bridge, skirting a bluff that overhung the river. Kudzu blanketed the ground and scaled the trees. The Mississippi moved invisibly far below them. A barge crept along its surface, a black mass demarcated by tiny blinking lights. After Arkansas, after the rain, it all seemed faintly exotic, no matter that they'd come by way of a 1984 Chevy Cavalier.

Jim cracked open another beer and held it up. "Here's to running like rabbits from all that ails us."

"To running like rabbits," Abe said.

They hit Panama City Beach by morning, and once they'd lugged the bags up to their third-floor suite, blinking like troglodytes in the unfamiliar sun, they made their way to the water, not chancing any time on sleep. In the end, they spent only a few hours beneath the glorious empty sky before rain drove them from the beach, a storm sweeping in over the Gulf. They returned to their cars in shoes still crusted with Arkansas mud, anomalous and sand-filled and hot, but they were happy, drunk with that extravagant sunshine, and they found a restaurant nearby and soaked sweet crab meat in butter as rain streamed down the foggy windows, and didn't care at all about the rain. In spite of the wet, or perhaps because of it, the shops outside were busy. Knots of youthful scroungers in every doorway, huddled under awnings and umbrellas. Bright clothes everywhere and bright skin, and Repeat insisted that this should be them—Repeat could have gone for days on the mere sight of all that skin and color—but the others insisted on the motel and sleep.

It wasn't until late in the evening that Repeat managed to rouse them. He flipped on the lights and flung open the curtains, the rings making a teeth-gritting sound as they scraped along the metal rods, and found the radio and turned it up. "It's dry outside, boys," he said, dancing into the bedroom to shave. "The rain's gone to bed, and it's time for us to rise and shine. We have got to hit the *town*."

Blearily they rose, splashing water on their faces and making trips to the open door to see for themselves. The sidewalks were damp, but the air was warm and clear. The sky, not yet dark, was a vault of deep blue, with streaks of orange and pink on the horizon. Pigeons burbled from the roof overhead. Standing at the door each of them sniffed, spat, and nodded in turn. It was a beautiful evening.

They packed themselves into the Camaro and eased out into the traffic. The Strip was jammed with cars. They crept along with the windows down, the warm air soft on their faces. Repeat had bought wine coolers and they poured them into empty soda cans and drank from the cans. Cars honked up and down the street like geese passing the word. Tipsy clusters of half-clad youth strayed smilingly into the jam, approaching stopped cars for impromptu conversations, attempted seductions. The streets and sidewalks were spilling over with people, with the hordes of the young and the want-to-be young. Tan skin, bare legs, long blue shadows under the streetlights; wide-open radios, seismic basses, engines doing the rev and grind. Every minute it was playing out, the ceaseless, hilarious, damned routine of unfigured lives: the jiltings and acquisitions, the loves negotiated, begun, and ended, the sweet liquors purchased and sucked down and vomited in vast quantities. From the back seat Abe watched the people streaming by. He spoke wryly with the groups of girls who called to them from the sidewalks. He listened to the excited chatter of his friends. He laughed and talked crazily, feeling a little happy and a little hopeless and overcome.

At a red light Repeat jumped from the car and ran to join some girls who had called out to him, leaving the driver's seat empty. Kylie climbed over and took the wheel. Jim and Roberto got out of the car too. Abe started to follow and then thought: You can't leave Kylie.

The light turned green.

"What the hell you want me to do?" Kylie yelled out the window.

"We'll be here," Repeat said, waving him on. "Come back and pick us up."

Jim looked back over his shoulder for Abe, frowned, gestured for him to follow, then understood. He shrugged and waved. "See you in a bit," he called. He looked very small next to Roberto and Repeat, his legs thin and pale, with the first tinge of sunburn coming on. But he seemed happy. He had one foot in the future, and it was doing him good.

Abe climbed up into the passenger seat.

"Can you believe this shit?" Kylie was saying. "We get stuck with the car? I can't believe it."

"We can find a place to park it if you want."

"Yeah, that's an idea. Let's park the son of a bitch somewheres and walk back there. I don't want to be stuck in a car while they're out meeting girls. I mean, come *on*. I bet you Repeat'll get laid before we even make it back there."

"I doubt it."

"I'll bet you a hundred dollars."

They couldn't find a place to park. They couldn't even turn around. The traffic moved in spurts, a few feet at a time. Abe sat with his arm out the window, watching the people go by. Sometimes he made eye contact with girls in other cars; sometimes he drew a smile. One girl in a car full of girls blew him a kiss, laughed, and waved good-bye. He smiled back and in delayed response lifted a hand to wave, but she never turned to see it.

"This is unbelievable," Kylie was saying. "Look at all these chicks, man. They're all just looking for a good time. Just dying to have some fun. Which that is *nothing* like back home. And we're stuck in the car. We've got to get out there and talk to them, Pitt, you know? Make something happen. We can't spend all the time alone in this car."

Abe was watching the disappearing taillights of that last one in the side mirror. "You used to bitch about not having a car," he said irritably. "Now you're in this Camaro, which you have always coveted, you're cruising in Florida, and you're bitching about it. Make up your mind."

"No, it's one thing to have everybody in the car together, and it's another to be trapped with the car and not be able to get away from it. You know? He should *not* have skipped on us like that. That was cheap, man. Which I guess I shouldn't expect any different from Repeat."

They drove a mile before managing to turn around, and by the time they reached the place where the others had jumped out, an hour had passed. A cluster of pasty-pale high school boys stood uncertainly under the streetlights there, looking not so much fresh-arrived as just picked up and deposited. They looked, Abe realized, like younger versions of himself and the others. The boys saw him and Kylie looking at them, and they stared back, almost hopefully, as if they wanted their lives explained. He nodded hello. One of them waved. But Repeat and the others were nowhere to be seen.

"Shit!" Kylie said, pounding the steering wheel. He'd been prepared to be furious. "I can't believe this!"

"Calm down."

"What do we do now?"

"Whatever you want. We're not that far from the motel. They can find their own way back, as far as I'm concerned. Maybe they already went there."

"Yeah, maybe so. Should we circle around one more time, see if they show up?"

"I don't care."

Kylie grew quiet, considering. Abe turned the radio up, leaned his seat back, and tried not to think. Kylie looked left, then right, then studied the rearview mirror. "I don't know what to do," he said at last. "You want to check the motel?"

"Sure."

It took another half-hour to reach the motel. Their suite was cold from the air conditioner, and empty. Kylie kicked a plastic shopping bag into the air and swatted wildly at it. "Those assholes!" he yelled.

Abe went outside. A drop of rain landed on the back of his neck. He'd been thinking of going down to the beach, taking a walk, but he was not in the mood to get rained on again. He leaned against the railing. There was a decent view from this height; you could see a good way down the Strip. He turned and started up the stairs.

Kylie had come to the doorway. "What are you doing?"

"Just going up to look around. It's starting to rain again."

"I'll come with you," Kylie said. He seemed calmer. "Serves them bastards right. They'll get rained on."

Abe doubted it. He imagined they'd found their way into a nightclub somewhere. He climbed the stairs to the fourth floor with Kylie behind him, and together they went down the walkway, passing room after room with the window blinds drawn. The motel seemed deserted.

They leaned against the railing as the rain came on. Beneath the eaves they were mostly dry, getting only the occasional tingle of spray when wind caught the rain. In the distance, along the Strip, the colored lights of cars and traffic signals grew misty and blurred, the traffic sounds muted. From somewhere nearby Abe heard the strains of a television. He searched the windows until he saw a flickering blue light beneath a shade three rooms down, and felt an absurd desire to knock on the door and ask to be let in. He felt suddenly old and yet ridiculously young. He thought, Somehow this happened to you. You got too old to be young and too young to be old. You missed your chance, and you don't even know at what. Then he spat into the rain, feeling stupid for thinking it. He pushed back off the railing and moved farther down the walkway, past the room with the television.

Kylie followed him, saying, "Does this stuff ever go away? Will it ever stop?" Trying to pacify Abe now, make up for complaining so bitterly about Repeat and the others by complaining about something else. "It's raining even in goddamn Florida? I mean, you come to Florida you want sunshine, you know? Get a suntan, see the girls in bikinis and all that. Jesus."

Abe stopped walking. They had come around the last corner of the building. The swimming pool lay below them and off to the right, glowing a pale, smoky blue. Rain chopped the water into a thousand tiny waves.

"How was college this year, Kylie?" Abe asked, hoping to derail the griping.

Kylie brightened. "Oh, pretty good. I'm still trying to decide on my major."

"I thought you were going into computers."

"Yeah, but I didn't know you've got to take a ton of math. I never was good at math, you know, and you've got to take a ton of it. So I been thinking about going into recreation."

"Recreation?"

"You know, sports recreation? It's like, teaching different sports and all that. But I haven't decided for sure."

"Plenty of time, I guess."

"Yeah, it might take me a little longer this way, but what the hell."

They watched the rain chopping up the swimming pool.

"You ever miss it?" Kylie asked.

"College? No."

"Did you just hate it or what? People ask me sometimes, and I never know what to tell them. You never tell me this shit."

"I don't?"

"Hell, no."

"All right," Abe said, "I'll tell you. I miss my idea of college, but I don't miss college itself."

"Now what the hell does that mean, your *idea* of college?"

"Forget it. It doesn't mean anything."

"Repeat said you just partied yourself out."

Abe resisted an urge to laugh. Of course Repeat would say that. "You see him much when y'all are up there?"

"Oh, sure. He's pretty busy doing track stuff, but we go to parties. At one of them, man, this one hot chick, I mean hot, she was all over him—Which, girls are always like that with him, you know? I just don't get it. With his screwed-up voice and everything, but it doesn't even seem to matter. It doesn't seem right."

Abe was absently fingering the coins in his pocket, no longer listening. He found a penny by size, pulled it out, and with a quick snap of his arm flung it out over the swimming pool. The idea had come into his mind only the moment before: What the hell, make a wish. He closed his eyes briefly, not so Kylie would see, and thought: anything at all. The penny spun out into the pool lights and plunked into the water.

"Hey, great idea, Pitt!" Kylie said, interrupting himself. "Yeah, man. Good thinking. I'm gonna make a wish too."

Now Abe was embarrassed, but it was pointless to lie. He looked out at the place where the penny had sunk while Kylie dug into his pockets.

"Damn! I only got this quarter. You got anything smaller?"

He checked his pocket. "Nope."

"Damn. I guess this'll just have to do." Kylie closed his eyes, squeezed the quarter, and jerked his arm in the direction of the pool. The quarter sailed off to the left of it, jingling on the concrete and rolling to a stop two feet from the pool.

"God damn son of a bitch!" Kylie cried, flailing his arms furiously in the air before him, like a novice boxer attacking the speed bag. "That's just perfect! That's just the way my life is going!" He stopped flailing and began to pace.

Abe closed his eyes.

"Okay, I'm gonna tell you something," Kylie said. "You want to know what happened to me last year? I haven't told anyone else about this. It was midterm, right, and I met this girl downtown, and we were getting along good, right?"

Abe realized he had heard this story. Repeat had told him.

"We start going out pretty heavy, and a few weeks later I find out she's only seventeen. Can you believe that? But I don't care, I love her, man. She's beautiful and smart and just real, real sweet. She's got family problems. Then her sister finds these pictures I took, you know what I mean? Personal pictures. Of me and her. And she gives them to Kristi's parents. They freak out, tell me I've got to marry her. But hell, I loved her, so I said I would do it. Which it wasn't such a hard decision, I'd marry her just to get her out of that house. She was so great, Pitt, I'm serious. I was fixing to get married and I didn't even care. But she told her parents she wouldn't do that. She wouldn't marry me. She wasn't going to bring me down, she said. And then she told me we couldn't see each other again."

"The parents let you get away with it?"

"Her dad called to yell at me every day for a while. Called me a walleyed mongrel bastard, I'll never forget that. He was real messed up in the head. I mean she had real bad family problems. But then after a while he quit, and it kind of just faded away."

"What about what's her name? Kristi."

A pained look came over Kylie's face. He stopped pacing and stared out into the rain. "She started dating some other college guys." He lowered his voice. "*Black* guys, Pitt. I see her downtown with them, just a-laughing and having a good time like nothing ever happened. She won't even look at me anymore. She acts like she never seen me in her whole life."

Abe nodded. He had heard most of this from Repeat. "You still have the pictures?"

Kylie looked at him out of the corner of his eye. "Yeah. I kept the negatives."

"Did you print them?"

Kylie glanced at him again. Nodded.

"You ever look at them?"

"I never told anybody," he murmured, which Abe suspected was untrue. But then, Repeat had not mentioned it, so maybe it was true after all. "Yeah," he said, "I look at them."

Abe nodded again. He would imagine so. To his surprise, though, Kylie reached for his wallet and dug out a folded envelope, the edges crinkled and bent. From the envelope he took a thin stack of trimmed photographs and held them out.

"You keep them in your *billfold*?" Abe took the photographs and looked questioningly at Kylie, who just shrugged, waiting to see his reaction. They were terrible shots, but they captured enough. Breasts, genitals, flat buttocks, slack mouths. Partly out of politeness, partly from his intense discomfort, he concentrated on the ones that focused only on Kristi's face. A very skinny girl. Black hair falling on bare, bony shoulders. Crooked teeth.

Her eyes red from the flash. Abe felt sad and embarrassed. He handed them back.

"She seems pretty."

Kylie nodded. "I thought so." He gazed at the photos before putting them back into his wallet.

If there was ever a moment to be quiet and let Kylie talk, this was it; but Abe didn't have it in him. He sighed and said, "Well. There any of those wine coolers left?"

"I think one or two, maybe."

"Let's go get them, watch a little TV."

There was one last wine cooler in the car, and they took it back up to the suite and sat on the sofa and cranked up the television volume, propping their feet on Repeat's overnight bag. Abe left the door open so that the damp breeze blew into the room. He let Kylie drink the wine cooler and tried to lose himself in the music videos, with their beautiful women and outlandish backdrops. He hadn't seen any of them. He didn't own a television and only watched it at other people's houses. Kylie had seen them all, and commented on each one until he realized Abe wasn't answering him; then he fell silent. Almost immediately he was asleep, as if talking had been the only thing keeping him awake.

Abe went to the door and looked out. Still raining, though not much. The hell with it, he thought. He glanced back at Kylie, whose expression, soft with sleep, was uncomfortably familiar now that Abe had seen those photographs. He left his shoes by the door and went out into the rain.

The beach was deserted. The ocean seethed in the darkness, a heavy, sleeping sound. Foam slid up the beach and ran cold over his feet. In the distance the blurry yellow lights of a pier stretched over the dark water, and between him and the pier was the flicker of a bonfire. He headed in that direction, curious to see who he'd find trying to keep a fire in the rain. He walked barefooted through the wet sand, wary of crabs, though he saw none. He remembered how powdery the sand had felt earlier in the day, nothing like the beach sand of an Arkansas lake, rough grainy stuff you were just as likely to shovel into a concrete mixer as throw a beach towel on. This fine sand, when it was dry, was soft and hot and blindingly white. Beautiful stuff. Squeaked like snow when you walked through it. Now, in the rain, it was crusty and stuck to his feet. He thumped over it, glad to be alone.

When he neared the fire, he stopped several yards off and crouched behind a dune. A lone man sat at the fire, bearded and long-haired, wearing ragged jeans. His shirt was spread out like a blanket, and he was sitting on it, drinking from a bottle of fortified wine. The fire crackled and hissed in the rain. The man had accumulated a pile of wood. He reached without looking, took a stick from the pile, and laid it across the fire so slowly Abe was surprised his hand wasn't burned. The fire flared, changing colors, then settled back into its steady yellow and orange. The man took a pull from the bottle and stared into the fire.

The rain wasn't much, but Abe couldn't see how the flames held out so well. He watched the man lay another stick across it, just as slowly as before, and take another pull from the bottle. The man's movements, so exactly as they'd been just a minute ago, gave Abe a disturbing feeling of déjà vu, as if his mind had slipped a half-notch in time. He backed away, moving out toward the water, and passed by at a distance. The man never looked up.

He pressed on toward the distant pier, feeling uneasy. Odd that such a simple thing could trouble him, he thought. And he kept thinking about it, until finally he realized that the déjà vu came from something he had seen a few years before, a brief vision he had almost forgotten.

The night had been balmy, like this one, the air shrill with crickets. His feet were sore from a long shift at Jackson's, but he'd changed into comfortable shoes now. Sandals, even, because at Hendrix College men wore sandals too, and Abe was trying them out. With an overstuffed bookbag straining his shoulder, he was walking across campus toward the Mills Building to study. The campus was a self-contained neighborhood of red brick, trees, a profusion of flowers. He found it beautiful but had no time to enjoy it the way he'd like, maybe by taking a bench on the pecan court as he saw some students do, studying away the sunny afternoon, or just letting everything go for an hour or two, sitting by the fountain, watching people pass. He could imagine it, but he never did it. Tonight, despite the pain in his feet, he was taking a meandering route, putting off his studies because he was tired from work and knew that, once again, he would cash out before he'd made it halfway through his reading. The thought made him queasy. His first class started in seven hours. He wasn't doing well in it.

It was late and hardly anyone was about. Above the shimmer of crickets he heard the far-off splash of the fountain and, strangely, the sound of voices singing. He wandered in the direction of the singing, which came from the chapel, and as he drew near he saw that some sort of late-night service was being held there. The stained glass windows, softly lambent, cast patches of colored light on the grass outside. He felt both isolated and charmed. He hadn't heard about this service and wouldn't have come if he had, but now that he had stumbled across it in the night he felt a kind of mysterious thrill. Quietly, he entered the foyer and peered in through the open doors into the chapel.

There was no special service after all. A lone man stood facing the altar, upon which he had set a large portable stereo, wearing simple blue jeans and sandals, an untucked white T-shirt. He had a bald patch at the crown of his head, but his hair was black, and from behind he seemed young and trim. Abe couldn't see his face. He was waving his arms back and forth as if directing the unseen choir. His bald spot shone with sweat. Beside the stereo on the wooden altar stood a bottle of furniture polish and a wadded rag. A barely detectable buzzing accompanied the music as the stereo vibrated against the altar—the bass was turned up too high—and as Abe watched, the bottle of furniture polish eased slowly across the gleaming wooden altar as if impelled by an invisible hand. Finally it tipped over the near edge and fell soundlessly to the carpet. The man, still directing with one hand, stooped and righted the bottle with the other.

Sleepy and more than a little disoriented, Abe had backed away from the door and forgotten about the man until just this minute, walking the beach. He couldn't remember what had happened after he left the chapel. Probably he had been asleep in less than an hour, exhaustion draining him of all fear and motivation. He thought back. It had been a sticky night and loud with crickets, and the flowers were in bloom, so it must have been late in the spring term. Within a month of that night, then, he would lose his scholarship and go home.

Despite the rain, the pier was crowded. Men in slickers and hats were spread out all along the railings. Pails stood at their feet and forbidding displays of block and tackle, nets and hooks, and folding chairs. A strong, sickly odor of fish hung in the air. The people were quiet—only a low, courteous murmur of conversation and the businesslike movements of fishing. Rain ticked on their plastic slickers. The wood groaned. Abe moved along the walkway with his head down against the drizzle. He passed an old married couple fishing from their chairs, the woman short and fat, the man short and lean. In their chairs they were the same height, and they wore the same fixed expressions. After he was past them he heard a cackle and a flurry of excitement. The woman had snagged something. He looked back over his shoulder but never saw her haul up the fish.

At the end of the pier was a small open space between two broad-shouldered old fishermen. He edged into it, drawing glances from both sides. He said, "Just taking a look."

The man on his right smiled. "That's what we're all doing, looks like. Fish ain't biting for shit."

"No luck?"

"They just playing with us."

The water was a long way down. The fishing lines trailed off, disappearing into blackness. He leaned against the railing, letting his head hang over so that he saw nothing but black ocean far below him. He couldn't see the rain hit the water. It fell through the pier lights and vanished. With his head down like this, rainwater dripped from his forehead. He listened to the low mutter of the fishermen, the creaking of wood, the water lapping against the tarred pilings. He listened to the rain on wood and plastic, the distant moan and rush of traffic on the Strip. He felt sleepy, lulled. His thoughts seemed to settle, to become at the same time more lucid and more dreamlike. He thought, This is the sound of the world when it's good. Somewhere behind him a fisherman laughed, as if he'd heard Abe's thoughts.

He straightened abruptly, inexplicably embarrassed, and held dizzily to the rail for a moment as the blood left his head. This is the sound of the world . . . He couldn't remember the rest. He smiled. He felt a little giddy from the headrush. You're tired, he thought. Sleeping on your feet.

"Well, good luck," he said to the man who had spoken to him.

"I sure do need it."

He turned and headed back down the pier. The old woman was on her feet, cursing under her breath. She had lost her fish. Beside her, her mate was digging in a pail with the same expression on his face, ignoring her.

The others returned late in the night. Hearing voices, Abe came to the door of the bedroom and saw a party of red-faced men and women around the kitchenette table. "Pitt!" the men cried. Empty bottles and cans littered the floor and the table. Jim wore a look of sheepish solemnity that probably meant he was drunk. The others were far gone too. They were loud, but Kylie was sprawled out in corpselike oblivion on the couch; no one had bothered trying to wake him. Abe was in his underwear, so he went and pulled on some shorts and came back. He shook Kylie awake.

The two women were not the same ones Repeat had run out to see along the Strip. They were drunk, not particularly interested or friendly, just looking for something to do. Abe said hello to them, promptly forgetting their names, and sat sleepily at the table while the others played drinking games.

"Why do they call you Pitt? Are you the pits?" asked one of the women, laughing. She had a red, puffy face, and when she laughed her eyes squeezed so tightly shut her eyelashes disappeared.

"Yeah, I'm the pits."

"You are?" she said, surprised.

"What I want to know," said the other one, "what I want to know is, why do they call him Repeat?"

"His name's Pete Peterson."

"We already told her that," Jim said.

"But I don't get it," the woman said.

"Well, I'm not explaining it again," Jim said.

"But you have to," she insisted. "I'm not stupid."

"No, I'm not saying that, but you've had too much. Words don't seem to make sense to you. Sentences are too complicated. You're like a . . . like a . . ."

"Like a what?"

"Just forget it. Just take my word for it. Words are too complicated for you."

"Oh, come on," she said. "Come *on*."

"Okay, listen," Kylie said. He was kneeling at the table because there weren't enough chairs. He had squeezed in between the two women and was touching their hips with his shoulders. "Listen carefully and I'll explain it to you."

"Okay," the woman said, seriously. "I'm listening."

"Pete and Repeat sat on a bridge. Pete fell off. Who's left?"

"Kylie," Jim said. "Don't do that."

The woman was frowning with concentration. "Repeat," she said, after a moment.

Kylie smiled and said it again: "Pete and Repeat sat on a bridge. Pete fell off. Who's left?"

"Am I missing something?" the woman asked.

"Kylie, cut it out. It's bad enough already. She doesn't even understand words, Kylie. They're too compli—"

"Say it again," the woman said. "Say it real slow, and this time I'll get it."

Kylie said it again.

"Repeat?" the woman said, uncertainly. She looked to the others for help. With an expression of false sympathy, Kylie put a hand on her shoulder and said it again.

"Kylie, for God's sake, shut the hell up."

"But I don't get it," the woman said. "Isn't it Repeat?"

"Every time you say that," the other woman said, "he repeats it. Don't you get it?"

"I must be missing something. I just, I don't quite—"

Repeat pointed a warning finger. "One more time, Kylie, and I'm kicking the shit out of you."

Eventually Abe gave up and went back to bed. He awoke late to the pain of his sunburn kicking in and bright sunlight pouring through the window. The women were gone. In the living room Kylie lay facedown on the couch, having reclaimed it in the wee hours by passing out on it. He was wearing no shirt, and Abe saw that yesterday's haphazard slathering of sunscreen had resulted in white patches across his shoulders and back that were shaped like blurred fingers, fringed by pink sunburn. His bald spot, though, was perfectly tan, protected by that polish he put on it. Roberto lay on the floor with his head out of sight in the open closet. The others were sleeping in the second bedroom. Abe kicked them all awake.

After a silent breakfast in the motel café, they took to the beach again. The sun was painfully bright. White clouds trailed the ocean horizon. They went down to a beach shop and bought headache medicine and a tube of zinc oxide, and all but Roberto, who hadn't burned, smeared the bright green stuff over their noses and foreheads and ears until they looked like children gone rebellious with fingerpaint. Roberto, in spite of his vicious hangover, kept laughing at the sight of them.

They walked the beach and swam for a while, not because they felt like it but because they could, then one by one dozed off on their towels. By early afternoon, shadows began passing over the sun, and they were awake again—not stirring, but listening to the squeals of children chasing their runaway air mattresses. The fine white sand lifted and swirled, stinging their skin, and overhead a gull was flapping, making its mournful cry, gaining no headway. People were clamping their sun visors to their heads and fleeing the beach. But the five of them were tired, and they knew this was the last of it, so they lay there a while longer, stretched back on their towels, watching the clouds scud in and cover the sky, like the wiping away of a dreamed-up world.

Chapter 2

Marie was dreaming of the road when lightning woke her. She opened her eyes and it was gone, the bedroom dark, and highway dashes still tickered past in her mind's eye. She might yet be dreaming. Then the thunder struck, huge and heavy, and she came fully awake with a startled cry. Rainwater sang in the gutters. Outside her window the wind was shaking the plum tree; the branches tapped and squealed against the panes.

There was a timid knock at her door. "Marie?"

"I'm awake," she croaked, sitting up and gathering the blanket to her chin. She glanced at the clock. Just after five.

Her father stepped into the room, his figure lit softly from behind. The kitchen light was on down the hall. So he'd been up for a while. "I thought I heard you in here," he said.

"The thunder," she said.

"Yeah, it got me too."

He clumped into her room, not turning on the light. She peered down at his feet. Boots. He was in soaking wet shorts and a T-shirt. "Don't you ever close your drapes?" he said, looking out her window. He clicked his tongue. "I need to trim that plum."

"You're wet."

"I put your car in the garage. It started hailing. Hear it knocking on the roof?"

So that was the irregular thumping she'd been hearing. She straightened up to look out the window. Another lightning flash revealed chunks of white ice like ping-pong balls bouncing up from the driveway and rain pouring down in torrents. A moment later thunder smashed the house like a physical blow, rattling the window in its frame. Her father jumped back.

"Whoa doggy. That was something."

"I never saw it rain so hard," said Marie.

"Me neither. Not in many years."

"How long's it been going on like this?"

"Don't know. I just woke up a few minutes ago."

"I don't suppose you're going back to bed."

"Who'd want to? This is incredible."

She sat back. "I think I want to."

"Oh. Right. You go back to sleep," he said, going quickly to the door. "Sleep tight."

Marie slid down beneath the warm covers, but she couldn't fall back to sleep. She still wasn't used to this. This house, this bed, her father—all of it was unfamiliar. It had been less than a month since she had showed up at the door in the rain, wearing her best clothes, clutching the ripped-out page of a phone book with his address on it. Her good clothes—which weren't much, black dress pants and a cheap satiny blouse—were soaked through and clung to her skin, her scuffed high heels ruined. Opening the door, her father took one look and had to step back. He pulled his glasses off. His face registered shock, then confusion, then concern. She actually watched it go through the stages. Then, like a fool, he didn't beckon her inside but stepped out into the rain to embrace her, so that he got drenched too. At first glance, he told her later, he'd thought she was her mother, unchanged after all these years. But that was impossible, and once his mind worked that out, he knew it was Marie.

She pictured him stepping out into the rain to hug her. A mostly bald man with glasses dangling from his fist. Skinny legs in checkered shorts, rough yellowish feet in house thongs. She had remembered him as a big man, yet he wasn't big at all. He was hardly taller than she was, and although over the years he'd developed a slight paunch, he still seemed slender. Or maybe he'd always been thick around the belt. Maybe it wasn't the sort of thing you noticed as a child.

Everything she'd brought with her from Little Rock had fit inside the trunk of the old Corolla and was now put away in the closet. Her father had been calling this her room, though it could have been anybody's. There was nothing on the walls. But she'd been sleeping here, and maybe she would stay. He was making her feel welcome—not as though she'd just stepped out of the past with no explanation, no job, nothing but need; not as though she burst into bewildering fits of anger he braved like summer squalls. He didn't know what to do about her, but he was welcoming, so maybe she could stay. Maybe she would try to get something for these walls. She didn't know what. It struck her, not for the first time, that her father had lived in this house for years and never put anything up himself, at least not in this room. And in the other rooms he'd hung only a few prints, cheap framed posters of blown-up book covers, an old world map. No pictures, no photos of her mother or herself—or anyone else, for that matter. After all these years. The house might have been a stranger's.

She pictured him stepping out into the rain again. It really was a foolish thing to do.

At six o'clock the radio alarm went off, a news announcer buzzing on and on about warnings and watches. Marie shut it off, vaguely irritated there hadn't been music. She'd fallen asleep after all and wished she hadn't. She felt much sleepier now. Her father came to her door again, this time wearing dry clothes and wielding a spatula. "Rise and shine and give God the glory," he said. "Pancakes are ready." He disappeared again.

She didn't feel hungry, but she couldn't refuse him. She pulled on a sweatshirt, freeing her hair from the shirtneck with the backs of her hands. Her hair crackled with static electricity. She tried to smooth it down, felt it clinging to her hand, gave up. Put on sweatpants and an extra pair of socks because her father kept it so cold in this house. She'd never known anyone to keep a place so cold in the summer, had never known anyone who could have afforded it.

In the kitchen her father was humming, keeping watch over bacon sizzling in a black iron skillet. A stack of pancakes stood on a platter by the stove. The smells hit Marie hard. Bacon and fried batter and coffee. She was suddenly very hungry. "Lord, does that smell good," she said.

He flipped a half-dozen strips of bacon onto a plate. "Well, eat up. Help yourself to the pancakes." Pointing with the spatula at the miniature television on the counter, he said, "Mess out there, isn't it?" The screen showed a map of Arkansas with a mass of color spreading across the middle like a bruise. The weatherman, looking harried and hot, was pointing out trouble spots.

"What's going on?" Marie said, her mouth full of bacon. She washed it down with coffee to get that dark, smoky taste she'd learned to like as a kid in roadside diners. After that taste you wanted some strawberry jelly on your pancakes, not syrup. She went to the refrigerator and found the jelly jars. He had three kinds.

"Tornado watch," her father was saying, "flash flood watch, thunderstorm warning. They showed a picture of a milk truck with the window busted out from the hail."

"Don't you think it'll ever get tired of raining?"

"I think today it may wear itself out."

She poured herself more coffee and refilled her father's cup. He winked at her. He'd finished the bacon and was frying up a thick slice of Spam.

"Are you going to cook everything in the fridge?"

"Just got a hankering," he said.

She could say this for her father, the man did his grocery shopping with zest. She'd never seen a refrigerator hold so much food: milk and chocolate milk, two kinds of juice, beer, soda, all sorts of cheeses and meat, large brown eggs, relishes, two kinds of mustard, sauces she never heard of; and the crisper was packed with lettuce, peppers, celery, green onions, mushrooms, carrots, tomatoes. With all this food around you'd expect him to be a fat man. Then again, maybe he'd bought groceries like this only because she was here. For all she knew, he'd been living for years on cheese sandwiches and pickles.

He joined her at the kitchen table and they ate together quietly, Marie still shaking her grogginess, her father dividing his attention between the newspaper and the television, alternately sliding his reading glasses up and down his nose. After a while he set the paper aside and removed the glasses, rubbing his face.

Marie was watching him. "Why don't you try for some more sleep?"

"I think I might."

"You do that. I'll get moving." She rose with the dishes.

"Marie, you don't need to go out in this. It's not like you'll get any business."

"I'm going in, Dad."

"Well, not if it's hailing, at least. You'll ruin the paint job on your car."

Marie went to the sink window, studying the back yard in the weak gray light. Hundreds of hailstones were scattered in the green grass—the lawn looked like a driving range—but there was only rain now. She shook her head.

"All right," he said, "but there could be flooding downtown, so make sure you park back in the warehouse. Don't leave your car on the street. And if it starts hailing while you're driving down there, you pull over right away, try to get under an overhang or—"

"Okay, Dad. Got it. You go lay down."

"I think I'll just set in the living room."

"Go in the living room, then." She stopped by his chair, tentatively put her hand on his shoulder, and bent quickly to kiss the top of his bald head. She'd had the impulse before, but this was the first time she'd acted on it. He reached back up behind him, patted her shoulder awkwardly.

They were getting on well together, better than she would have hoped, though it had taken some time to shake the tension from their first confrontation, which came the day after she arrived. Her father had stayed home from the bookstore to be there when she awoke. Marie had risen at noon. She found him in the kitchen clearing away the long-cold breakfast he'd cooked her and dishing up chili and crackers for lunch. Ravenous and grateful, she wolfed several bites before she noticed he hadn't touched his.

She stopped chewing and looked at him. At the question waiting to be formed. She had briefly been his daughter; now she was a vagrant in a nice man's kitchen. Well, if he *knew* her he wouldn't have let her inside his house in the first place. She'd spent her entire life consorting with addicts, crazies, and thieves, including her own mother, and had married a man and seen him buried and arrived here in the same clothes. And she was not yet twenty. But she was determined not to have such memories, such a past—it was a brief past, all things considered, brief and absurd, a bad film. She had no intention now of giving it consideration. And so she swallowed the food and all of the answers with it and said, "I don't want to talk about it."

"Some things we've got to talk about, honey."

"No."

Her father studied her. "I think I at least ought to know if someone's coming after you. I should know if you're in trouble."

"You mean with the police?"

"For starters, yes, with the police."

It shouldn't have surprised her. He had, after all, been married to her mother, who had accustomed him to trouble. And Marie herself, though her father couldn't have known it, had at one time or another been suspected of everything from shoplifting to assault. Yet the notion that her father should think of her in this way, however reasonably, outraged her.

"No," she said, slapping her spoon down. "I'm not in trouble with anybody but myself, all right?"

Her father was calm, much calmer than Marie would have been if someone had spoken to her in that tone. He had a way of looking you in the eye without intimidating you, which was more than she could say for most men she'd known. Perhaps it was the way his face was shaped, with its constant, almost imperceptible squint and the perpetual hint of a smile, as if he were slightly confused.

"Can you tell me what that means? Are you sick, honey? I just need to know what we're dealing with here."

"I'm fine."

Her father took off his glasses, rubbed his face, put the glasses back on. He was considering, she thought. Considering whether to send her on her way. Why should he have to put up with this? Finally he said, "One more thing, then, and I'll quit bothering you."

She looked at him sullenly.

"Is there a man after you? Are you running from someone?"

Marie blew up. Looking back, she realized she'd been waiting for the chance. Let herself cause a scene and be kicked out—she knew she'd half-wanted that, though she could hardly have said why. "Why would you ask me something like that?" she snarled. "You think I'm so stupid I'd be with a man I'm afraid of? You think I'd let anybody slap *me* around?"

"No, I don't—"

"Then why ask me something like that?"

"Well, because otherwise I couldn't figure why you came to me after all this time. Why you didn't go to your mother instead. I guess I thought if you came to me, maybe it was because you needed to be protected."

"You think *you* can protect me?"

He didn't lash at her for the contempt in her tone, as she might have expected, or just leave the room, which was probably more his style. He only flinched, and said after a moment, "I'll sure try, honey."

As if she were still a child. As if her words had no effect on him. She leaped from her chair and yelled, "Then quit asking me your goddamn questions! No, I'm not in trouble. No, I don't need protection. No, nobody's coming after me. It's just me, all right? Isn't that enough?"

By the way he was looking at her she knew he was wondering if something was wrong with her. She'd seen that look before, plenty of times, and it made her more furious. And there was that lying part of her brain that believed he'd meant to hurt her, that he knew everything about her, every detail of her jettisoned life, and wanted to make her think about these things only to wound her. For a moment she believed this, and needing to hurt him back, she said, quite easily and without having to consider, "I thought you'd be different this time."

Her father closed his eyes. He didn't flinch, but she knew she'd struck home. It took all the guts out of her, having done it, made her feel despicable and sick. This was always how it was. The irresistible thing was the thing you most regretted.

She hesitated, not knowing what to do. She didn't want to go, not at bottom, yet now she surely couldn't stay. She tried to figure a way back, a return to the night before, when there was nothing between them but empty history. Before she could think of what to say, her father opened his eyes, smiled ruefully, and said, "I'm sorry, honey. Sorry I upset you. You don't have to talk about anything you don't want to."

Marie sat down, confused.

"I'm sorry," he said again. "It's okay."

"I just don't want to think about it. I'm trying to forget all that."

"That's fine."

"I just want to—" She gestured impatiently, as if waving somebody away. "I mean, yesterday doesn't matter. Whatever happened doesn't matter, right? I just want to move forward."

Her father nodded, with a plain expression of relief, and Marie realized he had misunderstood her. He thought she was forgiving him. Though she'd never felt he had anything to be forgiven for, she decided to let him think it. She let him think it partly because it made her feel better, but also because he seemed to need that. He wanted to start over as much as she did.

Marie got ready quickly. It was her second week opening the bookstore alone, and she still felt nervous. There was nothing to it: unlocking the doors, putting cash in the register, cleaning a little. But over the weekend it had begun to seem foreign and intimidating again. What was she doing opening a store? Who was she to be doing this?

Her father had suggested it. He was tired of the place, he said. Twenty years sitting in the same chair every day, he could use a break. Marie's showing up was the perfect excuse. If she wanted the job, it was hers. So she took it, not knowing what else to do, and they spent a week together in the store. It wasn't such a big place—in a day he showed her everything she needed to know: the account books, the inventory, the register, the tiny warehouse in back with its boxes of unsorted books and just enough room to squeeze your car. If she had any questions she could call him. Any real problems, he could be there in ten minutes. There was nothing to worry about, but still she got nervous.

Last week, on her first day opening the store alone, she had willed herself out of bed early to make breakfast for him, both as a sort of thank you and as a way of taking some control. She'd covered the long counter with sausage, butter, cheddar cheese, eggs, vegetables. When her father shuffled into the kitchen, the iron skillet was on the stove, and Marie was putting out silverware, finishing off a glass of chocolate milk. He wasn't going in that day, but out of habit he was ready to go. The thin gray bands of hair on each side of his head had been neatly slicked back over his ears with a wet comb. It was darker when wet, almost charcoal. When he'd had a full head of hair, it was jet black, like hers. That was the way she remembered it.

He looked at all the food in surprise. "She can cook."

"If you aren't hungry you don't have to eat it."

"I never said anything of the kind."

"Okay, then." She hadn't cooked in weeks, hadn't realized how she'd missed it. Not just the cooking, but the satisfaction of seeing a man heap the food onto his plate, wanting to eat what you had made. It seemed a normal thing to feel, and for that reason she liked it. For her own breakfast she drank another glass of chocolate milk. Too edgy to eat. Her first day.

It had been raining then too, of course—rain every day since she arrived—but it was warm outside, warmer than that icebox of a house, and she'd paused in the doorway, shaking off the indoor cold. It was a fine drizzle, rain light enough to rise and swell when a gust of wind caught it, shifting like smoke. Two blown sweetgum leaves were plastered against the windshield of her car, resembling the tracks of a giant bird. Like an omen, she thought. Wasn't there some mythic bird that brought needy souls good fortune? There ought to be.

All across the neighborhood—a decent neighborhood, like no place she'd ever lived—water gurgled in the gutters of brick homes, streamed in well-kept drainage ditches, puddled on tarp-skinned swimming pools. Upturned magnolia leaves drifted down the ditches like gondolas. You could hear the cars hissing past on Central Avenue, two blocks west. Marie stood soaking it all up, lulled by the whisper and mutter of her new city under rain.

At the bookstore she'd parked on the street, not wanting to wrestle with the heavy warehouse door, and unlocked the front door at seven-fifteen. Most businesses along Central Avenue wouldn't open until nine or ten, but Hamilton Books, her father said, had always kept longer hours, and people were used to it. The store was part of an old building situated on an incline, not uncommon for buildings in downtown Hot Springs, where the streets lay flanked by wooded hills. The tiled floor sloped gently upward to the back, where a swinging door led into what her father called the warehouse, though it was hardly more than a garage. There were a few comfortable reading chairs, a desk, a coffee pot and table. Off to the side, near the bathroom, a private room held filing cabinets, a dusty mounted fish, and the antique safe her father had bought when he opened the store. That was twenty years ago, in 1970, when Hamilton's was the only used bookstore in the city.

Marie opened the safe and counted out the money for the register. It was curious to think he trusted her with the money. It seemed right—she would have been angry had he not—yet she found it surprising. But then, there wasn't enough money here to set him back if she took it. Most was in the bank. If anything, this was a trap, to see what she would do. She felt a sudden burning resentment. Well, if that's what he expects, she thought, rising with a fistful of bills and looking to the door.

She checked herself. "You're nervous," she said aloud. "So just go about your business. Count the money and clean the damn store."

She did, mopping the aisles, which were sullied with muddy footprints and sediment, then dusting bookshelves. The desk radio played softly, and she began to hum absently along. She had never minded work. It held an almost exotic appeal for her, this doing normal things for normal money; she enjoyed it. She was sharp about details, and work was nothing if not details. Shoving the register aside, she dusted beneath, which she doubted had ever been done. Her father should have hired her long ago, she thought; she was allowing herself the fantasy of having spent her life differently when the doorbell jingled.

In the entrance a miniature old woman stood with her half-folded umbrella out in front of her, dripping onto the floor. She was trying feebly to close it as Marie hustled up to greet her. The woman was not quite five feet tall. Her bushy hair, perfectly white, was massed beneath a straining, transparent hair net, so that she looked like a cotton swab. She wore a powder-blue summer sweater and polyester pants, and a tiny gold change purse dangled from her shoulder, interfering with her efforts to fold the umbrella.

"Morning, ma'am," Marie said. "Can I help you with that?"

The woman looked up, grinning. She had clear blue eyes and a faint white mustache. One of her front teeth was gold. After a moment she said, "What, dear?"

"Can I help you with your umbrella?"

"Oh, yes. Thank you, dear."

Marie folded the umbrella and propped it behind the door. "What can I do for you?"

The woman peered into her face, the pale blue eyes jittering in a mildly unsettling way. Marie waited for a reply. After a long pause she thought she'd have to repeat herself, but finally the woman said, "You Jimmy Hamilton's girl?"

"Yes, ma'am. You know my dad?"

Again the woman gazed at her a moment before responding. Words seemed to take a while to reach her, as if they must travel a great distance, though apparently they arrived intact. She smiled again.

"Oh, heavens, yes. Yes, yes. I know Jimmy. I've known him since he was this high." Her trembling right hand jerked slightly upward, failed, and dropped to her side. She raised it again immediately, this time succeeding, lifting it as high as her own head and holding it there a moment. "Since he was this high," she said again. They both laughed. The woman fumbled to take Marie's hand and held on to it. Her skin was like suede; her hand trembled Marie's. "You look a whole lot like your mother, honey."

Marie, caught off guard, blinked and tried to smile. "Oh," she said, in a politely casual tone, as if talking about the weather. "Is that right?"

"Oh yes, yes," the woman said, squeezing her hand. "I helped deliver her, you know."

"You—helped deliver my mother?"

"Oh Lord, yes! What a strange-looking baby your mother was! Her head was longer than her body. I'll never forget that. Ugly as the day is long. And what a screamer. We was all sure something was wrong with her, but she turned out a beauty in the end, didn't she? I swear you look just like her. And bright? Lord, that girl was smart. Smarter than all the boys, that's for sure," she said, laughing again. "I bet you take after her in that too."

Marie felt hot and flustered. "I don't . . . Would you . . . Can I get you a chair? Would you like some coffee?"

"Oh, not today, sugar, but thank you. I'm making a cake for my great-grandson. It's supposed to have a picture of some mutated something-or-other on it. Do you know what I mean? Some kind of turtle?"

"A ninja turtle?"

"That's it, whatever that is. They make the most fool things now. I thought Jimmy might have a children's book with a picture I could copy from."

"Let me run see," Marie said, gently withdrawing her hand. She went to the box of comic books in the children's section. There was one with the turtles right on top, but she took a minute, pretending to search. When she felt calmer, she returned to show it to the woman.

"Oh, thank you so much, honey. Now ain't those the most fool-looking things?" she said, peering at the cover as she unsnapped her purse. "How much do I owe you?"

"This one's free."

"Oh, nonsense," the woman scolded.

"No, it's free. You just come back and visit me sometime."

"Well, my stars and garters," the woman said, grinning. She reached up toward Marie's face. As before, her hand failed in its first attempt. Marie bent forward when it came up again, and the woman patted her cheek softly. "What a dear you are."

Marie retrieved the umbrella and started to open it.

"Oh, gracious, don't do that in here, honey," the woman said, frowning. "You know better than to open umbrellas indoors. It's bad luck."

"It is?"

"Well, where were you raised?" the woman said with a smile. But the smile faded at once, and her bright eyes looked regretful.

"Oh, I remember now," Marie said. "I don't know what I was thinking. But here, let me get this for you." She stepped quickly around the woman and opened the front door. Standing outside on the step, she held the door open with one foot and unfolded the umbrella.

"Thank you," the woman said, still turning. "You move so fast I can't hardly keep up with you." Carefully she negotiated the step and took the umbrella. "Now what was your name again, sugar? Was it Marie?"

"How in the world did you know that?"

"Well, it was your mother's name too, wasn't it? And anyhow I knew you when you were just a little thing. Lord, you were such a ornery child. But you've grown up nice, haven't you?"

"I'm sure trying."

The woman gave her gold-toothed smile. "You're doing fine, honey. I'll come visit you sometime soon."

A man was waiting for her in a green Cadillac parked at one of the meters along the curb. From the doorway Marie watched him climb out and open the door for her. Rounding the back of the car, he saw Marie and gave a polite wave. He was gray-haired and slender, but not so frail, not nearly so old as the woman. Perhaps her son.

Marie waved and went inside, watching through the display window as the car drove away. She was annoyed with herself for not asking the woman's name, but she'd felt strangely guilty for not knowing it. The woman knew hers, after all. Well, that shouldn't have been surprising. Many people in Hot Springs must have known her mother; it was not such a big city. Still, she'd been gone so long—they both had—Marie hadn't expected to meet anyone who remembered her.

Surely it wouldn't happen often. Would there be others? Only her grandfather came to mind—her mother's father—and he hardly counted, was hardly in the world. He lived out at the Valley Lodge Nursing Home near Lockers Creek, a bloated old man who never rose from his bed. He had once been a professor of some kind. Marie had a distant memory of visiting him. She'd stood at the foot of the bed, terrified by his bulk, distressed by the smells of the place. Although her mother and father were surely both there, she couldn't picture them, only the huge man propped up before her. He was demanding animal crackers and peppermints (and she had some to give him, she remembered now; her parents must have known he'd want them) and lecturing incoherently on the decline of America. Sometimes he referred to it as "Rome, America." Marie had understood very little. His vigor had quickly waned, like a radio with dying batteries, and she remembered the sudden alarming silence in the room when he finally stopped, as if he had died yet still sat there blinking at her.

Her father had told her he was alive even now. She hadn't known the name of his nursing home or even if it was in Arkansas. She'd never tried to find it; she wouldn't have wanted to. But her father knew. He took care of the arrangements for the old man. Even drove out on weekends to visit him, the crazy father of his lost wife.

He'd told Marie this mostly as a warning, in case she wanted to come with him sometime. She'd seen the hopeful look in his eyes but had told him that she didn't think she did, and he had let it go.

The rain was so heavy Marie had to lean forward, squinting to keep the road in sight. Her wipers rocked at high speed, but it was as if someone were emptying a tub over her windshield. Red taillights appeared ahead of her, she stomped on her brakes, and the car ahead pulled forward again, disappearing into the rain. It was disconcerting how utterly it vanished into the wall of water—a kind of horizontal sinking. In her headlights now she could just make out what the other driver had seen: water bubbling up through a grate and streaming across the road. You're a fool to be out in this, she thought.

At the store she pulled off the side street and parked with her bumper almost touching the warehouse door, headlights beaming. She found the key for the padlock and leaped from the car, feet coming down in ankle-deep water. No point in hurrying; she was drenched at once. She heaved against the warehouse door, rolling it sideways in its track, and slogged back to her car. Lightning crackled just beyond the hill as she pulled into the sudden quiet.

In the faint light from a high, dirty window, Marie walked, shoes squishing, through the warehouse to the front of the store. She set coffee to brew, first things first, then stripped out of her soaked clothes in the bathroom, wringing them into the sink. In the mirror she saw her black hair slicked to her head, bangs demolished. Her mascara had run onto her cheeks. The harsh bathroom light made her skin look deathly pale, her face like a mask. "Who the hell are *you*?" she asked aloud. She squeezed water from her hair, dried off with a handful of paper towels, pulled the damp clothes back on. Her socks she left hanging from the edge of the sink, her shoes overturned on the floor.

Counting money from the safe in the little private room, Marie reflected on how much quieter her insistent cynic had become already. Every day she counted the cash seemed less like a trap and more like a job. Just a job, which pleased her, though it wouldn't do to let her guard down. Not three days before, she'd circled the block twice before pulling into the warehouse. Had been doubting her chances, was thinking of the interstate. It took so little effort to think of her father as a stranger and this town not her town. In no time she could be elsewhere, remembering her father as a man who set traps, Hot Springs as a place where it always rained.

As she rose from the safe, Marie became aware of a whispering sound outside the room; her hair stood up on her neck. At once she returned the money to the safe, closed and locked it. Let them try, she thought, heart pounding, and went to peer out from the door. It was only a leak: Two rows down, a stream of water fell from the high ceiling, pattering onto the tile floor, just missing the shelves of first editions. A yellow stain spread across the ceiling, stretching out in a bruised oblong from the leak at its center. A pretty heavy leak, too. Rain must be pooling in the attic.

Marie laughed at herself. How quickly she'd protected that money!

She'd like to think it was an act of allegiance—protecting her father's hard-earned cash—but she knew it was sheer defiance. Well, she thought, gathering herself. Whatever it takes.

She set a coffee can under the leak, and by the time she'd mopped the floor, the can was full. She dumped it into the mop bucket and put it back, squinting suspiciously up at the leak. Nothing to be done about it right now. She still had to open the store. Unlocking the front door, she looked out the big display window at the storm. The rain obscured everything across the street; the tall buildings were great dark shadows looming indistinctly. The daylight-sensitive street lamps were in confusion, flickering off and then immediately back on. Water ran in the street, splashing against the tire of a lone car parked at the curb, shallow but swift.

The metallic tinkle in the coffee can had gone to a deep-toned gurgle. She emptied it into the mop bucket, and now the bucket needed emptying. She dumped it over the floor drain back in the warehouse, but then the water didn't drain. It spread out across the floor, lapping over her bare feet. She leaped away, remembering the bubbling grate in the street, and now realized what it meant: there was nowhere for all this water to go but up.

You would have thought she'd worked here all her life. Suddenly and without thinking, she became all business. Trotting down the rows of boxes stacked on pallets, grimy feet slapping the cement, she emptied a rubber trash barrel and lugged it down into the store. The coffee can was full again. She replaced it with the barrel, the water splashing into it with a satisfying, hollow rubber drumming.

Back in the warehouse she discovered still more water on the floor, coming in through a gap under the warehouse door. Scrabbling through boxes, she found a heap of dirty rags and stuffed them into the gap. Useless—a dozen fluffy towels wouldn't have done it. Finally she spotted an old tarp covering a stack of boxes, and rolling the door open just enough to squeeze through, she dragged the tarp out into the storm. Rainwater rushed downhill toward Central Avenue, running over her ankles. She muscled the door closed with one end of the tarp still inside, then stamped the tarp down so that water ran over it. The weight of the water held it there, pressed between the warehouse door and the driveway, a makeshift seal. She didn't pause to admire her work—the rain was hitting her face so hard it hurt. She headed for the front door, splashing downhill with the runoff almost carrying her feet out from under her, and turned the corner to find the entire sidewalk under water.

"Lord have mercy," she said. A phrase of her father's.

Inside, she wiped her face from the chin up as if coming out of a pool—blinking exaggeratedly, slicking her hair back—and the gesture called up memories of a hundred motel mornings, her mother with a buyer in their squalid room, trading the illicit contents of their duffel bags, with Marie sent out to swim or otherwise amuse herself. Sometimes she circled the building to stand on her toes and peek in beneath the drawn curtains, even though her mother had caught her once and screamed at her for it. Times like those, people didn't want eyes at the window, not even little girl eyes. But what Marie managed to see was nothing she wasn't used to, nothing to hold her interest—just a lot of nerves and money. Usually she swam.

When she had blinked the water from her eyes Marie was looking out again at the car parked against the curb. The water had risen halfway up its hubcaps. A ruined orange hunter's cap had caught against one of the tires, held fast there by the current. Now and then other pieces of trash drifted past. She lingered at the window, her clothes dripping. The city seemed so strange, entirely new and unreal, and somehow less substantial than her childhood memories of it. She could never have guessed the present might feel less real than the past, for how could something be less real than nothing? "Well, it can't," she said aloud, without conviction.

The trash barrel was singing a bass note. Over half full now; a chunk of plaster floated in it. She looked up at the leak again, but found the lights had gone out. She went searching for the circuit breakers. It was even darker in the warehouse; she got in her car and switched on the headlights. When she found the breakers it made no difference. No power.

She was thinking about the plaster in the trash barrel. Pictured the entire ceiling caving in, water cascading over her father's books. Maybe she should look in the attic, see if she could do something. It was a cramped, unused space that ran the length of the store; she'd find it pitch dark up there and probably teeming with spiders. She considered, standing there dripping in the headlights. Well, she could at least take a look.

The attic entrance was a trap door in the ceiling, about fifteen feet up, in the back corner of the warehouse. To reach it you climbed metal rungs fixed into the concrete block wall. It was an awkward climb, too—she had big feet, and her toes kept kicking the concrete. At the top, she pushed with one hand against the sliding trap door, but it didn't budge. She tried again, throwing her shoulder into it. The door made a sucking sound, lifted about an inch, and dropped heavily back into place. Filthy water splashed into her face. She swore, wiping her face with her upper arm. Now she had something in her eye that felt about the size of a match. She thought, This is fucking ridiculous. Then, unexpectedly, felt ashamed, as if her father had heard her.

The entire attic must be under water. It seemed unlikely she could do any good. With her free hand she swiped gingerly at her eye; she blinked a piece of insulation out. But you might could spare his ceiling, she thought, maybe save all those books. She stared up at the trap door with a feeling of nausea, as if she were looking at maggots.

You could just pretend it didn't occur to you, she thought.

Beads of oily water hung trembling from the door, occasionally smacking on the cement far below. "Oh, for Christ's sake!" she snarled, and closing her eyes and ducking her head, she thrust one hand up against the door and shoved as hard as she could, forcing it aside.

A torrent of black water poured onto her head. She shrieked as it came, grabbing the rung with both hands now, holding tight, squeezing her eyes shut. She'd hoped the worst would be over quickly, but the filth gushed steadily out. After a while she gave up and descended the slippery rungs, barely managing to keep her grip, and at last stepped out of range.

She blew water from her nose, wiped her face. The water drained in sheets from the open attic door, sending up a dirty spray from the floor. In the headlights it looked strangely pretty, like a hidden waterfall in a dark grotto. It muddied the warehouse floor, but the book boxes were safely stacked on pallets. After a while the outflow lessened, streaming from the edges but no longer gushing. All that water. The leak would surely have burst wide open if she hadn't relieved the pressure. That, at least, was what she was going to believe. You didn't want to do something like that for no reason.

The warehouse floor lay under a dirty skin of water, some of which had seeped downhill and wet the store's main aisles. A long day's mopping job was all. Marie went into the bathroom, stripping yet again. She rinsed her face, and was going to rinse her clothes, when the faucet water faded to a trickle and disappeared. "Oh, come on!" she shouted, twisting the faucet handles. Nothing came out. She took a deep breath. She wasn't as furious as she might have been. In fact, to her surprise, she felt pretty good. Well, what the hell, she thought. She wrung what she could from her clothes, brown water and tiny pieces of rotten wood, yellow-brown insulation. She flapped them out in front of her, trying to shake the excess filth. Stepping out of the bathroom for more room to maneuver, she heard the deep thrum of water in the trash barrel.

Dropping her clothes to the floor—what did it matter?—she went to move the overflowing barrel. It was like trying to lift a refrigerator. She got downhill of the barrel and dragged it to the front door to dump it outside, only to discover water coming in through the crack beneath the door, and at the *side* of the door, between the door and the frame. Through the display window she saw that the street was gone, a river in its place. So this was how it would come out. After all that trouble, nothing to do but watch the floodwaters pour in.

She might yet save some books, though. She went to work on the shelves near the leak, removing books by the armload, stacking them on a cart, rolling them away down the aisle. She took care of the first editions and rare books on the top shelves, then cleared the lower shelves along the front aisle, where she thought the water might rise high enough to reach them. The leak, at least, was letting up, so maybe the ceiling would hold.

When at last she'd finished, Marie was suddenly cold. The sweat was cooling on her body and her hair was drenched. The thought of those damp, filthy clothes sickened her, so she walked naked up the wet floors to the coffee maker. The coffee, by some miracle, was still hot.

She dragged a chair to the window and sat down, crossing her legs for warmth. She leaned forward over the coffee cup and took a sip, felt the heat from it against her damp breasts and neck. Water oozed against her toes, but she didn't bother looking down. It was strange how quickly you got used to it.

Your life's not even real, she thought; it's something made up.

The floodwaters were lapping against the bottom of the window, and still the rain came. Gusted raindrops slapped the glass like pellets. All the streetlights had given up now but one, which glowed and faded across the street like a beacon. And now a shape hove suddenly into view, large and dark and slowly spinning. The flood had taken up the car at the curb. It floated swiftly away, half-submerged.

Minutes later another drifted past, almost striking the glass. Marie pulled her chair some distance from the window and sat down again. Now that she'd done what she could, she enjoyed sitting and watching this way. Like being at an aquarium. Strange and peaceful. The world on a day like this didn't pertain to you. You didn't have to forget anything because the world was doing the forgetting for you.

She sipped her coffee.

The floor of the first aisle lay under several inches of water. Outside, the new river roared, rain chopping the waters. Rain beat noisily on the roof. A lightning flash brightened the street, and Marie thought she saw heads sticking up out of the water, a line of people up to their necks in the flood. But that couldn't be. Who would risk such a thing? She stood up, waiting for another flash.

Parking meters. Of course. Nobody takes such risks.

She dropped into her chair again, but she was unsettled. Almost happy. The city seemed so strange.

Chapter 3

Abe pinched himself hard on the arm. The coffee hadn't helped, and there was no one to talk to; the others were dead asleep. He'd been driving for hours, making awful time in the rain. Now he was headed into a full-fledged storm. He had to concentrate to see the road, which considering his bleariness would have been challenge enough without the rain. But it was almost dawn; they were almost home. He would just have to bear up. He tried the radio again: nothing but static.

Slowly along the winding wooded highway, headlights feckless in the rainy dark, rain hammering the roof. It was blowing in a nasty one. A blast of thunder shook the car, and Kylie sat up in the passenger seat, looked out the window as if searching for something, then leaned back again and closed his eyes. Probably hadn't even awakened.

It seemed a different life altogether that they'd been in Florida, loading the car in a steady rain. Floorboards muddy and full of trash, damp towels and clothes wadded in the seats. Abe had looked at the car with revulsion. All evening and all night he would have to ride in that mess. His sunburn was bothering him: his face felt tender and strangely taut, as if his skin had been tucked and fired. And his nipples were raw from the ocean, so that even his T-shirt chafed them.

He and Jim had said their good-byes, which weren't good-byes at all. They had sat in the motel café drinking coffee, sections of a newspaper scattered between them on the table, both of them tired and irritable. Jim's face was grapefruit-red and slippery with aloe vera, and he looked scruffy, having been too badly burned to shave. He said he'd bought some cigars for the occasion but had accidentally packed them away.

"Probably better," Abe said. "I feel too queasy to smoke."

"I'll mail it to you, maybe."

"I guess you really mean to stay down here, then," Abe said. His heart wasn't really in it to joke, but neither did he feel up to being serious.

"As long as I'm down here already, I guess I will."

"But who do you propose I talk to?"

"I propose you pick up the phone and talk to me."

"Suppose it's the middle of the night."

"Then you call Repeat. Anyway, whatever happens in the middle of the night?"

"Nothing," Abe admitted. "That's the problem."

"So just wait till morning. What difference does it make?"

Their waitress came with more coffee. They shook their heads, but she didn't notice them or didn't care, and filled their cups anyway. Jim dutifully stirred cream into his.

"Seriously," he said. "What are your plans now?"

"You think I'll just wither away and die with you gone."

"No, listen, I'm being serious."

Abe frowned into his coffee cup. "Same as I've been doing, I guess."

"Which is what, exactly?"

"Have you been saving this?"

"I'm just asking," Jim said.

"Well, I don't know."

"You ever think about going back?"

"I've thought about it."

"And?"

"I don't really see the point in it."

"You won't be content with roof work the rest of your life, that's the point."

"I like roof work well enough."

"Well, you can like something and not be content with it. Don't tell me you sold your horses and went to college because you wanted to be a roofer. It doesn't exactly wash."

"Can you tell me why we're talking about this now?"

"Because now you can't change the subject. Because now you have to answer my questions, because this is the last time you'll see me, and you feel obligated."

"In that case," Abe said, "what I guess it boils down to is I went to college and nothing came of it. That's it. End of story. So when you ask me what I'm going to do, my answer is, I don't know. I already did the only thing I knew to do, and it didn't work."

"You can't think it's as simple as that."

"It's really not a question of simple."

"But surely you don't think that's just it. You act like it's too late. Look at me, for God's sake. I'm just getting started. All you have to do is get started again. You have some money saved up—"

"Listen, I really don't want to talk about this, Jim. I appreciate it, I honestly do, but I'd rather not."

"Well, why the hell not?" Jim said. "It's your last chance to tell me what's really been rattling around in your head. You act like nothing ever happened, like you never went away or even wanted to go away, but you did. I of all people know that you did. Don't get me wrong, it's been good to have you around. Lord knows I'd have gone crazy these past couple of years. You've listened to me bitch about my parents and my job and I don't know what all else, and you haven't hardly said a thing about yourself. Now I'm giving you your big chance. I am one hundred percent all ears. So why not talk about it?"

"Because it embarrasses me," Abe said.

Jim was in his arguing habit and started to respond. Then he checked himself. He watched Abe pick up his spoon, stir his coffee, and put the spoon gently down on the table without taking up the coffee. After a long pause he said, "Well, hell, Abe, I'm sorry. I wouldn't ever have thought . . . well, hell. I'm sorry. But that's ridiculous, you know. You of all people. You've got absolutely nothing to . . ." He stopped, scowling. Finally he said, "All right. Sorry. Let's forget about it."

"Okay."

"But you know I don't agree with you. And nobody else does, either. You really are crazy to feel like that. You've got to know that."

"Okay."

"Well, hell," Jim said, looking defeated.

A few minutes later Kylie appeared at the window. He rapped on the glass, beckoned them irritably, and stalked away. The mere sight of his cranky expression brought them a kind of relief. They smiled at each other.

"The more things change," Jim said.

With the car loaded, they all stood in the motel lobby, checking their watches and looking out at the drizzle. Nobody knew how to start them off, so finally Jim said, "Well, girls, I'd better hit the road. I've got a long drive ahead of me, you know. Not like you."

"Tallahassee, here you come," Repeat said cheerfully. He was trying not to act impatient, which for Repeat was a real act of heroism. He'd been itching to come; now he was itching to go.

They shook hands all around. The others went out to the car while Abe and Jim lingered in the lobby. They found nothing else to say, only stood there together looking out. Abe waited until the others piled into the Camaro. Then he said, "Well," and they shook hands again and went out.

Kylie was in the passenger seat of the Camaro, already arguing with Repeat about the way out of town. Abe watched from the back seat as Jim flashed his headlights and pulled out of his parking space. He'd expected their parting to be different, but he couldn't have said how. Turned out it was just wet and uncomfortable, one more moment in a life full of moments. Turned out Abe just wanted to get on the road.

In the front seat there was a blur of movement and a thud. It happened so fast it took Abe a moment to realize what had happened. Repeat had shot out a fist and punched Kylie in the shoulder. He didn't know why. He hadn't been paying attention to them.

"Shut the hell up!" Repeat yelled, his voice cracking wildly. Kylie's eyes watered, and he drew up his own fist. Repeat's face took on a warning look. "You want to get out of the car?"

Kylie kept his fist up. He sniffed and said in a strangled voice, "You can't just hit me like that, goddamnit! Goddamnit, Pete, you can't just hit me like that."

Abe closed his eyes.

Roberto said, "I have to separate you two?"

Kylie lowered his fist and looked away, shaking his head.

The engine roared to life, Repeat gunning it angrily. The windshield wipers began their incessant moaning. Repeat said, "Kylie, sometime you've got to learn when to keep your damn mouth shut." He pulled out of the parking space, tires spinning on the wet pavement.

At the lot exit Jim sat in his car, waiting for a break in traffic. They pulled up behind him. "Here's Jim again," Repeat said flatly. Jim had noticed them. He lifted a hand, looking back at them in his rearview mirror. They all lifted their hands.

Feeling the crunch of gravel, Abe pulled the wheel left. Though he knew the highway well, it was difficult to follow. In some places water covered the road. He wouldn't see it so much as feel it, the sudden looseness in the steering wheel and the guttural splashing against the undercarriage. Clenching his teeth, he'd squeeze the wheel, holding it square, and plow through.

"This is crazy," Roberto said from the back seat.

"You awake back there?" He didn't chance looking in the mirror. He heard Repeat groan sleepily behind him.

"I mean this is goddamn crazy," Roberto said. "Just look at this stuff."

"I'm about give out from looking at it," Abe said. "Thank God we're almost home."

Roberto leaned forward. "Are we?" he said, peering out through the windshield. It was impossible to see anything but the road in the headlights. "*Dónde estamos?*"

"Highway 5."

"You serious? We been asleeping that long?"

"You, maybe."

Kylie sat up, blinking and clearing his throat, and said, "Where are we?"

"Almost home."

Soon the sign for Big Creek appeared in the headlights, and as they hit the bridge, Abe felt the steering wheel jerk left. He swore and pulled against it. Immediately Repeat and Roberto were leaning over the seat, staring intently out into the rain. Kylie braced a hand against the dash. No one spoke. They all felt the car slipping sideways, could see the blurred yellow line passing from left to right before them. A moment later they were across the bridge, and Abe had pulled back into the right lane.

"For God's sake, Pitt! What the hell was that?" Repeat said.

Abe clutched the steering wheel, wide awake now. "We lost traction—I was steering us straight into the right rail, and we were still sliding over. There was water all over the bridge."

"Drains must be clogged up with leaves and shit," Kylie said.

Abe let out a deep breath. "Felt like I was driving through a lake."

"Well, maybe you ought to just slow it down," Repeat said, still testy, though Abe was driving slowly already.

"I about pissed my pants," Roberto said.

The highway sign for Crows materialized out of the gloom, and Abe pulled carefully onto the turnoff to Jackie's house, operating on memory almost as much as sight. The steep woods road was all mud, even worse than before, and cratered with deep puddles. Repeat touched his shoulder.

"Pitt. Hey, man, you think you could walk the rest of the way up?"

He'd guessed this would come. The road was in poor shape; it did seem unlikely the Camaro could make it. But he was in a terrible mood and resented being asked. He stomped the brake and the car skidded to a stop.

"Yep," he said tersely.

"Sorry, Pitt," Repeat said, trying to be gentle now. "Just worried about the car."

"Not a problem."

"You want your stuff now, or—"

"Hell, no. I'll come to your house tonight and get it."

"No, I'll bring it by your place."

"Fine."

He sat a moment longer. Steam rose from the hood of the car. In the headlights you could see the hard rain sending up a fine spray of mud that hung like brown mist over the road.

"Well," he said.

"We gonna wait here, make sure you get your truck out," Roberto said.

"All right." He sighed. "See y'all later."

Repeat was half-standing, head bent forward, ready to climb up into the driver's seat. He clapped Abe on his sunburned shoulder. "See you tonight, Pitt."

Abe splashed uphill through the puddles, mud sucking at his shoes. His truck sat alone in the yard, strange to see. He'd rarely seen the house without Jim's car in front of it. Jackie's little foreign job was gone too; she must already have headed in for her early shift at the hospital. She'd left the porch light on, however, probably for his sake, and Abe felt a disproportionate pang of gratitude for this simple act of kindness. He slogged over to his truck.

On the muddy road his truck slipped and skidded, branches squealing against his window, but he hardly cared. At the highway he found the others already gone. It was one thing for Roberto to say they'd wait, another for Repeat to actually do it. In a few minutes he was passing through Owensville, where the Camaro's lights appeared off to his left, heading away up the county road. He eased past at thirty miles an hour. Every few seconds lightning flickered, intensely bright, and the larger world appeared like a series of photograph negatives. Trees and road and streaks of white rain. He passed the Valley Lodge Nursing Home, a lonesome blur of painted cinder blocks, and then the Garland County highway sign, which meant he was almost home.

A rock cracked against the windshield. Abe pumped the brakes, thinking he'd come up on a log truck that he couldn't see in this rain—their tires were always throwing up debris. But nothing showed in his headlights except the white boil of rain on asphalt. Two more stones struck his windshield in quick succession, and no sooner had he realized it was hail than he was in the thick of it, white chunks clattering on his hood and roof, exploding into smears of powder against the windshield. The noise was deafening. That's it, he thought, looking for a place to pull over. But now he'd come to the South Fork bridge, and when his headlights lit up the ripple of current in the water ahead of him, he understood, with a sudden shocked clarity of retrospect, that the drains in the bridge over Big Creek hadn't been clogged: the creek had overtopped it.

Too late to avoid the bridge, he aimed for the right side, not hitting the brakes but keeping his head, knowing he wanted those tires turning, seeking pavement. When he turned the wheel to the right he saw no bridge railing there, and the beam of his headlights didn't follow the direction of his wheel but swept downward and to the left, illuminating a turbulent gush of water where he expected concrete and metal. He felt a rising in his gut, a sharp pain as his forehead hit the windshield. Water rushed over the glass. He still didn't understand. He knew the truck was moving; he thought the creek was pushing him along the bridge rail. At last, too late, he realized there'd been no bridge at all.

This is it, he thought, with profound disbelief, and felt himself lifted and flung through the cab. He struck the passenger door and crumpled into the floorboard. His hands moved sluggishly through water; his legs were in the seat above him. Dazed, only dimly aware of his situation, he hauled himself up from the floorboard as if out of a full tub. The truck had stopped. The headlights were off. It was completely dark. He heard the groaning of metal as the truck swayed.

After a moment, his head cleared, only to panic, and he lunged for the door handle. His ear smacked the window and began a painful ringing, as if he'd been boxed—the door hadn't budged. But he felt the truck moving again, the sway opening into a broad turn. It had been uneasily perched against something, a tree or jutting bank, and now it was free. Abe cranked the window handle, keeping his hold as the creek water poured in over him, his shout of distress choked silent at once. He yanked himself through the window and was snatched away.

At first there was no swimming. He slapped his arms against the water and went under, felt himself pressed down, down, down, swallowed by the creek, lost in it, until his knees scraped gravel and he was up again, head above the surface, coughing water and snot. This time he kept afloat. His arms paddled slowly, in ridiculous proportion to the speed of the current. He saw no creek bank, only water and the trunks of trees swiftly passing. To get clear of the main channel he swam for those trees, and after a few desperate strokes, a sycamore trunk caught him in the midriff, knocking the wind from him. Abe clung to it, its pale trunk faintly luminous in the darkness, his forehead pressed against its peeling bark. His breath returned in a rush, leaving a sunken feeling in his gut. Water splashed over him, split around the sycamore trunk, roiled past. He was above what used to be the creek bank.

The current had shifted to the west, following an invisible bend in the creek bed. He wasn't free of it but sensed he was close. He kicked off from the sycamore, swimming hard. The water caught him as if on the lip of an eddy, swinging him along the fringe of the current and then, abruptly, releasing him. He drifted into the trees, where the water grew swampy and still. He stopped swimming and treaded water, his breath coming in gulps.

It was loud in the woods. Rain beat heavily down, despite the canopy of trees, and hailstones skittered through branches to plunk into the water, rising to bob like corks. The high bare branches of dead trees clattered tonelessly together, and all about him the wood creaked ceaselessly, a thousand attic doors. He could hear better than he could see. He could just make out the trees close by, although, when lightning flashed, the woods got deep and huge, and he could see even the faraway trees swaying in the wind.

Before long Abe discovered that the water came only to his chest here and, by the oozing feel of mud under his left foot, discovered, too, that the creek had torn away his shoe. He stood resting for some time, waiting in vain for his side to stop aching. Now and then a hailstone glanced sharply off his head, and the wind freshened the sting of the scrapes laced across his cheeks and neck. The rain was constant, and soon he hardly noticed it.

Eventually he started back toward the creek, intending to follow it out. It was a short distance but slow going. The ground was uneven, the water sometimes to his waist, sometimes over his head, and he had to pick his way through hidden brush and briars. At the sight of ripples in the water ahead of him, he froze, the back of his neck prickling. He could sense it, the deep and dangerous pull of the current. He felt a stab of fear, as if he'd come across a living beast, something enormous and unknown in the water with him. He retreated a few steps and headed upstream, keeping the creek to his left.

Minutes later he was stopped again, the first hint of unseen current plucking at his shirt. The creek had taken a sharp bend to the right, across his path. He'd been prepared to follow it until lightning had lit up the trees in a long succession of flashes, and in its light he'd seen something moving off to his left. As thunder rolled over the woods, he watched it draw closer and finally sweep by, only an uprooted pine sapling. But it had come from the left.

Abe sank back against a willow tree to rest, staring at the place where the two swollen creeks converged. He couldn't quite muster a bitter laugh.

The willow proved easy to climb, its branches low and sturdy. Abe pulled himself up, his clothes sagging heavily, water streaming from his pants. Now that he was in the wind, goosebumps rose on his arms and he began to shiver. At the first branch broad enough to sit on he stopped, wedging himself against the trunk, crossing his arms for warmth. The muddy sock on his left foot drooped from his toes. His right shoe was streaked with mud, its laces matted with stickers and cockleburs. Even a flood couldn't stop the damn cockleburs.

He sat uncomfortably, crowded by the narrow branches, considering. Despite the gloom, he could see the two creeks more clearly from this height, judging them more by the flotsam borne along their currents than by any distinct boundaries. Downstream they joined to form a single channel; upstream they diverged in a broad Y-shape and disappeared into darkness. Either branch could be South Fork Creek, but perhaps neither was: perhaps South Fork Creek converged with one of them farther upstream or with another creek that went on to converge with one of these. In these woods the lesser creeks branched and crossed each other and branched again; there was a wide and intricate network, and all of them would be flooded now. What he needed was a compass or at least the sun. He looked up through the high swaying willow branches, shielding his eyes from the rain, but though by now the sun must have risen, he saw only the gray underbelly of storm clouds, flickering now and then with sheet lightning.

The willow branches swayed in the wind. He kept looking up at them. Something had registered in a darker part of his brain. Not the swaying of the branches, but a certain oozing motion, an unwinding. The lightning came again, and his eyes seemed to focus for the first time. The branches were alive with snakes. Every bough, crook, and twig, draped with the long dark bodies of water moccasins. Even as he looked, one swung suddenly loose from a branch above him like an unfastened hook on a screen door; it dangled twisting for a moment, recovered, and roped itself around the branch again.

Abe straightened abruptly, needing to disengage from every surface at once. Losing his balance, he clutched instinctively at a nearby branch, saw a muscular black body writhe away from his touch, and withdrew his hand without ever touching snake or branch. He jumped as he fell, pushing off from the branches, leaping as high and far out as he could, having seen in an instantaneous panoramic vision the snakes below him, snakes on the very branches he had moments before gripped to pull himself up, snakes wrapped around the low thin limbs that bowed and finally disappeared into the water below.

He descended through the branches in an arc, hitting with a splash and striking out away from the tree. His leap had carried him almost to the verge of the creek, and now he swam directly into it, feeling the grip of the current before he could stop himself, and was instantly dragged off and under. Twenty yards downstream he came up coughing and struggling. After a while he was free of it, drifting once more into still waters thick with brush, where he grabbed the bole of a birch sapling to keep himself afloat as he gasped for breath.

It occurred to Abe he might die in these woods. But that was absurd. He grew up here. The highway was probably five minutes away. Calm down, he told himself; nobody dies in second-growth pine woods. He forced himself to look around. The creek passed off to his right; somehow he'd crossed it. He set out again.

Wary now of everything that moved, he traveled more slowly than before. After a while it seemed he'd gone far too long without finding the creek fork, and he climbed another tree—not without scanning it first—having begun to suspect he'd passed the confluence without realizing it. Though he could see the creek below him in the gloom, it faded quickly into broad boundless water, boundless shadow and woods. There was no movement and no break in the trees. He didn't have a proper fix on direction. He might move parallel to the highway for miles without noticing. When lightning illuminated the woods in a long sequence of flashes, his eyes swept greedily in all directions; still he saw nothing to help him. When the lightning was gone, however, he did.

Some distance off—perhaps a quarter of a mile—shone a small, dull circle of light, low to the ground. He could see it between lightning flashes. It seemed fixed there beneath the trees. A spotlight, or the parking light of a truck. Maybe a logging road cut through the woods there. Maybe even the highway itself, and he too disoriented to know it.

Setting his course firmly in mind, Abe descended into the water and headed out. He couldn't see the light from here; a low ridge lay in his path; nor could he see the ridge as a ridge, exactly, but as a darker swelling in the shadowy woods, like a storm cloud against a night sky. It grew distinct as he drew nearer, a great hump rising out of the murk. Staggering up onto rocky soil, he climbed to the ridge's crest, slipping now and then on sodden mats of pine needles—but, oh, the relief of solid ground. His appearance triggered an alarmed flurry of movement: The white flag of a deer's tail flashed in the darkness, followed by the quick clump of its hooves, and Abe glimpsed its flank melting into the gloom. Squirrels screeched at him like cats from the branches above; snakes coiled and flared and twisted away. Abe stood frozen, heart racing. Every creature in the woods had crowded onto the high ground.

He scrutinized a broken pine branch, kicked it sharply, hopped back. A copperhead kinked into view, sliding off away from him. He kicked the branch again. When nothing else crawled out, he picked it up and swung it before him, scraping the ground, hoping to scare a clear path. But the snakes had already retreated.

He found the light again. Low off among the trees, not a hundred yards away. His excitement mounting, Abe worked down to the water's edge, where slick turf gave way to mud, and waded in again. Plunging ahead in thigh-deep water, he'd hardly taken twenty steps when from behind him came a sharp report like a gunshot, followed by a long, squealing groan that sounded like an animal mad with pain. With bile in his throat he whirled to see a tremendous black oak coming down off the ridge, moving toward him through the dark animate trees like something prehistoric and furious and big beyond reckoning. He saw it caught in three separate lightning flashes as it fell, which gave it the sense of something alive and coming for him, and he stumbled backward, awestruck and numb with fear. Then it was down. Its huge, muffled splash overcoming even the rain and thunder. Abe stood shaking. The oak was lost in the darkness; he couldn't tell if it really had been close to him or if he'd been fooled by the storm. When lightning came again he saw nothing in its greenish light but the water, the ridge, and the undergrowth and upright trees around him. He turned and went on.

He was nearing another creek, could feel the first tug of its current, and he moved more cautiously as the water deepened. It was quieter than you'd expect: no great roar, nothing much louder than the rain beating down. At last he began to see the movement of the water, foam splashing up as the creek rolled over hidden boulders and crashed against trees lining what once had been the creek bank.

Just downstream of him the light beamed up through a translucent wall of moving water. It lay submerged some four or five feet in front of a massive oak. Fighting back an oppressive disappointment, despairing at the absence of any hint of road, Abe took a few moments to realize what he was seeing—the single functioning headlight of an overturned car, pinned against the tree by the current.

He moved quickly now, thinking of how long the car had been underwater, how long it had taken him to reach it. Soon he came alongside the car and the oak tree, perhaps ten yards away. He clung to a bent sapling, his legs drifting out to the side, pulled by the current. He was on the fringe. The headlight offered scant light, its dim circle pushing a weak, truncated beam into the murk. Floating clumps of leaves and tree branches passed in front of it. The tires protruded upward from the underside of the car, the two farther ones clearing the surface. The creek tumbled over the front tires in two round hillocks of water.

The oak, broad and thick, grew up from the creek bank now underwater. Beyond it the creek bent away; Abe could see the flotsam following its course. The car was pinned flat against the tree, its front and rear ends sticking out on either side of it. He'd once seen an aluminum canoe caught against a tree in just such a way. The river had bent the canoe around the trunk until it looked like a horseshoe.

He couldn't think of anything to do. If someone was trapped inside, he had surely drowned by now. It would be ridiculous to risk drowning just to find a dead man. The current here appeared swift, and Abe was already exhausted. He stared at the car, afraid of it, his anger mounting. Of course he would have to try.

"Damn it!" he shouted, and his voice sounded wild and strange, muted by the rain and rushing water. He held to the sapling, studying the car, wondering how to get at it. It was a long ten yards. A squirrel's nest floated past the headlight and was gone. Lightning strobed the woods, a long sequence of burning flashes, and in that light Abe saw the eyes behind the car. His stomach turned. When the lightning was gone he could still see them, faintly reflecting the light from the water.

Thunder exploded overhead and ripped away toward the hills. As it receded, a voice drifted ethereally across the water, as if from a long distance: "Are you real?"

Abe shivered and cried, "What?"

The voice rose, a woman's voice, quickening with emotion: "You're real? You're real! Oh thank you, God! Thank you, God!" She was crying now, weeping so that he could plainly hear her gasps: "Help me," she sobbed. "Please help me. I'm stuck here. I'm stuck—"

"I am," he said, heart thumping madly. "Just a minute. I've got to figure out how to get over to you."

"You have to hurry!" she cried frantically.

"Just a minute," he said again, searching the water. He saw mud sifting like smoke through the beam of the headlight, but nothing to grab onto. He would have to move upstream and swim for it, try to reach the car before the current carried him past.

"Where are you going!" the woman screeched.

"Be quiet!" he yelled, before he knew what he was saying. Her scream had scared him; he'd felt her panic in his gut. "Be quiet! I'm just going upstream a little. I'm going to swim over to you, okay? Just calm down."

She called after him, still weeping. "You should've told me first. You have to tell me."

Abe, guilty, didn't answer, only picked his way cautiously upstream. When he judged he was far enough, he yelled, "Can you hear me?"

"Yes!"

"I'm going to try to swim down to you now." From here he could no longer make out her eyes or the outline of her face. Only the hulk of the car, the tree, and the single short beam of light. He thought of something: "If I don't make it, I'll come right back, okay?"

"You have to make it," the woman said.

"I think I will, but if I don't, I'll come right back, okay?" He got no answer. "Lady, okay? I'll come right back!"

"Yes," she said at last.

He pushed forward, kicking off from a tree, swimming hard out into the current. Seconds later he felt his knees bang against metal. He groped blindly and caught hold of a submerged tire. His legs swung around, the creek pulling at them, but he held himself in place.

He had grabbed one of the front tires and was stretched out in the current above the car. Holding his breath, he reached down and found a strut, then an axle, and moved back across the car until he was near the woman. Bracing himself against the tree with one hand and the car with the other, he lowered himself beside her. Water rushed over his arms, but he found he could hold himself there in the lee of the car.

He could see the woman's face now; he was only a couple of feet away from her. She was about his mother's age. Her hair was plastered to her forehead, and her chin was tilted upward, the crown of her head pressing against the tree. She was absolutely still. The water streamed over the car and passed just below her chin. Spray flecked her cheeks, forcing her to squint and her eyelids to flutter constantly.

"I've been here so long," she said, her voice trembling. She turned her eyes toward him without turning her head, and only then, with agonizing certainty, did he know her. It was Jackie.

She recognized him at the same time. "Oh, Abe," she said, "Abe, Abe, is Jim here with you? Where did you—? Are you still here? Did you not go? Abe, I think my legs are crushed. I can't feel them."

"Can't feel them at all?"

"No, no I—Abe, where's Jim?"

She must be in shock. He looked into the water but couldn't see more than the shadow of her body and the car. He said, "Jim's not here, Jackie. Now tell me, what should I do to help you?"

Her eyes flicked away from his, then back, as if she didn't understand the question. She said, "Well, y'all need to just, just push the car off while you—"

"Jackie, I'm alone."

She was confused, her voice turning desperate again. "Well, didn't you call somebody? Isn't somebody coming?" Her chin dipped briefly under the surface. She raised it quickly again, spitting water.

"I don't think anybody knows. I'm lost."

"What do you mean?" she cried. "Didn't you see me from the road? Can't you just flag somebody down?"

"Jackie, we're lost! I can't see the highway. I don't know where it is."

"Oh, God," she said, searching his face intently. She wanted it to be a lie, but couldn't understand why it would be. Then her eyes wandered, and she seemed to forget him.

"Jackie," he said. "Jackie, let me try to push the car off you."

Her eyes returned to his face with a hungry look in them. "Yes," she said. "Yes, get the car off me."

"Can you swim at all?"

"I doubt it," she said. "You'll have to help me."

"Okay," he said, having no idea how he would manage. "I'm going to try to pull this end around. Maybe the current will help if I try to swing it around."

"That's right," she said. "Swing it around."

He moved out toward the front of the car, holding on to the bottom of the frame with his fingers, his legs drifting behind him in the current. He had to throw his head back to keep his mouth above water. When he reached the tire, he wrapped his arms around it, took a deep breath, and dropped under. He forced his knees forward against the current, bringing his legs down. His feet sank into mud, skidding as he strained against them, and bumped against the car. So the car was on the ground. He'd thought the current was holding it up. It was a small car, though, and sitting this way with its top in the mud, with the creek pushing against it, he thought he might yet be able to turn it. He tried to step back, to pull the tire with him. And right away he knew he would never move the car; it was like trying to pull down a tree. Still he stood there and strained at the tire until he was out of breath.

He came up for air, careful not to lose his grip. He might hold himself against the current, but he could never swim against it. Jackie was staring ahead, brows furrowed as if in great concentration. "It's no use," he said. "It won't budge."

"Try it again," she demanded.

"Jackie, I tried as hard as I—"

"Try it again!"

"Jackie, it's a goddamn car! It's too heavy! It's stuck in—"

"Try it again!" she screamed, her frantic eyes turning toward his. "Try it again! Try it again!"

"Shit!" he shouted, and sucked in a deep breath, jabbed his feet into the mud. He could hear himself straining, the groan in his throat loud and warped under the water. This time he stayed under too long, sucking in a mouthful of water as he came back up. He stayed at the front of the car a minute, coughing and struggling to get his breath, before he moved back in to her.

He said nothing at first. Jackie was looking straight ahead again, with that constant fluttering of her eyelashes against the spray. He waited for her to speak—she must know he was here—but she was quiet. "Listen," he said finally, as gently as he could, "it just—"

His voice triggered hers. "Try it again, Abe! Try it—"

"Jackie!"

"Try—"

"Jackie, shut up!"

She fell silent, gulping for breath. Her eyes were on him now, huge and white and wild.

"Don't say it again," he warned. "You're panicking, okay? I can't move the goddamn car. We've got to do something else."

Jackie kept her eyes on his, and he gazed back, waiting for a response. She held her head in an eerie, unnatural stasis, never shifting it. At last her eyes went forward again, and she said, calmly and firmly, like the Jackie he knew, "You've got to help hold me up, Abe."

"Okay!" he said, relieved to have a plan. "Right. How do I do that? Are you—are you treading, or—"

"I'm pinned," she said sharply. "I told you."

"Yes, but—" He peered into the dark water, trying to figure out the problem. Her face was above water and she could breathe; he couldn't see what she needed him to do. "What is it you—"

Desperation edged back into her voice. "I've got to press down with my arms and hold my chin up like this or else my face goes underwater and I can't breathe. I can't breathe because of the water. You see I've got to—"

"Oh, Jesus."

"It's only a few inches difference," she said, "but no matter how I turn I can't keep my face out of the water without arching up like this. So you've got to hold me up and let me rest or I'm going to drown. You've got to hold—"

"Okay, Jackie. Where do I—"

"I think if you can pull yourself up here in front of me—"

"Right," he said, already moving. He reached forward, probing the guts of the car for handholds, and pulled himself into the current. The water surged against his face. Spitting water, he brought his legs up and forward, poking them down into the car and steadying them as he shifted position. He turned, easing down until he was squatting directly facing her; then, feet firmly placed, he braced his knees against the tree on either side of her. The current pressed from behind, but he had leverage now. He slipped his hands under her shoulders and leaned back.

Her forehead dropped against his chest. "Oh, thank you," she said in relief. "Thank you, Abe. Thank you, Abe." She relaxed in his arms, letting her own hang loose in the rushing water. The water tumbled over his forearms, bubbling in the space between their chests. And still the rain came down. He held her quietly. At first it seemed almost easy. Soon, however, he felt the strain. He shifted his footholds, his knees, testing different positions. None of them proved any easier. He gritted his teeth and held on, fire creeping out through his limbs.

Jackie was crying against his chest. Her arms were over his shoulders now, clinging weakly to his neck. He lowered his head toward hers and, speaking softly, said, "I'm going to have to move a little, okay? This is killing me. I've got to move my legs. Can you hold yourself up a second?"

She nodded against his chest. He'd expected her to resist, but almost at once she disengaged herself, sinking back. Water rushed over her face but she quickly brought her chin up, spitting water as if from long habit. A look of deep and deliberate concentration came onto her face.

Abe worked his legs up out of the car, felt the burning in his knees and thighs worsen as he unbent them. There wasn't room to straighten them entirely, but he managed to get them into a better position than before. He was sitting on the frame of the car, low in the water now, his feet braced against the tree on either side of Jackie. When he reached around her this time, locking her shoulders in the crooks of his arms, she seemed lighter. He leaned back against the current, his legs squeezing her sides, and she lifted easily toward him. She relaxed again, hanging her head forward in the lee of his body, moaning with relief.

He let his own head drop back and looked up through the tree tops. The hail had stopped without his noticing, but in the sheet lightning he could see the high rain, falling steadily from the iron gray wadding of cloud beyond the branches. It was strange how you forgot the rain. After a while it became like air. And the thunder might just be the blood in your ears, or the rumbling of the water. You forgot the sky and thought only about the creek.

"What are we going to do?" Jackie said.

"We have to be close to the highway. I'll go look for it after you rest a little bit. I can wave somebody down."

"I don't want you to leave me," she said. She seemed suddenly lucid and calm. "My back hurts and my neck's cramped from holding my head up."

"Here," he said. Still supporting her in the crooks of his arms, he began to knead the muscles of her neck with his hands.

She winced. "Too hard," she gasped. He stopped to let her recover, then started again, more gently. She winced but said nothing.

"Well, I can't hold you up like this forever. You need to rest a little, and then I'll have to try something else." He'd meant to speak confidently, but he heard the uncertainty in his voice.

"But I don't think you should leave me. I don't know how long I'd last."

"Let me think. You rest and let me think of something. Maybe I can find another way to get you out."

What he needed was a lever. A stick, maybe. It would have to be a big one, and strong. Jackie had leaned forward to rest her head against his chest. She said something he couldn't make out; he could feel her lips move against his collarbone.

"What did you say?"

"I said the creek's still rising. I can feel it."

"No, I don't think it is."

"No?"

"No. Just hold on a minute. I'm thinking."

He looked to his right, at the tires sticking up from the water, hoping a branch might have lodged against one of them. There wasn't anything, but one might come downstream any moment. He should be alert, ready to make a grab for it. Water rushed around the tires, ragged black mounds battered to hell on their trip through the woods.

"The tires," he said. "Jesus, I'm an idiot. Have you got anything in your car, Jackie? A tire iron or a jack?"

"Oh, yes!" she said. "Yes, in the turtle hull, under the floor. I mean the floor lifts up. But I think it's bolted down or something. It's one of those little jacks, the new kind."

It was probably just a wing nut holding it down, he thought. He should be able to unscrew it with his hands. "Can you hold yourself up while I go look for it?"

"Just give me another minute to rest."

He tilted his head forward, his mouth close to her ear. Wet through as she was, her hair still smelled bitterly of hair spray. It made him think of his own mother, of sitting on her bed as a boy while she got ready for work. The hair spray would come last, his mother squinting against the acrid spray as she swirled the can around her head, then waving her hand in front of her face. He would wait for her, watching her, and after the hair spray she would smile at him and say, "Ready?" as if she and not Abe had been the one waiting.

It must have been the same for Jim, he thought. He must have seen it done a thousand times.

He put the thought away. "Jackie," he said softly, into her ear, "do you think your legs are inside the window?"

"I don't know," she said. "I've been trying not to think about my legs."

"It's okay."

"Are we far, Abe? I mean are we far from the highway?"

"No," he said. "We're close."

"So after you get the car off me you can go for help?"

"That's right. We'll find a place you can rest, and then I'll go."

"Okay," she said, pulling her arms from his neck.

"Okay I can go for the jack now?"

"Yes."

"I'm going to need the keys to open the trunk. Are they still in the ignition?"

"I don't know. But there's a little lever down next to the seat, you know where I mean?"

"Down to the left of it?"

"Yes, that pops the turtle hull."

He eased her into position against the tree and lowered himself next to her. "Okay," he said, "I'm going under to pop the trunk. Don't worry. I'll be right back."

Taking a deep breath, he pulled himself down, first by the bottom of the car frame, then by a door handle. The dirty water stung his eyes and he had to close them. It was too dark to see anyway. He searched the side of the car by feel. He touched something soft, one of Jackie's legs, and followed the leg down with his hand, expecting to find an open window to pull himself through. But the glass was closed. That was the rear window, then. Her legs lay completely straight against the tree, not half-out an open window as he'd expected.

"You get it?" she said when he came back up.

"I'm on the wrong side. I have to climb over in front of you."

Abe pulled himself up into the stream again, made his way around to her other side, and went under, this time finding the open window easily. The car was upside-down, he reminded himself, the lever would be near the surface. Reaching in, he felt around between the floor and seat. His hand closed on a knob. That would be for adjusting the seat. Too far. He moved his hand and found two short levers. One for the gas tank panel and one for the trunk. He pulled them both, and from a few feet away came a muted, metallic ping. He surfaced.

"Got it," he said. "Going back to the trunk now."

He struggled over to the back of the car, only to recognize his mistake. The car lay upside down; the trunk opened down, not up. He spat, disgusted with himself, but went under anyway to investigate. The current felt stronger here, coming around the back end of the car. He could barely keep his grip. The trunk was pressed against the ground as he knew it would be. It opened a few inches, into mud, and then no more. He came up.

"Jackie," he said. "It won't open."

"But it has to," she said, the panic back in her voice. "Alls you need to do is—"

"Jackie, listen to me. Can I get into the trunk from the inside? Can I lay the back seat down and get into it that way?"

"Can you—? Oh. Yes. Yes, you can lay the seat down. You just need the key."

"Which key?"

"The same key. The starter key."

"And where does it go?"

"It goes up at the top."

"Top of where?"

"The top of the back seat, in the middle there."

"All right. Just hold on."

He returned to the open window and groped around for the ignition, praying that the keys would still be there. His hands closed on them, a small bunch of three or four. He dragged himself into the car, where instantly the current lost its grip on him, and in this welcome, almost peaceful stillness, he hunched next to the steering wheel, his feet against the ceiling beneath him. The dying headlight filtered weakly through the mud-covered windshield, tempering blackness to muddy gray, but Abe still couldn't see anything, and he closed his eyes. By touch he found the release button on the steering column, pulled the ignition key free.

Not even half a minute had passed; he decided to lay the back seat down before surfacing for air. It wasn't hard to slip between the top of the driver's seat above him and the car's ceiling below, and in no time he was running his fingers along the top of the back seat. Near the middle he felt the fabric disappear, the coldness of metal, a distinctive grooved circle. He worked the key into the keyhole, turned it easily, heard the catch spring. Now he had to think a moment, reorient himself. His mother's car had a seat like this. You pulled the bottom toward you, and the back lowered down into the trunk. But the bottom was above him now. Crouching low to give it room, he reached up and tugged on the seat. It came smoothly forward, the bottom flattening out above him, but the back wouldn't hold itself up in position. When he let go it sank down again, its weight pulling itself closed.

His chest had started to burn, but he was so close he didn't want to give up yet. He pulled the seat out again and quickly thrust his head and shoulders beneath it into the open trunk. The seat dropped gently onto his shoulders. It was a deep trunk and he had to move forward a few feet before he reached the end. His hands, sweeping around on either side of him, found only emptiness and the metal hull. He began to feel panicky and was about to retreat when he realized he was probing the top of the trunk and not the bottom. He flipped onto his back, exhaling through his nose to keep the water out, and clawed at the false panel above him. It was a flimsy square of particle board, and when his hand tore at the handle, the sodden panel yanked sharply down and split open. He was suddenly smothered by weight. The spare tire came down onto his face, tools and cables spilling onto his chest and shoulders.

His eyes opening to pitch blackness, Abe screamed, his voice gurgling and buried and lost inside his head. He thrashed wildly, and his arms became tangled in the jumper cables. He pushed up against the tire but it dropped back down as soon as he released it. He twisted onto his belly, confused, and tried to escape by pulling himself forward, which brought him against the front of the trunk, the outer hatch. He scrabbled at the seams, pushing his fingers through a crack and feeling them press into mud. He strained against the crack, trying to force the hatch open the wrong way. Then he pushed the other way, but still it didn't move. The tire weighed against the back of his head and shoulders. He tried to scream again, but his breath was gone. He sucked in water.

He had forgotten how to get out of the trunk. There was no way out. He arched his back, trying to free himself from the tire, but it had nowhere to go. He smashed what was left of the broken particle board but the tire still sat on his shoulders. At last he wormed backward on his belly, not with any idea of escaping the trunk—he couldn't think that far now—but only to get out from under the tire. The loose seat rubbed along his back, and he kept moving, shoving the tire up and forward with his hands. It fell into the cleared space in front of him. He felt the tread rub against his face as it dropped. His hands came up against the seat bottom.

And now he had a vague idea of what was happening. He was in a car, he could remember that, somewhere in the lake. He couldn't remember which lake, though, or why he was here. How had he forgotten? It hurt like hell to forget.

When the back seat lowered behind him, one of the jumper cables that was wrapped around his arms got caught inside the trunk. He didn't know what was mooring him there. He felt a pressure against his arms as he tried to back away but couldn't see what caused it. He swiped at the cables, snakes or something on his arms, he didn't care. He remembered he wasn't afraid of snakes anymore. Not that he wanted them hanging off his arms like that. He brushed them away and turned to go. He felt guilty and sick to his stomach. He had come into the car for something, but he didn't know what. Something of his mother's. Hair spray? Well, she would have to buy more. He couldn't find it.

"Abe!"

She was angry. She would have to get over it. He needed to hold on.

"Abe, are you all right? Abe!"

She kept calling his name. He tried to blink water from his eyes, but the wetness wouldn't go away. His face was down in the water. He straightened his head and looked toward the voice. Too dark to see anything. He tried to call out, "Say something else, I can't see you!" But when he opened his mouth he vomited.

"Abe! Abe!"

He remembered he ought to be breathing. He vomited again. Spluttering, he dipped his face into the water to wash it clean, brought it up again. He blew out through his nose, felt a sharp pain, sucked in a quick breath through his mouth. His lungs filled with air, and he began to cough.

"Oh, God, you were down so long, and the light died. I thought you weren't coming back."

He opened his eyes, coughing and coughing. It was raining. Water rushed over his shoulders. He was next to a woman, his hands out of sight in the water beneath him. They were holding on to something. The car. He looked at the woman. Jackie.

"What?" he said, in a choked voice, still coughing.

"Abe, are you all right?"

He nodded. "You're stuck here." It was making sense now. It was her hair spray he'd been looking for. No, not hair spray. Something else. The jack.

"Abe?"

"Just a minute."

When he brought one hand up to feel his face, the arm moved sluggishly, as if in slow motion. He expected his face to feel strange, alien, but it seemed the same as before. His nose hurt, he was covered with scratches, but it was the same as before. He felt as if he were waking up from one dream into another. He lowered his hand again, holding to the car, and waited.

"Abe?"

"Just a minute."

He held himself there, breathing, not moving. He let his head hang forward, his chin just touching the water. He was sleepy, but he didn't sleep. He kept his eyes open and waited. Something was going to happen. He could tell. And then it did. He felt a violent spasm rip through his body, and he vomited again. He groaned, exhausted.

"Abe?"

He didn't answer.

"Abe, what happened?"

"I got stuck or something. In the trunk. Give me a minute." He squeezed the metal frame of the car, getting oriented. The world seemed hazy, but he remembered it all now. It was the same place. The flooded woods, Jackie, the rain, the car. Only the headlight had gone out. He hung there in the water, resting.

"Abe?" Jackie said finally. It had been a few minutes.

He nodded and shakily began to pull himself up. "You need me to hold you for a while?"

"No," she said. "We need the jack."

The dream came back to him now with hideous clarity, and terror seized him. "What!" he shouted. "Are you fucking crazy? You want me to go—"

"Abe—"

"No!" he shrieked. "I won't do it! I won't do it, Jackie!" He shook his head violently. "No!"

"But you have to!"

"I won't go back down there!"

"You have to!"

He struck at her face, but the current swept him sideways when he let go his grip, and his hand splashed down just short. He quickly caught his grip again. "If you don't shut up—"

"I'm going to die," she said, beginning to cry again. "I'm going to drown. I'm going to die."

He glared at her, seething with rage. Their faces were close. She quit talking but was sniffling, weeping. His mind was wild. He was thinking, You have to be calm, calm down, talk her out of this.

"Jackie, I can't go," he said.

"I'm going to die."

"God *damn* it!" he screamed. "God *damn* it!" He dove under water like a man slamming a door. Wriggling furiously through the window, he swam to the rear of the car, pulled out the back seat, and felt around inside the trunk. There were the jumper cables; he remembered them clearly now. He raised the seat farther and shoved his head and shoulders inside. Angrily he groped about, finding the tire, then the plastic pouch of tools. He shoved the pouch into the front of his jeans. By touch he made out the jack, found the wing nut that held it there, unscrewed it, and backed out of the trunk.

"How does this thing work?" he asked, gasping for air. Tiny points of light shifted around in his head. He held the jack up with one hand and squinted at it. Just a small metal block, solid and heavy. He'd seen this kind but never used one.

"You got it?" she said.

"Yeah, I got it," he said. His anger had subtly shifted, without his knowing it, into a sort of small joy. He studied the jack, saw the silver thread of a long screw. “Yeah, okay, I’ve got to hook the wrench inside this little hole.” The jack was only a few inches tall, with a narrow lifting platform, but the wrench would open it up and push the car away from the tree. They didn’t need much room, only enough to free her legs. Once the jack was wedged firmly into place he could pull her out himself.

He needed both hands to work it. Struggling up into the belly of the car—he felt very weak now and was hindered by the jack—he held himself there with his feet against the metal frame and the crown of his head against the tree. He kept the jack low beneath the frame, so that if he lost his hold the jack would drop down into the car and could be retrieved. That’s good, he thought. You’re thinking again.

He dug into his pants and worked the wrench out of the pouch with his fingers. The wrench was a miniature tire iron with a hook at the end, shaped like the handle of a pencil sharpener and not much bigger. Carefully he hooked it into the jack and lowered the jack into place against the tree. He wasn’t looking at Jackie but could feel her eyes straining toward him. He started turning the wrench.

“Is it working?” she said.

He twisted it round and round. “It’s going to take a minute. It’s not even touching the car yet. But it’s moving. It’s going to work.”

“Oh please,” she said. “Please work.”

“It’s going to work.” He turned the wrench, twisting and twisting.

“How long will it take?”

“Not long now. It’s getting closer. Once I get it good and tight against the car, I’ll just—”

As he spoke, the wrench suddenly slipped free and his hand plunged down, carried forward at first by momentum and then in a desperate grab for the wrench, but it was gone, out of his hand, instantly and irrevocably gone into the dark rushing water. And he was falling forward. He dropped the jack and caught at the tree to stop his fall. He pushed himself up, staring after the jack. It too was gone. There was only the creek.

She’d seen him lurch forward. “What is it? What happened?”

He couldn’t speak. He couldn’t tell her.

“Abe!”

“It broke,” he said at last. “It broke off right in my hand.”

“No!”

“There was nothing I could do. I tried to grab it but it broke off—”

“How could it break!”

“I don’t know,” he said, his voice cracking. “I don’t know. It just did. Maybe it was rusted or something.”

“But how could it—? How could it—?” She fell silent.

He hung there for a minute, sick. The lights spun dizzily in his head, like tiny iridescent fruit flies. Then he was climbing right back into position, placing his feet against the tree, taking Jackie into his arms. She turned herself over to him, sagging into his support, her head resting against his shoulder, and wept.

Minutes passed. He saw the wrench go again and again into the water. Then the jack, into the water, again and again. Jackie slowly stopped crying, until at last she simply lay still against him, breathing. Lightning flickered twice and was gone. The thunder might have been inside his head.

"Don't feel bad, Abe," she said.

He didn't speak.

"Don't feel bad you dropped that thing. It was impossible. Nobody could have done it. Nobody can do anything." She didn't raise her face, but she lifted a hand, weakly rubbed his shoulder, and dropped the hand again. She spoke again, in a murmur this time, and he couldn't understand.

He bit his lip, holding his face there, feeling her cool wet hair against his cheek, not smelling the hair spray anymore. His nose was clogged. His eyes stung, and there were those pinpricks of light behind them. Remembering her cramped neck, he lifted his head back and began massaging her.

"Thank you," she said. She didn't cringe anymore, either too exhausted or too used to the pain.

"We have to think of something else. I should try to find the highway. I should go for help."

"Don't leave," she said. "If you leave, I won't be here when you get back."

"Don't say that. I know you're worn out, but I'll let you rest a while and then you'll just have to hold on. I'll go as fast as I can."

"Rest won't help," she said, listlessly, almost impatiently, as if she were speaking about another person, someone she didn't know or didn't like. It seemed not to concern her. "I've lost blood. Even if I don't drown, I'll be gone when you get back."

"Jackie. No you won't. Your legs are just busted up. It doesn't mean you're bleeding to death."

"I think it does."

"Now listen to me. You're going to rest, and then I'm going to look for the highway. I'm going to find help, and we're going to get you out of here, and you're going to be fine."

"Okay."

"Right?"

"Okay," she said again.

"First we'll let you rest a few more minutes."

"I don't need a few minutes. You can do it now."

"Are you sure? Jackie?"

She nodded, numb; her face was slack. When he set her back, though, it tightened from the effort and pain. Her chin lifted, and this encouraged him. He looked all around, trying to memorize the trees, the shape of the distant ridge. He couldn't lose this place.

"Just hold on," he said, and launched himself out into the water. The current seemed to have lessened, but he was weaker now, he couldn't swim as well, and the creek held him longer than he'd expected. When at last he broke free into still water, he turned and hurried back upstream, alternately walking and pulling himself and swimming along, straining his eyes for any sign of the highway. He passed the car but didn't call out. It might discourage her to see how long it took him just to return to the starting point.

Upstream he came across another confluence of creeks, but the second was an offshoot of the larger one and wasn't strong. He swam across with little trouble and continued along the first, walking waist-deep now. His eyes scanned the murky woods. The tiny lights in his head flitted irritatingly about. He thought maybe too much time had passed. He kept seeing the wrench slip free of the jack. At one point his hand shot forward in the water to catch it. Alarmed, he stopped walking. He'd been falling asleep.

He should return to Jackie. But he still wasn't thinking clearly: He was thinking that if he surrendered himself to the current, it wouldn't take long to reach her. Another jolt of alarm, and this time he gave himself a fearsome slap. Turn back, he told himself. Find something else to use as a lever and go back.

He turned back.

On his way he found a strong green hickory branch caught in a clot of sticks and leaves, and he dug it out and carried it with him. Knowing where he was headed seemed to help him make better time. When he was well upstream from the car, but could see it in the gloom, he hollered to Jackie that he was coming; then, awkwardly holding the branch, he struck out into the current. He'd been too bold, however, had forgotten the strength of the creek and his own weakness, and he missed his grip on the first tire. Flailing out desperately to catch the second tire, he lost the hickory branch.

But if Jackie saw him drop the stick, she said nothing. He spat, caught his breath, and worked his way in along the car toward her. She was just as he left her, pinned in the surging darkness, eyes staring helplessly out into the trees.

"Okay, I found the highway," he lied. "Let me help you rest for a while and then I'll go back for help. I can find it easy now. You just have to hold on." He started getting into position to hold her up, then dropped back down beside her. She hadn't answered. "Jackie," he said, "I'm here."

She didn't move or answer. Her eyelids were still, her skin ghastly pale. The features of her face seemed wavery and distorted. At last he saw that he was looking at her through a veil of moving water.

The storm had begun to subside. Even as he stayed at the car with Jackie, the creek dropped enough in an hour that her eyes were clear of the water. It hadn't been rising after all. He smoothed her hair back from her face. Her eyes regarded him with a blank and watery gaze. He looked away, up through the branches above him. The sky was leaden and flat. Rain pattered on the leaves and wood. He looked at her eyes again.

"Do it," he told himself.

But he couldn't. He couldn't close them. And eventually he left her there, staring blindly and without grace into the trees.

When he broke into the open, he saw not highway but a broad, flooded clearing in the woods, a field that was now lake. The sun weakly permeated the cloud cover. A few last pieces of half-melted hail drifted in blue-white chunks. As he stood there a gust of heavier rain swept in over the clearing, the raindrops coming toward him across the water's surface in a discernible line. He moved out to meet it, crossing the open with water at his hips.

Beyond a thin stand of trees he found another clearing. It lay in a wide, flat basin, with rocky pine ridges rising on two sides. The water deepened as he went down into it, and he stopped, not wanting to swim again. Far off to his left, at the verge of the trees, a sloping platform rose from the water—the steep slant of a roof. An abandoned farmhouse, almost entirely submerged, its roof littered with clumps of leaves and twigs, a rusted can, broken branches, a squirrel's nest. A muskrat scampering along the peak. Water lapping under the eaves.

Next to it grew an aged oak, a one-time shade tree with its upper branches spreading out over part of the roof and its lower branches now underwater. Abe hauled himself up. He thought from the peak of the roof he might spy some old road leading out. He crawled along a thick bough, found a clear spot below among the broken limbs, and lowered his feet onto the roof, hearing it groan. He waited, still with an arm over the bough, to see if it held his weight. After a moment he let go of the bough and took a step.

The wood buckled beneath him with a terrific crack. One of the tree branches whipped around to look at him. He saw the eyes, the sudden bloom of white cotton as it reared and hissed, and he felt a shock of horror, urine warm on his leg as he broke through the rotten wood and the huge water moccasin disappeared from sight.

He fell through space into water. Floundering, indistinctly afraid, he came up for air inside an empty room. The water was up to his eyes. Rain and murky gray light poured in from the new hole in the roof. He whirled around, his movement sending out tiny waves that slapped against the walls and rocked back toward him. Rotten wood floated around him in the choppy water. There was an echo in the room, like when he was a boy and would swim up under the floating dock at the beach and would hang there beneath the floorboards among the support bars and beaded spiderwebs and blocks of foam. Later he would dream of this, that he had fallen through a roof into his childhood.

He swam along the wall, seeking a window. His bare foot got tangled in a web of some kind, something gauzy. An old curtain on the floor. He kicked free but couldn't find the window it had belonged to. He paused. Something had changed. The cadence of the rain, the dim light—something almost imperceptible. At the hole in the roof he saw the dark angular shape of the moccasin's head. Water dripped from the snake as it poked its head in through the hole, rain draining around it and splashing into the room. It gazed dispassionately at the water, the head pointing down with a glass-eyed, fixed expression, like no living thing. Then it began to drop, and with part of the roof crumbling beneath it, the moccasin spilled through the hole and into the room with him. Its head slapped against the water before its body was halfway through the hole.

Abe swam for the dark doorway across the room, the top of the frame just visible. He must have passed close to the snake, but he didn't look toward it. In a moment he was through the door and still swimming, until his hands and then his head struck the far wall of the next room. He spun and faced the doorway. He tasted blood in his mouth now, warm and sticky. This room was darker, but he could see the doorway; there was more light in the other room from the hole in the roof. He edged along the wall, watching the door. The water chopped all around the room, lapping against the walls with that hollow echo.

The moccasin slid into the room, easing silently along the surface, its head elevated. The head was broad, thick, and heavy, with the snout slanted up, so that from Abe's perspective it looked absurdly like a frog gliding over the water. It swam as far as the wall he had bumped into, turned toward him, and was still. The snake lay in shadow now, away from the door, and even as he stared at its dark shape in the dark room, it disappeared.

Desperately he searched the wall beside him, his knuckles scraping against wood, until at last his hands slipped through into nothingness and he ducked under and kicked through the window and came up swimming. He swam until the ground rose up and he could stand waist-deep. Only then did he turn and look back.

The horizon was a fringe of pines. Wind swept whitecaps across the water. By sheer accident he had found the old road, a narrow path through the trees west of the house, rising uphill. He followed it, emerging from the water with his clothes clingy and dripping. The road continued steeply uphill until he was trudging ankle deep in brown mud, shivering in the wind.

He walked for some time along high ground, the road crowded by somber green pines. He stopped often to rest, stooping with his hands against his knees, every muscle quaking. The road sank into a slough stirred up by the rains. Old dead trees slimed with mold and algae floated languidly, lifted by the water from the mud where they had lain bogged and decaying for years. After a while he came out of it. One last precipitous ascent, and the road crested onto a narrow ridge overlooking Highway 5. He struggled wobbly and blown onto the ridge, flushing a possum from where it lay in a bed of pine needles. It hissed pink-mouthed and moved stiffly a few paces off and watched him. Abe looked down at the highway. He'd never been more than a mile from it.

The possum hissed again when he moved to descend. He took up a knotted stick of pine and flung it angrily, almost falling down with the effort. The stick hit the possum near the tail and knocked it onto its side. He left it feigning death and picked his way down to the highway.

He was about a quarter of a mile uproad from the washed-out bridge. It was lighter out now. Off to the east, thunder sputtered like a dying candle. The rain was soft. A crow cawed from somewhere beyond the ridge he'd just descended. He headed west, the asphalt cool and rough against his bare left foot, which had lost its sock without his noticing. His legs were rubbery and disconnected, and he walked erratically along the shoulder as if drunk. There were no cars. He sometimes heard a sound like that of a car approaching from behind and would turn expectantly, but each time it was the wind coming off the mountains, shaking rain from the trees and sweeping wet leaves over the highway.

He walked the deserted highway, misjudging the familiar terrain, expecting each bend to reveal the town straddling the highway in the distance. Half a mile out, he stepped on a broken beer bottle. Heard the glass crunch beneath his shoe and felt, a moment later, pain in the heel of his other foot. Pulling up the foot to investigate the cut, he lost his balance and fell into the wet grass at the side of the road. A shard of clear glass dangled from the tough skin of his heel. He touched it gingerly and it fell away. The cut wasn't deep and hardly bled, but the rest of his foot was a mess of bloody scratches. He sat looking at it until he felt his eyes losing focus. He got up onto his knees. Then to his feet.

It took him an hour to walk the two miles into Lockers Creek. When he came into town the plastic triangular flags over Purdue's used car lot were fluttering in the wind, and three men stood smoking under the striped front awning. Emma's Café, the low brown building on the near edge of the strip, seemed desolate and still. All the lights were out. The floodlights over at Purdue's, the neon sign in the café's front window, the tall illuminated sign down at the Phillips 66 station—everything was dark.

He crossed the highway toward Emma's. The men under Purdue's awning hadn't been looking in his direction and didn't see him until he crossed the road in front of them. One of them lifted a hand in a wave as he passed, but he couldn't return it. Before his back was to the group he saw one man point at him with his cigarette hand, flicking the ashes away with the same gesture. He knew Purdue and had never liked him and did not want to talk to him now. He climbed the short cement steps to the café, stumbling at the top and catching himself with his hands against the door. He heard a spurt of laughter from across the highway.

The café was empty and dark. The waitress, Laine, a young woman he knew but slightly, was sitting on the counter painting her fingernails. She leaped down, surprised.

"The power's out," she said, a bit defensively.

He stood in the doorway. "I just want some coffee," he said after a moment. His teeth chattered when he spoke.

She went around behind the counter, blowing on her fingernails. "You got it. It should still be hot. You just sit wherever you want."

He walked to a booth with vinyl-covered seats. He sat shivering and wrapped his arms around himself, his head bowed. Water dripped from his nose onto the formica table. "Phones out, too?" he said without lifting his head.

"What's that?" Laine asked. She came with his coffee and was about to set it down when she got her first good look at him. "Oh my God," she said, clattering the cup and saucer onto the table. His hair was slicked back, so that even with his head lowered she saw the cuts and swellings on his face. She recognized him now and bent over him tenderly, lifting his chin with one finger to see the rest of his face. "Abe? What happened to you?"

The softness of her touch made tears start into his eyes. He brushed her hand away and clenched his jaw. "Your phone out?" he said again.

"No," she said, more coldly now. "No, the phones are working fine.

Emma just called while ago to say they probably won't get the power back on today. I was fixing to close up when you come in."

He nodded. "I'm going to need to use it here in a minute."

"Okay," she said, a little wonderingly. She straightened, crossing her arms and regarding him.

The coffee cup was hot and burned his fingertips, but he held onto it with both hands and lifted it shakily to his lips. His teeth made a stuttering noise against the rim of the cup, and he had trouble tilting his head far enough back to get any of the coffee.

She watched with widening eyes and then spoke in a soft voice again. "Let me get you some pie," she said, heading back behind the counter. "I was just getting it out of the oven when the electricity went out. It should still be warm."

When she returned he was just setting the cup down onto its saucer again. Coffee dribbled over his fingers. She slid the cup and saucer to the side, his fingers still laced around the cup, and set a slice of pie in front of him. "You look like you need some hot food inside you."

"Okay," he said.

He let go of the cup and took the fork she held out for him. His hair fell forward over his eyes and she reached out and slicked it back, and this time he didn't resist her. The pie was hot and sweet, a Dutch apple with a crumbly, sugared crust. He swallowed a bite with difficulty, felt it move in a lump down his throat.

"How is it?" she said, laying a hand gently on his shoulder.

The fork in his hand rattled violently against the table top. He tried to release it but couldn't. The features of his face bunched up as if drawn together with a cord. He took a deep breath and nodded and said, "It's good."

He saw the look of concern on Laine's face, felt her sliding into the booth next to him to hold him. Her arm shook against his shoulder.

"It's okay," she said soothingly. "It's okay."

He understood then that it was his shoulders and not her arm that shook, and when he realized this he felt the warm tears come into the back of his throat. He coughed them up, coughed furiously for a moment, and then felt the tears and snot on his face but couldn't stop himself. He wailed and wailed in the dark café, and he clung to the waitress until he was too spent even to hold his seat. And after she had phoned and they came for him, they found him on the floor beneath the table with Laine sitting next to him smoothing his wet hair, and though the lights had come back on, his eyes were squeezed closed and his face was hidden in his hands, and he didn't know it.

Chapter 4

It wasn't hard work, but he'd been at it all morning, and Marie found herself scolding her father into taking a break. His entire head—cheeks, brow, bald pate—was pink from exertion, and he glistened with sweat. The sun beat down on the wet streets and sidewalks, setting the whole downtown asteam. People were wiping their brows, tugging at the necks of their shirts. The gawkers and picture-takers dripped with sweat just from standing around. Marie leaned her mop against the wall and joined her father outside. He wouldn't sit still if she kept working; she'd finally figured that out.

They perched on the narrow stone sill of the display window, her father holding the shovel as if reluctant to waste energy setting it down and taking it up again. He looked like something from a picture, she thought, one of those mine workers or railroad builders during the Depression, sullied but cheerful, gazing with weary interest upon the downtown hubbub. The sidewalks teemed with workers—people moving among mountainous piles of mud and glass, the twisted metal of ruined gutters and collapsed awnings, stacks of merchandise carried out to allow for cleanup inside the stores. From all sides came the monotonous scrape and clang of shovels against tile and cement and stone, as store owners scooped mud from their floors and front sidewalks. The street gutters were clogged with trash and muck. Far down Central Avenue, men stretched tape measures against the sides of buildings and scribbled in notebooks, recording the high water marks.

They'd already passed by Hamilton Books. The mark on the store window was 4.75 feet, they said. It wasn't the highest they had seen, and they expected more dramatic findings down along Whittington Creek. Marie felt as if she and her father were supposed to be disappointed. She'd told them in an acid tone to be sure and let them know who won the prize. All of them, including her father, who'd been joking with the men, seemed embarrassed.

Two doors down a man was stacking boxes of waterlogged shoes onto a particle-board table warped by moisture. He had already scrawled "100 Year Flood Sale" onto a sheet of butcher paper and hung it in his front window. He was talking to a couple from Texas as he worked. The woman wore a T-shirt that said "Don't Mess With"; the man, a shirt that said "Texas." Marie heard them say they'd come into town for a convention, but the Convention Center's electricity was still out. The shoe man was explaining the flood.

"What happens is that all along Bathhouse Row here"—he pointed up and down Central Avenue, at the storefronts and derelict bathhouses—"you basically got nothing but a drainage basin for West Mountain and Hot Springs Mountain. It ain't hardly three hundred feet wide, okay? And you're right downstream of where Hot Springs Creek and Whittington Creek comes together. Now, they're suppose to run out through underground tunnels, okay? But when them things fill up, where do y'all think the creeks is gonna go?"

"In the streets," the woman said helpfully. Her mate wasn't listening. He kept sneaking looks at Marie, eyeing her bare legs.

"In the streets," the shoe man said. "Exactly."

Marie put her hand on her thigh, just at the hem of her shorts, and unobtrusively turned it so that the middle finger pointed up. When the man glanced her way again, she saw him twitch. He turned his back to her and began paying close attention to the shoe man.

The shoe man was telling them about all the town disasters, but Marie knew the details already. She and her father had gone through the newspaper together over breakfast. The power in their neighborhood was still out, so Marie had cooked up some perishables from the refrigerator on her father's grill. She'd spent a good many days of her childhood with the electricity out, in much less comfortable circumstances than these, and hardly felt troubled or even inconvenienced by it now. With the television strangely blank and silent and a kerosene lamp for light, she and her father had read all the newspaper stories.

A foot of rain had fallen in one day. There were photos of mudslides, demolished trailers, front lawns strewn with hailstones. Thousands were still without power, repair service hampered by damaged and destroyed bridges all over the county. And one woman had been killed in a flash flood east of Lockers Creek, found dead by a man whose truck had also been swept off the road.

At this report Marie's father had grown concerned for old Dr. Hodgkins, whose nursing home was just outside of Lockers Creek. A nurse on the phone assured him his father-in-law was fine. The floors had flooded, but no one was injured. Still, the nurse told him gruffly, there was a lot of cleanup work to do, and their phone kept ringing. How could they be expected to get any work done with the phone ringing off the hook?

All morning Marie had been thinking about the old man, spread puffily upon his bed with water on his floor. Trapped on an island in his own room. She'd been trying to tweeze some sympathy out of her revulsion.

Now the shoe man was talking about how bad it was out by Lockers Creek, and she said quickly, before she could change her mind: "When do you think we should go out and see Grandpa?"

If her father was surprised, he didn't show it. He leaned forward against his shovel. "You want to come along?"

"I think so."

"Well, that ought to please him if anything could. I'd say tonight, but it sounds pretty hectic out there right now. Might better wait till the weekend, when things have settled down."

She watched him askance. He'd spent the morning carting around boxes of books while she shoveled and mopped the muddy floors, and his face was still flushed. Yet in spite of the mess, he seemed content. Last night he'd kept saying how lucky he was that Marie had been here, until finally she got cranky and told him to stop. Now he sat with a bemused smile, squinting against the sun, watching a tow truck pull a sedan from a store window down the street.

"She sure went out with a bang, didn't she?" he said.

Later Marie drove over to Ouachita Avenue to buy sandwiches at a café that opened the moment electricity was restored. Coming back through the warehouse, she found the store empty. Through the display window she saw her father out on the sidewalk talking to people. The old woman she recognized at once, and the slender, gray-haired man who stood holding a newspaper over her bushy white head to shade her from the sun.

With them was a woman Marie hadn't seen before. She couldn't be older than fifty, but her hair was perfectly white, cut in a bob that fell just below her ears. Petite and trim, dressed smartly in a sleeveless blouse and pleated pants, with simple hoop earrings and a gold locket around her neck. Her smile was white and even, and she held herself like a beauty pageant contestant, with that same lift of the chin, that same posture and frankness. Even the crows' feet at the corners of her eyes, showing clearly as she smiled, gave her a look of wisdom that makes even an old harbor fisherman seem handsome. She was beautiful, and Marie felt a flash of hatred for her—she didn't know why.

"Well, here she is," the old woman said, when Marie stepped out.

From the corner of her eye she noticed the beautiful woman start, eyes widening, as if Marie had just walked into view out of a stone wall. But when she looked at her directly, the woman smiled agreeably. Marie took the old woman's outstretched hand and gave it a gentle squeeze.

"Mrs. Baker says y'all have already met," her father said.

"That's right. How are you, Mrs. Baker?"

"Oh, I'm just fine, sugar, thank you," Mrs. Baker said, after her usual pause. "I'm just out here a-jabbering on while your daddy wants to be working."

"I doubt that."

"No, I'm plumb worn out," her father said. "I needed the rest."

Mrs. Baker kept her hand. She turned toward the other woman. "This is my daughter, Angela West—"

"Angela Baker," the woman corrected, giving Marie's free hand a firm, friendly shake. Her skin was silky and pleasant to touch. She smelled faintly of apricot. "Pleased to meet you, Marie."

Mrs. Baker, watching them exchange greetings, had that look of wonder on her face Marie was getting used to. When Angela stepped back, Mrs. Baker said in a stage whisper, "Angela just got divorced."

"It's been three years, Mother, and I doubt Marie is interested."

Mrs. Baker gave Marie a look, shrugging exaggeratedly, as if they were sharing a joke. Marie wanted to laugh but felt it might be impolite.

"Don't worry, Marie," Angela said. "Mother likes to tease me, but really she's pleased I got away from him when I did. She always thought Bob was a scoundrel."

"Speaking of scoundrels," said the gray-haired man, "I'm Vincent."

Marie moved to shake his hand, then saw that he was one of those older men who'd been taught to shake hands only with other men and hadn't quite outgrown the custom. So he didn't meet her halfway, and because Mrs. Baker still held her other hand, she found herself covering her gesture with a ridiculous sort of half-curtsy. Everyone laughed. As if this really were her, just a brash and good-natured jokester, perfectly at ease. She laughed with them, but felt confused.

"Vincent's my baby nephew," Mrs. Baker said.

"Still a baby after all these years, I'm afraid," Vincent said. He had a hook nose that jerked to the side like a bird's when he regarded you. Circumspect but good-natured. His pale blue eyes gazed frankly at her as he nodded and smiled. It was a family of pale blue eyes. Mrs. Baker and Angela had them too.

Vincent had been telling a story, which he continued now, about a time when electricians were in his attic and he'd come into his kitchen to find a man's legs dangling through the ceiling. Marie liked to hear him talk. He spoke with an odd, old-fashioned eloquence, the kind she'd seen in movies but never in life. He made elegant gestures with one hand, while with the other he shaded his aunt with the newspaper. Below his rolled-up sleeves his wrists were delicate as a child's, though spotted with age. An expensive gold watch flashed in the sun when he gestured.

"I told the fellow to stop apologizing," he concluded, "that seeing my own kitchen as a surrealist painting more than compensated for the trouble."

"Was your clock all melty-looking too?" Marie's father asked, grinning.

"I half-expected it to be."

Marie had no idea what they were talking about now, and Angela, perhaps sensing this, touched her elbow and said, "Jimmy told us what you went through to spare his ceiling, Marie. That's what got Vincent started."

"Yes, indeed," Vincent said. "Nice work, Marie."

"Well," she began, then didn't know what to say.

"Why don't y'all come inside out of the sun?" her father said.

"Oh, we'd love to but we can't," said Mrs. Baker. "We were just walking back from looking at the mess and wanted to say hello. Vincent's got an appointment, and he's probably late as it is."

Vincent checked his watch. "No, Aunt Catherine, I'll be on time, but I do suppose we'd better get on." He looked at Marie apologetically and said, "You know how doctors are. Keep them waiting and they prescribe the wrong medicine out of spite."

"Are you sick?" Marie asked, then seeing the subtle change in her father's face, regretted it. What seemed to her the polite thing to ask always turned out to be the worst possible question. She felt blundering and coarse, and her cheeks burned.

Vincent, however, appeared to be amused. "All old men are sick, my dear. It's the burden of responsibility. Women age like wine, but men, well, we age like machinery. We fall apart."

"I'm sure you don't mean to say that men have more responsibility, Vincent," Angela said.

With a look of mock-fright, Vincent said, "Oh, dear, certainly not. I simply mean to say that men are burdened with it. Women, being the stronger sex, bear it easily." He turned to Marie. "It's been a pleasure," he said, "and now I had better quit while I'm ahead."

It was a relief to go inside the store after the others had left. The air conditioner was working now, and already the air had improved. As Marie spread out their lunch, her father dropped heavily into a chair and mopped his face with a napkin. He gulped almost all of his drink before he even touched his sandwich. "You let yourself get too hot," she said, scolding him this time just because she felt like scolding. She was feeling peevish, still picturing the shift in his expression when she asked Vincent if he was sick. She was angry because he'd shamed her, although she knew he hadn't meant to.

"I'm better now," he said, chewing happily.

"Well, and by the way," she said, in the same scolding tone, "did you realize you called Angela 'Angie' when you said good-bye?"

"That's her name."

"No, Mrs. Baker called her Angela."

"Oh, well, we go way back. Used to all go to church together down at First Presbyterian. She used to sing these beautiful solos. That woman's got a voice, now, I'm telling you."

"How long ago was that?"

"Seventeen, eighteen years maybe. Your mother and I used to go down there. In fact you might have gone there once or twice yourself. You'd have been pretty little, though. You probably don't remember."

She didn't remember. She wondered why he happened to stop going there, whether it had to do with her mother leaving him. That had been around the time. As a child it had never occurred to her to wonder how their leaving had affected him. Now she wanted to know. She didn't see how she could ask about that, though, without bringing her mother into it. After receiving her first couple of terse replies, her father had been careful to avoid the subject; she thought his mentioning it now might be a sort of hopeful invitation. But she didn't want to talk about her mother. Instead she asked, "What's she doing now?"

"Angie? I think I heard a while back that she was still teaching Sunday school there. Or maybe it was at Amity Presbyterian. Course she just retired from being a schoolteacher. Taught for twenty-five years at Fountain Lake. She and Bob divorced right after she retired."

"Why?"

"I don't guess I really know. Though it did seem to coincide with their kids getting out of the house. Maybe they were waiting for that. Or maybe she just got tired of Bob. Which I couldn't say I'd blame her. Bob made a ton of money but not a ton of friends."

"You seem to know a lot about them."

He shrugged. "It's not that big a town."

"What else do you know?"

"About what?"

"About anything. About Angela. She's pretty, isn't she?"

"Nobody ever argued that."

"So what else do you know about her?"

"I don't know, honey." He squinted at her curiously, finally cautious. "What did you want to know, exactly?"

"Never mind."

"You okay?"

"I think I just have a headache."

"You been working too hard," he said. "I should have made you slow down."

"I'll be all right after I eat."

She ate, but she didn't feel all right. She spent the afternoon tracking the years in her mind. She'd been very young when her mother took her away for good, without her father's permission but also without his interference. It had been coming for some time, though for how long Marie couldn't say. She remembered her father becoming a friendly stranger. In her memory it seemed an abrupt change, but it must have taken a while. Once or twice a month she would see him, an evening or an afternoon, rarely more than that. You could never predict how long her mother would let them stay. Her father had eventually moved out of their house into a cramped apartment near the bookstore, a place she remembered only vaguely. More distinct in her memory was the house the three of them had once shared—though not with him in it. No, she remembered that house only after he was gone, when nobody seemed to live there, not even Marie and her mother, although they did stay there, coming and going. It was an empty house.

They'd often stopped there as they passed through, sometimes for a week, but when Marie thought of the house now, most of her days there blended together. Listless afternoons alone in her room, making carpet angels in the shag. Reading tattered comics by a shaft of window light, watching the dust motes swirl when she flipped a page. The house always had that empty-place feeling. Marie much preferred the car, which felt occupied even when you were alone in it. In a car it only took one person. The house needed more, more than Marie and her mother; in the house she'd felt like an indistinct person, and her memories of the place were no different.

She remembered one time with clarity, remembered waking hours before dawn with the dark house bitterly cold, her mother calling from the kitchen. She was older by this time, seven, maybe eight, and she could tell by her mother's voice that she was wired, just as she could tell when her mother was sleepy or frightened or lying through her teeth. She sat up in her bed, pulling the dirty sheets and blanket around her, tight around her neck to keep out the cold, and stared without focus into the darkness of her room. There was no electricity; her mother had neglected to pay the power company again. A bill and two written warnings had been in the pile of letters beneath the mail slot when they arrived the afternoon before. The telephone was still connected, though, and her mother had called the power company, complaining and entreating, but it did no good. She sat down and scribbled out a few checks, and Marie licked and stamped the envelopes and put them into the mailbox.

Then her mother had called for a pizza and said she'd be back in a minute and left the house before the pizza was delivered. Marie had paid the man from a loose stack of bills on the kitchen table. He stood peering from the doorway into the cold, dusky house, snowflakes drifting past him into the kitchen. He had delivered a pizza here before, more than once, and maybe he remembered the young mother, curvy and sleepy-eyed and hair sometimes tangled as if, he thought, fresh out of bed with someone. But she wasn't here tonight, apparently, and he left the pizza with the kid and kept the change without asking.

Marie could find nothing in the dark, mold-speckled refrigerator but beer and a single can of soda. She opened the soda, leaving the metal pull-tab on the counter because the trash was overflowing, and drank it warm with her pizza at the kitchen table. She felt sticky afterward, and twice went to the sink to wash off, but there was no water. Outside the sun was setting, and before it grew totally dark she used the bathroom, tried without success to flush the toilet because her mother had flushed it earlier and it hadn't refilled, and went into the bedroom and crawled under the sheets in her clothes. She awoke hours later to the sound of a man's voice in the kitchen, fell back asleep, and awoke again when her mother called her.

"Marie, are you getting up? We have to leave in a few minutes," her mother called, her voice uneven and jittery. And she could tell by her mother's voice not only that she was wired but that the two of them were alone in the house again.

"Yes," she called back, her own voice scratchy from sleep. She was thirsty, but there was nothing to drink unless her mother had brought something home. She stayed under the covers, drawing her knees up, feeling the sheet bunch beneath her because she had left her shoes on and the rubber soles pulled on the sheet. There was no need to rise until her mother came to the door; she didn't have to dress, couldn't brush her teeth or wash up. She rested her forehead on her knees and dozed.

"Marie," her mother said from the doorway. A click sounded as her mother hit the light switch. The room remained dark. "Honey, it's time to go. Are you ready? I've got your coat."

Marie stood as her mother stuffed her arms into the sleeves and fumbled agitatedly for the zipper. She caught it at last and zipped it all the way up to her bare throat, pinching her skin.

"Ow," she whined, flinching away.

"Sorry, sweetie. Sorry, sorry, sorry."

"It's too cold."

"The car will be warm," her mother said. "Once it warms up it'll be warm. Now put your mittens on and let's go."

"Go warm the car up first."

"There's no time, honey. Come on."

Marie found her mittens in the coat pockets. "I'm thirsty."

"We're going to stop somewhere for breakfast, okay? I want to look at myself in a mirror anyway, somewhere where there's light and a sink that works."

"I need to pee," Marie said, though she didn't really.

"You'll have to wait till we get somewhere. The bathroom stinks. You can't flush it."

They went to the kitchen, where her mother handed her the little gym bag to carry. She could tell by the weight and feel that it was full of money now, which meant they were headed for Mena. Sometimes in this house she lost time and forgot whether they had come from the east or west. But it was the money now, and so they had come from Memphis and were headed to Mena. She held the bag in both arms, squeezed against her chest like a stuffed animal. She was waiting for her mother to open the door, dreading the blast of air, but when the air hit her it didn't feel much colder than she already was.

They stepped outside into a flurry of snow, and above them the covered sky cast back an unexpected glow of orange. "Jesus!" her mother hissed. All the windows of the neighborhood danced with the reflection of fire. Down the street, the two-story house on the corner was crackling with flames, crazy and ragged under a low ceiling of black smoke. Above the snow-blanketed hush of the neighborhood they heard the fire's heavy rumble, the deep exhalation of the burning house. Marie pressed against her mother.

"Jesus," her mother said again.

Dozens of dark figures scurried across the face of the bright house: Neighbors carrying furniture, armloads of books, clothes, blankets. They streamed like ants in a long line across the back yard to the tool shed. Already furniture was massing outside the shed, no more room inside, and clothes were draped across the chairs, the books and drawers stacked on tables and then on the snowy ground. A man shouted from the back of the house. "No more!" he was saying. "That's it!" It was the father, holding back his older son, who wanted to go inside again. He pushed against his son's chest and then put his arms around him, holding him and walking him backward away from the house. "That's it!"

"Come on, honey," Marie's mother said. "We have to go."

She got into the car as her mother brushed snow from the windshield and the back window with bare hands and then jumped in herself and started the engine. She backed down the driveway into the dead-end street, no way out except past the burning house. "What a terrible terrible thing," she said, grinding the gears. "Those poor people."

The car crawled forward, her mother feeling anxious and vaguely disrespectful to be driving away like this, leaving these people to their tragedy. As they passed the house next door, Marie saw silhouettes in the front picture window, a man and woman and two children in a lamp-lit room. Their heads were bowed and they held hands, like a paper cut-out family. They were praying. She watched the car's reflection pass like a ghost across their window.

At the end of the street a man jogged down the driveway from the burning house. One of the neighbors. He was obviously coming to meet them, so Marie's mother stopped the car and rolled down her window. A gust of heat blew into the car, carrying with it the sharp tang of smoke. Marie's eyes blurred; she wiped at them with her mittens. Behind the man the yard was full of people, most of them just watching now, milling around and generating a helpless murmur, small people beneath the towering flames and smoke, ashes and sparks and snowflakes drifting out among them like angry swirling insects. A woman sobbed into another woman's neck. One of the sons came over and put his arms around both of them.

The man outside the car leaned forward, thrusting his hands into his pants pockets. He wasn't wearing a coat, and his face and bare arms were smudged with soot. "Thanks for coming," he said, his teeth chattering, and Marie felt a flush of shame. "But really there's nothing else to do."

"What?" her mother said.

"They're all okay," he said, not catching the confusion in her tone. "We got a lot of the stuff out, most of the important stuff. Fire started upstairs, so we had a little time. No going back in now, though, and the shed's full, so we're just going to carry all the rest of it over into my house. We've got plenty of help. No need for you ladies to get out in the cold."

"Oh," her mother said. "Oh, well, all right."

The man kept talking, shivering with his arms drawn in against his sides, his hands in his pockets. He was excited, charged with adrenaline and cold and no way left to spend it. "It's a goddamn shame," he said. "Excuse my language, but it's just a shame. They say the fire truck got in a accident, hit a icy spot on the bridge, and now supposably there's a huge mess out there and nobody can get by. I don't know if anybody got hurt. Linda kept calling the station, and they kept saying a truck was on the way, but then finally they found out what happened. I don't know where the police are. Looks like somebody ought to have shown up by now, but I guess if they're trying to come out the highway they're all getting caught up in that mess at the bridge. There ain't going to be nothing left by the time they get here, though."

"Well, okay," her mother said, and began pulling slowly forward again.

The man stepped back, surprised. "Oh, okay," he said, patting the hood. "Thanks again. You ladies take care."

Marie watched him turn and head up the driveway toward the burning house. It stood huge against the night, the fire roaring through the opened roof, sparks leaping and spinning out into the darkness. The upstairs windows, their frames now empty of glass, appeared as dark hollows in the midst of the seething orange fire, staring out through the flames like eyes in a face. As the car crept forward, she twisted in her seat, staring at the face, which, like an old jack-o'-lantern, was slowly sinking in upon itself.

Come Friday night, Marie's nerves were a mess. She'd spent the week dreading the visit, regretting she'd agreed to go. It amazed her how, in her father's world, even the simplest things could be intimidating. But this is it, she told herself, this is where you stick. And so after work on Friday she bought ingredients for cookies, and in that way roped herself into going home and baking them instead of climbing into her car and driving off to who knew where.

She did allow herself to wonder—just for a minute—where she might have gone. Back to Little Rock? Melt back into her old life, or what was left of it? She could do it so easily. This was one of the many things she would never tell her father—that she'd come here from Little Rock. Partly to avoid wounding him with the knowledge that she'd been so close all these years yet hadn't sought him out, partly to keep closed those doors she preferred closed. If her father knew she'd lived in Little Rock all this time, he would surely, eventually, press for details. And what would she say? Would she enumerate all the lies and petty failures, all the wounded, wasted lives? The sick, the violent, the strung-out, the dead—everyone she had loved or tried to love? She was too cynical for such disclosures. She was nobody new. She was not the only messed-up girl with a messed-up life. She had known plenty of others, had spent too many hours in group sessions listening to girls recount their stories with such drama and feeling that it was clear they would cling to their horror until they died. The horror was all they knew—it was their life-raft, and they did their utmost to keep it inflated.

Marie didn't want that, wasn't going to be that. Anyway, there was the practical side of things. Give your father even half the facts, and the next thing you know you're in counseling; you're on suicide watch. And so you say nothing, and you don't—she reminded herself sternly—even think about it. You put it away.

"For God's sake," she breathed aloud. "Put it away."

In the evening it rained—a sweet, soaking rain. As Marie baked the cookies, her father mixed up whiskey sours with finely crushed ice. He put a lot of effort into getting them right, and just when she slid the cookie sheet into the oven, he put the glass into her hand, and they clinked glasses and drank. "To a hard week's work," he said. The drink was delicious, not too strong, and she practically gulped it down. He made her another one, still sipping his. The stereo played softly in the den, some jazzy tune she didn't know but to which her father was humming along.

She felt suddenly very content and very sad. It was strange how the two feelings could sit so comfortably together. Her father had begun telling her about some oddball who'd come into the store once, a man who wanted every book available on rainbows, including fiction, including westerns and romances. Rainbows, her father said, shaking his head. Marie smiled, a little sadly, wondering if she was the only one ever to hear these stories. Her father sometimes spoke of his friends, including his brothers, but they all seemed to live in other places, and he never used the phone. His quiet isolation moved her. She felt greedy about his throwaway stories, enjoying the notion that she was the only one to whom they'd been told. She soaked them up, stories of nothing, stories of his life.

As the evening progressed, her father made them both several drinks, and it occurred to Marie that he, too, was nervous about tomorrow, but she was getting sleepier and couldn't sort her thoughts about it. By the time the cookies were baked and they'd watched a television movie, she could hardly keep her eyes open.

Saturday morning she came hard awake with sun in her eyes and dread in the pit of her stomach. Her body was always the first to remember when she had an unpleasant task before her. A flush rose in her cheeks, and dressing before the mirror she thought she looked stupendously ugly and unkempt, the skin splotchy on her chest and neck. Her hair was tangled until she brushed it; then it frizzed. She fled the mirror to find her father in the kitchen dressed neatly in gray slacks and a white oxford shirt, as if he were still courting the old man's daughter and wanted to present himself well. There was a nick on his cheek and he smelled of spicy aftershave. He stood at the stove tying on an apron before cooking, something she'd not seen him do before.

"You look nice," he said.

"Don't even try."

"What? But you do."

She shook her head. "Just don't."

He nodded with mock solemnity. "Only the food for you this morning."

"Only the food."

"No talking."

"No talking," she repeated.

The empty streets downtown, in the shade of the sidewalk magnolias, were still cool. As her father drove, Marie gazed out upon the recently repainted storefronts like her father's, but also upon those moribund and those long dead, and the once-glorious bathhouses now defunct. They went past the Ramada and the Vapors Club—where people like Tony Bennett used to sing, her father said, though not anymore—past the run-down bars and motels and apartments, a part of town more like the kind Marie was used to. Although the streets were quiet at the moment, they were coming awake, having slept fitfully at best. Trash lay in the street gutters, detritus of a Friday night, and a skinny white man swept up bottle glass in front of his pawn shop, talking to a skinny black man who sat on an empty planter, smoking. A limping, frail-looking woman carried grocery bags down the sidewalk as her children followed with ice cream cones, kicking broken pieces of pavement. At the sight of all this Marie felt an unexpected surge of pleasure, the sweet comfort of familiarity. She caught herself thinking of her father's peaceful neighborhood as a dead one and this shambled place as a living one. Then despised the thought, which was born of looking back.

From Park Avenue her father took the highway out of town, where they came immediately into country. The sky was a cornflower blue, and along the highway the grass seemed almost desperately green, as if, too long overshadowed by rain, it would now insist upon attention. The banks were scarred here and there with muddy ruts, and branches and debris were scattered on the shoulders. Water stood deep in the ditches. At Lockers Creek her father followed a detour sign off the highway. Like the country around it, the town had been swamped. Even now, people were cleaning up sidewalks, lugging junk down to rubbish bins, replacing storm shutters that had blown free. The stores still had sandbags stacked in front of them, and freshly sunburned workers clambered over their rooftops, scraping and hammering shingles and hanging gutters. Stacks of shingles stood awaiting the roofing crews in almost every driveway.

Marie's father followed the detour signs, many of which were hand-made and nailed to telephone poles and trees. Until the new bridge was built over South Fork Creek, highway traffic had to follow an elaborate detour to get from one county to the other. A back-road bridge had been washed out too, so the route, mazelike, wound around and switchbacked and used blacktop and gravel and dirt roads alike. The signs took you out of town into more rural country, where in the shadow of the hills the bottomland farms looked boggy and unworked. The creeks under the bridges were swollen, if no longer dangerous. On higher ground kingfishers and crows stalked the puddles where fish had been trapped when the floods receded. Marie and her father were on these back roads for miles, so long that Marie could almost pretend they were on a leisurely country drive without destination. But eventually they were shunted out onto the highway again, and suddenly—too soon—they had arrived at the Valley Lodge Nursing Home.

The place reminded Marie of all the bland institutions through which she had passed herself—all those sterile premises in beautiful surroundings. The building was a long, low, cinder-block affair, painted beige, with uniformly spaced windows lining the two wings. It sat at the foot of a thickly wooded hill, and the raised edge of the tiny parking lot, where asphalt met gravel, was furred with an accumulation of rust-colored pine needles and twigs. The lot itself had been hosed off and swept clean, and small knots of visitors and residents stood among the cars talking and enjoying the sunshine. Nobody ventured from the asphalt—the walking paths were all puddled and slick with mud. Marie absorbed the subdued scene with an old feeling of revulsion.

"I should warn you," her father said, before they got out.

"That's okay."

"He used to be real smart. I mean, he still is. But now he's kind of . . . unpredictable. It can be hard, is what I'm saying."

"I'll be fine," she insisted, though she didn't feel it at all.

"Well, I know you will. I'm just saying."

They gathered their gifts and walked briskly and solemnly across the lot, passing through a funnel of gnats outside the foyer doors, each waving a free hand to clear the air. It was bright and air-conditioned inside. The foyer, freshly mopped, smelled of lemon, but the baseboards were dingy and water-stained. The reception area was a turmoil of people—some standing and chatting casually, some bustling about with clipboards and pushing carts—and Marie immediately wanted to retreat to the damp, dreary parking lot. She took measured breaths as her father checked in at the desk and led her down the hallway.

The door to her grandfather's room was open, but her father knocked on the doorjamb before they stepped inside. The room was a tidy one, recently mopped, with sunlight pouring in through the window. A rolled-up area rug leaned against the wall. Slippers and books and neatly arranged boxes lined the tops of the chest of drawers, the television, and the coffee table, all taken off the floor during the flood and not yet replaced. A slightly stale odor hung in the room, whether from the old man or from creeping mildew Marie couldn't tell, but it was cut through with the pungent smells of shoe polish and the lemon-scented floor wax.

They hesitated in the doorway, her grandfather having made no response yet to the knock. A fat, jowly old man with a sad and drooping look to his face like a hound dog's, he sat on his bed in the corner with his legs stretched out before him, gazing out the window. His hair was bristly and gray, but his ruddy cheeks were smooth, as free of stubble as a young boy's; he didn't appear to grow whiskers at all. He wore thick woolen socks, a billowing blue denim oxford shirt, and gray sweatpants, which, judging by the creases down the front, appeared to have been pressed. Not turning from the window, he said, "They told me you were coming," as if to let them know he was not surprised.

"How are you, Dr. Hodgkins?" her father said, going over to the bed and extending his hand.

The old man looked at the hand out of the corner of his eye. He shook it limply. "Reasonably well," he said in a dull tone, "under the circumstances. And how are you?"

"Oh, we're both fine. I brought my daughter along today."

Pulling two chairs close to the bed, he sat in the one near the foot of the bed and left the other for her. Marie sat down, tentatively touching the old man's arm. "Hi, Grandpa," she said. "It's Marie."

Again he looked askance, but upon seeing her face he turned his head toward her and placed his hand upon hers. It felt like cold rubber. "My darling girl. Did you bring your daddy some peppermints?"

"It's your granddaughter Marie, Grandpa," she said, taken aback. Her mouth went dry. "My dad has your peppermints. Mr. Hamilton has them. See, I baked you some cookies." She showed him the platter covered in plastic wrap. Her father was digging in his sack for the bag of mints and the animal crackers.

"No crackers?"

"Dad has your crackers too. I thought you might like these cookies, though. They're chocolate chip."

He squeezed her hand and nodded and reached abruptly for the platter. She loosened the plastic wrap from it and set it on the edge of the bed, holding it as he chose a cookie. He took up three or four and inspected them for chocolate chips, setting them back down in search of one with more chips than the others. His fingers, fleshy and pale, began to smudge with chocolate.

"They're all yours, Grandpa. You don't have to choose. You can have them all."

"All of them?"

She nodded and tried to smile. He settled on a cookie and ate it quickly, crumbs sticking to his lips and falling onto his shirt. He reached for another.

"What did you think of that flood, Dr. Hodgkins?" her father said. He had set the animal crackers and peppermints on the foot of the bed where the old man could see them. "Give you a lot of trouble?"

Her grandfather regarded him suspiciously for a moment, then seemed to remember him. "Oh, the floods," he said, still chewing. He swallowed, cleared his throat, and leveled his gaze not on her father, but on Marie. "The floods."

"Kind of a mess, huh?" she said.

He exhaled loudly through his nose, his breath whistling. "The floods are older than man," he declared, in a voice so forceful it startled her. "And man believes they serve the good—always, he says, the will of God. Always, always, always. The deluge was sent first to cleanse God's earth of evil men and later, as baptism, to cleanse man himself of evil. But I ask you, how much smaller can the flood become? What remains to be cleansed, do you know? How sharp has the focus of God become?"

Marie looked to her father, whose expression was deliberately impassive. He only shook his head. She cleared her throat and said, "Well, Grandpa—"

"Tears," the old man interrupted. "Tears are the final flood. They cleanse not God's earth nor man himself, but man's own fervent, man's own religious belief in himself. Tears bring man to God, because in tears—are you listening, Jimmy?—in tears man loses his sense of self-sanctity, in tears he learns again that renewal is not in the filling up but in the emptying of the soul. Tears are the last baptism and flood, and God in his wisdom offers them to all men, not only to those steeped in the ritual and ceremony . . . in the ritual and ceremony of cleansing, but to their predecessors too, and those who wander, and those who inhabit the farthest reaches, and the anchorites, and the ignorant, and the hopeless, and the prayerless." He halted abruptly and smacked his lips, then added, in a soft, lugubrious voice, "Yet we are a nation of the tearless. I myself am a tearless man."

He was peering behind her now, toward the doorway, with a guilty look on his face as if he'd been caught at something. A nurse had stepped into the room, an older woman with a pug nose, deep wrinkles, and no expression whatever. She smiled in greeting, but her eyes didn't change. She came to stand by his bed.

"It's tears again, is it, Dr. Hodgkins?"

He scowled at her. "Yes, it is, Mrs. Garner," he said. "Even for you."

"Even for me," she said blankly. "Well, ain't that nice of you. Okay now, time for your meds."

Marie was leaning in her chair to be out of the way, but the nurse's hip still pushed against her shoulder. She scooted her chair over. Mrs. Garner moved closer and held out a small paper cup of pills and another cup of water. Dr. Hodgkins took them both. He began to drink the water, but Mrs. Garner said, "The pills first, Dr. Hodgkins. Otherwise you'll start talking and I'll have to go get more water."

"There's plenty of water, isn't there?" he said. "I was telling them about the disaster."

"I know you were. Take your meds now, please."

He looked to Marie's father. "It took them three weeks to clean my rug, can you imagine? How difficult is it to clean a rug? And my slippers were floating in the closet like junk boats. Floating around like little bitty Chinese junk boats. With no candles in them."

"Three weeks, my butt," said Mrs. Garner. "The flood was on Monday, Dr. Hodgkins, and they cleaned your rug yesterday. Remember? Me and you sat in the kitchen drinking lemonade while they pulled it up. Now please take your pills."

He frowned at her and dumped the pills into his mouth. "My daughter brought me these cookies. I suppose you don't want me to eat them."

"You can eat them till you upchuck, if you want to. Now go on and swallow them pills. You know I can't initial the book till I see you swallow them."

He closed his mouth and sighed the whistling sigh through his nose. He glared at her for a few seconds to show her he couldn't be hurried, but Mrs. Garner pretended to look out the window while she waited. Finally he tossed back the water and swallowed noisily, and she plucked the empty cups from his hands.

"Thank you," she said, hustling out. "Y'all have a nice visit."

The old man's eyes settled on the plastic bag of peppermints at the foot of his bed. "May I have one of those peppermints, Jimmy? The pills leave such a foul taste."

Her father gave him a peppermint. Dr. Hodgkins untwisted the wrapping deliberately, squinting as he worked, but when he finally freed the mint it dropped onto the floor and rolled across the tiles into the corner. Her father dug out another.

"They wouldn't roll around that way if my rug were down," her grandfather said.

"We'll help put the rug down again before we leave," her father said.

"That would be very nice, thank you. Very nice. Very . . . Marie, be a good girl and bring me that card from the coffee table. It's standing upright. Yes, that's it."

He didn't take the card from her. He seemed to want her to hold it.

"My sister—your aunt Dorah—sent this to me. She lives in a retirement home in Sausalito, California, with both her grown daughters. All together in the same home again. Isn't that something? You remember your aunt Dorah, don't you? And your cousins, whatever their little names are?"

She was looking dutifully at the card. It was dated from the year before, and there were three signatures, all in the same handwriting. "It's your granddaughter Marie, Grandpa," she said gently. "My mother isn't here."

His look of bewilderment quickly transformed into a fierce, accusatory expression, and he stared at her until she averted her eyes in embarrassment. No wonder, Marie thought angrily. No wonder. My mother must have hated you; she could never have stood such a look.

"What do you hear from Dorah?" her father asked.

"Oh, she cabled me the other day. She insists that the presidency is under attack and that I should write a letter to the editor. But I told her, as I have told her so many times before, Jimmy, that I will not see my words printed on the same page as the words of those cowards. Journalism is as jaundiced now as ever, as jaundiced as ever, and I have often said that I feel about the papers as the aborigines felt about photographs, that they will capture my soul—do you follow me?—that they will capture my soul if I lend them my image. And make no mistake, Jimmy, I've told you a hundred times if I've told you once, a man's words are his image just as surely as his face or figure is. But Dorah—," he sighed, "Dorah never listens. She believes we should first swell the ranks and then mass against the generals. She claims never to understand my opinions. Did I tell you?" he said, brightening suddenly. He chuckled, his great belly trembling. He touched Marie's arm and smiled a happy, cookie-crumb smile. "Did I tell you? She once chided me that my telegrams were like missives from the Oracle, she couldn't make heads or tails of them!" He gave a wheezing, high-pitched laugh.

They smiled hard until his laughter subsided. Her father said, "I see you're wearing the new shirt—"

"You are nothing like your aunt Dorah," Dr. Hodgkins said to Marie. "Don't worry. Not Dorah. Good grief, girl. You are nothing like Dorah. Now put that card right back where you found it. Right there on the table. That's it. No, to the—yes, right there. Thank you."

He took a deep breath. His voice had dropped almost to a murmur. "I'm getting tired, Jimmy."

"We'll go here in a second."

"It's just that I get too tired."

"I know. We don't want to wear you out."

The old man looked at Marie and said softly, almost drowsily, "I hope you aren't behaving foolishly anymore, Marie. You are a sensible and smart girl, just as your mother was. Not like your aunt Dorah at all. Don't even say such things. Your mother would have been proud to see you. And your daughter, your little girl, I'm sure she will be just like you. Though you shouldn't name her for yourself, Marie—that's such foolishness as I've never heard. But you're a good girl, and she will be just like you, regardless. Smart and sensible. Won't she, Jimmy? You can see already how the little one will favor her mother, can't you?"

Her father was slumped forward in his chair with his forearms on his knees. He looked dejectedly at the old man and nodded. Her grandfather watched him, waiting, as if the nod didn't satisfy him.

"Yes, sir," her father said at last. "Yes, I can."

They didn't stay much longer. The old man fell silent and ate a few more cookies, then just turned toward his window again. They tried to talk a little, but he wasn't listening and didn't respond. So they sat for a while, her father looking at his hands and Marie, like her grandfather, looking out the window, until finally her father said they ought to go.

"We'll put your rug down first," he said. "You'll only have to get up for just a minute."

The old man shook his head. "Not right now. I'm going to watch the television now."

"Are you sure? It'll only take a few minutes."

He shook his head again. "Later."

"All right. Mrs. Garner and the others can put it down for you later, then."

"That's fine, Jimmy. You see how tired I am."

"Yes, sir. We'll be going."

In the car, they rolled down their windows, and Marie turned up the radio so they could hear it over the wind. It was almost noon, the sun was brilliant, and Marie took deep breaths of the clean country air. She wanted to clear out the nursing-home smell and, with it, her memory of the place. That had been her grandfather. She had come from him. It seemed ridiculous. You might as well have told her she'd sprung fresh from a lake; she couldn't have imagined it with less difficulty.

"You know," she said, turning down the radio, "I didn't like the way that nurse treated him."

"Mrs. Garner? She's kind of sharp, it's true."

"Treated him like a baby, is what she did."

"I used to get aggravated by her too. But, you know, your grandfather's not what you'd call a meek man. I've seen him bully her around and give her grief more times than I can count. She takes good care of him, though. She's been there a long, long time. Longer than he has. They're both the kind of people that what you say slides right off of them. In a way it's kind of a blessing, I guess. They go good together."

"I still don't like her," Marie said, wondering how in spite of her dislike for the old man she could feel such an undercurrent of loyalty. Loyalty ought to have a better foundation than that.

"Well, maybe you're right. Maybe I've just gotten used to them."

He was slowing the car to a stop. Sawhorses blocked the highway ahead, one of them bearing a sign that said "BRIDGE OUT," under which someone had spray-painted "for lunch." Beyond the sawhorses you could see where the road simply disappeared, picking up again a hundred feet farther on. On the far side of the creek sat a bulldozer, a cement truck, and an assortment of discarded equipment, all of it temporarily abandoned. A lank dog was nosing among the equipment, wetting the truck tires.

"That creek must have been a monster," her father said. He turned off onto the detour route, taking a sidelong glance at her. He was worrying about her now and trying not to show it. But she could always tell.

"Tell you what," he said. "There's a little café in Lockers Creek I usually go to when I come out here. Why don't we get some lunch? You'll feel a lot better with some nice, greasy food in you."

Marie gave a slight smile. The more road under her, the better she felt, the easier it was to forget. She said, "Okay, that sounds good."

"Yeah, some good old greasy food'll fix you right up. Put some meat on those bones." He flickered one eyebrow mischievously.

Marie pulled down the sun visor and looked into the mirror and tried to raise one eyebrow. They only drew together in the middle. She slapped the visor up again.

Emma's Café was noisy and crowded with men. The bridge construction crew was having lunch there and took up three tables, cluttering the formica with their empty dishes and full ashtrays. The place smelled of smoke and grease, which for Marie were welcome smells, and she relaxed despite the confusion. She and her father slid into the one empty booth as a young waitress hustled over to them. A heavy woman with bottle-blond hair teased into absurdly high, sheer bangs, wearing jeans too tight for her under a stained apron, the waitress was attractive nonetheless. She had a disarming smile and wore just enough makeup to set off her bright green eyes, so that you noticed them first thing.

"How you doing today, Mr. Hamilton?" she said, filling their water glasses. "I see you brought somebody with you this time."

"What's this 'mister' stuff? This is my daughter, Marie."

"Marie Hamilton?"

Marie nodded, and the waitress surprised her by frowning and putting a hand on her shoulder, cocking her head as if suspicious. Marie was suddenly shot through and tingling with alarm. Somehow this woman knew her and was going to spread Marie's life out on the table, before she could think to stop it. She could tell at once this was the kind of woman the waitress was, someone who would say anything without giving it a moment's thought.

"Now, did you ever go to Lakeside Elementary?" the woman asked. "Like, when you were five or six?"

It took a moment for her question to register, and when it did the relief was so gratifying that Marie instantly liked her, as if she really had known more painful things to mention but had chosen to spare her. "Off and on," Marie said, glancing at her father. "Yes, I did."

"Oh my God," the waitress said, her eyes widening. "I'm Laine. Laine Sanders? Don't tell me you don't remember me. We were best friends."

"Laine Sanders," Marie repeated, and an image flashed into her mind of a bright-eyed girl in dog-ears, a jump-rope in her hand. "Lainey Sanders?"

The waitress burst into a snorting peal of laughter. The workers at the next table looked over. She covered her mouth. "Oh Lord. I ain't been called that in years."

"Lainey Sanders. I can't believe it!" Marie stood up, and they hugged, Laine holding her water pitcher awkwardly to the side. "It's been such a long time."

"Don't I know it. Just look at you, girl. Marie Hamilton, of all people." She frowned teasingly at Marie's father. "Here you been coming all this time, and I never knew you were Marie's dad."

"We went to school together way back when," Marie said.

"*Way* back when. She was the first friend I ever had."

"Well, I'll be," said Marie's father.

Laine waved irritatedly at the other tables in the café. "Listen, we're real busy right now, but once these hogs get out of here it ought to slow down, and I'll come back and visit, okay? You want some coffee, Mr. Hamilton?"

"Jimmy."

"You want some coffee, Mr. Jimmy?"

"Please."

"How about you, Marie? What can I get you to drink? Oh, I just can't believe it's you. Look at you!"

"Maybe some iced tea when you get a second."

"Oh, don't you worry, honey, y'all get priority." She squeezed Marie's shoulder and stage whispered, "And guess what else?" She held up her left hand, bent forward at the wrist so Marie could see her fingers.

"Oh! It's beautiful! Who is it?"

"Bill Smith? Big hairy monster? I don't think you'd know him. He's from Jessieville. Anyway, y'all sit tight, and I'll tell you all about it here in a bit." She went back to the kitchen.

"Well, that's a nice coincidence," her father said.

"Lainey Sanders. God, she was something else. Quite the talker, I remember. We were always getting in trouble together."

"That was at Lakeside?"

"Isn't it strange? I'd almost forgotten I ever went there."

"I don't guess you're in touch with many of your old friends?"

"No. I don't guess I'm in touch with anybody."

"Not a soul?"

The question, she knew, was prompted by his stirred-up memory of that time, of the days when she and her mother had lived with him. She'd been jolted by the memory herself. That had been the neighborhood of the burning house. She'd been in school there hardly a year before her father moved out, and not long after that she'd begun to miss school days, traveling with her mother, until eventually she was gone from there altogether. With that same memory fresh in his mind, Marie realized, her father couldn't help but press, but still it made her feel cornered and crabby.

"It just seems like I ought to know more," he said, when she didn't respond. He was embarrassed. "I don't mean that you ought to tell me more, but that I ought to know. As your father. I mean I just don't feel right about it. After you and your mother left, you just kind of—"

"Well, like I said, I don't guess I am."

"—kind of slipped away from me," he finished.

They each took a drink.

"Don't guess you are what?" he said.

"In touch with anybody."

"Not anybody?"

"Not anybody," she said roughly, and he let it go.

It had been a rare lapse for him. Which was far more than she deserved, Marie thought. Who was she to come soak up his life and offer none of her own?

"Dad," she said, "you're one of those people who makes lemonade out of lemons. Anybody ever tell you that?"

He grinned. "Once or twice."

"I don't see how you do it."

"Well, you can't have lemonade without lemons."

"That's not what I mean."

"You've got to do something with them. All those lemons lying around?"

"Forget it," she said, shaking her head. "You're a goofball."

"You don't have to get ornery about it."

"You're the ornery one."

Eventually Laine brought their food, and she made Marie scoot over and slid into the booth beside her. Lightly touching Marie's knee, she said, "You have gotten so pretty. I can't get over your hair. Last I saw it we were both wearing dog-ears."

"Well, Lainey, look at you. Getting married— "

Laine snorted. "Girl, you have got to stop calling me that. It cracks me up just to hear it. Really, though, you don't think I look terrible? I'm a lot fatter than I used to be."

"Oh, for Pete's sake!"

"No, I am, I know I am, but I'm going on a diet now that we finally got some swimsuit weather. Could y'all believe that rain? It like to never quit. I was just going crazy from being inside."

"You don't need to go on a diet. You look great."

"Stop it. You really think so?"

"Definitely."

Laine smiled, clearly pleased, and looked at Marie's father. "Now Mr. Jimmy, why aren't you eating? You don't like the looks of that catfish?"

"No, it looks great," he said. He picked up his fork.

"You, too, Marie," Laine said, waving at her plate. "Y'all don't be so polite. Go ahead and eat. I can only set here for a minute, anyway. We've been covered up all day. But first, come on, now, you got to tell me what happened to you. You just up and vanished on me, and not a bit of warning. My little heart just broke."

"We moved out of town," Marie said. "I just recently got back."

"My God. And after all these years. What— "

"You were going to tell me about Bill Smith."

Laine seemed delighted. "Oh, yes. Well, I wish you could meet him. He owns a construction company, and he ain't but twenty-five. He's just like a big old ape, and he is such a sweetie-pie. You're gonna have to meet him." She held up her hand again so they could admire her ring.

"I can't believe you're getting married."

"Well, we had to, you know," Laine said, suddenly serious, putting a hand on her belly.

"Oh? Oh, congratulations! When's it due?"

Laine cackled riotously and threw her arms around her. "I'm teasing you, girl! You're just the sweetest thing. 'Oh, congratulations.' You are something else, Marie. You must've raised her right, Mr. Jimmy."

Her father, drinking his iced tea, looked relieved.

"I can't believe you," Marie said. "You're terrible."

"Well, what about you, girl? Where's your ring? Haven't you got her married off yet, Mr. Jimmy?"

"Mm-mn," he said, his mouth full of cornbread. He swallowed. "Not yet, anyway."

"You men. Y'all don't even care."

More workers appeared in the café door. "Oh great," Laine said. "Speaking of." She took a compact mirror and a lipstick from her apron pocket, but after looking in the mirror she decided her lipstick was fine. When she stood up she pointed at Marie's plate and said, "You hardly touched your food. No wonder you're so skinny."

"I'm not done yet."

"Mr. Jimmy, you make sure she cleans her plate. Now listen here, Marie, I'll tell you what. We're all going out to Charleton next weekend, a whole bunch of us. And you have to come. Don't even think about saying no."

"What's Charleton?"

"Oh, come on, you know Charleton, it's that campground out on 270? We're going to have a cookout and go swimming if it's sunny. It's got the coldest water in the world. It'll freeze your—" She cleared her throat dramatically, glancing at Marie's father. "I mean it'll just freeze you to death."

"Well, I might could come—"

She crossed her arms and scowled. "No, ma'am, no might could to it. You have to say yes right now. I mean it."

"Okay, then."

Laine wrote her number on a napkin. "No changing your mind. You can come to my house and ride out there with me and Bill. It'll be fun. We can catch up."

"Okay, I'll call you this week."

"Don't let her change her mind, Mr. Jimmy."

"I'll try not to," he said.

Marie watched Laine's retreating back with a mixture of dread and delight. The prospect of enduring another onslaught of questions left her cold in the belly. But she could evade questions better than most, and whatever evasion didn't resolve, she could address with wicked meanness. She didn't so much articulate this to herself as feel the old reassurance of her abilities. She would go. People, she told herself, real people have friends.

At home her father changed into cut-offs and a paint-stained shirt and went out into the yard, the grass being finally dry enough to cut. Marie turned on the stereo and set to work inside. First she washed the living room picture window, watching her father in the front yard as he mowed. Skinny white legs in sports socks and tennis shoes. He had on a baseball cap to protect his bald head from the sun, and looked pleasantly foolish. The buzz of lawn mowers sounded throughout the neighborhood. Across the street a woman was trimming her bushes in cut-offs and a tube top, her shoulders pink with sunburn.

Marie finished the windows, started a load of laundry, cleaned the bathroom. She could do this—she could work hard. She could clean a house and not feel like an imposter. Maybe she hadn't learned it from her mother, but she had learned it regardless. She dusted and polished until the whole house smelled of furniture cleaner, then turned the stereo up louder and vacuumed the floors and left the music loud when she finished. Scrubbed the kitchen sink and mopped the linoleum and cleaned the oven and the stove. Between tasks she folded laundry and started new loads. When she finished the kitchen, the house was clean, the laundry hampers were empty, and it was only five o'clock. Her father had finished mowing and was pruning the plum tree outside her bedroom window. She took a hot shower, and afterward the air-conditioning was almost painful on her skin. She slipped on sweats and socks.

The sun was still high in the west, and the day seemed as if it might go on and on. Marie stood in the front doorway breathing in the sweet smell of cut grass. She had grown so used to the rain she hardly knew what to do with an open afternoon of sunshine. Her first free sunny day in Hot Springs. A breeze rustled the azaleas and the plum tree outside her window. She strolled down the driveway in her socks and checked the mail, but the box was empty. She never got mail anyway, and when her father did, it was generally bills. Walking back toward the house she saw trees and sky reflected in the picture window. Sunshine and blue sky and no place to be.

Was this it? Marie thought, her heart throbbing unexpectedly. The yard, the neighborhood, the city, the entire world—it all seemed open and empty as the sky. You could die and no one would find you in all that emptiness. They could hardly find you if you lived.

She found her father in the den watching a baseball game, freshly showered and, it seemed to Marie, perfectly content.

"Hey," he said, "the house looks great."

"So does the yard."

"Well, I should've taken care of that plum before now," he said absently. He was intent on the game.

"So do you have plans for the evening?"

"Hmn? Oh, I thought I'd just set around and take it easy. What about you?"

These were polite questions. Neither of them ever had plans.

"You want to pick up a pizza and rent a couple movies?"

"What if we go after this? The game's almost over."

"No hurry," Marie said.

They ate the pizza on the back patio and drank cold beer as the sun sank behind the magnolias and sweetgums. The patio flagstones were warm from the sun; she could feel them through her socks. Somewhere in the neighborhood someone was grilling out, and they could smell it on the breeze, the tang of charcoal smoke and meat. They sat outside until the evening turned blue and lights glowed in the windows all down the street. The crickets had started up, and lightning bugs drifted over the bushes with that peculiar, lazy listlessness, like balloons following unseen currents of air.

Afterward her father fixed her a White Russian, which Marie had never tasted. She liked the drink yet was in no mood to enjoy it. Something about this absolute calm made her restless and strangely watchful. She huddled up in a blanket on the couch and sipped the cold drinks her father made between movies, heavy on the chocolate stuff and light on the liquor, and they watched three movies back to back. She kept expecting the phone to ring but couldn't say why. It seemed like it should. In a house you expected the phone to ring sometimes. Her father went to bed when the last movie ended, Marie on the couch pretending to be asleep.

Finally she did fall asleep, and at four in the morning she awoke on the couch shivering with cold and did not know where she was.

Chapter 5

They stopped working only when it became too dark to see. In the mornings they rose in darkness and drank their coffee and packed their lunches and left their homes when the sky first hinted of gray. Abe had grown so tired he no longer bothered to fix a separate breakfast, not even cereal and milk, but ate a couple of slices of cheese and sandwich meat as he made his lunch. The coffee would be ready when he finished packing the lunch, and he would wash the food down with a cup of it and pour the rest into his thermos. Outside on the trailer porch his cats mewed when they heard him stirring. He would step out into the porch light and open a rubber barrel and scoop cat food into the hubcap in the corner, and the two cats would nose into it with their shoulders touching. He left the porch light on because it was dark when he left in the morning and dark when he returned.

It was almost dusk again at yet another job site, the second of the day, and in a minute they would load up their trucks and go. He had come down for water and stood in front of the house watching the sun touch the trees. He spat in the dirt and looked up again and could swear it had sunk visibly farther during the moment he had glanced away. He looked at the sunlight threading through the treetops.

"Heads up."

He heard the words, but they seemed meaningless. Certain things you heard so many times you no longer noticed them. He realized he was flagging. During the day he worked hard, and only seemed to pick up momentum as the heat increased, but in the evenings he lost his strength and found his mind filling up again, and he worked slower and slower and took frequent breaks. No one said anything to him about it.

He considered this as he watched the sunlight in the trees.

"Pitt!" Roberto said sharply.

It startled Abe into attention, though he still didn't know what was happening. Roberto charged over and shoved him. He went reeling backward, almost losing his feet. As he staggered back he saw the half-coiled power cord drop into view behind Roberto, thudding heavily in the dust. Abe was stunned and instinctively angry about the shove. It would take him a moment to collect himself and say something appropriate. He bent and picked up his water cup.

Roberto was shouting angrily up to someone on the roof. "You almost hit him, you stupid—"

"I said 'heads up' and nobody said nothing."

"You got to look!"

"Hey, I waited and nobody said nothing."

"It's my fault, my fault," Abe said, coming over. He saw Lester frowning down at them from twenty feet up. "Sorry, man," he said with a wave. "My fault." Lester shook his head and withdrew from sight.

He looked at Roberto. "Knock me down, why don't you?"

Roberto scowled and waved his arms. He was in a rare state of agitation. "Well, goddamnit, Pitt—"

"Hey, I'm kidding. Sorry. Thanks for the push."

"You lose your ears or what?"

Abe began coiling the power cord. It was yards long and weighed several pounds. Dropped from that height it would have knocked him flat. "Just tired, I guess."

"Man, you need to take a day off or something. Pierce, he'll let you, no problem."

"I'm fine."

"We only working a half-day tomorrow anyway. You ought to just sleep in. Get some nice sleep."

He put the power cord on the truck. Behind him the sound of hammering sputtered and stopped. It was Friday and everyone was tired. Most had been working dawn to dusk for ten days straight. Abe had been at it for seven. He'd meant to help gather the materials, but he lacked the will. Instead he leaned against the truck and gazed into the bed as if looking for something. The truck's radio was on, tuned to a country music station because today was Lester's turn to choose. Abe found the twang of steel guitar soothing. He hummed softly and poked around in the bed of the truck.

The others began descending from the roof. In a few minutes the yard had filled up with men. They were laughing and roughhousing in spite of their weariness, and though they'd be up again at dawn there was talk of driving into Hot Springs and hitting the bars. They had no weekends now, but they did have pay days, and today was one of them. Pierce came over to Abe and Roberto to confirm that they were only working half a day on Saturday.

"Where y'all going again?" he rasped. He turned his head away and exhaled smoke through his nostrils. It was a familiar sight but strange this time, because he had approached them with his hands in his pockets and no cigarette in his mouth.

"Out to Charleton."

Pierce nodded. "I know that place. Freeze your little dingies off. Y'all still plan on working Sunday, I hope."

"Yep," Abe said. Roberto looked at Abe but said nothing.

"All right. I won't be here. Kids want to take me out to lunch for my birthday. Get me some steak at Sizzler, I don't know. Anyhow if we get done here tomorrow we'll start on the one down at Cedar Road on Sunday. You might just run by here first to see."

"Think you'll finish it tomorrow?"

Pierce took a pack of cigarettes from his shirt pocket and tapped it against his palm. "Yeah, I think so. It's a big old house, though, and y'all are cutting out early." He shrugged. "You know I remember the last time a roof got put on this house."

"You do it?"

"Me? Hell, no. Some dumbasses from Benton. Tore the shingles off the whole damn roof in the morning, what with rainclouds and weather forecasts and you name it. Course they didn't get half the shingles laid down before the rain come. Guy told me his light fixtures looked like water fountains."

"I guess they learned something."

"Bunch of dumbasses," Pierce said again, lighting a cigarette. "Y'all are brain surgeons compared to them guys." He snapped his lighter shut. "Well, getting late. Guess I better go talk to the man."

The evening was sinking to full dark. The mosquitoes had come out, and the men were slapping their arms and legs as they talked. Pierce stood under the porch light talking to the man who owned the house, waving bugs away from his face. Abe lingered for a while, listening to Roberto and the others make their plans. He had rarely joined them on such outings in the past, and now no one seemed to expect him to come. Finally he left. He gave a kid named Mitch a ride home, then headed out Merrill Road: past the turnoff to his parents' house, another two miles, and down the long gravel driveway to his trailer.

The trees on either side of the driveway fell away to open pasture. His haggard old trailer sat at the edge of the pasture near a stand of white poplars that gave it shade. Beyond Abe's half-acre the land belonged to Arthur Simmons, whose cattle grazed sometimes right up to the barbed wire fence behind the trailer. Certain summer mornings as Abe got dressed he'd see the cows standing a few yards away, watching him through the screen window. He would talk to them a little, and they seemed to listen, though not with much interest. In the evenings they would be gone.

A quarter mile to the east lived Arthur Simmons and his family. At night Abe could see the lights of their big farmhouse through a screen of trees they'd planted to hide his trailer from their view. Beyond Simmons's pasture the Ouachita foothills rose up in piney ridges. That first summer Abe had come back and moved out here, he used to squeeze through the barbed wire and cross the pasture to those woods, taking long walks even on the hottest days, following the faded trails on which he used to ride his horses. He would hike up to a high ridge where the trees broke open and offered a view of the land—the pasture and his trailer and even the highway in the distance, and on each horizon the swelling of forested hills. On very hot, breezeless days, when the trees were still, you could almost believe it was a painting, that it wasn't real. It was oddly comforting. Then a red-shouldered hawk would glide over the field and break the spell.

But when the first winter came he'd lost the habit of those walks and taken to reading his days away. Work being intermittent, he rarely went out except to stock up on groceries and books or occasionally to visit Jim. It got to be his pattern, and he only sank deeper into it. Summer came again, and he worked and went out with Repeat and the others, had a few three-week relationships he simply let die, went back to his trailer to read. Sometimes Jim came out and they talked into the gray hours, but then he'd leave and it was just Abe and the cats in the trailer again. In this way two years had passed. It didn't seem like two years. It didn't seem like anything. If someone told him it hadn't happened he might almost believe it.

He climbed stiffly out of his truck and turned to look at it. On the highway the tires had sounded louder than usual, and sure enough, the front left tire was going flat. They were always picking up roofing nails. Right now every tire shop and garage in Garland County was backed up with customers having the same trouble. A roofing crew moved into a neighborhood to repair a damaged roof, and within a couple of days car owners began to notice their sagging tires.

He dug his jack out from behind the seat and set it in place. It wasn't easy. After a long day of scraping and hammering and packing shingles up to the roof, he could hardly move his fingers without wincing. When he had the jack in place he stared at it, felt his knees falter, and went over to vomit into the ditch. He looked up into the overcast sky to clear his head. There's nothing, he told himself. In the overcast sky there was nothing.

His head still wasn't clear, though, so he walked down the driveway to the road. A few minutes later he came back, chewing on a handful of sheep grass to kill the taste in his mouth, and set to work again.

Lucky came down from the porch to bump against his leg as he worked the jack. Abe had picked Lucky from a litter Roberto's cat had delivered. He'd been the runt of the lot and was scrawny even now. Abe scratched him under the chin and looked around for the other cat.

"Where's Tab?" he said. Lucky flopped onto his side and writhed in the gravel. Abe returned to his work. He wondered if this time Tabby wouldn't return. She was a very old cat, a calico he'd had since he was a boy. She had always been a wanderer, and over the years he'd given her up for gone a dozen times or more. Sometimes she turned up at his parents' house, prowling old territory. It was strange the way a cat could remind you of your past, in this case just by walking down the road to it. Not that there was much of a past there. His past in that house had been characterized by its lack of a present; it had been all about elsewhere, about the future.

Which is right now, Abe thought. Right now's your future. He rolled the tire over to the side of the trailer and heaved it into a plastic tub. Water splashed over the sides, soaking his shoes. He turned the tire around in the water, looking for telltale bubbles, but the porchlight didn't quite reach to where he stood. He would have to empty the tub and drag it into the light and fill it again from the hose. He decided to patch the tire later. He was too tired now.

In back of the trailer was another spare he thought was in good shape, though it had lain in the yard all winter. He had to tug it free from the weeds and creepers that had grown up over it, but it seemed fine. He checked it with a tire gauge. Low, but then all his tires were low. He would air them up again tomorrow.

As he finished changing the tire he saw Tabby trotting up the driveway as if returning from a day at work, her eyes reflecting the porchlight as she drew nearer. Lucky leaped down from the warm hood of the truck and went to greet her, but she hissed and boxed at him as she always did, and he veered away. She was a cranky old cat and looked a mess. Her matted fur was caked with mud about the flanks and paws, her haunches spotted with sticktights. She had a musty odor, too, like something out of an attic. She came obliquely up to Abe, more skittish than ever in her old age. Wouldn't let him take a brush to her and only occasionally let him pet her. Her right eye was clouded up, so Abe came at her from the left. She let him rub the scruff of her neck for a moment, then shied away as if he had tried to trick her somehow.

He put away the jack and went inside.

The trailer was hot and stuffy as usual, and Abe turned on the fans and opened the windows, taking care with the one that had been cracked during the storm. He had sealed its cracks with masking tape, but someday soon the glass was going to fall out and he would have to buy a new one. Whatever windblown thing had damaged the window had knocked his screen off too—he'd found it hanging against Simmons's barbed wire fence, the barbs poking through the mesh—and though he'd hammered the screen back into shape, it was in dire need of a patch.

In the bathroom Abe stripped and regarded himself in the mirror, no longer surprised to see the sunburned brow and the cuts and scratches that laced his neck and face. They had healed and faded considerably but were still obvious. The original sunburn had peeled off and been replaced with a fresh one. This one, less severe, was tanning up rather than peeling, and so his face was speckled and striped pink and brown. At least he'd grown used to the discomfort. He hardly thought about it. His knees ached from the long days on the roof, and his ribs, though much improved, were still sore, but he took aspirin every morning and went to work and almost forgot about it. That was his plan of attack these days, forgetting.

The funeral had been like a dream to him, a feverish, disorienting dream, the kind in which people appear out of the past as if they've never been gone. Jim was suddenly back, and Mr. Townsend and Jim's sister, all of them stricken, with bloodshot eyes. It was the kind of dream in which you've done some terrible thing and cannot account for it and cannot take it back. The kind in which nothing is as you remember it except for the very worst of it, which you know to be real. The preacher repeated what the sheriff had said, which Abe knew to be untrue—that Jackie had died quickly and without pain, in a state of shock. And Abe listened, knowing the truth, wondering vaguely if the sheriff had lied for the family's sake or if he believed it himself.

Abe had lied too, of course, had told the sheriff she was already dead when he found her. No one had questioned that, but after the sheriff had been out to the woods, he did come around to speak privately with him. A stout man, the sheriff, with a face like a ham. His breath whistled in his nose. Abe had lain in bed pressing his temples against the raging headache that hadn't left him since the café, where it had blossomed in a wild, electric rush as he sat in the booth with Laine's arms around him. Concentrating on the conversation was almost beyond him.

"You know," the sheriff had said, "I found her keys in the back seat, and the jack out on the ground. Way it looks to me is when you come acrossed her there, you thought the decent thing to do was to get that damn car off of her, even though she was already dead, as you say, but it turned out to be too much for you under the circumstances. Which nobody, and I mean nobody, son, could blame you for that. Ain't that pretty much the way it happened?"

"Pretty much," he said, thickly.

"Course I can see why you didn't mention it. Far as I'm concerned, details like them are just too gruesome to talk about. For the family, I mean. Best not to give them too much of a mental picture. Best to just let them details lay, don't you think?"

Abe held his head, the sheriff's words pounding into his ears like waves slapping the shore. It was all he could do not to cry out, For God's sake, shut up! Shut up! Shut up! He squeezed his head and looked at the blurred image of the man looming over him.

"Don't you think, Abe?" the sheriff said again, and again the waves came, four spikes in quick succession.

"Yes," he said. "Yes, thank you."

At the funeral Jim had been stoic, walled up like a stranger. He wore an old, ill-fitting suit and seemed physically uncomfortable, his cheeks raw from shaving too closely, his skin bright pink with that sunburn from the beach. He nodded as people spoke to him but said hardly a word. Even when Abe greeted him he only shook hands and nodded. No falling apart in the arms of his friend, as Abe had half-feared, nor did he ask the questions for which Abe had been preparing. He nodded, without quite meeting Abe's eyes, and went to sit with his father. Mr. Townsend, smartly dressed in an expensive new suit, looking fit and tan and well groomed, was weeping uncontrollably, in great heaving sobs, a wreck. Jim and his sister sat on either side of him, holding his arms.

Abe was too weak to go to the burial service. He could hardly stand. Before the funeral, and after it for three days, he had lain in his old empty room at his parents' house, nursing the headache, his mother salving his cuts and bringing food into the room and insisting he eat. Jim left town again without calling or coming to see him. And Abe had simply lain there, desperate to leave, too anxious to leave. Whenever the headache faded he would fall immediately asleep, so that it was always there when he was awake and seemed unrelenting. His friends came once and stood around his bed like more absurd figures in the dream. He spoke to them a little. They even tried to joke. Afterward he asked his mother to keep them away.

Then his father had finally walked into the room one morning while his mother was in the shower and asked him if he ever planned to get up and work. And he had said, "Yes, sir," felt his anger burning through the headache, pushing him out of bed, and tugged on his shoes and left the house before his mother got out of the shower. His father stood at the door, smoking, and watched Abe go, having mistakenly thought that Abe might keep working with him, hanging sheetrock.

Abe showered with the hottest water he could stand, for his back, then the coldest he could stand, to help keep him cool once he got out. He left his hair wet too. He put a frozen dinner in the primitive, one-setting microwave that came with the trailer, went to his bookshelf, and flipped through a few books. He'd read everything already. Eventually he settled on *Bleak House*, for its thickness, and took his dinner from the microwave. Refried beans, Spanish rice, and enchiladas, burned on the edges and cold in the middle, but no longer frozen and therefore edible. He opened a can of soda and settled onto the carpet in front of the box fan, with the food on a scarred-up coffee table. He read with his back propped against the couch. Water trickled from his wet hair down his neck and onto his bare back.

He read fast, eating without noticing the food, changing positions whenever his legs and back ached too much. After a while he was out of soda, and Lucky was scratching at the screen door. He let him in and stood for a moment at the screen, watching a monstrous garden spider wrap up a moth. The spiderweb trembled between two porch rails. The moth had stopped struggling, and the spider webbed it up matter-of-factly. Abe turned off the porch light and returned to his book.

He was sleepy now but still not quite enough to do the trick, so he stretched out on the floor with the book in front of the fan, holding the pages to keep the wind from turning them. A quarter of the way into the book, he laid his head on its open pages and fell asleep with the fan ruffling them at the edges.

Coming out of his dreams in the early morning, he found the pain worse, as usual. He sat up, feeling it in his lower back. The trailer had cooled off considerably. Abe climbed up onto the couch, hugging himself for warmth. Like a street tramp in your own home, he thought. Lucky was clinging to the screen, trying to get at a June bug. His claws made metallic popping sounds. Abe put him out and sat on the couch again. He was sleepy but didn't want to slip back into his last dream, and was too bleary to read. In lieu of making a decision he sat cross-legged, his head hanging forward, and picked at the scab on his heel.

Some time later he awoke with pain shooting in his knees. Gingerly he unfolded his legs. He could tell by the character of the darkness that he might as well stay up. The field sparrows were starting up their staccato songs—flat, dry peeps that quickened into flat, dry trills, like Morse code for morning. Abe took a few aspirins, bending his head under the kitchen faucet to drink. The sulfurous taste of the well water brought him further awake.

After he'd started the coffee brewing, Abe sat down to write Jim a letter. He'd written several already but had only mailed two. Among those he'd destroyed was one in which he'd told Jim the truth, thinking he deserved at least that. That was wrong, though; Jim didn't deserve that kind of truth. Yet Abe couldn't help feeling as though he kept it secret only to protect himself, to hide his shame. As long as he kept that secret he would feel like a coward, no matter the true reason. Or perhaps both were true reasons, and like a coward he clung to the notion that he would have behaved otherwise if only he'd been granted the fair chance. He'd written this, too, in one of the letters he destroyed. This morning's attempt was nothing so reckless, and he sealed it up and stamped it, though it still felt all wrong.

By the time he left for work, the other birds had come awake. The meadowlarks and red-winged blackbirds perched on fence posts in the darkness beyond his porch light, and grackles edged sidewise along his rain gutters, like trailer gargoyles. Lucky crouched in the dewy grass watching them, his tail swishing. Abe could hear thudding and shuffling sounds in the pasture, familiar sounds that reminded him of his horses, the nervous thump of hooves on dirt, the switching of tails. But these were Simmons's cows he heard. He could see their bulky shadows moving out in the darkness.

The interior of his truck smelled of mildew. He noticed it only in the mornings—by the end of the day he smelled mostly himself. The radio was broken. He drove in silence with his arm out the window, taking advantage of the few hours of cool. As he passed the turnoff to his parents' house he saw the lights of his father's truck coming down the road toward him. He lifted a hand. They hadn't spoken since the day he left the house. Though on lunch breaks he sometimes stopped in at Ridgeway's Grocery to see his mother, he hadn't gone to the house again. Now he saw the headlights flash a couple of times and knew his father had recognized him. He drove on.

The Phillips 66 was just opening; Billy Cantu was unlocking the front door. Abe pulled up to the air compressor, and Billy waved and said he would turn it on. Abe waited until the lights came on inside the store and he saw Billy disappear into the back room, then hit the compressor switch and knelt on the concrete, wincing a little. His knees would loosen up after a while. He fit the hose onto the tire stem, heard the hiss of air passing through.

His father pulled in and climbed out of his truck, one hand holding a thermos cup of coffee and the other a half-smoked cigarette. "Morning," he said.

"Morning."

"Truck sure took a banging, didn't it?"

"Yeah. Taking it in next week for body work."

"Running okay, though?"

"Yes, sir. Pretty good."

"Well, Bates does good work."

"Yep," Abe said, checking the tire. It still looked low. "I haven't even paid him yet. He told me to drive it a couple weeks first."

"That's the way he does it. They don't do it that way much anywhere else, but Bates has always been like that. And now looks like his boys'll take over and do it the same way."

His father rarely talked this much in the morning and never this cheerfully. Abe wondered if he'd taken to drinking in the mornings too. "Well, I bought it off you in good shape. You took care of her, that's for sure."

"Well, it's a good truck," his father said, snapping away his cigarette butt. "You trying to pop that tire? You been airing it long enough."

Abe checked the tire, which now looked as if it had melted. It was entirely flat. "What the hell?" he said, disconnecting the hose. "I could've sworn this tire was good. It just went flat right while—" He scowled, straightening up and putting his ear to the compressor. "Well, no wonder," he said disgustedly.

"Compressor ain't on?"

"No." It was a dismal moment, a moment for the old contempt, and he waited for it. But his father just laughed.

"You been sucking the air right out of your tire. It'll take you a *real* long time to get them filled up at that rate."

Abe flipped the switch back and forth. "I guess Billy forgot to turn it on."

"You sure the tire's good?"

"Yeah, the tire's fine."

"Guess I'll take off, then."

"You still working up in Crows?"

"No, I'm out at that Jesus' Name church near Rubicon. Got a lot of water damage, walls peeling right off. The preacher's been helping me hisself."

"The preacher's helping you?"

"I didn't see why not. He's working for free, and you can't really tell a preacher no. Anyway, he's a good hand." He lit another cigarette and looked up at the bluing sky. "Well," he said. "Take her easy."

Abe had a curious feeling of having spoken with someone who looked like his father but wasn't his father. He watched him drive off.

Billy Cantu was counting money into the cash register and jumped when Abe banged on the window, looking out with wide eyes. His hand went to his head. "Sorry!" he called, hustling to the back room with money still spread out all over the counter. An earnest kid, if not very keen. Abe filled his tires, and he bought gas and a couple of candy bars too. Billy was nervous now and gave him too much change. Abe counted it back to him.

On his way to the site he passed Mitch the Kid, as the crew called him, and stopped to give him a ride. The kid had walked two miles with sleep still in his eyes. It was just after six. The site was empty except for Roberto's truck parked at the side of the road. Roberto always arrived early and dozed until the others showed up. Abe tossed one of the candy bars through the window into his lap. Roberto opened his eyes and looked down at the candy bar.

"Hey," he said. "I thought it was a damn bird landed on me."

"If a bird landed on me I'd be freaking out," Mitch said.

"Roberto doesn't freak out easy."

Roberto rubbed his eyes. "Not when I can be asleeping."

Mitch went to lie down beneath a tree in the yard, and Abe, leaning against the truck, told Roberto about flattening his tire. Roberto had a friendly sense of humor, didn't persecute you the way Repeat or Kylie would. He just chuckled and said his cousin in Obregón had once done the same thing, only in his cousin's case the air compressor was broken, he had no spare tire, and his trunk was packed with stolen goods.

"What'd he do then?"

"He went to the jail is what he did."

"I guess it can always be worse."

"When you going to fix that thing? It look like something terrible. Or you plan to just keep driving it that way?"

"Next week, maybe," Abe said. After a pause he added, "I never did ask how you guys got it out of the woods."

"We don't. Police or somebody, I think. They got them this winch with a long-ass cable? And they just pull it up the creek till it come to the road."

"How far down was it?"

"You don't know? They say about a hundred yards, I think."

"That all?"

"What they say. You sure I didn't told you this?"

"I guess you might have, but I don't remember."

"Well. You was pretty out of it. Okay, Bates, he see that they bring the truck into town, so he have them take the truck to his place, and he call Repeat to tell him about it. He got it fixed so fast too. Must have went straight to work on it."

"I remember you telling me that."

"Well, okay, that's all."

"How did they get Jackie's car out?"

"Jackie's car?" Roberto looked at him, scratching his jaw, as if he couldn't understand the question. Finally he said, "They don't. It was too far out there. I mean, it was way out there, like half a mile."

"They couldn't get it out?"

"Well, they have to build a road or some goddamn thing. Jim, he say it ain't worth it. He don't want it anyway."

Robins were hopping in the yard around Mitch, tugging up worms. He was fast asleep. Lester and two others drove up in the company truck and parked in the driveway. The robins scattered into the trees.

"So the car's still out there?"

Roberto nodded. "It's a strange, man, sitting out there in the middle of the woods."

"You mean you've seen it."

Roberto blinked his eyes slowly and looked ahead through his windshield. Abe could tell he hadn't meant to mention it. "Yeah," he said. "Me and Repeat went out there to look."

"You and Repeat," Abe said. "And who else? Did Kylie go? Did all of you go out there together?"

"Hey. Calm down, man. You getting mad?"

"I am calm. I just want to know."

Roberto hesitated.

"I just want to know, Roberto."

"Okay, lots of people has gone out there, okay? Kylie, he don't go with us, but I think he went later with some other people."

"You think?"

"He told Repeat he did. But that's Kylie, you know, maybe he's lying just for the hell of it."

"No, I'm sure he went. And you say lots of people went out there? What people? Who all went out there?"

"Pitt. Hey. Take it easy."

Pierce had driven up while they talked. He called across the road to them. "I didn't know you boys was taking the morning off too."

Roberto got out and looked at him with that same set expression he always had. Abe stared angrily down the road at nothing. But Roberto waited for him, and after a minute they went up the driveway together.

Abe worked harder than usual, at a foolish pace, and the others kept glancing at him but said nothing. By nine it was very hot on the roof, and he flung his shirt down into the yard and kept at it. Pierce asked him to haul some trash to the dump, an obvious ploy to get him off the roof and out of the heat. It wasn't the first time Pierce had done something like that. Earlier in the week he'd made Abe go run estimates, something Pierce usually did himself. Abe felt furious and still more ridiculous, but he hauled the trash and came back an hour later and worked hard again until it was time to go.

"Can I go too?" Lester said to Pierce. The others were all dropping down onto the grass and digging into their lunches. "Abe's already did my day's work."

"I don't doubt it," Pierce said. "You think you get paid for setting around on your butt."

Abe and Roberto went down to their trucks.

"We picking you up, right?" Roberto said. "In a half hour?"

"Right. Half an hour."

"You okay?"

"Yeah. Sorry about that."

"You don't got to say that."

On his way home, coming down the long gravel driveway, Abe was overcome by an unexpected feeling of dislocation. A sense of returning to a place he hadn't visited in years. With the rain and then with working dawn to dusk, he hadn't seen the trailer in full sunlight for more than a month. The dew on the grass had dried, and in the slight breeze the leaves of the white poplars looked silver and metallic as they fluttered. Grasshoppers buzzed in the pasture. Abe could see the cows grazing in the distance, and the empty skeleton of Simmons's new barn. The sun glinted off the trailer windows and the roof. His cats were nowhere to be seen. It looked like an abandoned place.

When he shut off the ignition he was instantly, miserably hot. He climbed out of his truck, stooped for a rock, and pitched it hard at the side of the trailer. It bounced off the siding with a bang. A second later the bang echoed off the ridge across the pasture. He got another rock and flung it as hard as he could, so wild that he overshot and the rock disappeared over the roof. He never heard it land, and after the bang and echo of the first throw, the silence irritated him. His next two throws smacked against the siding. The echoes came again. Then he was spent, his arms trembling and his grip shot, and he went inside to clean up.

Chapter 6

Marie showed up at Laine's house feeling more than a little spooked, but when Laine came skipping out to hug her like the prodigal daughter come home, her mood improved. It was nice to hug Laine: She was soft and smelled sweet and squeezed you hard.

"Ain't it just a perfect day for a cookout?" Laine exclaimed. "We're going to get so rowdy! Here, show me your suit. I want to know how hard I'm going to have to hit Bill when he looks at you."

"Right here in the driveway?"

"I don't see why not."

Marie lifted her shirt to show the swimsuit, a black two-piece she'd bought at a discount store on the way. Laine made her turn around a couple of times.

"You look good," Laine said, shaking her head. "I mean you look *damn* good. You don't even have a butt, hardly. I'm mad at Bill already."

"I'm sure he's only got eyes for you."

"It's not just his eyes he's got for me."

"Lainey, you're terrible!"

"Well!" She gave Marie that daring expression she had, widening her eyes and cocking her head. Laine was always acting as if she ought not to have said something but was pleased she had.

They sipped iced tea on the living room couch, waiting for Bill. The window unit, rattling softly, dripped condensation, and the cold air came from the vents smelling musty. Laine insisted Marie kick off her sandals and take the seat nearest the window unit.

"We've got to be kind of quiet, though," she said. "Mom's trying to sleep."

"Okay."

"I'd take you back there to say hello, but she's not feeling so good. She's still down from a hysterectomy."

"Is that right."

"She's fine now, but she's been sleeping in."

"That's good," Marie said, noting the false breeziness in Laine's tone and wondering why Laine should lie to her. "I'm glad she's fine."

"Oh yeah, she's fine, she's fine. Y'all can visit tonight maybe. She'll probably be up when we get back. I'm so glad you're staying over. We can stay up all night talking, and I'll have a good excuse not to go to church. That tea sweet enough for you?"

"It's great."

"Well, I am just so glad we run into each other again. All my best girlfriends have babies now and that's all they want to talk about, how this one's poopy come out all weird and yellow and how this one nearly died cause he swallowed a lighter."

"I figured you liked babies."

"Oh, shit yes, I love them. I babysit for my friend Darla all the time. Her and Dwayne and their little squirt's coming today, so you'll meet them. But, you know, I'll have a baby of my own soon enough. Right now I don't want to talk about babies. I just want to talk about sex."

Marie laughed. "You're so bad."

"Well, it's true," Laine said, flashing that look of hers. "And speaking of, everybody else that's coming today is single, or at least almost single, so feel free to sleep with any of them you want to."

"Thank you. I probably will."

"Really, I can't wait to see them boys look at you. You ought to just wear your shorts and that bikini top. Then you can see their eyes pop out when you get out of the car."

"Uh-huh."

"Why not? When I was skinny you couldn't hardly get me to wear nothing else. Mom would scream and tell me to put some clothes on every time she saw me."

"Well, that's you."

"Yeah, okay, Miss Priss, that's me. So anyway, back to the subject of who you might sleep with."

"Is that what we were talking about?"

"Now, like I said, anybody but Bill."

"I was thinking about Bill, actually."

"You watch it, honey. He's my old ape and nobody else's. Besides, you wouldn't want Bill. He's too hairy. I mean even his *butt* is hairy. Now do you really not have a boyfriend? Not that it matters."

"Not really."

"How come?"

"How come I don't have a boyfriend?"

"I mean, you ain't driving down a one-way street, are you?"

"What?"

"You ain't—you know, kind of fishy?"

"Oh! Give me a break."

"Well? I don't know. How am I supposed to know? You can't tell me with a body like that you don't have *somebody* on the line. Or did you leave someone behind when you come back?"

"Sort of," Marie said. "I mean, yes, I left. But it's neither here nor there."

"And you don't want to tell your sweet old friend Laine about it."

"Not really."

"I knew it. You got it written all over your face. Well, forget him, honey; he ain't worth the hair on your legs."

Marie nodded. This was not a subject she intended to get into, with Laine or anyone else, and she put away the unwelcome image that had lit up in her head, of Tom's rugged but plain face, a bland face, gazing intently at her over a plate of runny eggs. This was always the way she remembered him, despite more dramatic images her brain could choose. Eating his eggs he was easier to put away. In her mind she just rose from the table and went to the sink.

She was looking away now, at the husk of a dead fly that trembled atop the vibrating window unit. "You know what I always used to wonder as a kid? How flies died. I mean those that didn't get swatted or stuck on a fly strip or something. There's always dead ones on the window sills, scads of them. Banged their little brains out on the glass, I guess. Or got fried by the sun. But do you think any of them ever just sort of wink out in midflight?" She was picturing it now, as she had when she was a girl: the buzz stopping short, a last silent dropping arc, soundlessly striking the soft carpet. That wouldn't be such a bad way to go.

"Uh-oh," Laine said. "I didn't go and make you mad at me, did I?"

"No, of course not."

"You sure? Suddenly you're all interested in flies dying. Sometimes I got a big mouth, I know."

"Lainey, I'm fine," Marie said.

"Well, good," Laine said, plainly relieved. "And now here comes Bill. That stupid car, you can hear it a mile away. Hear that engine?"

Marie nodded. It was impossible not to hear the metallic death rattle in the driveway.

Laine rolled her eyes. "Now tell me quick, before he comes in. You're not planning on going away again, are you?"

Marie felt strangely exposed, as though she'd been caught at something underhanded she hadn't even been aware she was doing—like telling lies simply out of habit, no longer thinking of them as lies. She'd been guilty of that before.

"No," she said, wondering if it was a lie. Now she wasn't sure. "No, I don't have any plans."

"Really?" Laine said, and the obvious delight in her face made Marie forget her discomfort. "So maybe I can hook you up with somebody here in Lockers Creek, and you'll move out here and we'll be neighbors and raise our poopy kids together?"

"Why not?" Marie said, laughing.

Bill came in without knocking, sweaty and still wearing his work clothes. He was indeed a hairy man, and so big in the doorway he looked like an adult in a child's playhouse. His beard and hair were black and curly, he had no neck to speak of, and his broad shoulders rose slightly as they went out from his chin, so that his head looked like a bowling ball on a sagging shelf. Laine took one look at him and slapped his beefy arm.

"You think we want to ride in a car with you smelling like that?" she scolded.

"You said you wanted me to hurry," he said, grinning. "I figured I'd just wash up in the creek."

"You figured wrong. You get in there and take a shower. And be quiet, Mom's sleeping. This is Marie, by the way."

He extended his hand, but Laine slapped it down. "Don't you touch her with that nasty thing. Go get cleaned up and let's go."

He dawdled as if to talk to Marie. Laine clapped her hands against his chest and shoved him, but he didn't budge. "Get *in* there!" she said. He leaned toward her, forcing her off balance. She cocked her head. "I'm about to slap the fire out of you."

He laughed and leaned to kiss her, but she leaped back out of his reach. "If you don't hurry up," she said, swatting at him again as he turned to go down the hall. When he was gone she said, "I swear I don't know what to do with him. Did you see the way he was looking at you?"

"No."

"Well, I did, and he's going to regret it."

From Lockers Creek it was a long drive to Charleton. You went down Highway 5 to Highway 7, which took you into Hot Springs—where banners all over town advertised cheap body work and paint jobs, hail damage being the boom business of the season—and you drove along the north side of town, along Central and Ouachita and West Grand, to Albert Pike, then across a stretch of Lake Hamilton, where below you the built-up bay glittered and the ski boats etched wakes that spread and faded like jet trails. You passed marine shops and gas stations and strip malls and flea markets. You passed two catfish restaurants. Then the highway straightened and the businesses thinned to occasional lonely outposts, until the roadsides emptied entirely and you were in the Ouachita Forest, with the pine and oak and sweetgum thick along the road, and you felt properly on your way.

Despite the air-conditioning it was uncomfortable in Bill's El Camino. Bill was so large that with three of them in the seat Marie found herself squeezed against the passenger door. Heat rose shimmering from the highway, the more distant cars appearing tremulous and ghostlike through the heat, as if seen through water. Marie was gazing out at the trees, remembering the last time she'd seen her mother. They had driven together down this stretch of highway on a blustery, clouded day, an afternoon nothing like this one.

"Marie," Laine said, "what're you so quiet for?"

"I'm not being quiet."

"Bill, is she being quiet or isn't she?"

"I don't think so."

"You are so aggravating," Laine said. "Do you just *try* to aggravate me?"

"Well, you asked me if she's being quiet, and I told you what I think."

"But she *is* being quiet. You're just trying to aggravate me. Marie, if you're gonna be so quiet, why don't you find a station on the radio you like? No, not that one, try 98. We need to wake you up."

Marie found the station on the radio.

Laine said, "Now will you just *tell* me, Bill? Is he coming or not?"

"How am I supposed to tell you if I don't know? Kylie said he'd ask his friends. That's all I know."

"I can't talk to you. You're just ornery." She reached and changed the radio station again.

"Is who coming?" Marie asked.

"Are you just pretending you weren't listening or weren't you, really?"

"I guess I really wasn't."

"See? Bill, this is what it's like when a person is *honest*. Bill won't tell me if Abe Pittenger's coming or not."

"I'm not telling you cause I don't know," he said. He shrugged his big, sloping shoulders; Marie briefly lost sight of his ear.

Laine ignored him. "Bill's cousin Kylie's supposed to be bringing some friends and Abe's one of them. I'm just worried about him, is all. Did you hear about poor Abe?"

"I know Repeat's coming," Bill said, "but I don't know about the others."

"I'm not listening to you, Bill."

"Did you say his name was Repeat?" Marie asked.

"I know, isn't that stupid? And his voice cracks like he ain't but twelve years old. But a body? Lord have mercy, does that boy have a *body*."

"Hey now," Bill said.

"Well, it's the truth. Anyway he's supposably got a girlfriend up in Fayetteville, so he's out. And then there's Roberto. He's Mexican or something, or I mean he used to be. He's kind of cute, but he's got a girlfriend now, and she's coming. Julie Ann something or other. So you can forget about him too."

"Were you going to tell me something about Abe Pittenger?"

"Do you know him?"

"You just said something happened to him."

"Well, did you hear about that woman getting killed in the flood? Okay, well, Abe was the one who found her. I saw him right after it happened, and he was bruised up and scratched all to hell and just crying like a baby. It was his best friend's mother who died. She was a nice lady, too."

"He was crying?"

"I know, isn't it awful? And now it's like he has nobody, and I feel a little worried about him."

"I'm sure Abe can take care of himself," Bill said.

"You hush. I'm not talking to you."

"Well, you shouldn't tell people about a guy crying."

"For God's sake, Bill, I'm not broadcasting it. I'm just telling Marie."

"What about his friends?" Marie asked.

"Oh, he's got plenty of friends, I guess. But he's kind of a loner? Lives out in a beat-up trailer by himself. He went to college a few years back, and then he come home without finishing. They say he partied too much."

"You don't know that," Bill said.

"I know it's what they *say*. I didn't say it was true."

"Which I don't see why we're talking about it then."

"Bill, would you please just mind your own business?"

"I am minding my own business," he said. "And you'd better find something else to talk about, cause we're here."

Charleton lay in a narrow wooded valley with a creek running through it. Dammed at the far end of the campground, the creek spread out in wide shallows and then, against the dam, deepened into a swimming area. The day-camp road led across a low bridge over the shallows, where smaller children splashed and waded, their arms cuffed with inflatable rings and some with their legs poked through holes in styrofoam floats, paddling about. Bill tapped his horn at them as he drove down the shady road.

They spotted Repeat's Camaro and parked beside it on a mat of brown pine needles, where just behind the cars a cement grill and picnic table stood, sheltered by pines. A slender man in cutoffs and a white T-shirt was brushing spiders and pine needles from the table with a beach towel. Three others were unloading lawn chairs and ice chests from the Camaro. One looked Mexican and one had a perfect physique, so Marie figured

Abe Pittenger was either the man at the picnic table or the gangly one already digging into the ice for a wine cooler. It was the latter, she suspected—for some reason she'd pictured him gawky. But when the man at the picnic table turned, she knew by his damaged face that he was Abe and realized too that she'd already met him.

He had come into the bookstore the week before to give her father an estimate on the roof. Abe had told him straight out that if he wanted it fixed quickly, he ought to hire a different crew, because his boss's crew was booked up for weeks. Her father said it was the same in Hot Springs, that's why he'd called. So Abe gave him an estimate, then volunteered to crawl into the attic and take a look at the ceiling. When he came down, dirty and pouring sweat, he said his father would be a good man to fix it, but he also mentioned another man in Hot Springs who would do a fine job. Her father had liked him for that, Marie could tell.

All the time Abe and her father were talking, she'd noticed he kept glancing at her, as if to include her in the conversation, though she hadn't spoken a word and didn't intend to. She was mending some dust jackets that had been torn when she'd frantically moved the books during the flood. She didn't feel compelled to participate. But when her father stepped away to help a customer, Abe tried to engage her.

"Must be nice to work around books all day."

"It's okay," she said, glancing up. She wasn't sure how to look at him. It was impolite not to look him in the eye, but then she felt like she was staring. She figured he'd been in a fight, because of his black eye, and probably with a woman, because of the scratches. She'd seen men who looked much the same, for that reason. She had in fact done that kind of damage herself.

"I was in a wreck," he said, as if he sensed her thoughts. She must have been staring, after all.

"Oh."

"I guess I'm still in one," he said, and gave a little laugh.

Marie had no idea what he meant, but she smiled.

"You do much reading?" He seemed bent on talking to her.

"In the mornings when it's quiet. Which is most mornings, I guess."

"What do you read?"

"I don't know. Books."

"Books," he said. "Of course."

She thought that was the end of it, but after a moment he said, "Any particular kind of books?"

She sighed. "Oh, this and that. Romance novels, mostly."

"I don't guess I've ever read a romance novel."

He seemed to be serious, which made her laugh. "Why would you have?"

"Why would I have. That's a good point."

He smiled and looked down as though embarrassed, and that was that. Marie returned to her work, disappointed. He'd taken her hints at just the moment she'd decided to quit dropping them. But it was just as well, she thought. Her father came back and finished talking business with him, and when Abe said good-bye she nodded but didn't speak. She hadn't learned his name, hadn't even thought about it until now.

This time, however, knowing a little about him, Marie was more curious. She liked that he'd been through misery. It wasn't a proper way to feel, but she couldn't help it. She wanted to speak to him. She smiled as Abe walked over to greet her. He had recognized her and seemed pleased about it.

The other men got to her first; Laine had to introduce them all. When Kylie's turn came, he took her hand and leaned in close. He smelled of musk cologne and had bulging, crooked eyes and prematurely thinning hair. An unfortunate-looking man with an expensive watch, a thin gold necklace, expensive sunglasses on a cord around his neck.

"I think I met you, once, Marie," he said, shaking her hand and then holding on to it. "At a party, maybe."

"I don't think so."

"You sure? Cause I know I've seen you somewhere."

She looked at him skeptically. "I really don't think so. Either way, I'm going to need that hand back."

Repeat guffawed. Kylie seemed unfazed. He let go her hand and started to say something else, but Laine cut him off, turning Marie by the arm to face Abe.

"And this here is Abe Pittenger," she said.

"Nice to see you again," Abe said, smiling. "How you been?"

"Just fine. You?"

"Can't you tell?" Kylie said, quickly stepping around to include himself. "This boy's been through hell. Tell her what happened to you, Pitt. He drove off a goddamn bridge."

Abe frowned without looking at Kylie. "I'm good."

"I heard about that," Marie said.

"I was just saying his face looks like a speckled trout," Kylie said.

"Will you shut up?" Repeat said.

"You thought it was funny two minutes ago."

"He's right," Abe said. "It does look like a trout."

"Oh, it does not," Laine said scoldingly. She looked as if she wanted to hit somebody, but Bill was unloading the car. "Have y'all been in yet?"

They all headed down to the wooden diving platform on the bank. The platform boards were slippery and dark at the edges where swimmers had stood, dripping, before jumping into the water again. Ahead of them two sunburnt boys cannonballed in tandem. The water was so clear you could see the boys even near the bottom. They swam underwater over to the dam and hauled themselves up onto it. The top of the dam was low to the water and broad enough to serve as a walkway from one bank to the other, and the boys ran along it to the far side, where sunbathers crowded on lawn chairs and towels. Beyond them the grassy bank rose uphill into pine trees.

It was a cozy place, Marie thought. She and her mother had passed the entrance countless times—she'd recognized the sign as they drove up—yet she'd never known what was back here in the trees. So many things you could drive right through. The whole world might have been two fences framing the highway.

"Who goes first?" Bill said, brushing past her. He hunched forward as if to scoop up Laine and toss her into the water.

"Don't you dare," she said, and he took her warning look seriously and straightened again, smiling. Laine said to Marie, "I like to go in slow, and he knows it. It's too cold."

"You go first, Kylie," Repeat said, but Kylie was making a small production of removing his watch and sunglasses, so Repeat hooted defiantly and raced across the platform. He launched himself high into the air, executing a reckless gainer. "Oh, mama!" he shouted when he came up.

As if by instinct the rest of the men charged off the platform together, trying to swamp Repeat. He disappeared under their splashes, and the swimming hole rocked in waves. Everybody came up with a cry of shock. Roberto yelled something in Spanish.

"Is it really that cold?" Marie asked, beginning to dread the water.

Laine said, "Oh, you get used to it. I always go down the ladder just a teensy bit at a time." She went to the platform's side ladder and began to lower herself, stopping when her legs were submerged to the hips. Bill swam up to stand behind her, the water to his chest.

"Let me help," he said, splashing her bare back. Her eyes widened, and she sucked in her breath as if she'd been gut-punched. It was the first real offense Marie had seen him give her—she expected hell to break loose. Instead, Laine just shrieked and laughed and flung herself down into his arms.

Marie went to the edge of the platform. The wood was slippery and warm under her feet. It was better just to plunge in, she thought, but she didn't jump. She'd let herself get spooked. Repeat and Abe had swum over to the dam and were sitting in the sun watching her. Kylie and Roberto treaded water, cheering her on.

"It's not that cold!" Kylie said. "Jump on in!"

Roberto said, "It's all nice and warm, like a nice bath."

She smiled, shaking her head to show she didn't believe them, and stared into the water. It was perfectly clear. She could see pebbles and sand at the bottom, six feet down. A sun perch swam by just beneath her, its shadow plain against the bottom.

"Go Marie!" she heard Laine call.

She held her breath and dove. Hitting the water was like coming suddenly awake after a life of sleep. The cold squeezed her breath from her and made her miserable and joyous all at once. She burst up through the surface squealing. The others laughed and cheered. Spluttering, treading water, she tried to catch her breath. She didn't see how you could ever get used to this. Some of the men had surprised looks on their faces, and she realized she'd been swearing.

Laine's face came creeping across the water toward her. Bill was swimming underwater, and she had hold of his shoulders, letting him tow her along. Her hair was still mostly dry, and a dragonfly had landed on it without her noticing. It looked like an iridescent green barrette.

"Nice going," Laine said.

"How does it get like this? This is unbelievable."

"Comes straight from a spring," Laine said. "Freezes your titties off, doesn't it? But listen, hon, you better not cuss so loud if you don't want those fussy parents to get mad at you." As she pointed toward the bank, Bill surfaced in a sudden uprush, and she squeaked and had to cling to his shoulders to keep from going under. The dragonfly shot away and hovered over the water a few yards off. Laine swatted the top of Bill's head.

"I've got to get out of this," Marie said. All she could think of was getting back in the sun. She climbed the ladder and stood with her arms crossed over her breasts, her skin prickly with goosebumps. In almost no time, though, she felt wonderful. The sun was lovely and warm. Her breath evened out. It was an entirely new feeling. She'd been in a thousand motel swimming pools, but pools were nothing like this. In a motel pool the pleasure was diving in and disappearing. Here it was all in the getting back out.

The men were taking turns leaping from the platform, doing flips and cannonballs and awkward dives. Marie watched contentedly from her perch at the side of the platform, soaking up the sun, her mind pleasantly fuzzy. She wanted to get good and hot before she went in again. Upstream Laine and Bill stood in shallower water, Bill holding Laine up in his arms.

They seemed to have forgotten everyone else. Marie wondered how such conspicuous people could seem so happily unselfconscious. She had never been in a public place herself without feeling as though she were being watched. In fact, she realized, she was being watched now. Repeat was coming over to her. The sun was behind him, and she had to shade her eyes to look up at him.

"Aren't you getting back in?" he asked. His voice split when he talked, like a yodel.

"In a little while."

"That was a good dive. I take it you're a big swimmer."

She shook her head. "I like it, is all."

"Well, you definitely look like you've spent some time in the water. You've got nice, strong legs."

"Laine tells me you've got a girlfriend up in Fayetteville," she said pointedly.

"She told you that?"

Marie stood up. "Looks like the others are getting here," she said, and walked up the hill.

Laine's friends Darla and Dwayne were passing their baby back and forth as they unloaded their car. Pulling in after them, in a short caravan, were a handful of Bill's friends from Jessieville, Roberto's girlfriend Julie Ann, and the two women she lived with, Carol and Gay, whose faces were nothing alike but whose makeup was exactly the same—the same two-tone eyeshadow, the same eyeliner, the same heavy shade of lipstick. They looked as if they were in some kind of show together. After Marie was introduced to everyone she found herself chatting with Darla, a plain-looking woman gone fat since her pregnancy, wearing an oversized Razorbacks T-shirt and culottes. She was talkative—probably the only reason Marie was in a conversation at all—but dull. It seemed unlikely that things were going to get rowdy, as Laine had said. Mostly there was a lot of passing the baby around.

Repeat was busy organizing a swimming race he was certain to win. They were all to dive from the dam and swim upcreek to the shallows, about fifty yards away, where Laine and Bill had gone to stand as judges. He could only get Roberto and Kylie and a couple of Bill's friends to take the challenge.

"What about you, Marie?" he called from the dam, where he and the others were already lined up side by side. She could tell he only wanted an excuse to pay attention to her. He was not a complicated man. She handed her sunglasses to Darla.

"Yay, Marie!" Laine shouted. "Beat the boys!"

The dam had regularly spaced notches along the top, each about two feet across, to form tiny spillways, and the water ran through them and down the slime-coated stone into the creek five or six feet below. The men were lined up one between each spillway. They seemed particular about the spots they'd chosen, and she had to edge past each of them to reach her place at the far end. When she got to Kylie in the middle, she realized he was making it hard for her to get by, so that she would have to brush against him. She threw her shoulder into him. He yelped, wheeled his arms, and toppled into the water.

Laughter and exclamations of surprise erupted from both sides, and the others made a show of giving her plenty of room as she went past them. They jeered Kylie as he hauled himself out of the water. He was grinning widely.

"I'll get you for that!" he called down to Marie. He was pleased with the attention. She should have just given him a contemptuous look.

Abe had agreed to start them off and stood waiting at the end of the dam. He smiled at Marie as she took her place. He was unusually smiley for a man, she decided. But not so much as to make him seem foolish. And then again, maybe it was because of her. It was obvious he liked her. She nodded and got into her ready position.

"On your mark!" Abe began. They all leaned forward. There was a long pause. Marie glanced impatiently toward Abe and caught him staring at her. His eyes darted away. "Get set!" he cried quickly. "Go!"

She plunged in, prepared for the shock this time, and kicked hard. Raising her head for breath, facing left, she saw the splash of the others swimming and the grassy bank beyond them. When she looked right she saw strangers in folding chairs watching her go. This felt good. She'd always been fast—she was a natural swimmer. Even as a kid she'd known to kick with her thighs more than her feet. Soon she'd pulled ahead of everyone except Repeat. She tried to push herself harder and yet keep herself composed, fluid, resisting the urge to flail madly in her lust for speed. There was no room for gaining, though, and the race was over just as she found her rhythm. The water went shallow, her fingers suddenly scraping gravel, and she stood up dripping in the warm sunshine. Repeat and Roberto stood nearby, smiling and panting as the others came up.

"You almost beat him!" Laine was exclaiming giddily. "A girl almost beat you, Repeat."

"How close were we?" Marie gasped.

Bill held his hands out a few feet apart. Laine frowned and pushed his hands closer together.

Marie was in a good mood now. She was happy. The sun was warming her up. She put a cold palm against her throat and could feel her heartbeat there. "I think he must've cheated," she said.

"What!" Repeat protested.

"That's right," Laine said. "You cheated, Peterson."

Repeat laughed, flexing his biceps. "Who needs to cheat?"

"Men always cheat," Laine said, giving Bill a slap on the shoulder and wading back to the bank with Marie. Bill followed them out with an open expression of contentment, as if he really had done something wrong and was proud of it.

Abe stood alone on the dam, watching them climb the bank. He had trouble taking his eyes off Marie. It wasn't just because she was pretty, with her dark eyes and black hair and that kind of savage smile, or that she was so scantily dressed—though he felt sure she'd seen him staring at her body and was embarrassed by that. It was more that she reminded him of something he couldn't name. And never would, he thought, because really it wasn't a particular thing he was reminded of; it was only the feeling you got when you were reminded of something, that conflated moment of search and relief. Except with Marie the relief didn't quite come; she just made you search. Even in those few minutes at the bookstore he'd noticed it. She was young, probably no more than twenty, but seemed older—or not older, exactly, but as if she'd grown up in another country. Abe couldn't figure it out and wasn't really trying to; he just kept thinking about her, hoping he was a quiet sort of fool and not an obvious one.

He joined the others at the picnic spot, where Bill got the grill going and set about cooking hot dogs and steaks. It was late afternoon and still hot, but the cement picnic table and benches had been in shade since morning and were cool to the touch. Everybody dug into the ice chests. The men stood around the grill. Marie and Laine had pulled on their shorts and sandals but not their T-shirts, and for this reason the men took frequent, furtive glances toward the table where the women sat talking.

Julie Ann and Roberto went off on a trail together, holding hands. Kylie left with them but returned alone a few minutes later, looking sullen. He came over to the grill, where Abe stood with a bottle of beer in one hand and waving away smoke with the other. Taking Abe's bottle, he pulled deeply from it, then tried to hand it back.

"Go on and finish it," Abe said.

Kylie finished it and went to an ice chest and brought back two wine coolers, handing one to Abe. Except for an occasional joke, the men stood quietly, watching the heat shimmer over the charcoals and listening to the meat sizzle on the grill. To Abe it seemed vaguely tribal. The silence suited him—he and these men had little to talk about, anyway—and he found he enjoyed this odd sort of communion. He belonged there simply by virtue of being a man. It was easy. You could just look at the coals. You didn't have to think.

Eventually Bill served up the first plate of hot dogs, and Abe carried them over to the table for the women. Behind him, almost at once, he heard Kylie talking about him. The momentary feeling of peacefulness slipped away. He went back to the grill.

"Hey, Kylie," he said. "Would you please shut the hell up about it?"

"Don't you tell me to shut up," Kylie said, face darkening. He looked ready to fight. He already had several drinks in him. To distract him Abe handed him his half-full bottle, trading it for Kylie's almost empty one.

"Don't talk about me, then," he said.

"I wasn't saying nothing *bad*. Damn, you're sensitive."

Abe was aware of the eyes turned on him. He drained the rest of the wine cooler, dropped the bottle onto the pine needles at his feet, and said flatly, "I'm going to take a piss."

"All right," Kylie said. "Wait a second, I'll come with you." He guzzled his own drink and likewise dropped the empty bottle.

Abe wanted to scream at him, but there was no point in being disgusted with Kylie. It didn't help anything. They went together across the dam and up the path to the public restrooms. The bathroom smelled rank. The tile floor was muddy, and beads of condensation dripped from the exposed pipes. Granddaddy longlegs massed in the sills of the open windows. One of them fell from somewhere above Abe and landed on top of the urinal. He looked at it, the tiny brown body like the head of a kitchen match, spindly legs like jointed hairs. He felt slightly drunk.

"You ever hear that granddaddies were poisonous?" he said.

Kylie stood swaying at the urinal next to him. "Only if you eat too many of them," he said. They laughed. Abe laughed so hard he dried up and had to wait a minute to finish.

"That's pretty funny," he said.

"Yep," Kylie said. "Only if you eat too many." He grew serious and said, "Hey, listen. I wasn't trying to embarrass you back there."

"Just let up about it, okay? I don't like to hear about it."

"I wasn't saying nothing about Jackie, you know. Just about you going off the bridge and all that. I don't see what the big deal is."

"Well, would you just let up about it, for me? As a favor to me?"

"All right," Kylie said. "Listen, you ever want to talk about it, I'm here. I mean that."

"I appreciate it."

"You want to talk about it?"

"Not right now."

"Well, when you do, you know."

"I appreciate it."

They took the long way back, down across the bridge over the shallows and along the grassy bank, weaving among the sunbathers lying out on towels. Kylie stared indiscreetly at the women until he remembered he'd taken off his dark glasses and they could see him looking. When they were a short way off he told Abe what he'd done, in a voice loud enough for all the women to hear. Abe couldn't help but laugh at that too.

At the picnic site the others were all eating now. There was one steak left, and Abe knew Kylie would argue for it, so he forked a couple of hot dogs onto his plate. Laine looked up when he came to the table and said, "You boys going to pick up after yourselves now?"

He raised his eyebrows questioningly, and she pointed at the bottles lying on the ground by the grill. Marie was smiling at him, apparently amused. He relaxed. "I was leaving those for you."

Laine cocked her head warningly, and he smiled and went over to pick up the bottles, which were already flecked with black ants.

Repeat was sitting next to Marie, and there were no empty seats, so Abe leaned against a pine tree and tried not to watch them. The more he drank, the more he hated Repeat. He realized he was getting too drunk. He was much too tired to be drinking. He switched to soda pop and reminded himself to watch his mouth. The afternoon was waning. Abe kept quiet, listening to the conversations, waiting for one of the women to ask Marie something about her life. It was always the women who did the polite thing. But no one did. Instead there was a good deal of talk about who was pregnant and who had children and which pregnant women had been married long enough to thwart suspicion. The men talked mostly about their jobs, and Repeat and Kylie, the only ones in college, told exaggerated stories of wild fraternity parties, stories Abe had heard before. He hadn't cared for them the first time, either.

The sun dropped behind the hill, and everything went into soft focus. The group stayed clustered under the pines and drank more and talked. Abe forgot his resolution to stick to soda pop. The air was still warm but not as sticky as before, and all around the campground people had started using their evening voices, a little quieter and with a little more laughter.

Darla's baby began to cry in Laine's arms. Laine had come to stand near Abe—trying to include him—and when the baby started whimpering she said, "Would you hold him for just a second? I've got to find his binky."

Abe's face turned panicky, and the women laughed. Taking the baby, surprised by its weight, he cradled it awkwardly until Laine showed him how. He felt the crinkle of diaper beneath the soft blue jumper as he adjusted his arms. Darla, he noticed, was taking sidelong anxious glances. But as Laine searched around for the pacifier, the baby grew quiet in his arms, looking up at him with wide eyes. He widened his own eyes. The baby smiled a gummy smile.

"Would you look at that?" Laine said in a hushed voice. "Maybe Abe's the real daddy."

"I wouldn't doubt it," Dwayne said. Darla scowled and pinched him.

"Probably it's just because he's warmer," Marie said matter-of-factly.

"You think that's it?" Abe said.

She came over to stand beside him. "Men get a lot warmer than women."

"They do?"

"Sure they do," she said, standing with her shoulder touching his and widening her eyes at the baby. The baby looked surprised. She twirled her finger and touched it on the nose. It laughed and flailed its arms.

Abe rocked the baby gently, afraid it would cry again and he would have to give it up. Marie stood close to him, talking softly to the baby, and Abe listened to her murmur and coo. When she leaned over to bring her face close to the baby's, Abe inhaled deeply but smelled only the baby's sour breath. It was getting heavy, too.

Having found the pacifier in the dirt, Laine and Darla had gone to the restrooms to wash it off. Repeat was talking to Gay now. She appeared to enjoy the attention. Gay was partly deaf and wore hearing aids; Abe wondered if she was really hearing him. She seemed rapt as Repeat talked about track and field, about his future as a coach.

"So Marie," Abe said, quietly, not wanting to startle the baby, "do you live in Hot Springs or just work there?"

When she stepped away from him he regretted having spoken, but she was only positioning herself to look at him more directly. He remembered his face and had to fight a self-conscious impulse to turn it away from her. Marie was tugging absently at the shoulder straps of her swimsuit, gazing off into the trees. "Right now I'm living there, with my dad."

"I take it that was your dad in the store," he said. "Y'all look kind of alike."

It was apparently the right thing to say. Marie gave him a look that seemed almost grateful, as if he'd flattered her. "You think so? I guess we do."

For a while, then—for a long while, Abe noticed—they talked about her father. She told Abe some of the stories her father told her, and a good deal about how much people liked him, and about how he visited her mother's father even though he wasn't with her mother anymore. Abe was surprised by the way she went on. Until now she hadn't seemed much of a talker, but now she had got wound up and wasn't winding down. She was unusually frank, occasionally wry. She spoke the way people do when they're slightly annoyed, even though she was calm.

"Have you been staying with him long?" Abe asked, when she seemed to be losing steam. "Laine said you just got back in town."

"I did," she said tersely, and that was all. She snapped closed like a trap.

Dismayed, Abe only nodded. Did she think he'd accused her of something? You need to keep your mouth shut, he thought. But then even as he was thinking it, he said, "Well, I wish I got along so well with my dad."

She nodded but didn't take it up. He watched her face slowly relax, though. He could actually see the tension fade from it. You need to be careful, he thought. You can't tell what gives and what holds. It's like climbing shale.

"I hear you used to have some horses," Marie said. She was making an effort.

"You like horses?"

She shrugged. "I never cared much one way or the other."

"I see."

"I mean I like them, I just haven't been around them." Marie tilted her empty bottle to her lips, lowered it, and looked at it. "Why do I keep trying to drink from this empty bottle?"

"Maybe you emptied one too many."

"This is only my second," she said defensively.

Abe got flustered again. "I was joking. I figured you had to be drunk to come talk to me," he said, and was instantly mortified. He heard the words but couldn't believe he'd said them.

Marie frowned. "Why?"

Abe tried to cover. "Well, nobody wants to get stuck with the guy holding the baby."

"I *like* babies."

"Oh, I do, too," he said. "You gotta have babies."

She gave him a puzzled look, but this time he kept his mouth shut, and it seemed all right.

"Can I hold him?" Marie said.

"You have to be very, very careful," he said, in a mock-serious tone.

"Oh, I will be," she said, in the same tone, and then Abe knew it was all right.

"I mean it," he said. "Babies aren't toys."

She laughed and took the baby from his arms and held it snugly against her chest. He straightened his arms, feeling them tingle. They stood quietly as she rocked him. Soon Laine and Darla were back. Darla laid the pacifier on the baby's belly.

"Sometimes he won't go back to sleep without his little sucker," Darla said. "If he gets cranky, just pop it in."

Marie nodded. Darla lingered for a moment, watching her baby's eyes grow heavy. Abe noticed she rocked back and forth along with Marie—a young mother's habit; he'd seen it before. Bring a baby into the room and all the young mothers start swaying. Abe found it pleasantly calming. Eventually Darla went to sit in Dwayne's lap. Dwayne had brought out a deck of cards and was playing poker with some of the other men. He had to look around Darla now to see his hand. They were betting with Fritos.

"I'm sorry if I was snippy with you," Marie said.

"I didn't think you were."

"I'm kind of touchy about some things. It's not your fault."

"It's all right. I'm sorry if I said something I shouldn't have."

"No," she said. "No, that's okay." Which sounded to Abe as if he had said something wrong but was forgiven for it. "I can get mean sometimes," she went on, "even when I don't really want to. Sometimes I just feel this urge."

"Maybe it's heartburn."

Marie squinted at him. "You like to joke a lot, don't you?"

"Sorry, I—"

"No, I like it. I'm just getting used to it."

"I do it too much. My father used to get mad at me because he didn't think I could be serious about anything."

"Your father sounds like a prick," Marie said.

Abe was so surprised he burst out laughing. The baby's eyes opened and its face screwed up. Abe shut up as Marie rocked the baby earnestly, both of them watching it with the same disproportionate fear, the universal fear of a crying baby.

"Put its thingy in," Marie hissed.

"Do what?"

"Its what-do-you-call-it, its sucker. Put it in."

Abe touched the pacifier to the baby's lower lip. The baby's bitter expression changed to one of bland purpose, and it took the pacifier in its mouth, sucking earnestly.

"I shouldn't have said that about your father," Marie said, when the baby's eyes had closed.

"Don't worry about it."

"I wasn't trying to be mean that time. I just didn't think. I'm sure he's probably nice enough if you know him."

"I wouldn't say that," Abe said. "He's pretty tough on people. I wouldn't say he's a prick, exactly, but he's pretty tough."

"Jesus, you must think I'm a terrible person for saying something like that."

"No, I don't. I like that you say what you think."

"Really? Well, sometimes I'm not thinking. That's the problem."

"There's worse problems to have, I guess."

"Well, I've got those too."

Abe grinned. Marie glanced at him and seemed pleased.

"I do," she said, smiling back.

Roberto and Julie Ann finally showed up looking tired and bedraggled. They scavenged among the food and trash on the table. "Look like a pack of wolves or something come through here," Roberto said.

"Where'd y'all go?" Carol asked.

"I could show you," Kylie offered, but Carol shook her head and said she was tired and didn't feel like walking.

The lightning bugs were out in full force now, glittering among the trees, and far off in the woods a chuck-will's-widow was singing out its name. With the arrival of dusk the mosquitoes had begun their onslaught, and Laine passed around a bottle of repellent. Abe finished with it and extended it awkwardly to Marie, but her hands were full with the baby.

"Want to trade?" he said.

"No, he's sleeping."

"Well, aren't they getting you?"

"Not too bad," she said, even as she shifted onto her left foot and rubbed an itch on her bare calf with the other.

"You want me to spray you down?" he said, gesturing with the bottle.

"That's okay."

"Lord, Marie," Laine said, coming over. "Give him here."

Marie handed over the baby. She shook her hands as if they were asleep and took the repellent from Abe. He watched her spray it into her palm and rub it over her legs and arms. Her back was bare and he noticed that she couldn't quite get to it, but this time he said nothing. She went over to the table and set the bottle down and put on her T-shirt, and then Laine started talking to her, and she leaned against the table and didn't return.

The evening turned full dark. Here and there among the campground trees, people stood around fires, their faces weirdly lit by the flames. Finding himself with nothing to do, Abe gathered wood and built a fire in the fire pit some yards uphill from the picnic table. He did it as his father had taught him, building a miniature teepee of pine kindling and getting that burning first, then slowly laying on larger sticks. He was patient, and using a bit of paper he managed to get the fire going without lighter fluid, although Kylie kept urging him to use it. In a few minutes the flames were good and high, and he stood up, feeling his knees creak. Repeat and Gay had come over to stand on the far side of the fire, without speaking to him. Repeat had his arm around her waist.

The poker players came to the fire with beers in their hands, and after a while the women followed. Roberto and Julie Ann had stirred up the coals in the grill again and were cooking the last of the hot dogs for themselves. The conversation had begun to die down. One of the car radios was playing softly, and you could hear the low murmur of Roberto and Julie Ann talking to each other over by the grill. The fire crackled and popped, sending sparks out among them; occasionally somebody would slap bare skin where a spark had landed. Dwayne was holding the baby now, standing with his back to the fire so the sparks couldn't reach it. Marie came around to stand by Abe.

He watched her come. He was using a solid green branch to prod the fire, and after he'd stoked it a few more times, Marie said, "Can I do that?"

She poked the stick into the fire aggressively, as if spearing a snake. Everyone stepped back, surprised, until the sparks settled. Marie let up, looking satisfied. She's an odd bird, Abe thought, somewhat dreamily. He laid the last piece of wood on the fire and would have been glad if not for Marie. He was dead tired. Soon there was nothing but a circle of charred sticks and dull red coals. The evening breeze carried intermittent gusts of cool air up from the creek. Abe felt sleepy and comfortable. His eyes were heavy, and he wished he could just stay that way, heavy-lidded and relaxed by the dying fire. He caught Marie looking at him and smiled drowsily.

"Tired?" she said.

"Not too bad."

Finally Repeat suggested they break camp and drive up the highway to Hickory Nut Mountain. Darla and Dwayne declined, and Carol said she would go home with them. It was clear to everyone Gay wasn't going to leave yet, so no one asked her. They set about picking up their things. Abe poured a few half-empty beer and soda cans over the coals. The coals hissed and smoked. He was alone at the fire pit again and felt disproportionately lonely, as if he'd been abandoned. Childishly lonely, he thought. He kicked dirt over the coals.

Bill's friends were headed for a party somewhere. It would be just two cars for the mountain. Repeat, in an absurd attempt to be discreet, pulled Roberto aside and asked him to drive the Camaro, then followed Gay into the back seat. Roberto and Julie Ann took the front.

Abe climbed into the bed of Bill's El Camino, nodding at Kylie to join him. But since Carol left, Kylie had drifted hopefully to Marie and was sticking close to her now. He waited while she got into the El Camino, only then realizing the front seat was packed and there was no room for him. Abe gestured again, but Kylie, frustrated and drunk, ignored him, climbing instead into the back of the Camaro with Repeat and Gay. Abe could hear Repeat protesting.

Laine put her head out the window. "Abe, don't be stupid. Get up here with us."

"That's okay."

"Get up here. Marie can sit on our laps."

He looked at Marie.

"Sure," she said. "Come on up."

He came up front. Marie half-stood as he squeezed into the seat, then sat dividing her weight between Laine's right thigh and Abe's left. Her shorts were damp from the swimsuit underneath it. Her bare calf prickled his shin. She braced herself with one arm around Laine's neck and one hand pushed up against the ceiling. It was obviously awkward.

"Marie, you can't be comfortable like this," he said. "Let me get in back again. It's nice outside anyway."

"I'm fine," Marie said.

"She's fine," Laine said. "Let's go, Bill."

Abe saw now that Laine was trying to get the two of them together. He couldn't figure her reasoning, unless it was pity, but he didn't want to think that. He didn't let himself.

The winding, wooded road up Hickory Nut Mountain was dirt and gravel all the way, with potholes that jounced Marie on their laps. Near the top Bill had to brake for an armadillo crossing the road—it bounded like a rabbit out of the headlights—and Marie's head almost hit the windshield. Laine snapped at him to be more careful.

"It's my fault," Abe said. "I should've known better than to squeeze in like this."

"Don't try to defend him," Laine said.

"Thanks, bud," said Bill. "But it ain't no use."

"Now what was I saying?" Laine asked.

"You said you wanted to ask me a question," Abe said.

"Thank you. Yes. Now what I wanted to ask you, Abe, if Bill doesn't kill us before I can ask it—slow down, Bill! For God's *sake!*—what I was wondering is what you think about Repeat and Gay."

"I'm not sure I know how to answer that."

"Well, Gay's my friend," she said.

"I know."

"Okay, then, speak up. Will he treat her right?"

"I guess it depends on what she expects."

"Lord. That's just what I thought. You men."

"I think Abe's right," Bill said. "Doesn't matter what you think, you can't control your friends."

"Bill, did I ask you?"

"I'm just saying."

"Well, don't."

They came to the top of the mountain, where the land was bald of trees and nearly flat. Miles from city lights, the sky here opened up, a huge canvas of stars and a fat yellow moon hanging low to the mountain rim. Across the broad gravel parking lot a stone gazebo stood backlit by the moon. The only other car on the lot was the Camaro, and Roberto and Julie Ann lay on its hood, their backs propped against the windshield, looking at the stars. Kylie was leaning against the car, waiting. He scowled when he saw Abe climb out of the front seat. He came over to them.

"It was chained off," he said, pointing toward the entrance, "but we just unhooked the chain. Wasn't even a lock on the thing. We'd better look out for rangers, though."

"You got a gun, Abe?" Bill asked. "We might need it if the rangers show up."

"I've got a pocket knife."

"But are you any good with it?"

"Alls I'm saying is we might get run off," Kylie said. "No big deal." He lowered his voice. "Repeat and Gay went for a walk."

Laine took Abe by the arm, and for a moment he thought she was going to scold him about Repeat. But she only led him up to the front of the car, like a schoolmistress with a pupil, and said, "You and Marie are guests, so y'all can sit up here on the hood. I'll get the chairs out of the back for the rest of us."

Abe climbed onto the hood, positioning himself in the middle with his back against the windshield. He knew Kylie would try to join them and was determined not to let him sit in the middle. Marie came up on his left and he slid over to make room for her. Sure enough, Kylie came up next to her, and so the two of them had to move again, until Abe's leg hung over the side. There wasn't room for three. Laine brought up a folding chair.

"Y'all look crowded," she said, a bit wonderingly. "Why don't you take a chair, Kylie?"

"I'm fine."

Marie said, "We are kind of packed, though." She was giving Kylie a look, but he wouldn't notice it.

"Kylie, come take this chair right now," Laine insisted. "I didn't carry it up here for nothing."

Kylie got down and turned the chair so that it faced them. Laine went back, and after a minute the car seemed to sink into the ground as Laine and Bill climbed into the bed. They weren't coming forward, after all. Kylie was talking again, but Abe wasn't listening to him. Instead he heard the engine pinging beneath them as it cooled, the tinny ebb and flow of crickets in the scrub, the barred owl hooting down in the trees, the infrequent shush of cars on the highway far below. Overhead, the stars were piercingly bright and close; the sky was vast. He caught himself thinking it looked like a map of stars.

They didn't respond much to Kylie. Soon Abe noticed he was the only one responding at all, with occasional grunts. Marie wasn't saying anything. Eventually Kylie quit trying, and they were all quiet, just looking up at the stars. A breeze ruffled his hair, and Abe looked sidelong at Marie because he wanted to see her hair move in the breeze. She was brushing a strand out of her eyes, tucking it behind her ear. She did it unconsciously and didn't notice him watching.

"What kind of bird is that?" she asked.

"I don't know," Kylie said, sounding startled. He might have been falling asleep.

"It's a barred owl," Abe said.

"Sounds kind of like a rooster."

"It does have that squawky sound."

Kylie didn't try to say anything else. Abe felt a twinge of hope. They were quiet again for a while, and Kylie began to snore. Marie looked at Abe and smiled.

"He's loud," she said simply.

"He had a lot to drink," he whispered, not to disturb Kylie.

"Well, it's a beautiful night if he'd just leave it alone."

Abe nodded. He didn't want to talk about Kylie. "During the day you can see the lake off that way," he said, pointing.

"I'll bet it's pretty," Marie said. She was whispering too, having picked up on his cue. It thrilled him to hear her do it.

"It is," he said. "You can see for miles."

"You ever go up on West Mountain downtown?"

"Sure. It's beautiful."

"I like it. The town looks like a playset from up there. It feels like you could just reach down and move the people around with your hands."

"That's right," he said. "It's just about that size."

"My dad used to buy us frozen Cokes and take us up there. I always loved that. There used to be some of those coin telescopes. I'd watch people down on the street and pretend I was part of their lives. Like I was with them, but just a few steps behind them, you know, and any second they would turn around and say, 'Hurry up, Marie.'"

Abe tried to picture her a little girl on her toes, eye pressed to the lens of a buzzing tourist telescope. "I thought you weren't from around here."

"I've lived here off and on. I mean, Hot Springs was where we'd always come back to. Because my dad lived here. And my grandpa, though we never visited him."

"You did a lot of traveling, then."

"Oh, sure," she said. "I basically grew up in a car."

"Is that right? You moved a lot, or—"

"Well," she said, looking at him askance, "my mom was a drug dealer, so we were always hopping around from one place to another. I mean constantly. We made runs all over the place. Tulsa, Arkadelphia, Little Rock, Memphis, just all over. I spent more time in the car than I did anywhere else—I definitely felt more at home in a car than I did in a house—but I liked Hot Springs. I always wanted to stay here. Because of my dad, I guess, though you know how kids are; maybe it was because I liked those frozen Cokes. A kid can have stupid reasons for things."

She'd said it all matter-of-factly. Abe had almost laughed at first but had caught himself in time. "Did you say your mother was a drug dealer?"

"Well, she was a user first, of course. Then she expanded."

"You sound like you're serious."

"I remember there was this one man who used to tell her she didn't just borrow trouble, she bought it in bulk. But I don't guess you want to hear about all this."

"No, I do," Abe said quickly. "I can't believe it. I mean I do—I'm just sorry, is all."

"It's no big thing. I don't usually talk about it. In fact I don't even know why I told you. I guess because you're nice? I don't know."

She was looking steadily at him now, and although she sounded as if she might regret having spoken, she appeared undisturbed, her face gone soft as though she were sleepy. He opened his mouth and closed it again. She gave him a sleepy-looking half-smile. Their faces were very close. He looked away, thinking. When he looked back she was still gazing at him. He stopped looking away.

"I don't know what to say."

"It doesn't matter."

"It does. I just don't know what to say."

"You can't say anything to change it."

"No."

"You won't tell anybody, though, will you? Not that it really matters, but—"

"I won't," he said. "I promise."

She seemed suddenly quite young to him, young and familiar. He felt strangely as though they were both children, and he loved her at once, the way he had loved girls when he was a child: anxiously and giddily, and more than a little bewildered.

Marie gave another sleepy smile. "Now you tell *me* something," she whispered. "You tell me your secret."

This caught him off guard, quickening his pulse. His secret. To his alarm, he felt the urge to tell her the truth. "I don't really have one," he said, stalling, expecting her to tease him. He would think of something else to tell her, something harmless.

Marie peered at him, her forehead crinkling, and Abe had the absurd, distressing thought that she already knew the truth and was testing him. As if to prove this, she said—not accusingly, but confidently: "You're lying."

"Why do you say that?"

"I can just tell."

"You're right," he admitted, and it was a relief. "I want to tell you, but I shouldn't. It can't do anybody any good. Not anybody. Certainly not me."

"Tell me anyway," she whispered. She moved closer, until her shoulder pressed his. She seemed excited, which excited him too. It also made him think he shouldn't trust her.

"We don't really even know each other," he said.

"I told you about my mother."

"I know."

"So tell me," Marie urged. "Tell me, and I swear I won't tell a soul."

They were perfectly alone. Kylie was snoring, the tireless crickets scraping insistently, the barred owl sending up its iambic squawks. They were alone, and Abe had the illogical feeling that the whole evening happened just this way so that he would tell somebody the truth. Tell a stranger, a strange woman he was falling in love with like a schoolboy. So he told her the truth about Jackie. He told her, and then he felt sick.

Marie's expression had hardly changed. "Are you all right?"

"No."

"Is it because you told me or because it happened?"

He thought about that, and his stomach settled a bit. "I guess both."

"Telling me didn't change anything," she said.

"No. I guess not."

"Except I'm glad you did. I'm glad you did, because it's nice to have someone trust you."

Only then did Abe understand why she'd wanted it. He hadn't been able to see it before. He said, "I trust you, Marie," although he didn't really think he did. And she smiled—she was smiling about this terrible, sickening thing, and it was like they were children, and in love.

They were quiet for a long time. The wind had picked up, moaning through the gazebo across the lot. Abe was thinking, Did this really happen? When the wind shifted, he smelled the mosquito repellent come off Marie's skin. The owl had gone silent in the trees. Then he thought, Does it matter? He watched her watching him with that soft expression. No, it didn't matter.

"I'm sleepy," she murmured.

"Go to sleep if you want."

"No, I don't want to."

He watched her blinking her eyes drowsily. He found her hand and squeezed it gently. She held on and closed her eyes. Her skin was cool. He caressed the soft down along the back of her hand. She didn't open her eyes or lean toward him but her lips still held a faint smile. He thought she might be asleep, and he felt as though he were the only person awake on the mountain—holding a stranger's hand under the deep night sky, with the wind moaning through the stone gazebo across the lot, holding her hand and thinking he might love her and not understanding a thing. He couldn't even identify what needed to be understood, though he felt powerfully that there was something. And it was like this for some time, with him awake and wondering, and never understanding any more than he had at the beginning.

The yellow moon had whitened and stood well above the gazebo by the time Repeat and Gay came back. Abe could hear their voices drifting across the parking lot, and the crunching of their footsteps on gravel. Marie opened her eyes and found him looking at her and squeezed his hand.

She seemed fully awake. There was a scraping sound as Kylie stood up suddenly from his chair.

"What?" Kylie said.

They let go each other's hand and sat up. Kylie was looking about confusedly. Repeat and Gay were coming toward them, talking loudly and laughing, their arms around each other.

"You were asleep," Abe said to Kylie. "It's okay."

Kylie looked at him as if he didn't know him. "What?"

"You fell asleep."

"Oh. No, I don't think I did."

Roberto's voice sounded from the Camaro, yards away. He was talking to Repeat. "About time, damn it. Me and Pitt, we have to work in the morning. I almost left you here."

"That wouldn't have been so bad."

"Goddamn," said Roberto. "You driving your own damn car this time. Get in."

Laine and Bill came up to stand next to the hood. Laine had been fast asleep and was rubbing her eyes like a small child. Bill was rolling his shoulder where she'd slept on it.

"Y'all get the world's problems all sorted out?" he said.

"Could you hear us talking?" Marie said.

"I didn't hear a thing," Laine said. "I fell asleep."

"I heard y'all whispering some," Bill said. "But I couldn't hear what you said."

"We were talking politics," Abe said.

"I'll bet."

Roberto came over to the car. "Can y'all give Pitt a ride back? We have to take Gay home."

"No problem," Bill said, folding up Kylie's chair and putting it in the back. Kylie stood there blearily, doing nothing.

"You sure?" Abe said.

"You live in Lockers Creek, don't you?"

"Yeah."

"Well, that's where we're headed."

Roberto looked at Abe and then at Marie, then back at Abe. "All right. I see you in the morning, Pitt." He checked his watch. "In about six goddamn hours. Come on, Kylie." He shook his head and went back to the Camaro. Kylie followed him, still dazed, not thinking to say good-bye.

Marie got into the car with Bill and Laine. Abe looked in through the open door. "I'm going to ride in back."

"Don't be a dork," Laine said grumpily. "Get in here."

This time he was firm. "No, it's too crowded. I'll be fine in back."

Marie gave him a sad and sleepy look. Sad for his sake. He shut the door. In the back Bill and Laine had laid out a beach-towel pallet; it was still warm from their bodies. The ice chests and folding chairs were pushed into the corners. He lay on the pallet and folded his arms behind his head. When Bill started the engine, his teeth vibrated. At the parking lot entrance they stopped, Bill getting out to clasp the chain again. Marie jumped out and climbed over the tailgate into the back.

"I'll keep you company," she said.

They lay together with their heads near the cab, and as the El Camino wound down the mountain they had to fight against the sliding ice chests. Finally they put them against the tailgate and propped their feet against them to hold them in place.

The sky was a narrow strip of stars above the highway as it cut through the Ouachita Forest. The moon was out of sight behind the trees. Abe heard a murmuring and turned to see Marie's mouth moving. She was talking, but he hadn't heard her for the noise of the wind and the engine and the thrum of the tires. He shook his head, leaned closer, and put his mouth to her ear.

"What?" he said, his lips brushing her ear. "I couldn't hear you."

She leaned toward him. Expectantly he watched her face draw closer. She touched his chin and pushed his head away so that she could put her mouth against his ear. "I said it's chilly back here, isn't it?"

He nodded and raised his near arm and she shifted closer, laying her head against his shoulder. He felt the goosebumps on her bare arm. She pressed her leg against his, and they lay like this without talking and watched the stars as the wind passed over them. From time to time they glanced at each other, their eyes watery from the wind. Abe couldn't sort his thoughts. It was as if everything in his life were happening just then, and he couldn't order it.

They came out of the forest and into Hot Springs, where streetlights flashed by overhead. The car stopped at an intersection, and they lay looking at each other as the engine idled. It was warmer and quieter with the car stopped. There was the sound of other cars behind them and on either side, but they couldn't see them. They smelled the bittersweet, acrid odor of the exhaust. Abe's windblown hair lay partly covering his face. Marie reached and brushed it back.

"You have pretty blue eyes, don't you?" she said.

He started to say something, he didn't know what, but the light changed and the El Camino pulled forward, and it was loud again and the air suddenly fresh and cool. She laughed as the wind blew Abe's hair back across his face. They passed through town and out again into darkness.

When they came into Lockers Creek, Abe recognized with a pang of sadness the familiar trees and the telephone poles, and could tell when Bill had turned onto Merrill Road. He shifted toward Marie, and she turned so that her leg lay over his. He put his mouth against her ear: "I'll come see you."

She tried to answer him, but he turned his head so she couldn't reach his ear. She drew back, frowning playfully. He kissed her and felt her leg press against his. He inhaled her breath. It was warm and sweet. Her eyes opened in the same sleepy way as before. She brushed the hair back from his face and watched the wind blow it forward again.

The car turned down the bumpy gravel drive to his trailer and in a minute was stopped in the dark yard. Marie sat up first. Abe felt the blood tingling in his arm like fire ants. He followed her over the tailgate. She caught him in a hug as he stepped down, and he buried his face in her hair. When she started to pull away he tried to hold her a moment longer, but she resisted and he had to let her go.

"They're waiting," she said. She glanced quickly around, at the dilapidated trailer, the beat-up truck, the stars over the pasture. "So this is where you live your life."

"Such as it is."

They went to the passenger door. Laine smiled groggily, scooting over to make room, and Marie climbed in. Bill nodded and said, "Night, Abe."

"Night," he said, leaning against the open door and looking in at them. "Thanks for the ride."

Laine said, "We're sure glad you could come."

"Me too. I'll see you, Marie," he said, reaching in and taking her hand. They shook in a formal way, and she smiled, almost laughing, and withdrew her hand.

"Watch your feet now," he said. He shut the door.

He stood in the headlights as Bill backed the car. Lucky had come out from under the trailer and was bumping against his legs. Abe picked him up and scratched under his chin and waved as Bill turned down the drive. The taillights disappeared around the bend. He heard the car fade down Merrill Road.

In the woods across the pasture a whip-poor-will was calling. Abe looked all around, still holding Lucky in his arms, trying to see what Marie had seen. It seemed a different place. He went into the trailer, turned on the fans but not the lights, and sat on his couch in the darkness. Lucky settled purring onto his lap. His heart was thumping hard, his stomach queasy and nervous. He tried to breathe steadily to calm himself.

Hours later he awoke to find he'd been crying in his sleep. His eyes were dry, but in his dream he'd been sobbing. He couldn't remember the dream this time, though he figured it was the same as ever, and the effect of it took time to fade. Lucky was scratching at the door, wanting out. Abe stood carefully and felt his back. He thought he'd take some aspirin and lie down again for a last few hours' sleep. But when he opened the door, he saw it was gray outside. Tabby was pacing the porch, growling her old cat's mew, waiting for her food. Out in the pasture, the field sparrows were calling up the morning.

Chapter 7

Laine stood at the stove in a thin yellow housecoat and fuzzy slippers. She was smoking a cigarette and exhaling the smoke toward the open window over the sink. She kept blowing after the smoke was gone, trying to push it on out the window. Marie watched her flip the bacon with one hand and stretch and tap cigarette ash into the sink with the other. When she noticed Marie in the doorway her eyes widened, and she made a frightened sound with her mouth closed. Then she laughed, and smoke came out her nostrils.

"I thought you were my mom. She'd kill me for smoking in the house."

"I'll take one of those," Marie said.

"On the table. Also, would you get the plates?"

She lit a cigarette as Laine flipped bacon onto the plates. Bread stood in the toaster already toasted.

"I don't normally smoke," Laine said. "But it takes the edge off of my hangovers in the morning."

"I didn't realize you drank that much last night."

"Oh, Lord, Marie, one beer does me in. I'm surprised you couldn't tell. Wasn't I all loopy and loud?"

"Not that I noticed."

"Good gravy, I don't know what that says about me. Now get whatever you want out of the fridge. We've got grape juice."

"I'll just have coffee."

"Pour me some too, would you? You want butter for your toast?"

"That's okay."

"You're right. I better eat mine dry too. All that fat."

"Don't be stupid. If you want butter I'll get it out."

"All right. Maybe just a little."

They finished their cigarettes and sat down to eat. Laine's father was at church, she said. Her mother was in bed.

"I hope she starts feeling better soon," Laine said. "I can't put off the wedding forever."

"You don't have a date yet?"

"It was supposed to be this month. But she doesn't feel so good right now, and we decided to wait."

"That was nice of you."

Laine shrugged. "Oh, I know, I'm all sweetness and light." She hesitated, considering, then in a lower voice said, "Okay, can I tell you something?"

"Course you can."

"It wasn't just a hysterectomy. Which, I don't know why I didn't just tell you straight off. I guess I thought it's too much to tell somebody who doesn't already know her. I mean what are they supposed to say? Well. Anyway. It's pretty far along. They couldn't get it all."

"I'm sorry."

"What can you do. She's raised a whole passel of us hellions and monsters. Probably she can use the rest."

Her voice faltered on the last word, and she ducked her head slightly, her hand going to her suddenly knotted brow, shielding her eyes as if from the kitchen light. Marie sat still in her chair. She imagined laying her hand on Laine's, as she had seen other women do. She imagined coming out of her chair and pulling Laine's head to her chest. But who was she? Instead she waited, miserably silent, until Laine took a deep breath and rose and went to the oven. She slid out a pan of orange rolls, taking a minute to compose herself as she slathered white icing over them. When she brought them to the table her eyes were red but her voice was back. "These are just about the best things I've ever had," she said, with forced cheer.

"They smell wonderful."

Laine licked icing from her fingers. "Don't they, though?"

Marie touched an orange roll. The icing was cold but the roll itself was hot. She didn't know if it was better to eat one now or to wait. She waited until Laine picked one up, and then she did too. They didn't speak. When Laine had finished her roll she sighed, brushed crumbs from her fingers, and shook another cigarette from the pack. She took it to the open window and smoked it halfway down.

"It's nice out," she said finally. She took another long drag on her cigarette. "Pretty day to be on the lake. That'll make Bill happy. He was going fishing this morning. Probably been out there for hours already. He sure loves to fish."

"Did I keep you from going?"

Laine didn't answer for a moment. She was staring out the window as if she hadn't heard. Then she glanced back. "What's that, honey?"

"Did I keep you from going with him?"

"Lord, no. I hate to fish. Never saw the appeal of it myself, especially with crickets the way Bill does. You got to put the hook right through their chest and then out—" She made a face, shuddering. She turned back to the window. "But Bill sure loves to go. Probably been out there for hours already," she said again, distractedly.

When she'd finished her cigarette she came back to the table, smiling a quick smile for Marie, a businesslike smile, as she stubbed it out. "Now then," she said, reaching for another orange roll, "forget all the serious stuff. I've got a accusation to make."

"You do?"

"Yes, indeed I do. Which is while Bill was kissing me good night last night, you pretended to fall asleep so you wouldn't have to say anything about you and Abe Pittenger."

"I did no such thing."

"Honey, nobody falls asleep that quick."

"Well, I did."

"Uh-huh. So what all did y'all talk about all night?"

"I don't know. This and that."

"You sure seemed to have a lot of this and that to say."

"Well, he's easy to talk to."

"I've heard that about him. Do you know Marcy Cook? I don't suppose you do. No? Oh, well, you aren't missing much. But I knew her in high school, and she went out with him for a year or so, and I remember her saying how he was the easiest thing to talk to in the world."

"He kind of is, I guess."

"Which I guess he'd have to be, if Marcy talked to him. She was so sulled up all the time. Kind of a smarty, if you ask me. But apparently it wasn't just her, she said. She was the kind of girl wants to act like she knows her man inside and out, you know, like she knew him better than he did. Anyway, she said people always wanted to tell Abe stuff they wouldn't tell nobody else."

"Huh," Marie said, feeling unpleasantly lumped together with the rest of the world. "Well, I didn't tell him much, myself."

"Which, if that's true, and I don't think it is, little Miss Liar, it wasn't because he wasn't listening. I saw the way he'd look at you while y'all were talking. He'd furrow up his brow real serious like this—" She brought her eyebrows together and nodded thoughtfully.

Marie laughed. "He *does* do that, doesn't he?"

"Yes, every little thing you say, and he's all—" She furrowed her brow and nodded again. They tittered.

"I can't help it," Laine said. "I think y'all would be a cute couple."

Marie scooped another roll onto her plate. Drank her coffee.

"I guess you're not going to agree with me, though," Laine said.

"I don't know."

"You sure didn't seem to have a problem last night when you two were laying in the back of the car together."

"I don't know what I was thinking."

"What are you talking about? It was so sweet, the two of you just laying back there, hardly even touching. Not that I was looking."

Marie shook her head. The night before seemed unreal and far away. She was amazed at herself. Had she really given herself over like that? She pictured his home, ramshackle trailer in a weedy yard. He'd sounded like her future and looked like her past, and she didn't feel up to accepting either one.

Laine was watching her closely. Marie picked up her orange roll and took a bite. "Yum," she said.

"Good?"

"Mm-hm."

"So you don't like him. That's what you're saying."

"No, it's not him. He's nice. It's just that—I told you I'm not looking for that right now. I need to just do my own thing."

"Well, that's a crying shame, cause he obviously thinks you are *it*."

"I doubt it."

"Oh, good grief. You couldn't see the way he was mooning at you?"

"I guess I could. I don't know."

Laine shook two more cigarettes from the pack. "Well, alls I can say is, a little sex tends to help that whole decision process."

That evening Marie came out of the shower and heard a man's voice in the house. She had grown so used to the two of them always being alone here, at first she thought her father must have turned up the television. Then she thought he was talking to himself—having a full-blown *conversation* with himself—and experienced a moment of panic. She froze, wrapped in her towel, and listened. No, there were two voices. A lively conversation, the rattle of ice in a glass. Then she recognized the other voice. She dressed hurriedly, checked herself in the mirror, was surprised to see the plain look of expectation on her face. She frowned and it was gone.

Abe Pittenger was leaning against the kitchen counter, drinking cream soda from a glass, listening to her father talk. He wore jeans and tennis shoes. His hair was damp as if he'd come right from the shower. He straightened when she came in.

"Well, here she is," her father said. He jiggled the ice in his glass. "Marie, you remember Abe Pittenger." Pretending to be sly.

"I know who he is."

"We were just talking about the book business."

"Is that right."

"He's almost got me thinking I should stay in it. But I'm trying to tell him not everybody reads like he does. Do you know how much this man reads? I'm telling you, though, not everybody wants to read like that. What people want these days is—well, I don't know what it is they want, but it isn't books. Computers or something, maybe, but it isn't books."

"Your business is doing fine."

"Course it is, honey. Don't get me wrong. We're just moaning about society."

"Society's doing fine too," she said, showing her irritation. She was uneasy. Her father seemed warmed up, enjoying himself in a way she wasn't used to seeing—his cheeks and bald head were slightly flushed. And here was Abe Pittenger in her kitchen.

Abe was clearly discomfited by her tone. "I had to come into town," he said, "so I thought I'd stop and say hello."

"Oh. Hello."

"Well," her father said quickly. Marie caught the puzzlement in his eyes; she wished she hadn't been so sharp with him. "I'll catch the weather and let y'all visit. Abe, nice talking to you. Glad you came by." He shook Abe's hand and disappeared into the living room.

Marie looked after him. She trusted him less now. Later she would realize it was because she hadn't been able to entirely predict him. If anyone could be trusted, it was surely her father, and she would be forced to recognize that she had long substituted predictability for trustworthiness. In this way her mother had been eminently trustworthy, as had any number of pushers, addicts, cops, and social workers. Now here at last was a decent man, talking about books in his own kitchen, and she'd felt her suspicions aroused. Later, when she understood it, she would loathe herself for this, for her inability to negotiate simple interactions the way anyone else might.

"What did you have to come into town for?" Marie asked, turning to Abe.

"I wanted to see you."

"Well," she said, glancing once more toward the living room with that nagging unexplained suspicion in her gut, "maybe we should go for a walk."

It was a breezeless night, the air heavy and warm, fragrant with cut grass and honeysuckle. They walked in the direction opposite Central Avenue, deeper into the neighborhood, where there were no sidewalks and they had to walk in the empty street. Marie hadn't said anything yet, and Abe, wary now, was following suit. They went down a short street that dead-ended at a stand of sweetgums whose leaves shone mint green in the moonlight. A nighthawk bleated overhead, fading off over the trees. Marie turned on her heel, but Abe held back. She stopped and turned again to face him.

"Did you have a good time last night?" he asked.

"Yes, I did," she said. "Can we walk?"

"All right."

They started walking again.

Marie continued, "I mean, it wasn't what I expected—"

"Me either."

"I mean it's not really what I planned on. It was nice, but it's not really in my immediate plans, is I guess what I mean to say."

"You mean me. I'm not really in your plans."

"No, it's nothing to do with you. I like you. I liked talking with you, and—well, all of it, you know, it was all nice."

He nodded, walking with his hands in his pockets, not looking at her. "Well, I thought so too. I thought it was very nice."

"It was," she said helplessly. "It really was nice."

He gave her a wry look. She had seen this before in other men, a sort of self-protection. He said, "I should just keep the ring in my pocket, then, is what you're saying."

"You should just—?"

"Forget it. A bad joke."

"Okay. I'm sorry."

To the south the houses were newer, bigger, more sporadic. Beyond the last one, the road ran out into a brief dirt lot, bordered at the back by a copse of pin oak trees and shortleaf pines. A plastic grid fence stretched around the lot, shadowy and weblike in the thin moonlight. Someone was grading the land for new construction. They stopped at the fence and gazed across the lot into the trees, almost longingly, as if they'd been thwarted, as if that was where they'd been heading all along.

Abe cleared his throat. "But you know," he said, "just for the record, I don't have a big problem with the short term."

She looked at him.

He threw up his hands as if to prove his innocence. "I'm just saying, is all. It doesn't mean anything in particular."

She laughed. "Just for the record, huh?"

"That's all I'm saying."

"That's good," she said. "Cause the short term's about all I've got in me right now."

Abe crossed two fingers and held them up. "Me and the short term are like this," he said, and Marie tried not to grin.

When at last they headed back to the house, with his left hand clasped in both of hers, they walked in a sort of stagger because she was leaning on him, feeling playful now, and he was tired. In the driveway they paused next to Abe's truck. The sound of the television was just audible from inside the house—a muted line of dialogue, a laugh track. The buzzing streetlight above them cast a hazy blue light over the driveway. Insects ticked against the bulb, swinging into view and out into the darkness again.

"You ever get to thinking about how everything around you has been made by somebody?" Marie asked. She leaned into Abe, who was braced against his truck. Pine needles were stuck to his shirt; she found them with her fingers and absently plucked them free. He folded his arms around her.

"Where did this come from?"

"I don't know, I was just thinking. All these new houses, and the TV, and the streetlight, and your truck. Even what we're standing on, the concrete. And your clothes. It was all made. Somebody made all of it. It's like it's not real."

"It's as real as anything, I guess."

"But it seems like it isn't."

"Are you trying to tell me something? Because I'm not quite getting it."

"No. I was just thinking, is all."

Abe shook his head. "I couldn't tell you the last time somebody said something like that to me."

"Oh," she said, and sagged a little. "I guess that was kind of a strange thing to say."

"Actually I'm standing here feeling grateful to have someone say something like that to me."

She leaned back away from him, frowning. "You're just teasing me."

"I'm dead serious."

"Really?" She pressed against him again. "I don't know, sometimes I just wonder about these things. Like how everything around us has been made by somebody."

"Well, there's the trees," he said, as if comforting her.

She smiled. "Yes, there's the trees. And you, I guess. And those bugs up there by the light."

He looked up at the streetlight. "And me," he said. "Me and those bugs."

They were desperate for each other. They parked on West Mountain—Marie with an awful taste in her mouth, but happy, ecstatic with his lips crushed against hers, or his teeth against her throat—both of them with hair wild and falling into their mouths, laughing and struggling to clear a path to their lips, their eyes mirthful and wide with a sort of mock fright of what they were doing, with that sense of the unexplained forbidden, and the unpredictable pleasure that lay moments ahead of them, as if they'd never known it. Her reason was lost to her, her control dissolved.

They parked on side streets coming back from the ice cream parlor, in an unsafe part of town. They went into the half-built house at the south end of her neighborhood, with a sideways grin of a moon shining in through the glassless windows. They went into the graded lot with its clods of dirt and upcut sod. They went into the sweetgum trees. They went night after night, and each time Marie wanted to stay out in the hot summer dark, unheedful of the gray dawn and nausea and headache that would be all that remained of the unslept hours, not thinking of the regret that would come.

On a sticky night when the newspaper had predicted meteor showers, Abe took Marie up to the roof of a taxidermy business Pierce's crew was reshingling. The building, solitary and square, lay on an empty dead-end road. A stuffed bobcat with illuminated eyes stood watch from behind the front window. Ladders had been left at the site, chained to a tree rather than lugged off at the end of the day, and Abe had the key to the padlock. They laid blankets near the roof peak and stretched out, only to watch clouds move in and cover the sky.

"So much for that," Abe said.

Marie rolled on top of him. She had taken off her shirt; her bra straps hung slightly loose from her shoulders. This had a profound effect on Abe, and he told her so.

"You like loose straps," she said.

"I do," he said, wiping sweat from his forehead.

"What else do you like?"

"I like your ribs. Though I think you need some meat on your bones."

"Stop it. Hey, I'm ticklish, stop it." She pinned his hands down. "What else?"

"Being alone with you on rooftops."

"Mm. Me too."

"I like how you make me feel."

"Which is how?"

"I don't know," he said. "Involved."

"What does that mean, involved?"

"It means sometimes I care what happens later."

She rolled off him, pushing hard against his belly so that he groaned. He couldn't see her eyes in the moonlight, but the attitude of her chin was one of attention, of concern. She was sitting up, staring at him.

"What?" he said. "What's wrong?"

"I thought we said this was short-term. Suddenly you're talking about later."

The edge in her voice struck Abe more as panic than irritation. "Are you all right?"

"Don't turn this around," she snapped. "Are you playing games with me, or—"

"Whoa. Marie. I'm not going to lie to you. I think it would be nice to spend more time with you. But—"

"Well, that wasn't what you said before," she said, her voice shrill. "If I'd known you were going to want that from me—"

"Marie," he said. "Okay. Fine. It's fine. Listen, when I said 'later' I meant as in the end of each day. Do you see what I mean? Sometimes when I'm working, I'm thinking about being with you that evening, and I like it. That's all."

There was a pause as his words registered. "Oh God," Marie said then, falling back and throwing her arm across her face. Abe got up on one elbow to look at her.

"Are you all right?"

"No," she said. "I'm a bitch."

He touched her arm. "I wouldn't say that."

"You don't have to."

"Well, I won't."

"Why did I have to say all that?"

"If it's how you feel, I guess." He shrugged.

"Well, shit. It's not, okay?"

"You don't have to take it back."

"But it's not how I feel, not really. I overreact. Aren't you upset?"

"It didn't make me feel especially desirable, but I suppose I'll make it."

"God, I'm unbelievable."

"Forget it, Marie."

"I won't," she said, grabbing him and pulling him on top of her. "Kiss me."

He kissed her.

"No, kiss me like I never said any of that," she said. "God, it's hot tonight. No, kiss me—Yes, like that. Like that."

"Let's just stay up here," she said later. "It's nice up here."

"All right. We can stay till daylight. But then people will start pointing."

"Let them point!" she cried, laughing. She scrambled to her feet and began gathering their clothes.

"Careful," he said. He made a swipe for his pants, but she pulled them out of reach, and he was too lazy to sit up.

Marie padded along the peak to the edge of the roof and looked down. "Would it kill me if I fell from here?"

"Not unless you went head first. Probably you'd just break a leg. Why don't you take a step back, all right? One baby step back."

In a convulsive gesture Marie flung her arms up and out, and Abe watched their clothes blossom in the air above her like a poor man's fireworks display. He sat up, surprised. She was laughing, watching them fall. One of his socks caught on the edge of the roof, and Marie plucked it free with her toes.

"You threw our clothes down," he said.

Marie laughed again and bent over to peer at them on the ground, her hands slapping down against her bare thighs. Abe could see her vertebrae distinctly, like a mountain range on a topographical map. She looked over her shoulder at him.

"My panties are in the azaleas," she said, grinning.

"Let me guess who has to go get them. Listen, will you take just a tiny step back from there?"

She moved back from the edge, though not enough to satisfy him, and made her way down to the ladder. She placed her foot on the top rung.

"I take it we're going?" Abe said.

Marie kicked out with such force that she lost her balance and fell back against the roof. The ladder shot forward and toppled into the yard with a tremendous metallic clank.

Abe had leaped up at the sight of Marie's arms flailing for balance. Now he stood blinking, his alarm fading to bewilderment. "You kicked the *ladder* down?"

"I scraped my butt," she whined, twisting up onto one haunch to inspect herself.

Abe came down to look at the ladder. Its top had fallen against the tailgate of his truck. "I can't believe that," he said.

"I think I'm bleeding."

"Let me see. No, you just scraped it good."

He sat down next to her. Without the blanket, the shingles were cool and rough against his skin. Marie was giddy, giggling to herself as she touched a finger to her tongue and then to the abrasion.

"Whoa, it stings!"

"What did you expect?"

"I don't know," she said. She looked at him, almost shyly, and snickered.

Now Abe laughed. It was too absurd, and she was too happy. The savageness was gone from her smile. He said, "What were you thinking?"

"That now we'll have to stay up here."

"Okay. That makes sense."

"Are you mad?"

"No."

"See? I knew you wouldn't be. That's one of the things I like about you. What I can't figure out for sure is whether you're just that way with me, or if you're that way in general."

"That's a good question."

"I know."

"What else do you like about me?"

"That's it," she said.

"That's *all*?"

She laughed and stood up. "You should come look at our clothes."

"I don't think I've ever seen you so happy."

Bits of shingle-gravel clung to Marie's buttocks. She absently brushed them off, then winced. "Yow," she said.

"You want me to kiss that?"

"In a minute. Come look at our clothes first."

He went with her to look. There were relatively few clothes, but dumped in the side yard that way they seemed to be more.

"I can't see my blouse," Marie said.

"Well, it has to be down there somewhere."

"God, what if I lost it? Can you imagine my going home without a shirt on?" She snorted.

"You sure are enjoying this. I'm surprised you didn't set fire to them first."

"Oh, wouldn't *that* have been something."

Abe began walking the perimeter of the roof.

"Do you see it?"

"I'm not looking for your blouse. I'm thinking about how to get down."

"That's another thing I like about you. You're always thinking. You're very smart."

"So there's two things now?"

"Yes, but just those two. So how are we going to get down?"

"I wish there were some way I could do it without telling you," he said. "But I don't see how."

"You wouldn't really want to go without me."

"The trouble is these damn azaleas on the sides, and—"

"What about the back?"

"See for yourself. There's buckets everywhere you look. I don't even want to think about what's in them."

"Why? What's in the buckets?"

"Actually I guess it's not organic or we'd be smelling it. But maybe he uses lime or something to keep the odor down."

"You mean like animal guts?"

"Probably not, now that I think about it. But I can't drop down onto a bucket anyway. That's just asking for a broken ankle. I'll have to try the driveway."

He left Marie wrinkling her nose and staring down into the buckets. At the peak of the roof he stopped and looked back at her—arms hanging loose at her sides as she peered into the darkness, hair falling forward over her bare shoulders, her strong, too-skinny body tensed from keeping balance at the edge. The moon was shrouded by clouds, and the light was scant; there was no glow about her, only a plain silhouette, but in his mind he saw the wrinkled nose and joyous, curious eyes, and the thought came to him clearly formed: This girl never played. He felt his throat tighten with sadness and love.

She turned to see him looking at her. "What? I'm being careful."

"Okay."

"So you're going to drop into the driveway? Won't that hurt?"

He went to the edge. "Falling barefoot onto concrete? Yeah, it's going to hurt like hell. Why don't you bring those blankets down here? That'll help a little. Please don't throw them off."

She brought him the blankets. "Why don't you lower me down? That way you won't have to jump."

"It would be harder than you think."

"I could hold on to the end of the blanket. We could tie them together, even."

"You realize you'd have to slide down naked against the edge of the roof? It wouldn't be comfortable, trust me."

"I'm already scraped up, I don't care," Marie said, sounding disappointed. She liked this notion of dangling from a blanket. He smiled and thought, What the hell. But then thought about the pressure on his knees, kneeling at the edge of a roof and lowering her down.

"You're thinking of running off with the ladder," he said.

"I'm not!"

"Sorry." He folded one of the blankets and dropped it to the driveway. It was heavy enough to fall flat without unfolding much. The other blanket was threadbare. He took this one and draped it over the edge of the roof to protect himself.

"Are you pouting?" he said.

"Yes," she said. "If you're putting that blanket down like that, why couldn't we have done it the other way?"

"It would have been too hard. Believe me. What if I dropped you and you landed on your tailbone?"

"Well," she said quietly. "I would have trusted you."

Abe was on his knees on the blanket now, getting ready. His back to the edge, his feet out over open space. He looked up at Marie. She stood with her arms crossed over her breasts, waiting for a response, and he had the mad thought that the whole thing had been orchestrated so she could say that to him.

"I appreciate it. I mean it. Now, don't be upset."

Marie swooped toward him with her arms out. Abe felt a jolt of fear. He clutched instinctively at her shoulders. But she wasn't trying to push him. She only grabbed him and kissed him hard on the mouth. "Don't fall," she said. "Be careful."

Abe had goosebumps on his arms, his heart was pounding. He wanted to laugh at himself, but he couldn't tell her what he'd thought she was about to do, not with this talk of trust. He took a breath. "It's not that dangerous, Marie."

"Still."

"How about another kiss, then?"

She kissed his ear, a quick smack against the hollow that set it ringing, and stood up again. Abe swung down, gripping the rough edge of the roof on either side of the blanket. His grip was weak from a day's hammering; in a moment he would have no choice but to drop. His feet were swinging, and he tried to gauge whether he was over the blanket. When he looked up at Marie, she seemed tall as an oak. From this angle it was hard to see exactly what he found so beautiful. Skin and bones towering over him. But he loved the sight of her.

"Are you going to let go?" she said.

"It's just that this is an unusual angle to see you from."

She backed away from the edge. "You better hurry up before I stomp your fingers."

Abe let go. The shock of landing made his teeth snap together.

"Did it hurt like hell?" Marie called down. "You hit the blanket, at least."

He sat rubbing his feet. "The blanket's a tease. It doesn't help much."

"So it really hurts?"

"Not so bad. They'll be a little bruised, is all."

"I'll kiss your feet when I get down."

"Oh, I'm not letting you down."

"You don't want to be kissed?"

"I guess when you put it that way." He got up and limped over to the ladder. Before he had lifted it, though, he heard a thump behind him, and turned in time to see Marie drop onto her butt on the blanket, scowling in pain and clutching at her feet.

"Shit," she hissed. "That fucking *hurt*."

Then she looked at Abe and burst into delighted laughter.

After they had dressed, Abe suggested they go to his place.

"It's not far," he said, chaining the ladder to the tree again. "And I have a couch. It's more comfortable than shingles, especially on a wounded butt."

"To your trailer?"

"You sound scared. I promise nothing will happen to you there that hasn't happened already on the roof."

"It's just that it's getting late."

"Late? This is early, for us."

"I'm just tired. I think it's catching up to me."

"Well, then," he said, nodding. "It's to bed with you."

He took her home, but the following evening Marie found herself driving out to Lockers Creek. She'd been resisting a visit to his trailer. She thought seeing him there would push her to end all this, that she'd be too strongly reminded of the dilapidated lives she'd left behind her—people strung out on failure, addicted to driftlessness—and would feel compelled to tell Abe it was over, they had come to term. When it occurred to her, however, that she was avoiding his trailer because she didn't want that to happen, that she was trying to make things last, she resolved to go after all. Starting your life over meant recognizing when you were deceiving yourself; it required discipline and not just the illusion of discipline. Stubbornness, sure, she had plenty of that. But Marie was in short supply of discipline and always had been. She needed to stock up.

At the gas station in Lockers Creek, the first person she asked was able to give her directions. "Abe Pittenger?" the man repeated. Bare-chested and sweaty, he was wiping under his arms with his shirt as he pumped his gas. "Well, sure. You don't know where he lives?" Sizing her up, as if no one could possibly have come here from anywhere else.

Abe was just home from work. He heard her car rolling up the drive and stood waiting for her in the yard, dressed only in his jeans, dirty and sweat-soaked and musky. Marie felt her throat catch. She was kissing him before he could ask if anything was the matter. They mounted the porch steps and went inside.

Later, he brought her a beer from the refrigerator. He had cleaned himself up, and with the fans going and the windows open it was almost comfortable inside. Marie was moving about the living room as if to explore it, but there was nothing to take in. No telephone, no television, no pictures on the walls. No furniture save the worn-out couch and coffee table. A shuddering box fan on the floor, a homemade bookshelf that seemed too large for the room. Abe had added on to the shelves the way poor people build additions on their homes—crudely, with whatever cheap wood was available. Marie stopped and studied his books. He had a lot of them. She ran her fingers along the spines.

"You want the grand tour?" he asked.

He led her through the tiny kitchen and down the narrow hall, opening doors. A bathroom, a laundry closet, a bedroom without a bed. In the bedroom she saw a chest of drawers, a doorless closet with a half-empty clothes rod, a guitar case leaning in the corner, and a row of cardboard boxes stacked neatly against the wall.

"I never quite got around to unpacking," Abe said, waving at the boxes. "That was what, couple years ago? Turns out I didn't need all that stuff."

They went back down the hall. "And here's the bedroom," he announced as they entered the living room again.

"You sleep on the couch?"

"It's not bad."

"No," she said, giving him a sly look. "It's comfortable." She walked to the door across the room and reached for the knob. "And what's in here?"

"Don't," he said sharply, and she jerked her hand back. He laughed. "No, I'm sorry, you can look." He touched her shoulder and opened the door. A second bedroom, dark and empty except for a broken telephone on the floor in the corner. The carpet seemed to sag toward the middle of the room.

"I just didn't want you to fall through," he said, closing the door. "The floor's rotting out in there and the supports are shot. I ought to fix it up, but I can't get motivated—it's not like I need the room for anything. I guess it's kind of pathetic, though."

"I'm just glad there aren't dead bodies in there. You scared the snot out of me."

"Well, it'd be pretty embarrassing if you fell through the floor of my home."

She went back to the couch and patted the cushion beside her. "I like your place, though. It's in a pretty spot."

"Spot's pretty," he said, sitting with her. "Trailer's a pile of junk."

She shrugged. She wasn't going to lie about it to be polite. "Lay back. I want to mess with your hair."

He laid his head in her lap. She set her beer down and ran her fingers against his scalp. She had no nails to speak of, but he purred and closed his eyes like a cat and moved his head back and forth.

"Sit still," she said. "I'm fixing your hair."

"Yeah, the trailer's a pile of junk," he repeated, "but I got a great deal on it. When I came back from college, I was looking out at the trailer park, but my mom told me about this couple wanting to sell their place and move to Little Rock. Apparently they inherited the trailer when the lady's parents died. No telling how old the thing is."

"You bought it straight out? Be still."

"Straight out, with my next year's tuition money. And I probably haven't bought anything since."

"Doesn't look like it."

"I haven't. I like to say that I own the land and everything on it. But that's the joke. You could fit all of it in one room."

"You own the land? I thought maybe you rented it."

"You aren't trying to braid it, are you?"

"I'm trying, but it isn't quite long enough."

"I own the land we're sitting on, but not the pasture. Just a half-acre that stops right at the fence out back. Everything around me belongs to Simmons."

"I can't believe he'd sell a half-acre of land—"

"And let somebody put an ugly trailer on it?"

"Well, yeah."

"He didn't. The people who originally owned the trailer owned the whole pasture, plus a lot of other land around here. When they retired they sold all of it but the half-acre and stuck this trailer on it. Probably it was state-of-the-art at the time. This was quite a while ago. They only lived here for part of the year. The rest of the time they drove around the country in a Winnebago. Apparently they had a monkey too. A gibbon or something, I don't know, they were a strange old couple. Simmons bought the rest of the land and built his house over there, just waiting for them to give up and die. He was pretty mad when he found out I'd bought the place."

"He probably wanted to buy it himself."

"Sure he did. But the younger couple—I mean the ones who inherited it and sold it to me—they never liked Simmons. They didn't like the way he'd pressured the lady's parents, and so they wouldn't even talk to him about it. Which was lucky for me, because I'm sure he'd have paid a lot of money just to get the trailer out of here."

"So now he's mad at you."

"Oh, we get along. Hardly ever see each other. He goes his way, I go mine."

"Which way is that?"

"My way is your way, baby."

"Whatever," she said. "Now sit up, I want to look at you."

"How do I look?"

"You look like yourself with your hair messed up."

"I want to see. Let me go look in the mirror."

"It's not worth it. Lay back down."

He lay back.

It was late when Marie left the trailer. They went out onto the porch, and Lucky sprang up from the shadows, emerging wraithlike through the railing.

"Well, hello," she said, kneeling to pet him.

"That's Lucky. Tabby should be around here somewhere."

He stepped over to a rubber barrel in the corner, popped the top off, and scooped dry cat food into the hubcap he used for a bowl. Lucky was purring and leaning into her knee, arching his back to be scratched.

"He's not hungry," she said.

"He prefers love to food, if he can get it. I only dumped the food so Tabby would come. She can hear it a mile away. I can call and call and she won't come, but if I dump food she just appears out of nowhere."

She stroked Lucky along the ridge of his back. He flopped onto his side and curled around her foot. Tabby came around the corner of the trailer, matted with stickers and cockleburs and dried mud. She didn't leap to the porch as Lucky had done, but trotted past it to use the steps.

"Here she is," Abe said.

"Oh! What happened to her?"

"Nothing."

Tabby came up the steps, pausing to study Marie with her one good eye, the cloudy one shining a dull green in the porch light. Then she veered widely around her, shouldering the rails, and sneaked to the hubcap.

"There's nothing wrong with her?"

"She's just old. She won't let me brush those tangles out of her. She'd probably fall apart if I did."

"She looks like she came back from the dead."

"Tabby, did you come back from the dead?" Abe said.

Tabby worked her way around the hubcap so she could eat with her eye on Marie, who had stood up again to go.

Abe walked her to her car. The night had cooled off and was perfectly still. Their footsteps sounded loud in the gravel. At the car door, Abe held on to her. She pulled back, still in his arms, and let him hold her that way, with her head and arms thrown back and the blood rushing into her temples. She said, "There's Orion."

It was so easy, she thought, the way he shifted to follow her gaze, his arms pulling her up again, the way she settled against his side. They stood beside each other looking up, his arm around her shoulder, hers around his waist. She held his other hand in hers and stood with her head still cast back, the beginnings of a lazy smile on her face. Abe moved his hand beneath her hair and stroked the soft nape of her neck, wishing she wouldn't leave.

"Let me try and see it in your eyes," he said.

She looked at him.

"No, you have to look right at it."

She looked back at the sky, smiling self-consciously. He looked into her eyes. They were bright, but he couldn't make out any stars.

"Can you see it?"

"Yes."

"You can? Let me try."

He looked for Orion. There was the belt, three sharp points of light, and there the sword stars, softer and slightly askew. He felt her warm breath against his cheek. Her face was so close, he couldn't stop his eyes from going to hers.

"Don't look at me," she said sternly.

"Sorry."

"I can't find it," she said at last. "Maybe it's the angle."

She didn't move away from him but made a soft, inward sound. A sigh.

A hum. Her eyes languid again. She kissed him sleepily too, sleepy as her smile, dreamily and softly. And her hair soft beneath his hand. Her breath warm and almost sweet. She laid her head back into his hand and it rested heavily there, and he leaned into her. The silky down of her neck, the taste of salt and a faint bitter taste of perfume. The slow, slow arc of her jaw as she lifted it, rolled her head away for him. Her hair falling against his face. He listened to her breathing, inhaled the apple scent of her hair.

Lucky was brushing against their ankles. Marie trailed one hand down Abe's chest and left it there a moment, flat against his breastbone. Then she let him go. He stepped back. She knelt and picked up the cat. "Good night, Lucky," she said. He purred and began kneading her chest. She held him out for Abe to take.

"You're not too sleepy to drive, are you?" he asked, partly wishful, partly misreading her look of contentment, though by now he should know better.

"I'm not sleepy at all," she said.

When Marie came to his trailer the next evening, she parked her Corolla recklessly and askew, its bumper almost taking off the porch step. She charged up the steps, banged on the screen door, and before Abe could open it she told him she couldn't see him. She reeked of cigarette smoke. Her eyes were furious. Abe backed away from the screen, and she followed him into the trailer, yelling. He thought he knew everything, she said accusingly, but he didn't. He didn't know anything. He thought he could just reach into her life and take what he wanted. He thought she should just drop everything and come to him, be some sort of goddamn whore for him, driving all the way out here in the middle of nowhere to his stupid shithole of a home. He thought he was so smart. He thought he knew her. He was so sure of himself, and she was sick of it.

Abe tried to get her to sit down.

She told him to leave her alone. She didn't need this. She was just getting her life together again, and she didn't need this. He wouldn't understand that. All these demands he made on her, as if he had some claim. Well, nobody had any claim, and he should quit acting as if he did. She was sick to death of it.

But Abe waited her out, and in half an hour she was spent, sitting dazed on his couch in the hot trailer. He soaked a washcloth and brought her some ice water. She drank the water off as he touched her cheeks with the cool cloth. He brought her more water, and she drank that too. And when, finally, she told him she was sorry, he told her it was all right, that he loved her.

"Don't say that," she said.

"All right."

"I guess I want you to say it, but—"

"Well, I do. I love you."

"No," she said, shaking her head. "Really. Don't say it."

She took the washcloth from him and put it under her shirt, against the hot skin of her belly. She put it against the back of her neck. She looked as if she were coming out of a faint. "I've never seen anybody stay so calm," she said. "Not even when they're wasted."

Abe said nothing.

"You aren't speaking now?"

"I'm being cautious."

Marie nodded. Of course he was. She looked at her fingers, still trembling from the broken rage. "I ought to call my dad. He doesn't know where I am. I didn't go home after work."

"I can drive you down to a pay phone. My phone's broken."

She flashed a look—it was almost contempt; he almost had to give up, because he couldn't do this under contempt—but it was just a flash, the last hiss of oil in the pan, burning away. Marie could tell how the look hit him; she was sharp about expressions. A few minutes earlier she'd have pressed it. But that was past, and now she took his hand and kissed his fingers, one by one, and gave him a penitent look.

"Why don't I fix us something to eat," he said, "and then we can drive down and give your dad a call."

"I want another cigarette first."

"You can have a cigarette first."

"Plus I'd rather eat somewhere with an air conditioner."

"I'll take you out, then."

She sighed, running her fingers through her hair, and said, "Don't you even want to know what set me off?" She still had a hint of challenge in her tone. Challenge, but not threat.

"I want to know everything you'll tell me, Marie."

She curled up on the couch with her head on his knee, facing out toward the room. He was in shorts, and she stroked the hair along his shin, up and down, as if petting the ridge of a cat's back. After a moment he realized she was waiting.

"What set you off?" he asked.

"You did," she replied. "You set me off."

"Me?"

She nodded.

"Well, tell me how, and I won't do it again."

"That's the problem. I don't want you to stop."

"Then I won't stop. We'll just deal with it."

"You really want to know everything that I'll tell you?"

"Yes."

"What if I don't want to?"

"Now you're just trying to mess with me."

She flipped onto her back and grinned up at him. "Now I'm just trying to mess with you."

"Imagine that."

"I'll tell you some things."

"I'm glad," he said, stroking her hair. It was very fine, and damp around her forehead and temples.

"Now, say you love me one more time, and then don't say it again."

"When do you want me to say it? Now, or—"

"Don't be funny," she said. "Say it right now."

"I love you."

"Good. Now don't say it again."

"Or else?"

"You don't want to know 'or else.'"

He stopped stroking her hair and studied her face. "I don't think I do," he said after a moment.

"Now put that washcloth on my forehead. Put it over my eyes. Yes, like that. Now kiss me."

He kissed her. Her lips were still cold from the ice water. They began to tremble, and he pulled back, thinking she might be crying.

"Are you all right?" he asked.

She sat up and took the washcloth away. Her eyes were dry and clear, but her mind seemed to have drifted. "I'm not living in the real world. None of this is real."

"I feel the same way sometimes."

"You do?"

"Sure."

"But for me," she said, "I think it's true."

He took the washcloth from her and placed it on top of his head. "Well, now that you're calmed down and speaking perfect sense, maybe we should go get something to eat."

She laughed. "I told you I want my cigarette first. Why haven't you gotten it for me yet?"

In Hot Springs he bought her a steak dinner, and afterward they walked the brick promenade just off the downtown strip, along the base of Hot Springs Mountain up behind the bathhouses. It was dark out now, but the promenade was lined by lamp posts and had overlooks where you could gaze down over the bathhouses and the sidewalk magnolias onto the lighted storefronts along Central Avenue. They sat for a while at a picnic table, the sounds of traffic filtering through the trees, pigeons quick-stepping across the bricks to peck hopefully at Marie's cigarette butts. Farther down you could stand at a railing above one of the springs, where the stones were slick with green slime and the steam rose up from the water so that you could feel the heat even high above. Marie wanted to lean out over the rail to feel the steam on her face. Abe held her secure by pressing himself against her. It excited him, holding her this way, but it made him nervous how far out she leaned. He pressed hard against her, heart hammering, fists squeezing the wrought iron rail with a tight grip.

"I love this place," she said, when he'd finally pulled her back. "I want to live here."

"You do live here."

"Oh, yeah," she said absently, turning away to look down over the city. "I suppose I do."

They walked the few blocks over to the Arlington Hotel, with its red carpet and bright chandeliers, still heavy in the atmosphere of the days Al Capone came to town. Passing nonchalantly through the lobby, where a swing band played for the paying guests, they found a creaking elevator that took them slowly to the roof. From up there they watched the streets, shining with traffic lights and reflections from storefront windows. The fountain sparkled and foamed in the median, but from the top of the Arlington, with the breeze in your ears, you could only hear the rush of cars. One building across the avenue had an old advertisement painted on its side: *Uneeda Biscuit*. For five cents a pop. In the streetlight the building facades looked like cutouts.

It grew late. They had parked near her father's store, and as they headed back there, walking along beneath the streetlights, Marie watched their reflections in the store windows across the street. In the glass they looked like any couple you might see downtown. She gazed up at the cut-out buildings. The upper floors were dark and deserted, but she knew things were kept there; her father had told her stories. Antique furniture, old Coca-Cola ashtrays, dusty stacks of casino chips. A wooden telephone with a crank handle, a radio cabinet as big as a television. Things belonging to people long dead.

They'd driven into town separately, parking along the quiet side street behind her father's store. Abe walked her to her car, but she didn't get in. Instead she found the store key and asked if he wanted to come inside with her where they could be alone for a while.

Of course he did, he said, taking her in his arms.

"But aren't you tired?" he asked. He could tell she was. Her eyes were red and puffy, and she was yawning. When he held her she leaned heavily into him so that he had to support her.

"I'm exhausted," she said. "But I don't want to go. Not yet. Do you want to go? We can go home if you want to."

"I don't want to go."

"Well, neither do I. It's been a real long day."

"I know."

"Sometimes after a day this long you don't want to go home, even though that's what you should do."

"I know just what you mean."

"But maybe I should. I don't want him to worry."

"It's okay if you want to. I'll see you again tomorrow."

"I don't," she said petulantly. "I don't want to."

"Well, let's go inside then."

"No," she said after a moment, holding on to him. "I can't decide. No, we'd better not go inside. Let's just stay right here."

"On the street?"

"Is that all right?"

"Absolutely," he said, holding her.

They were leaning against her car door, her head against his chest, her eyes closed now. He stroked her hair. Her hands lay flat against his belly, pressed between their bodies, so that she had to hold on to nothing but could just lean there comfortably, without effort. They were quiet for a long time.

"This is better," she murmured at last.

Part 2

Chapter 8

When her mother pulled up in front of the trailer in Mena, it was raining hard. Rivulets furrowed the gravel driveway. Orange and red maple leaves drifted in the ditch, accumulating in soggy masses at the culvert edge. Thunder rolled down from the hills. It didn't seem cold to Marie, but she could see her breath as they jumped from the car and hurried through the rain.

Joe stood inside the screen door looking out. He was leaning so that his forehead pressed the screen; when they came inside she could see the red imprint of the mesh on his skin. He was a short, wiry man, with dirty nails and prematurely gray hair and a sickly, fishbelly face that reddened when he was angry or high. He smelled of sweat and oil. In the corner of the murky living room a shotgun leaned against the couch, a wadded cleaning rag on the floor next to it. The trailer was littered with newspapers, potato chip bags, beer bottles, full ash trays. A black-and-white television with rabbit ears played on the kitchen table, a smoking cigarette in the ashtray next to it.

"What the fuck took you so long?" Joe said. They stood in the doorway, wet and shivering. Marie stood close behind her mother but didn't cling to her. She knew Joe hated it when she showed anxiety around him; if she acted scared, he was more likely to slap her. On the other hand, if she was too bold he would curse at her and throw her onto the couch and dare her to move. The safest approach was to be quiet, to answer quickly when he spoke to her, and to stay out of his way. She'd learned this lesson better than her mother, who once had her nose broken by him.

"We're right on time, Joe," her mother said, stepping forward. She came close enough to let him hug her if he wanted to.

"Well, goddamnit, Marie," he said, putting his arms around her. They kissed. It was a long, rough kiss, his hands moving up and down her mother's back. She watched them. Near the end of the kiss he opened one eye and looked down at her over her mother's shoulder. She looked away.

"What are you looking at, you little slut?"

"Joe—"

"I'm just giving her shit. Come here and give me a hug, Little Marie."

She obeyed, hugging him around the waist. She felt a hardness beneath his jeans and knew it came from kissing her mother. She'd noticed it before. He rubbed her hair with his knuckles, mussing it badly and hurting her scalp. She didn't resist, though, and after a few seconds he let her go. She moved toward the couch, where she might sit quietly and not be underfoot, but Joe made two quick steps and caught her by the wrist.

"What are you thinking?" he said, shaking her arm. A streak of fire ran up her shoulder and into her neck. "Don't you see that goddamn gun? Go into the kitchen and set down, you hear me? You don't go near that gun, you understand? It's dangerous."

"Yes, sir," she said, tremulously. Tears started into her eyes, and she was careful to hide her face. He swung her toward the open kitchen doorway and released her wrist. She dropped into a chair at the table and pretended to stare at the television screen. There were sparks in her head. On the table sat a plate with a sausage patty and a thick sheen of syrup on it. Fragments of pancake stuck here and there in the syrup. She could tell by the thickened, opaque grease in the crevices of the sausage that it was long cold. It made her sick to look at, but she dared not push it away from her.

Her mother stayed in the doorway, fretting nervously with her fingernails. Joe turned to her. "What took you so long?"

She checked her watch. "Joe. We're right on time." She checked it again. "We're early."

"I know, I know," he said, more gently. "I'm just antsy. Morton West called me this morning, and he wanted you there yesterday—"

"Yesterday!"

"That's what he said."

"He said tomorrow! You told me—"

"Marie!" he said sharply, and both mother and daughter flinched. "I know what the fuck I told you. Point is he called me this morning, and he's mad as shit. You know you can't argue with Morton. I told him you could probably make it today, and the son of a bitch said there was no probably to it, you better be there by four o'clock—"

"Four o'clock! Jesus, Joe—"

"Let me finish. He said there's these guys he told they'd get their shit yesterday, and now these guys are pissed at him and he's pissed at us—I know it's his own goddamn mistake, but that shit don't matter, you know that, Marie—and so he says either you're there by four o'clock, which is I guess an hour or so before he's supposed to meet these guys again, either you're there by four o'clock or that's it."

Marie's mother was looking at her watch again. She checked it against a clock shaped like a tea kettle that hung over the kitchen table. "Okay," she whispered, calming herself. "Okay, we can do that. We might even make it by three if we left right now."

Marie looked at the tea-kettle clock too, moving only her eyes so as not to draw attention to herself. Her mother had a good sense of how long it took to get places but never had any idea how long it took to leave a place. Marie knew they would not leave right then. Her mother would have to deal with Joe.

He was looking at her mother with his eyebrows raised. "Okay?" he said. He rubbed her shoulder. "I'm sorry I was all aggravated when you come in. I just wanted to have a minute to visit with you before you had to take off again. It's been so long. You want some coffee?"

She shook her head, and he led her into the living room, out of Marie's sight. "You got a little time, then?" he said softly.

"I don't know, Joe. We'd better get going pretty soon. If Morton—"

"I know, honey, I know. But you got a few minutes, don't you? It's been two weeks. I missed you . . ."

Marie heard them, the change in Joe's voice, the suppressed anxiety in her mother's, the rustle of caresses and the quiet wet sound of kisses between their words. She sat still at the kitchen table. The trailer floor creaked as her mother moved slowly with Joe down the hall toward the back bedroom.

Marie knew this trailer better than they did. She knew where to step to avoid creaking floors that called attention to you. She knew where Joe kept his pistol, where he kept the key for the gun rack in his bedroom, which arms of the rack would support the shotgun after he'd cleaned it. She knew where he hid the marijuana, the cocaine, the bennies, the cash. She knew how to cut the cocaine for the less important buyers—had helped do it more than once, sitting at the kitchen table with the adults. She'd seen both Joe and her mother utterly strung out and desperate, so desperate they would pick through the carpet searching for lost grains of cocaine, when Marie knew there was none left to be found.

The two of them had coked their way out of any profit and into a mounting debt. Once, a few years before, when the power had been shut off, a stack of money had gone untouched on the kitchen table for weeks—her mother and Joe lost to the world—until Marie had taken the money, walked into downtown Mena, and paid the electric bill and the phone bill with cash. She had bought groceries then and carried them home, dumping half of them into a ditch before she made it back because the bag was too heavy.

Someone had reported it, this little girl walking into town with all that money, and a police cruiser showed up outside the trailer that afternoon. Marie's mother had stood in the yard talking with two officers for almost an hour, Joe watching through the blinds and swearing beneath his breath. Her mother had just showered, was wearing a short pink bathrobe that revealed her long legs from midthigh down to her flip-flop sandals, and her wet hair and ruddy cheeks gave her a fresher look than she'd had in weeks. She told the police that Joe hadn't been home for several days, that she'd been sick in bed with a terrible case of summer flu. Her daughter had a mind of her own, she said, and was always worrying about things. She'd forbidden her to go into town, but Marie had sneaked out with some money to pay the bills.

"You do look a little peaked," one of the officers said.

"Yeah, it was a nasty old flu," she said. "Today's the first day I even felt like getting out of bed."

"Is the little girl around, ma'am?"

"Oh, yes," she said. "Marie, honey! Marie, come outside and talk to these nice police."

Marie didn't even glance at Joe, who was giving her a warning look. She stepped barefooted out into the summer heat. She was wearing terrycloth shorts and a striped tank top and was tan from the tops of her feet to her skinny shoulders from playing alone in the yard. She squinted and descended the trailer steps, lingering on the bottom one.

One of the officers came to squat in front of Marie. He was a burly man, with a huge jaw and incongruously tiny eyes, like a gorilla. "How you doing, honey?" he said.

"Fine."

"Can you tell us why you walked all by yourself into town yesterday? Don't you know it's dangerous for a little girl to go wandering around all by herself?"

"Yes, sir."

"So why'd you do it?"

She shrugged, hanging her head.

"She's scared she's going to get in trouble again," her mother said. "I already got onto her pretty hard. Marie, honey, it's okay. You can tell the nice policeman."

She glanced up at the officer, and he nodded his head encouragingly. "I wanted to pay the bills," she said.

"But that's grown-up problems," he said. "Don't you know that?"

She nodded.

"So why'd you think you had to do it?"

"Mommy was sick," she said meekly.

"Uh-huh. And you just thought you'd help out by paying all the bills. Didn't she tell you not to do it, though?"

"Yes, sir. I'm sorry. I didn't mean to do it."

"Well, now, that's okay. I don't guess we'll arrest you this time." He lifted her chin with one finger and winked at her, then straightened up again. "But from now on you don't go nowheres without a grownup, you hear me?"

"Yes, sir."

He tousled her hair, hitched his pants, and walked back over to stand with his partner and her mother. Marie disappeared inside the dark trailer.

"Good girl," Joe whispered as she shut the door. "Good girl." He was so grateful he seemed to forget for the moment that she was the one responsible for the visit. Or perhaps he was never fully aware of why the police had come. He squatted in front of the window in a T-shirt and underwear, sweating and trembling. The muscles in his thin legs stood out from the strain. His arms and legs were slightly tanned from earlier in the summer, when he'd spent time sitting in his yard with nothing on but fringed denim cutoffs, but his legs turned abruptly pale near the tops of his thighs. In the dimness of the trailer his pale haunches looked bluish, almost purple. He hugged himself miserably, careful not to brush against the blinds.

The two men stood talking to her mother for a long time, unable to take their leave of this fresh-scrubbed young woman in her short bathrobe. They talked, interrupting each other often, and Marie's mother listened closely, smiling and laughing. Finally they nodded good-byes and climbed into their car, backing slowly out of the yard so as not to raise the dust. Her mother stood there and waved.

When she came back inside, Joe said, "Goddamnit, Marie, you did everything but show them your tits."

"What was I supposed to do, cuss at them?" She dropped onto the couch beside him. At first he pushed her away from him; then he climbed on top of her. He was in terrible shape, shaking all over and dripping sweat. The window unit in the bedroom was the only air-conditioning in the trailer that worked.

"Too hot," she protested, pushing weakly at him, but he didn't get off. He seemed to be acting in spite of himself; he clearly felt too sick to continue, but he persisted. He tugged at the belt of her robe, accidentally tightening the knot, and the belt held tight. Abandoning it, he pulled the front of her robe open beneath it, revealing her breasts and her flat, pale belly. He groaned miserably, kissing her collarbone. "Too hot," she whispered again, hopelessly. She rubbed his sweaty back, pulling up his T-shirt to touch his damp skin.

Marie moved slowly from her spot on the floor against the far wall, crawling on hands and knees into the narrow hallway, then into her bedroom. A box fan rattled futilely near the door of her closet. Easing her bedroom door closed behind her, she took off her tank top and lay in front of the fan. The wind and rattle of the fan swept away all other sounds. She lay on her belly, with her chin resting on the backs of her hands and her face almost touching the fan's plastic grate, and spoke quietly into the fan. She spoke in the deepest tones she could manage, dragging out each word, listening to her voice turn robotic and strange.

"You are under arrest," she said, frowning. "There is no escape. Do you surrender. Come out. Come out. Come out."

She felt, rather than heard, her mother and Joe fall off the couch in the living room. She held her breath and listened, but no one came down the hall. They could not hear her if she spoke quietly.

"They cannot hear you," she said into the fan.

Marie watched the hands tick on the tea-kettle clock. From the television came the staccato beep of a weather warning; when she looked at the screen she saw a radar picture in the bottom corner. The radar line swept in smooth circles around a tiny map of Arkansas, revealing a dark patch over the far western side of the state. Words tickered across the bottom of the screen. Behind the radar image and twice as large, a woman in a glamorous evening gown was arguing with a muscular man in boots and jeans. When the beeping stopped, her voice came through again.

". . . a fool if you think you can get away with this! What happened—" A wave of static cut her short, rippling her image, and Marie looked back at the clock.

Outside, the storm was passing; the thunder sounded from farther off. From the bedroom came the thumping sounds of her mother hopping as she struggled back into her tight pants. Marie got out of her chair and stood quietly next to it. She listened for the squeak of bed springs as Joe stood up on the bed, the scraping sound of a ceiling panel sliding back, the thud of his feet hitting the floor again. Then the two of them appeared in the kitchen, Joe with his arm around her mother's shoulder, her mother clutching the gym bag. Both were sniffing and wiping their noses.

Marie was relieved. It had only taken a few minutes, and Joe didn't seem inclined to hold them up any longer.

"All right, girls," he said. "Y'all better make tracks." He swatted Marie playfully on the bottom. "You be good now, Little Marie."

"Okay."

"Take this, honey," her mother said, handing her the bag and hugging Joe. She kissed him freely now, evidently certain of his mood. When she pulled away he smiled and said, "Y'all be careful."

"We will," her mother said, looking for the last time at the clock on the wall. "We got enough time."

"Oh, shit!" Joe said.

"What?" She turned instinctively to look out into the yard, but nothing was visible through the screen door except their own car, rain sweeping sideways against it.

"I forgot. Old Brady called. He wants you to run some of his stuff to Tulsa."

"Brady? When?"

"Yesterday morning. I—"

"No, I mean when does he want me to come by?"

"I told him you'd come by today."

"Today! Goddamnit, Joe—"

"Hey!" he snarled. "Watch your mouth. I didn't know you'd be in such a goddamn hurry, and anyway it's right on your way. It won't take you five minutes."

"But how am I supposed to go to Tulsa when—"

"How am I supposed to know, Marie? Huh? How am I supposed to know? I think you can just go tomorrow. He just needs somebody with a car. Buster's is broke down or something. I just told him you'd swing by since it was on your way and we could use the money."

"Oh, God." She took a deep breath, rubbed her face slowly with both hands. "Okay. We can do it if we leave right this minute. Marie, get your ass in the car, honey. We gotta go."

"I'm sorry, baby," Joe said, suddenly gentle. "I just forgot. After Morton West called and everything—"

"It's okay. We'll make it. We just got to step on it."

Marie ran through the screen door into the rain. She had the bag in the trunk and was in the front seat before Joe finished hugging her mother. As her mother climbed into the driver's seat, the rain stopped altogether. They waved at Joe, who stood out front lighting a cigarette and checking the sky. He pocketed his lighter, exhaled a stream of smoke, and lifted two fingers in farewell.

"God in heaven," her mother said, jerking the gearshift into reverse.

With the palm of her hand, Marie cleared a circle in her fogged window, and through it she watched the woods pass—oak trees, hickories going yellow now, brilliant scarlet sumacs, the steady green of shortleaf pines. Water dripped from the leaves as though it still rained. The highway glistened under the bright, clearing sky, and behind the last of the westering gray clouds a cold wind was blowing in.

The woods ran deep, rising steeply on either side of the highway. To Marie they seemed dreary, with too much quiet and emptiness. She tried to imagine what they were like once the car had passed, once she was no longer there to see them: all that vast abandon of forest, not even a solitary girl's mind to consider it, just miles of trees and rain pattering the leaves, miles of damp earth and banks of moss on half-buried boulders. She felt a gut-pang of loneliness. It was too big to consider. Once you passed through these woods, they must simply cease to be. She looked at her mother, catching her just as she checked her watch. "Who's Brady?" she said.

Her mother's eyes returned to the road without glancing at Marie. It was the way they traveled and talked—hours of silence between them, either one speaking or refusing to speak at any given time. But Marie wanted to get her mother talking, to calm her down.

"You know Brady," her mother said.

"No, I don't."

"Well, you've met him two or three times, at least. I don't know how you don't remember him. You remember everything else in the world."

"Who is he?"

"He's sort of like your uncle, I guess."

"What does 'sort of like' mean?"

Her mother's brow furrowed, and she shifted in her seat. "Well, I don't know, Marie. Let's see. Okay. He's my grandfather's brother's wife's . . . husband? Brother. My grandfather's brother's wife's brother. So that makes him my . . ." She spluttered her lips exasperatedly and checked her watch again.

"Great-uncle-in-law?"

Her mother shrugged. "I guess." She looked frowning at Marie. "How do you know that?"

"I don't know."

"Okay. Anyway. What was I saying?"

"He's your great-uncle-in-law."

"Right. Or whatever. We'll call him that. I always just called him Uncle Brady. So if he's my great-uncle-in-law, then he's your—"

"Great-great-uncle-in-law."

"Right," her mother said, nodding slowly. "Your great-great-uncle-in-law." But she wasn't convinced. Still frowning, she chewed her bottom lip absently and went over the chain again in her head. After a minute, her face changed, and Marie knew she had given up on the problem.

"You got lipstick on your teeth," Marie said peevishly. She watched her mother lean up to the rearview mirror and use her finger to scrub at the red smudge on her front teeth, wincing a little and sucking in her breath when she applied too much pressure.

"Watch the road."

"I'm watching it, Marie. You watch your attitude. Right now isn't the time to play games with me."

"Why do you scrunch up your face like that when you rub your teeth? Does it hurt?"

"You're just trying to aggravate me now."

"No, I'm not. Does it hurt?"

Her mother sat back in her seat, reaching up to adjust the mirror again, and said in a resigned tone, "Yeah, I got bad teeth, honey."

"Why?"

"Why what?"

This kind of answer, so typical of her mother, infuriated her. She shouted, "Why do you have bad teeth?"

Her mother flinched, saying nothing. She brushed her hair back from her face, tucking a strand behind her ear. Marie studied her: The dark brown roots beginning to show beneath her short bleached hair. The straight ridge of her nose, with its slight hillock at the center, which Marie thought looked like a knuckle. That was where it had broken. Along the curve of her jaw there was a light blond fuzz. Her lips were full and pouty. The chords of her slender throat stood out even when she sat relaxed. She was supposed to be beautiful.

Her mother gazed silently at the highway. She wasn't going to answer. Marie half-turned in her seat and put her hand on the gearshift, running her finger over the smooth grip. She looked away from her mother's face.

"Mom," she said softly. "Why do you have bad teeth?"

Her mother sighed. "Cause I don't eat right, I guess. I don't know."

"Does the coke hurt them?"

"I suppose it does. They say it does, anyway, if you do too much."

"Are they going to fall out?"

"No, I don't think so."

"But do they say it makes your teeth fall out?"

"I don't know, Marie. I suppose they do. I really don't know."

"But—"

"Don't keep asking questions, honey," she said. "I can't think straight with you talking."

"What are you trying to think straight about?"

She didn't answer.

Marie tried a different tack. "What's the stuff you're getting from Brady?"

"Oh, just some moonshine, honey. That's another word for liquor. Brady's an old-fashioned bootlegger."

Marie knew what moonshine was. She had read about it in comic strips, always picturing it as lovely glowing white stuff, incongruously stored in jelly jars. "Why does he need you to get it? If it's just liquor."

"Well, it's a dry county, Marie. There's lots of dry counties. You're not supposed to carry that stuff across the lines. It's stupid, really."

"But why—"

"Marie," her mother said. "What did I tell you about questions?"

The road to Brady's house was a long, muddy, rutted track that made an impracticably steep ascent through the damp woods. Their car wasn't suited for it. In first gear the engine whined, in second it shuddered and died. The tires slipped and spun in the mud, dropped in and out of ruts that threatened to founder them. Twice her mother passed turnoffs without giving them a second glance. She knew exactly where they were going.

"Have I ever been to Uncle Brady's?" Marie asked.

"Once," her mother said, "about three or four years ago."

Marie searched the woods and the road for a landmark, for anything familiar, but found nothing. Eventually the road smoothed into a gradual curve leading out of the trees and onto level ground. Before them lay an open field rimmed by wooded hills—it looked to Marie like the base of a giant's bowl—and Brady's house, tiny against the backdrop of hills, sat at the near edge. It was a rude and weatherbeaten cabin, hardly more than a shack.

They drove along the muddy driveway, greeted by the yodeling bellow of hunting dogs penned out of sight on the far side of the cabin. A rusted pickup truck sat on blocks outside the cabin, tall grass and weeds growing up through its engine, its hood propped open by a support rod long since rusted in place. Beyond the roof of the cabin rose the taller, peaked roof of the barn. Except for patches of weeds and obstinate grass growing in scattered clumps, the yard around the cabin was slick and glossy with mud. The driveway simply disappeared into it.

Marie remembered the place now, remembered wearing white cowboy boots her father had bought her in Hot Springs—white boots with white fringe. She was very little, dressed in tight polyester shorts and a button-up western-style blouse, white like her boots. She'd stayed in the car while her mother was in the cabin, until a dog came to scratch at the car door. Then she'd screamed, and a man appeared in the cabin doorway and hollered at the dog. He had come over and picked Marie up, pulling her out through the open window of the car, and carried her inside. That was where the memory ended, except for walking back out to the car later and losing one of her boots in the deep mud. She must have cried pitifully. Her mother had dug for the boot, tossing it into the car floorboard, and peeled off Marie's muddy socks and stuffed them into the gullets of the boots. She had driven away with Marie in the passenger seat howling and sobbing at her soiled boots. Now she couldn't even remember what had become of them. She couldn't imagine caring so much about cowboy boots.

Her mother was out of the car, agitated, unconsciously smoothing her pants against her hips, straightening her blouse. She hurried over to the door, her pumps slipping a little in the mud, moving with the stiffly erect bearing people have when walking on slick surfaces. Marie followed, hopping from one clump of grass to the next. Near the door sat a boulder as large as Marie. She sat on it to kick the mud loose from her shoes. It was damp from the rain. She found a half-whittled stick at her feet and used it to dig the mud from the grooves in her soles.

Her mother was peering futilely through the screen door into the darkness of the cabin. The sun was out, and there were no lights on inside. She knocked on the frame. "Uncle Brady? Are you home? It's Marie!"

"Who?" returned a rough, old man's voice.

"Marie! Your niece! I've come about the—Joe said you called—"

"Marie? What the hell you doing standing outside, girl? Get yourself in here."

Her mother opened the screen door, the door spring crying out harshly, like a blue jay. Marie leaped up and followed her inside, hanging close. The cabin was dark, lit only by sunlight from two small windows, one on either side of the living room, which appeared to be the only room. There was a sink and counter, a stove, a small table, and a refrigerator inside the entryway, but these things didn't so much make a kitchen as imply one. The air was musty and redolent too of cigarette smoke; at the same time, it was vaguely, inexplicably sweet. In the living room sat an old man in jeans and a brown flannel shirt, slightly hunched in a recliner, picking through a bowl of dried beans. The dim light from the window behind him fell on the bowl in his lap, but it was clear the light did him no good. When he turned his head toward them, lifting his whiskery chin in greeting, his cloudy old eyes stared into an unseen distance. His round, bluff face was ruddy and dry, and a mole protruded from his forehead. His hair, cropped short into a thick bristle, barely exceeded the stubble on his face.

"Well well well," he said to her mother, in a gruff voice, "if you ain't gone and growed up on me." He bent and turned his head away with a rapid, habitual toss of the chin, spitting a stream of tobacco into a plastic tub that sat on the far side of his chair. Marie heard the squeak of the spit passing between his lips and then the droplets hitting plastic. This was the sweet smell, she realized. A tub of brown spit. She pressed against her mother's hip.

Brady's head swung around, and his eyes, as if they still served him, narrowed in Marie's direction. "And who the hell's this little thing?"

Her mother glanced down at Marie as if noticing her for the first time. She pressed a palm against Marie's shoulder blades, urging her forward. Marie resisted, taking only one small step and then retreating again. "This is little Marie. My daughter. You remember her? She's grown up some since you seen her, I guess."

Brady burst into laughter, a wheezing, phlegmetic laugh that startled them both. "Well I'll be damned!" he said, shaking his head. "That's right. Two little Maries." He shifted forward in his seat, as if preparing to stand. He started to set the bowl of beans on a coffee stand beside the chair, but it was covered with empty beer cans and a sauce pan. Indecisive, he held the bowl in his hands. "I got some horehound candy in a drawer around here somewheres. She like horehound?"

"Oh, no thank you, Uncle Brady," Marie's mother said, then lied: "She's got a loose tooth. She's not supposed to eat candy."

Brady gave a toothless grin. "You'd better brush them teeth if you don't want to end up like your old Uncle Brady, honey!" he said, laughing again. The two stood uncomfortably, unconsciously swaying in unison, shifting their weight from foot to foot.

"Well, set down," Brady said, pointing toward a rocking chair across the room, next to a cold wood stove. "Pull up a chair, girl. We ain't seen each other in no telling how long."

"Well, we don't have time really to—"

"Now don't go telling me all them tales. You set down for a minute and let's talk. I ain't talked to a young girl since I don't know when."

Her mother brought a chair from the kitchen table while Marie climbed into the rocker. Her feet didn't quite reach the ground; still, she was able to get it rocking. The wood creaked and made a soft, regular thump against the boards.

"You like that chair?" Brady cried.

She started, looking up to see her mother's anxious face turned on her, as if blaming her for this delay. Brady was smiling his gummy smile, chin up as he waited for her to respond.

"Yes, sir."

"Thought you would. My daddy brung it with him from Oklahoma. It was his mama's chair. You know how my daddy moved to Arkansas, honey?"

She shook her head.

Brady waited, raising his bristly gray eyebrows.

"No sir," she said.

He gave a bark of laughter and shook all over, dropping the bowl of beans into the crook of his lap and vigorously rubbing his thighs with his palms. "She got manners now, don't she?" he said to her mother, but her mother only nodded, forgetting to speak. He said, "She knows her sirs and ma'ams, all right.

"Honey," he continued to Marie, "you come from a bunch of goddamn outlaws. My daddy and his brother, they stole a train in Oklahoma—this was way back before your uncle Brady was born—anyhow they stole that train and they drove it till it plumb run out of track. Back then they was just beginning to run new tracks up here in the Ouachitas, for the timber. My daddy and his brother drove that train right up into these woods till they run out of track, and then they each went their own separate ways. That wasn't hardly two miles from here, over that a way," he said, pointing off to the west. "And, listen now, you see that big old rock outside the door when you come in?"

"Yes, sir," Marie said. Her mother stared at her, pleading with her eyes, but what could she do except answer? "I sat on it."

"Well, you ain't the first one to set on that goddamn rock!" he bellowed, delighted. "That rock been there over eighty years. When my daddy seen this field—he was a big strong man, my daddy—he carried that rock down off of the ridge and set it right where it's setting now, and he told hisself that that was where he'd build his home. Do you know how heavy that rock is, honey?"

"It looks pretty big to me."

"You goddamn right it's big!" he said, wheezing with laughter. "I spent my whole goddamn life trying to pick up that goddamn rock, and do you think I ever moved it?" he said, raising his eyebrows.

"Not even a little bit?"

Brady swung his head down and spat tobacco juice into the plastic tub. "Well, yeah, I did move it some, but I never got it full off of the ground. And strong—honey, I was real strong in my day. Runs in the family. We're all of us strong from the get-go. You're probably strong yourself, ain't you?"

"I don't know."

"Well, you give it time. But I mean to tell you, your old uncle Brady was specially strong. I used to keep a copper still in those woods out back," he said, jerking a thumb at the wall behind him. "Bout a mile from here. And every single night I'd wait till it was real dark, then I'd haul up and walk into them woods with a five-gallon wooden keg on my back, fill it up at the still—now we're talking about five gallons of moonshine in a wooden keg—and I'd put it on my back again and walk back out of them woods. Hill and dale, hill and dale. Five ridges in all I had to get acrossed. And do you know what happened to me one night when I come down that last hill with that keg on my back?"

She stopped rocking. "What happened?"

"Well, I'll tell you what. I was stumbling down that hill when all of a sudden I hear a goddamn rattlesnake kick up right in front of me—I mean right in front of me, honey, no further than from me to your mama here," he said, pointing back and forth between his own chair and that of her mother, who sat despondently with shoulders sagging, "and then another one starts to rattling right behind me, like I must've just stepped right over it. Course it was pitch black in them woods. I couldn't see a goddamn thing."

"What'd you do?"

"I'll tell you what I did. I jumped as high and as far as I could, with that five-gallon keg on my back, and I hit the ground running!" He flung himself back into his chair, nearly upsetting the bowl of beans in his lap, laughing his raspy hoarse laugh and rubbing his thighs. Marie was impressed.

Brady straightened up in his chair again. "Yeah, you bet I was strong in them days. But I still wasn't nowhere near as strong as my daddy was." He cleared his throat, settling the bowl of beans into his lap again.

Her mother opened her mouth to speak.

"Come here, girl," Brady said to Marie, "let your uncle Brady have a better look at you."

Marie didn't see how that was possible, but she obeyed. Brady took hold of her bare arm, squeezing it so hard she winced, but she could tell he didn't mean to hurt her. He had a powerful grip. He smiled. "She's got them bones, all right. She gonna be a big old girl like her grandma was before it's all said and done with." He let go her arm, then on an impulse reached for it again, but she had already backed away. His hand swiped empty air. "She's a quick one too," he said with a laugh. He straightened in his chair and looked at Marie's mother.

"So you're gonna run some jars for me?"

"Yes," she said, looking relieved, "but I have to go to Memphis first. That's where we're headed right—"

"Shit, girl, that's one goddamn hell of a long ways out of y'all's way. But listen, I don't care how you get there, so long as you get there. You know I used to could make a run from here to Tulsa without driving one mile on a paved road. Back roads the whole entire way. It'd take me all night sometimes. I got chased once or twice, but never once got caught, and that's a fact. However," he said, looking now toward Marie, who had climbed into the rocker again. "However. I'll tell you a time I about shit my pants, though."

Marie cast a glance at her mother, whose despair radiated in the room like a furnace. She couldn't imagine how the old man didn't feel it; Marie felt it painfully. But then Brady was not a man to be turned from his course. This was exactly the moral of his ceaseless narrative, which slipped naturally and easily from one conflict to the next, and it would continue to be the moral as he headed steadfast and sure to his grave.

"I was about forty miles from the state line on a back road," Brady was saying, "and it was one goddamn rainy night. I mean it was raining like a son of a bitch, and I'm driving without my lights, when all of a sudden whoomp, I run up onto something and stop dead in the road. And what do I hear? A woman screaming like a goddamn banshee. Alls I can think is, 'Oh my Lord, I done killed some woman,' cause the front of my car is rose up, and I know I've done run up onto something. So I get out and run up front, and you know what?"

"What?" said Marie.

"Laid up there under my car was about the biggest goddamn sow I ever seen."

"A what?"

"A pig, honey," her mother said quickly, trying to keep the story moving toward a conclusion.

"She don't know what a goddamn sow is? She don't—? Well. So now I'm stuck on this goddamn pig, honey, and it's pouring rain and thundering and lightning like you wouldn't believe, and I got two cases of moonshine in my trunk, and the sheriff might come by any goddamn minute, and there I'd be. So you know what I do? I just get right down and jack up my car, and she goes running off into the ditch without a goddamn scratch on her, just as pretty as you please!"

His palms hit his thighs again, and this time Marie laughed too, relieved about the pig. Her mother stood up, looked around confusedly, and sat down again, the reasons for her urgency momentarily lost in the urgency itself. Marie had seen this happen to her before. She'd once watched her mother shifting a box back and forth in the closet, not realizing in her confused state of panic that it was the box itself she'd been looking for.

Brady had stopped laughing to catch at the bowl of dried beans in his lap, which had begun to slip. He cleared his throat to speak again.

"Why do you have those beans in your lap?" Marie asked quickly. She was hoping to divert him from another long story, but her mother looked at Marie not with gratitude but furious disbelief.

"Honey, these here beans help your uncle Brady keep count of his business. Looky here on the side table in this little pot," he said, taking hold of a battered sauce pan and lifting it up for her to see. It made a slight rattle as he shook it. "I got ten beans in here. That's ten jars I sold today." He set the sauce pan down again, spat tobacco, and leaned forward, resting his elbows on his knees. His voice took on a less jocular tone, not businesslike, but serious and almost sad, partly self-pity and partly an old man's delicateness when speaking of grave matters to a child. "Your uncle Brady can't see no more, honey."

"But what are the beans for?"

"Well, the beans," he said, shaking the bowl for emphasis, "the beans is how Uncle Brady keeps track. See, you can't always trust folks that come up here. They might give you a sawbuck and tell you it's a twenty, you see what I mean?"

Marie didn't know what a sawbuck was, but she understood deception. "So you count with the beans."

"That's right. I count out the beans for what I'm supposed to have, and at the end of the day my nephew Buster comes up here and counts the bills for me, and if there ain't enough money to match the beans, I know I been cheated."

"And then what?"

Brady's blind eyes blinked deliberately, and his voice changed. "Then Buster goes and gets my money," he said flatly. Then his tone was gentle again. "But it don't happen much, honey. Most folks is honest with you."

Her mother stood up. "Well, speaking of business, Uncle Brady—"

"All right, all right," he said peevishly. "Let's head out to the barn." He spat into his tub again and rose, still carrying the bowl of beans. His shoulders were slightly stooped, but Marie could see that he had once been a man of considerable size. Even with his stoop he was the same height as her mother, who was tall herself. Stopping to set the bowl on the kitchen table, Brady said, "You know what I do with them beans if I don't sell no jars, honey?"

"What?" said Marie, a little horrified. She couldn't imagine.

"I cook them up for dinner!" He laughed and turned toward the screen door. "Ladies first," he said, waiting for them to go out. He let the screen door shut between them, and for some reason both mother and daughter knew not to open it again. A few moments passed. Marie heard a shuffling sound beyond the door. Then the door opened, and Brady stepped carefully out into the muddy, sunlit yard. To Marie's surprise, his cloudy eyes squinted in the bright sunlight, deep crow's feet gathering at each corner. "Well, come on, girls," he said. "It's round back."

The dogs, a handful of beagles and other hounds, dared not bay when Brady passed their pen, but the beagles whimpered eagerly and trotted back and forth, tails quivering like fresh-stuck arrows. Brady said sternly, "Hey now, dogs," pointing at them as he passed, and the dogs kept quiet.

The decaying old barn lay just beyond the pen. One of its forward walls had half-collapsed, giving it the look of a wounded animal, front legs bent beneath it as it sank toward death. Inside, the barn was warm, foul-smelling, and abuzz with flies. Sunlight streamed through the doorway and the holes in the walls and ceiling. The walls were strung with rusted picks and hoes, half-rotted halters and reins, loops of rope, hoses, a variety of handheld saws. At the rear of the barn a stack of rectangular hay bales stretched from one wall to the other.

Marie, standing near the door, took all this in peripherally, being more concerned with the freshly gutted carcass of a deer that hung suspended from a rafter above her, the body crawling with flies. A viscous stain spread across the dirt and straw beneath it where the offal had spilled. Marie stood transfixed.

"She's a beauty, ain't she?" Brady said. "Buster shot her this morning right across that field." He pointed through the barn wall toward the field. "I told him, 'Goddamnit, boy,' I said, 'don't go shooting deer in my back yard. Like to scared me to death!'" He laughed and spat tobacco toward the wall. "I was setting on that big rock of yours," he said to Marie, "waiting for somebody. I didn't even know Buster was hunting around here. Course I recognized his shotgun, though, so after that first little scare I wasn't worried."

Her mother, bewildered and anxious, was turning in slow circles, searching the barn for any hopeful sign. Finally Brady moved toward the wall of hay at the back of the barn. "Buster'll come round again in a couple hours to finish her up," he said, jerking his thumb over his shoulder at the deer.

Her mother followed close behind. Every few seconds she ran her fingers through her hair, then tucked them back into her tight hip pockets in an effort to keep them still; she'd left her cigarettes in the car. She glanced at Marie, who had lingered to stare at the dead deer. "Marie Ann," she said sharply, not hiding her anger, and Marie hurried over.

Brady had walked over to the far left of the hay wall. With surprising ease he reached up and lifted a bale from the top of the wall, his rough old fingers curling around the baling twine and tugging the hay toward him. He set it aside. "I got no other use for this hay," he said, lifting the next bale, "but Buster keeps horses, so it don't look suspicious." He moved a third bale, then the bottom one, creating an open doorway. Suddenly he was all speed and business. He passed briskly through the opening without inviting them to follow. In the gloom beyond the hay wall Marie glimpsed only shadows and burlap. Half a minute later Brady squeezed through the opening again and set down a covered crate. He turned and quickly replaced the bales.

"Okay. Let's go, girls," he said, hefting the crate. He growled "Hush!" as they left the barn, before the dogs had a chance to bark. The dogs let out half-muted squeals, pacing their pen. By the time Brady reached the car, Marie's mother had opened the trunk and pushed aside the gym bag and suitcase to make room. She stepped out of the way, and Brady, somehow gauging perfectly where the open trunk was, bent his knees against the bumper and lowered the crate inside. His wrinkled old face was splotchy with heat now, the mole on his forehead gone crimson.

"Well, that's that," he said to her mother, breathing heavily. "You know the place, don't you? You know how to get there?"

"Uh-huh," she said, trying to sound patient.

"I know you're in a hurry, girl," he said, taking out a roll of bills. "Now, I'm paying you ahead of time cause you're family." She thanked him and handed the bills absently to Marie, who tucked them into her pants.

"Won't be no trouble in Tulsa," he continued. "Redfoot knows how much to give you, and he won't do you wrong. We been doing this longer than you been alive. Now, when do you expect to get back here?"

"I don't know, exactly, Uncle Brady. In a week or so?"

"That's fine," he said, waving her off. "I'll tell Redfoot to just give me a call when you get there, and I'll expect you the day after that. I know you ain't gonna drink up all the product, but I'd just as soon have the money safe back here after you get it. Good enough?"

"Oh, yes. Thank you, Uncle Brady. It was so good to see you again." She hugged him awkwardly, with a flurry of pats on the back of his shoulders.

"Come give your uncle Brady a kiss," he said to Marie. With a grimace of pain he bent to one knee on the muddy ground and held out his hands. She came and kissed his rough, bristly cheek, and he laughed right into her ear, making her wince. He didn't notice; he was chuckling and straining to stand up again, hands braced against his knee. "You're softer than a dog's ear," he said. He stood directly behind the bumper while they kicked mud from their shoes and jumped in.

"God, don't let me roll back into him," her mother muttered as she engaged the clutch. But the car did lurch backward, and Brady, sensing it, stepped neatly aside. Trying to stop the roll, her mother gunned the engine and sent mud spraying back in a short arc, spattering Brady's boots and jeans. He didn't bother to frown or even look down. Marie, turning in her seat, saw him waving cheerfully, pants flecked with mud, a stain on one knee where he'd knelt to kiss her good-bye. She waved back, forgetting he couldn't know it.

Her mother was hysterical. "I had no idea!" she shouted, spinning her tires as they pitched headlong down the mountain road. Marie bounced wildly in the passenger seat. "No idea it would take us this long. He talked and talked and talked! Jesus Christ!"

The car jounced and rocked, squeaking like bed springs each time they dropped into a rut. Terrified, Marie braced her hands against the dash. Another hard bounce—she felt her hair graze the ceiling. "Slow down!" she whined. "We're going to wreck!"

"Shut up, Marie!" her mother shrieked. "Shut your mouth! For once in your life shut your goddamn mouth!" The wheels spun, spraying gravel and wet leaves as they dropped in and out of the ruts.

Halfway down the mountain, sliding around a hairpin turn, the car stopped, bogged in mud. Her mother slipped the gear in reverse, but the rear only swayed from side to side, tires howling. "Oh no, no, no," she whispered, "Oh Jesus no," and slammed the gearshift into first again. She mismanaged the clutch and the car died. She wiped her forehead, said, "All right, calm down," and cranked the ignition. The engine roared to life; again she put it into reverse. The tires hummed a high note, the back end of the car swinging gently to the left, to the right, to the left again. Marie, her forehead against the side window, looked back at the whizzing tires. Gray mud coated the rear of the car. The tires were half-buried.

Turning her eyes away, she stared into the deep woods. The sky had brightened considerably since the storm passed, and sunlight fell in patches on the wet, leaf-covered ground. Yellow leaves fluttered and whirled down from high boughs. She saw two gray squirrels spiraling briskly up the trunk of a shagbark hickory. Saw the tail of one squirrel and the head of the other, then the head of the first squirrel and the tail of the second, like the stripe on a barber-shop pole. She wouldn't speak or look at her mother now. Her stomach was tight as a drum.

Her mother worked the gears desperately, and the car became more and more hopelessly mired. "Get out and push!" she shouted at last. Marie turned to her with scared eyes.

"I can't—"

"Get out and push!"

Marie was fumbling for the door latch when a man's face appeared in the window. She screamed, and was sickeningly aware of what a little girl's scream it was—how tiny and thin it was against the roar of the engine, the moaning of the tires, the vast desolation of woods. She closed her eyes, covering her face with her hands.

"Kill the engine," a voice was calling. Her mother didn't hear it at first, but when Marie squealed, she looked and saw the man outside the passenger window. A gaunt, pale man in a red flannel shirt, his face whiskery and angular. He was running his finger across his throat. "Kill it," he said again. A shadow crossed her shoulder, and another man stepped up outside her own door.

This man was larger and much older than the first, probably in his forties, wearing jeans and a filthy T-shirt. His black hair, streaked with gray, came down almost to his shoulders. His face was red and chapped. Bending forward, a cigarette between his lips, he motioned for Marie's mother to roll down the window. When she did, he took the cigarette from his lips and blew smoke back over his shoulder. "Cut the engine, little girl," he said. "You're stuck good."

She did as she was told, glancing back at the other man, who was coming around to join his friend by the driver's window. Marie sat in the passenger seat, rocking back and forth with her knees drawn up and her arms over her head. Her mother smiled at the older man. "We're so glad to see somebody. We're in a big hurry, and it's kind of an emergency."

"I imagine so," he said languidly. "Why don't you step on out and let Lance drive for a second? He's a good hand with a stick shift."

"Oh, that would be just great," she said with a dramatic sigh of relief. He opened the door, and she smiled again as she climbed out. "Thank you so much."

Lance had come to stand close to the door. He flattened his back against the car as if to make room for her, but as she stepped past he slapped her on the hip. She jerked her head toward him, laughing uneasily, and he smiled back. "Them are some tight pants, girl," he said. "You looking good."

She tried to smile. "Well, y'all are nice to stop and help us. Like I said, we're in a great big hurry— "

"We heard you, we heard you," Lance said, giving no sign of moving. He was looking at her breasts, glancing up at her eyes to see if she noticed. She crossed her arms across her chest and forced herself to hold the smile.

"Y'all are sweet," she said, in a weak, coquettish voice. "Do y'all live around here? Because you know, I could come back and visit with you. Right now we're in a hurry, but— "

"What's your big emergency?" the older man said. He was standing in the same spot, close to her, staring not at her but into the interior of her car. "It wouldn't happen to be that you got some illegal liquor in your car, would it?"

"No! No, it's just that we're supposed to meet somebody, and they're expecting us, is all. Like I said, I appreciate y'all helping—"

"Lance," the older man said, "take them keys and check what's in the turtle hull. Don't look like there's nothing in the car but a lot of trash and that little girl." He turned his eyes on her again, appraising her. "That your daughter?"

"What? Oh, yes, that's Marie. She's a sweetie-pie. Marie, honey, say hello to these nice men. They're going to get us out of the mud so we can go."

Marie didn't look out from under her arms.

"She's shy," her mother said.

"What you got in the turtle hull, girl?" he said brusquely. He flicked his cigarette butt at Lance, who flinched and swatted it to the ground like a wasp. "I told you to get them keys."

"Just some clothes and stuff," she said, looking anxiously from one man to the other. Lance had made no move to get into the car, but was leaning against it, staring at her. "I thought y'all was going to help me out here," she said petulantly.

"We are, we are," Lance said. "Ain't that right, Carl?"

The older man pressed impatiently between them. He reached into the car and snatched the keys.

"What do you need the keys for? Can't y'all just give us a push?"

"You are a fine-looking woman," Lance said. "What's your name?" He pushed off the car with his hips and moved close to her. Leaning in so that his face was inches from her neck, he inhaled deeply. "Mmm. You smell good, too. What kind of perfume is that?"

She held still. "It's . . . it's called—What are you doing with my keys?" she cried. Her voice, a playful whine, broke into a false giggle. Carl just looked at her as he headed for the trunk. She moved to intercept him, but Lance grabbed her arm at the elbow.

"Where you going? You can't stop Carl once he gets his mind set on something. Might as well stick with me. You ain't in that big a hurry, are you?"

She didn't take her eyes off Carl. "Yes, I am," she whispered. She felt Lance's hand slide up her arm onto her shoulder. His grip had relaxed. He began to trail a finger down along her collarbone. She stepped quickly away from him.

"Hey now," he said in a surprised voice, swiping at her arm and missing. She hurried over to the trunk just as Carl opened it.

"You sure you ain't been up to see old Brady?" he asked, looking at her with his eyebrows raised.

"We was just up . . . driving up to . . ." She tried to step between Carl and the open trunk. He didn't step back, and she ended up pressing against him. She placed the palm of her hand against his chest, trying to push him gently back. "Please. This is our personal stuff back here. Can't y'all just help us—"

Carl looked down at her hand on his chest, then back up to her face. "I done seen what your personal things is. And if you didn't buy it from Brady then I don't know what."

Lance had come up from behind her. He took her by the arm and yanked her roughly toward him. "That wasn't nice," he said in a jocular tone, "walking away from me like that."

"I'm sorry, I just don't want y'all digging through my things like this." She looked imploringly into Lance's eyes. "Can't you tell him to stop? That's my stuff he's getting into."

He glanced back at Carl, who was lifting the burlap-covered crate out of the trunk. "I'll give you a little money for it. Like I said, you can't change Carl's mind for nothing."

"But they're not mine! They're Brady's!"

"I thought you said you didn't know Brady."

"I thought y'all might be the police or something. They're Brady's, I swear. I'm supposed to run them somewhere for him."

"Why you lying to us?" Lance said calmly. "Brady never had no girl run jars for him."

"But I'm his niece! He told me to—" Her eyes welled with tears. "He told me to—"

Carl was toting the crate up the hill toward a muddy pickup truck parked in the road above them. He looked back over his shoulder to Lance. "Get them bags, too," he said. He slipped in the mud, stumbled, caught his balance just in time to avoid dropping the crate.

"No!" she screamed, slapping at Lance's arms. She tried to reach up and slam the trunk closed, but Lance pulled her away.

"You'd better just calm yourself down, girl!" he said angrily. She wriggled violently in his arms, pushing against him, and he used her momentum to swing her in an arc away from the trunk and up against the side of the car.

"No!" she shrieked, flailing at him. "You can't! You can't!"

With great effort Lance turned her away from him so that her arms were pinned between her body and the car. He pressed hard against her back with his body, squeezing the backs of her elbows with his hands, holding her there. She fought back against him, but he held her firmly, breathing into her ear. He lowered his chin and half-bit, half-kissed her at the base of her neck.

"No!" she sobbed, and her body went limp, dead weight against the car. Her shoulders heaved. Her voice went low. "No, no, no—"

"Hush now, little baby," Lance said, moving against her. His left hand dropped from her arm and slid along her hip. "Hush. Shhhh. It's all right."

"Please—"

"Shhh."

They felt the car dip slightly. Carl had returned and was leaning into the trunk, one knee against the bumper.

"Please! Please, I'm begging you—"

"Get back in the car," Lance said now, in a different voice. "Me and your mom is talking."

She tried to look toward the door to see Marie, who must have come out, but her face was pressed against the side of the car, with Lance's forehead against the back of her head. Lance didn't loosen his hold.

"Get back inside the car, little girl," he said again.

"Y'all better leave us alone," Marie said.

Lance pulled back to yell at Marie, and now her mother did manage to turn her head. Marie was sitting on her knees in the driver's seat, leaning out and bracing herself with her arms against the open door. Her eyes were swollen and red. Lance shouted for her to get back inside. Then she said, in a quavery voice, "My daddy's going to come along any minute and he's going to be mad."

"What's she saying?" Carl called from inside the trunk, his voice muffled.

"Says her daddy's coming."

"Tell her we don't believe her."

Lance laughed. "He said to tell you—"

"He had to go get something, but he's coming back," Marie interrupted. "He's still got to finish the deer he killed this morning." She climbed out of the driver's seat and stood in the mud. Her face turned resolutely angry. "If he sees you and Mommy like this, he'll kill you too."

"Marie, honey—," her mother said.

Carl came around the back end of the car, his hands empty, his eyes suspicious. He had sensed the shift in mood. "What's she saying?"

"She says—"

Marie began to cry. Her hands clenched into fists and she wailed, "My daddy's going to kill you! He'll kill Mommy too! Y'all better leave us alone!"

Lance turned his head nervously toward Carl. "Says her daddy killed a deer this morning and that he's coming back—"

"Hush, little girl," Carl said. He looked at Marie sternly, and she dried up, looking defiantly back at him. "Now, I don't think you're telling us grownups the truth. Y'all ain't from around here. Your daddy—"

"We're visiting him," she said, wiping her nose with the back of her hand. "He said he was going to bring me some horehound."

"Now, wait a minute—," Lance said.

"Shut up, Lance," said Carl. "What's your daddy's name, honey?"

"His name's Buster, and if—"

Lance released his hold on Marie's mother and jumped backed, as if he'd seen a copperhead. Carl looked at Marie's staunch red face, her tiny wrist wiping her tiny nose. He didn't seem to hear the rest of what she said. He turned his gaze on her mother. She, like Marie, was wiping her nose. They looked like the same woman seen from different perspectives; the girl was the woman seen from a distance.

"She telling the truth?" he said.

She nodded, swallowing her sobs and covering her face.

"Well, goddamnit, woman," Carl said. He turned half away from her as if to go, stopped confusedly, and turned back again. He looked at her, then at the girl, who was climbing back inside the car. "Well, goddamnit."

Lance stood frozen in place, watching Carl with wide eyes. His hands hung straight against his sides like a guilty schoolboy's. He shifted his weight uneasily from one foot to the other, the mud sucking at each boot in turn.

"Look," Carl said to her. "We thought you was someone else. If we'd have knew who you was—We wasn't going to hurt you. Okay?"

She nodded, making a little gasping sound as she held back her tears.

"Shit," Carl said. "We're sorry. We're sorry if we scared you."

"Yeah," Lance said.

"It's okay," she managed to say, dipping her chin in a tight nod. She sniffed and tossed her head back, gasping again as she regained her breath from the sobs.

"Well," Carl said quickly, "we know you're in a hurry. Why don't we help get you out of this mud?"

"Thank you," she said, not looking at them.

Carl stared at her a moment longer. "Shit," he said, shaking his head. "Come on, Lance."

The two of them trotted uphill to the truck. Carl slipped again and this time fell completely. He got up without even wiping himself off and lifted the crate out of the truck. "Get a couple them boards," he directed Lance.

He returned the crate while Lance slid two long two-by-four boards from the bed of the truck. He shut the trunk and gave the keys to Lance, who went up to the driver's side door, skirting widely around Marie's mother as if she might strike him. Carl worked the boards under the back tires.

Lance put the key in the ignition and waited for Carl to give the word. He glanced at Marie, who sat beside him, staring straight ahead with a flat, unreadable expression. He said, "You be sure and tell your daddy we helped get you out of this mud, you hear?"

Marie didn't respond. Carl shouted for him to throw it into first. He cranked the engine and stomped the accelerator. The wheels sang against the muddy wood, and Carl's violent curses reached their ears faintly and indistinctly, as if muted by distance. After a while Lance let off the gas. "Goddamnit!" Carl was shouting. "Get out here and help. Let the lady drive!"

Lance put the car in neutral and opened the door. He looked back at Marie, but she didn't turn her head his way. "You remember—," he began, then stopped. He got out.

Her mother sank into the driver's seat and shut the door. When Carl gave the word, she hit the gas. For a moment the car seemed to be lifted upward instead of forward, and under the noise of the engine and the spinning wheels they could hear the men behind them, straining and cursing with effort. When the tires found purchase the car launched forward with frightening speed, careening along the rutted track. She whipped the wheel quickly to avoid running off the road, and the car swerved right, bouncing and jolting again as before. Without one glance in her rearview mirror, without a word to Marie, she pulled the gearshift into second and sent them racing down the slippery, winding road.

The wind buffeted the car as they sped east into Hot Springs. Although the sky had cleared, the asphalt was wet, and a constant grimy film built up on the windshield. The wipers hardly helped. Her mother was smoking the last of her cigarettes.

"Marie, honey, check in the back and see if there's any more cigarettes."

Marie craned her neck, gave a cursory glance. She knew there were no more. She'd dug this last one out of an abandoned pack from beneath the driver's seat. There was nothing but wrappers and trash in the back. "Nope."

"Are you sure? You didn't even look."

"I'm sure."

"Oh, Jesus," her mother murmured. She took a deep drag, ashing the cigarette all the way to the butt. Marie heard the crinkling sound of the paper burning. "Oh God," her mother said.

They were going ninety; Marie was watching for troopers. She wished her mother would slow down—not because she was afraid of the speed or because she didn't want to be pulled over, but because she didn't want to get to Memphis. They were going to be very late. Every tick of the odometer, every passing car, flashing sign, looming billboard, every bend of the road took them closer to Memphis, where they were going to be very late. She held herself rigid in her seat.

They flashed over a bridge without slowing, the waters of Lake Ouachita chopping white beneath them. The bridge curved upward and dropped again, and as they crested the peak, Marie felt her stomach rise. It refused to come back down. The lake disappeared behind them, and soon they came to an intersection on the outskirts of Hot Springs. At a stoplight her mother checked her watch. She moved her lips, mentally calculating time and distance. Marie watched her.

"Let's not go to Memphis," she said.

Her mother, studying street signs, didn't respond. Her brow was furrowed. When the light changed they raced forward only to catch another red light, and her mother pushed her hair back from her face, leaving her palm flat against her forehead, apparently lost in thought.

"Let's not go to Memphis," Marie said again, louder.

"I'm trying to concentrate, Marie! Now, which way is it? Is it straight, or do I turn right on Central? I'm going to need to know when I get to it."

They had come this way a hundred times or more, and suddenly her mother couldn't remember. Marie's throat tightened. She glanced around at the intersection and knew it immediately, the 70-270 junction. They were on Albert Pike. Their route should edge the north end of town, keeping them on 70 East. Turning on Central Avenue was what you did if you wanted to hit 7 South and drop down to Arkadelphia. It bore no relation to Memphis.

"Turn on Central," she said.

Relieved, her mother said, "Do I? Is it Central? I thought I turned on Central, but I couldn't remember. I'm so, I'm just so—Are you sure, honey?"

Marie looked straight ahead. "I'm pretty sure."

"Okay, we'll turn on Central and see if it looks right."

Albert Pike, then Grand Avenue, then Central Avenue. Her mother got into the right lane and waited for an opening to pull in. Traffic was heavy, and twice she started to pull forward only to slam on her brakes again. "Somebody let me in!" she shouted.

Marie looked at her mother, who was leaning far forward in the seat, her breasts pressed against the steering wheel as she peered left, trying to spy an approaching gap in traffic.

They were intolerably late.

She saw the cars slowing across the intersection and knew they were getting a yellow light. "It's clear," she said.

Her mother started forward at once, nearly clipping a bumper. Her eyes widened, and she stopped to let the car pass. Before she could shout at her, Marie pointed at the empty lane ahead. "The light changed. It's clear."

They surged forward again, heading south on Central. Immediately her mother was fretting. "This doesn't look right. I don't think it looks right. We're going south."

"I think it's right," said Marie. She pointed at a highway sign. "Highway 7. Doesn't that connect with 30?"

Her mother shook her head furiously, finally remembering. "God, no, Marie! We wanted to stay on 70. Oh, sweet Jesus." She looked for a place to turn around. They were coming to an intersection.

There was a gas station on their right and fast food restaurants on all four corners of the intersection. Marie looked across the street at the Burger Chef. She remembered eating there. Her father had taken her a few years before. The light fixtures were colored globes, and each table had brightly colored swivel stools. She had liked that place.

"I have to go the bathroom."

"Marie! You do not—"

"I do! I've been holding it all the way from Uncle Brady's!"

"You'll have to keep holding it."

"I can't!"

"You'll have to, Marie Ann."

Marie pointed to the fuel gauge. "You're almost out of gas."

Her mother, suspicious, looked at the gauge. "Well, that's just great."

"It's not my fault."

Her mother cut the wheels sharply and pulled into the gas station, her right wheels climbing the curb and bouncing down again on the far side.

"I need some cigarettes anyway," she said, as if justifying the stop to herself in that way. She pulled up in front of the self-service pumps and leaped out.

Marie's heart jumped as she stepped from the car into the cool wind outside. The air smelled faintly of gasoline. Her mother was frantically unscrewing the gas cap. "Can I go?" Marie said. She was scared now, balking at her own half-formed plan.

Puzzled, her mother looked at her. It wasn't like Marie to ask permission.

"Can I go?" she asked again, listening to herself say it.

The gas pump meter whirred to zero and her mother began to pump, still studying Marie. "You have the money Brady gave us?" Marie nodded, searching her face. The suspicious look faded. "Well, get me a couple packs of cigarettes and pay for the gas, okay? Hurry up!"

Halfway to the gas station door she lingered, watching her mother bent over the hose as the gas meter ticked. Her mother's hair fell over her eyes, fluttering in the breeze. She brushed it back but it just fell forward again. She noticed Marie standing there. "Marie!" she said peremptorily.

Marie spun on her heels.

The attendant sat behind the counter reading a Bible. He was handsome but haggard-looking, unkempt hair tucked behind asymmetrical ears. He glanced up at her and smiled. "Two bottles of Jim Beam?"

"I need a key to your bathroom."

"Bathroom's unlocked. Just head around the corner and it's right there. Hey, does your mom want her oil checked, or any—"

But she had already trotted out the door. She rounded the corner of the building without looking back at her mother and went to the bathroom door, her breath coming rapidly now. For a moment she stood looking at the symbol on the door, the nondescript figure of a woman in a dress. Her hand went to the doorknob, her fingers just touching the cold metal.

She turned and ran.

Across the street, weaving among idling cars waiting for the light, and into the Burger Chef. A family sat in a booth just inside the door. The parents looked up at her, looked back to their children. At the counter people stood waiting to order. It was as she remembered, the colored globe lights, the bright swiveling stools. The back of the restaurant was empty save a tomato-faced old man drinking coffee and smoking a cigarette over a newspaper. She slid onto a blue stool several tables away from him and watched out the large window.

Marie could see her mother at the gas station, hanging up the hose. Now glancing impatiently toward the doors of the station, now checking her watch, now climbing into the car. A gray puff of smoke rose from the exhaust pipe. Marie swiveled back and forth on her stool, watching. She stretched her arms out on the table, rested her chin on her upper arm. She heard herself breathing heavily through her nose, the pounding of her pulse in her ears. Beyond her fingertips pressed flat on the table, with half-moons appearing beneath the fingernails, out through the thick glass, across the wide street, she saw her mother climb out of the car again and go into the gas station. She saw how muddy her mother's shoes were, and as her mother disappeared inside, she turned her gaze onto the car, onto its familiar shape and color, its rear fenders and tires caked with dried mud.

Her mother reappeared, two packs of cigarettes in hand, and stalked around the corner of the building. Marie saw her wrench the bathroom open. Watched her stare dumbly into the empty bathroom for a moment, slam the door, run back toward the car. Halfway there her mother stopped, hand flying to her mouth, and bent forward in an involuntary crouch of sudden terror. The sickness of understanding. Still doubled over, she went to the passenger side of the car and pressed her face against the window. Dropped to her knees and looked beneath. Then on her feet again, whirling, standing with her arms pressed back against the car as if trapped there in the face of an attacker. Her bosom rose and fell. Her face darted left and right.

The sounds of the world came all at once to Marie's ears, as if something had popped. She heard the bustle and murmur of the restaurant patrons, the crying of a baby somewhere across the room. Outside, the honking of car horns, the rumbling engines and squealing belts, the cooing of pigeons in the eaves. She watched her mother's mouth form her name—it created a grimace, her name, a horizontal stretch—and she heard it, or imagined she heard it, even from that distance. Her mother's mouth opened narrowly and widely, calling her name again, then a third time, the tendons in her neck standing out with the strain. She went back into the station, came out again, ran to the bathrooms. This time she opened both doors. She disappeared behind the building and seconds later came out from around the far corner, still running.

She peered into the car as if she must have made a mistake before. Whirled again in exactly the same way she had done the first time. "Marie!" she shouted, and began to sob, her shoulders jerking. "Marie! Marie! Marie! Marie! Marie!"

Marie watched her circle the car, hands in her hair. She stopped by the driver's door and called her name again. It was her own name too—she might have been screaming for herself. Her eyes swept the windows of the Burger Chef, and Marie pressed her chin against her arm, trying to make herself smaller, not wanting to duck.

And then she lost her nerve and thought: Find me.

But her mother saw nothing. She saw nothing, only turned again and again, searching in all directions, hoping her daughter's face would deliver itself to her of its own accord. She dropped her forehead against the roof of the car, holding herself steady with her hands. She seemed to be gathering herself for something. At last her head came up again, she threw it back, and she screamed "Marie!" in such a desperate pitch of appeal that everyone sitting on that side of the Burger Chef looked out the window, startled. Marie didn't move, because her mother hadn't found her.

Then she did what Marie had known she would do. She opened the driver's side door—frantically waving away the attendant, who had come running out to ask what was wrong—took one last wild pleading look around, and got into the car. She got into the car, and she slammed the door and pulled forward, forcing the attendant to back away. Shaking his head, he watched her go, her tires keening as she circled inside the lot. Her blinker came on, the wrong one, and after a moment's pause the car leaped out into traffic.

Marie closed her eyes and waited. She opened them again and the car was still gone. The attendant was gone. A pickup truck had pulled up to the same pump her mother had used. She closed her eyes again. Just with her hips, she swiveled slowly in the chair. The muddy tips of her shoes dragged across the tile floor, back and forth.

Some time later she heard a woman say, "Honey, are you here by yourself? Where's your mom?"

Marie looked up. A fat young woman in a mauve Burger Chef hat stood over her, an expression of friendly concern on her face. There was no real reason for alarm. It was a beautiful, sunny autumn afternoon; the rain had passed. All around them people were enjoying themselves, eating good, hot food. The woman smiled sweetly as Marie looked up at her.

"You're not crying, are you? Your eyes are red."

Marie shook her head.

"Are you lost?"

"No, ma'am."

"Is your mommy in the bathroom?"

Marie shook her head again. "She's coming," she said. "She's coming in a minute. I'm supposed to wait for her."

Chapter 9

Sometimes it was easy: They would laugh their way through dinner—at a sandwich shop, usually, but occasionally it was chicken livers and mashed potatoes, or shrimp and steak at Mollie's—and drive around the simmering town at night. Or Abe would take off on a weekend afternoon, and they'd tool along country roads, where morning glory draped the fences and the fields were white with Queen Anne's lace. On a gravel road, striped down the middle with weeds, they would tumble into the bed of his truck, breathlessly wrestling, burning themselves on the hot metal, with the drone of bees in the ditch clover. They went for their late night walks too and up again to the fresh-shingled roofs of empty buildings. The nights had stopped cooling off even in the wee hours, and the humidity was high—they would break a sweat and never lose it. They joked that they had never seen each other clean or kempt.

Sometimes, though, Marie would go sullen. She'd say this was pointless, ridiculous. What was she doing? She'd not meant to be here with him, not like this. She would start to get angry, and once started, there was no stopping her. When she managed to be less cruel—which, more and more, she did—she would turn the anger away from Abe, its more convenient target, and level it upon herself. She would call herself an imposter in a real person's life—declaring this with such conviction, yet so elliptically, that Abe often found himself momentarily doubting mundane things: the trailer, the town, the moment, himself. She could dislocate him with a sentence. She would insist her simplest plans were farcical and outrageously conceived.

Abe, always afraid this time she would make good on her intentions to leave, would talk her out. He'd say he didn't believe that; and in this way, trying to calm her, he teased out the details of her life. Compelled to prove him wrong, she would tell him almost everything: about her years in the foster homes—in Little Rock, in Benton, in Sherwood, in Little Rock again—and the group homes, and the halfway house. She was what they called a runner. At high risk to run, she said. Said it with a sneer, because she was always in a bad mood when she started down these paths. The solicitous case workers would check her into a locked facility—you could usually hear someone screaming in the background, she said wryly—and she would start looking for the exit before she'd unpacked her bags. She would quickly prove a model of comportment, would tell her counselors what they hoped to hear. No matter that "histrionic tendencies" was noted in her file, she would convince them nonetheless. This time was better. This time she understood. She'd had a breakthrough, she'd wept, she'd exposed her wounds and finally could heal. And at the first good opportunity—a fire alarm, a walk to the cafeteria, confusion boarding the alternative school bus—she would run. Just drop her things and fly. Where, she had no idea. She never had any idea.

"Not to your father?" Abe asked. He was rubbing her feet. She was smoking a cigarette, not looking at him. It was early evening on a Sunday. They were parked at an overlook on Hot Springs Mountain. In a nearby picnic shelter, raccoons were digging around in a garbage can. Abe had seen one of them knock the lid off with a practiced swipe of its paw.

"To my father?" Marie said, as if she didn't understand the question.

"You wouldn't go to him?"

"Oh, no. I couldn't do that."

"Why not?"

"Well, what would they do to my mother if they found out she'd abandoned her little girl, that's why not. If I went to my father he might tell somebody."

"You were worried she'd get in trouble."

"I knew she was in trouble. I thought she might get in more trouble. So no, of course I didn't go to him. At first, sure, that was exactly what I planned to do. But when I thought about it, I realized I couldn't."

"You'd think somebody would have contacted him."

"No way they could. I never told anybody my real name."

For a moment Abe didn't speak. He was astounded, although he didn't show it. With Marie he had learned not to show it. He said, "You spent your childhood with a fake name?"

"Most of it."

"What was it?"

Now she smiled, somewhat more easily. "Marie Burger."

"Your last name was Burger."

"It was the first thing that came to me, sitting there in that Burger Chef. That was where it occurred to me I couldn't go to him, that I'd have to lie. Hey, I was just a kid. It was all I could think of."

"Sure."

"The funny part is nobody questioned it, not once in all those years. Marie Burger. It doesn't even sound fake to me now. It hasn't for a long time."

"What I'm unclear about is why you'd run. If there were people taking care of you—"

She laughed. A vicious bark of a laugh that made him regretful. "Oh, they took care of you. My first foster father tried to rape me, so I ran. My second one was okay, but his foster sons kept trying, so I ran. At the third place the mother hated me, so I ran. And so on. They keep sticking you in homes with losers who need the money and a bunch of foster kids who've got nothing to lose. They'd steal from me, attack me, threaten me. For a while I'd fight back, you know; I'd give them serious trouble. I like to clawed a kid's eye out once. He had to wear one of those metal patches for a while. But when that didn't work, and it never did for long, I'd bolt. Some girls I met in the group homes never knew what to do. They'd just sit there and suffer until some social worker finally came along and yanked them out of their personal hellhole. Me, I always ran."

Abe said nothing. He switched to her other foot, and she shifted in her seat as he massaged it.

"The youth home in Little Rock was better," she went on, "but I was in the habit, I guess, and I kept it up for a while. Trying to run every chance I got. It was harder to get away from that place, though; they knew my history and took it seriously. Finally I figured out it was better to just stick, do the program, get my GED, get out." She lit another cigarette. "And that's pretty much all there was to it."

Abe knew that was not all there was to it. He imagined, although he hated to, that she had found her way into work that required no GED, the barter of drugs or body or soul, or she'd stumbled onto some darker path he could hardly imagine and had only recently stumbled back out. But he'd learned not to press her once she'd talked herself to a stopping point. She wouldn't go further; they would only argue, and anyway he was anxious about what he might learn. So he nodded and rubbed her feet as she smoked. A truck pulled up by the picnic shelter, muffler blatting, and they watched startled raccoons come piling out of the garbage can like clowns from a clown car. One was still nibbling a corn cob as it fled.

"Let's get something to eat," Marie said, snapping away her cigarette. "I'm starved enough to eat trash myself."

They went to their usual sandwich shop on Albert Pike, in a hot, ugly part of town where businesses were housed in low cement buildings with flat roofs and the city seemed somehow stickier. There was a bank next door and a neon supply company across the street. An odor of exhaust hung in the air. But the sandwich shop was cool and clean inside, suffused with the smell of fresh-baked bread. It was empty, as usual, which was why they liked it, despite the fact that its emptiness would doom the place. The proprietor, a squat, red-bearded man, came out of the kitchen. Although he never remembered them, he wore the solemn expression of a businessman who took his customers' needs seriously. "How y'all doing?" he said, drying his hands with a white towel.

"Any specials today?" Marie asked.

"You name it, you get it special. How's that?"

They ordered and sat down. A family came in. A skinny black man in shorts and sandals, and his wife, also skinny, dressed for work in a suit and heels. The son and daughter, knee-high to the man, were spinning with their arms out to dizzy themselves. They each had that toddler's characteristic thickness of rump, hidden diapers beneath their clothes. They staggered crazily about, laughing. Abe tried to picture Marie at that age. He tried to picture himself.

"What are you thinking about now?" Marie said. She was always suspicious after these disclosures, always imagined him to be having terrible thoughts about her.

"I was trying to picture myself at that age," he said, nodding toward the children.

"And?"

"It seems unlikely, somehow."

"Is that all?"

"That was all."

"Well, tell me something else. I'm sick of hearing myself."

"What do you want to know?"

"I don't know. Tell me this thing about your father."

"What thing?"

"You said he's acting different."

"Yeah."

"So what does different mean? And don't make me keep asking questions. Just talk."

"Okay. My father. Well, he's been this unremitting hard-ass all my life. As you know. You couldn't do anything properly around him, you couldn't talk to him, you definitely couldn't argue with the man. Nothing like your dad."

At this she gave a slight smile. It was generally a good way to bring her out of her funks, to say something about her father. But you couldn't push it. She was too smart for that.

"And then," Abe continued, "all of a sudden, he's turning into a saint. Cut down on his drinking. Trying to be nice. Last week he painted the house—which I know doesn't seem like much, but my mother's been asking him to do it for years now. I mean years. She finally quit asking. Suddenly he just up and does it. Asked her what color she wanted it, went straight out and bought the paint, and then spent the whole week working on it."

"So what happened?"

"No idea. What it makes me think of is how—well, you know how sometimes when you're sick, you feel better after you throw up? That's what it seems like. For years he's been getting worse and worse, and then one day he just turned around, like he finally threw up and started feeling better. My mother says it's because he's been talking to a preacher. Started going to church. What I'm not sure about is whether talking to the preacher has changed him or if he started talking to the preacher because he'd changed."

"Was he really that hard on you?"

"Oh, I don't know. Seemed like it to me, but maybe I was a touchy kid. I don't suppose it's a new story. I do know I never wanted to work for him again."

"But you worked for him for years. You must have liked it some."

Abe hesitated. At first he thought she didn't understand, that she couldn't grasp why you stuck through something you hated, or how for some people options don't seem like options but fancies. Then he knew he was being foolish. She understood. She was just antagonizing him. Either she was working something out in her head, or she simply hadn't got her hackles down yet.

He shook his head. "I think the only thing I ever looked forward to, when I was a kid at least, was wearing the stilts. But even—"

"Stilts?"

"They're these big metal elevator shoes about knee-high. I thought I'd be like a giant, tromping around all over the place. But by the time I was big enough to use them, I didn't give a damn about being a giant. They were just one more thing to drag around, and if you lost your balance you'd bust your ass."

"You ever lose your balance?"

"I can tell you want the answer to be yes."

She smiled and averted her eyes.

"You think it'd be funny."

"Well?"

"Of course I lost my balance. And the worst part wasn't even getting banged up. It was having your dad hear the racket and come in from the other room to check on you. The way he'd just look at you like you were wasting his time, like he was absolutely disgusted with you, and then go off again."

"I take it he never fell."

"Not that I ever saw. Maybe he did when he was younger."

"You don't sound like you believe that."

"I don't, I guess. No, I don't think he ever fell."

Their sandwiches came. Marie tore into hers, a sloppy meatball sub. The sauce oozed over her fingers. Abe watched her for a moment, trying to suppress a smile.

"Wha?" she said, with her mouth full.

He slid a napkin toward her, and she just laughed through her nose. She was cheering up. A cloudburst dumped rain while they ate and was over by the time they finished. When they stepped outside not even the clouds remained, and the blue dusk was damp but cool. They went walking, taking the sidewalk off the business strip back into the residential neighborhood along Prospect Avenue. The cement was uneven and crumbling, with weeds poking up through the cracks and a shallow puddle every few steps, but it was a pretty place. There were old homes on the hill, with porches and narrow yards, and a high canopy of oak trees and magnolias over the street. The mimosas were in bloom, too, their pink and white pompon blossoms perched atop the fanning branches, their heady, rain-freshened fragrance suffusing the air. A breeze soughed through the trees. There was a patter of leafdrip on pavement.

They sat on a bench, heedless of the damp, and watched a woman creak past on a relict, single-gear bicycle, hair clinging to her forehead. She had groceries in the bicycle basket, a sheen of sweat on her arms. The streetlamps were flickering to life as she passed them, as if purposely lighting her way.

"Tell me why you quit college," Marie said, taking his hand into her lap. She picked absently at his fingernails.

It was the first she'd spoken since they left the sandwich shop. Now he was sure she was antagonizing him. But not to hurt him. It was one of her ways of paying attention. "I told you that before," he said. "I couldn't afford it."

"You told me you spent your tuition money on the trailer."

"All right, it was like this. I had a scholarship. Not a full ride, but a small one, which saved me just enough money that I could afford the tuition if I worked full-time. I didn't realize how hard that would be. It was a serious place—people studied for hours every day. I never got started till the middle of the night, after I'd worked a full shift at a restaurant. I didn't know anybody, and I didn't do well. I lost the scholarship. End of story. It isn't very interesting."

"But you still had money," Marie persisted. "Couldn't you afford to go somewhere else?"

"I could have. Yes."

He was remembering a discussion with his father. He was going to take out a loan, had made the decision already, had started the paperwork. His father was calling him a damn fool. You don't throw good money after bad, he said. Any man worth his salt, he said. And Abe—who had lost the scholarship, who drove most days past the empty lot where he'd once kept his horses—not surprised, really, at this from his father, not surprised, but still stricken, took little convincing. He burned the paperwork in a yard barrel.

"Well, then, why didn't you?" Marie asked.

"I guess that kind of took the wind out of my sails."

"I don't know much about college, I suppose."

"Turns out I didn't either," he said.

"But you must be pretty smart. I mean they gave you a scholarship in the first place."

"Not the big one. I had a shot at the big one and I screwed up."

"What happened?"

"You know, I shouldn't have mentioned it. I don't really—"

"Now you have to tell me."

"I'd rather not."

"You have to."

"I think you're really trying to torture me tonight."

She kissed him. "Yes, I am. Now tell me."

So he told her. Told her how he had dressed for the interview in his one outdated suit and driven an hour and a half to get there. Standing nervously in a sitting room, waiting. No mirrors to check his tie. There was beautiful old furniture, a fireplace, a baby grand piano, a chandelier. He was early and had to wait. Another scholarship candidate joined him in the sitting room, a well-dressed, handsome kid who sat casually at the piano bench and picked out a tune. Abe thought of him as a kid because he didn't seem to have any manners.

"Was it just me," the kid said, "or was that test a joke? I mean, I'm surprised they only accept ten candidates. It's hard to believe anybody could have missed any of those questions." He fingered the keyboard delicately, playing a minor chord for the fallen, and sighed. "But I guess they must have. Or else it was the essays that did them in. There's only ten of us, after all."

Abe despised the kid at once. He crossed the room to study a bookshelf until it was time for his interview. He needed to use the bathroom but didn't want to ask anyone. Finally it got so bad he decided he really must ask someone, and just then the woman came and told him it was time. He climbed the stairs.

In a comfortable, sunny office he was met by the three interviewing professors: two middle-aged, frumpy women—frumpy but not prim—and a white-bearded man with venous cheeks and nose. They greeted him with handshakes and friendly smiles. He relaxed slightly. They all sat down in plump-cushioned chairs around a coffee table.

"I see here on your application," the man said, flipping through papers, "that you want to be a writer."

"Yes, sir."

"That's admirable," the man said. The women smiled and nodded. He liked them all immediately. They wanted to help him. The women wore loose-fitting, dull-patterned dresses; the man's suit was rumpled and old. These were comfortable, nice people. The man continued: "Under 'Goals' you wrote that you would like to win the Pulitzer Prize and the Nobel Prize. Now, I'm wondering, why the Nobel? Is there something in particular about the Nobel Prize, or does it simply represent to you the pinnacle of achievement?"

It was the latter, of course, but he felt somehow that this would be the wrong answer. Churlish, even. You couldn't say that was your reason. But he had nothing to say in its stead. Why on earth had he written that? He sat there, helpless.

The man tried to help. "What does the Nobel Prize make you think of?"

"Well, I know it was started by Alfred Nobel, the man who invented dynamite. He wanted to do something good. I guess that's just what I want to do."

They all nodded helpfully.

"Anything else?" the man asked. Giving him a chance. A chance to show that he knew anything at all.

"Well," he said. "I once read William Faulkner's Nobel acceptance speech . . ." He trailed off. He couldn't say anything more. He'd only spoken because he felt he must, and now he had nothing to say. A drop of sweat trickled down his side from under his arm. He tried to think. That acceptance speech, it was supposed to be a good example of some rhetorical style. What style? He couldn't remember. He sat there and said nothing.

One of the women smiled and said, "You like Faulkner?"

"Yes," Abe said, gratefully. "Yes, I do. I've only read 'The Bear,' but I liked it very much."

"Tell us about it," the white-bearded man said, "When you think of 'The Bear,' what comes to mind?"

He was quiet. He was thinking, Nature. Nature comes to mind. The importance of nature. But you couldn't say that. It was too obvious. You couldn't say that, and yet there was nothing else to tell. Surely he shouldn't just summarize the story. Surely he shouldn't say that he liked it because he liked the woods. He should say something meaningful. He cleared his throat.

"Well," he said, and faltered. "Well—"

"For instance," the man said, "when I think of 'The Bear,' I am struck by the importance of nature in the story."

"Yes," Abe said miserably. "Yes, that's true."

The women professors took their turns, asking him about civic responsibility, the significance of learning, what he would do with his degree. His answers were fumbling, bloated, grandiose, boorish. And all the while they tried to help him. They asked leading questions. They smiled; they even laughed at his few attempts at humor. But he was disappointing them. He would leave, and they would look at each other and shrug. They had done what they could for the poor kid. Give him one of the small scholarships. Bring in the next candidate, someone who can answer a question, preferably someone who can play piano.

So Abe went home with the small scholarship, and eventually he sold his horses to make up some of the difference. But he didn't mention this part to Marie.

"That's nothing," she said, punching his shoulder. "You act like you've got this sad, sad story, and then it's nothing."

He rubbed his shoulder. "I know it's nothing."

"I hope you aren't expecting sympathy."

"Listen, you told me to tell you, so I did. We can drop it."

"Oh, I'm sorry," she said, wrapping her arms over his shoulders. "Poor Abe, I'm sorry."

"Don't say 'Poor Abe.' It's fine."

She kissed him. "Couldn't get his big scholarship."

He laughed. "All right, that's enough."

"So tell me something else."

"With this kind of treatment? I don't think so."

"Come on," she said, kissing his ear. "Come on, tell me something else. Tell me something nice."

He turned to kiss her, but she pulled back.

"What do you want me to tell you?"

"Tell me something good. Tell me about your horses."

It was as if, having struck a nerve, she could follow it right in to the next one. In this way she would map his ugly courses and know him straight through. He was appalled and flattered at the same time.

"What do you want to know?"

"What were their names?"

"What were their names. All right. Their names were Bluebell, Dollar, and Enemy."

She laughed. "Those are some weird names."

"Well, Bluebell came already named."

"And the other two?"

"I was young, you know. I thought I was clever. I had a habit of naming things what they weren't. Dollar was a quarter horse, so I named him Dollar. Enemy was a palomino—or Pal for short—so I called him Enemy. Pal, Enemy. You see what I mean."

"You thought that was clever."

"I know," he said. "Like I told you, I was a kid. I just did things like that. We got a calico, and I named her Tabby."

"Well, that's cute."

"Oh, I thought it was a riot. I thought it was the funniest thing. Tabby the calico. Dollar the quarter. I amused myself to no end."

"How did you afford them? The horses."

"Working for my dad. He'd put up the money, and I'd work it off. It's all I ever spent my money on, was those horses."

"Okay," she said, "you've earned it now." She kissed him.

"I think I earned more than that."

She kissed him again but broke off laughing. "Dollar and Enemy?"

He thought about teasing her back. He could say something about Burger, but he didn't trust that one. She was happy now. He said, "Oh, you think you're funny."

She kissed him. "I don't, actually. I've never been funny. I mean, I try, but I can't make people laugh."

"Sure you can. You make me laugh all the time."

"That's different. You just want to make me feel good so I'll kiss you. But other people, all I can do is tell jokes. Bad jokes. I can't just make somebody laugh for no good reason."

"Tell me a joke, then."

"Really? I'm telling you, they're bad."

"I want to hear one."

"Okay." She leaned back and showed him her fist. "Do you know what this is?"

"No, what?"

She thumped him hard on the shoulder.

"Damn, Marie," he said, rubbing it.

She had a confused expression on her face. She looked at her fist, then at him, and said, "Oh, wait. That was the punch line. Let me tell it again."

He grabbed her hand. "Okay, that's it for jokes. Where'd you hear that?"

"I made it up when I was real little. My dad used to let me do it to him."

"He must be tougher than I am."

"I'm sure he is. Plus, I wasn't so big then."

"Well, damn. You keep hitting me tonight."

"Oh, I'm sorry," she said. She kissed his shoulder. "I didn't know you were such a baby."

"Well, I am. I am a baby. Everybody knows that."

She kissed him again.

They stood up at the same time and began walking. They did it without thinking about it or asking each other, and weeks later, when Abe was alone, he would remember this and wonder. The way people tune to each other. The way you can remember things to which you paid scant heed at the time.

Marie said, "He wouldn't always let me tell that joke, though. Sometimes I'd hold it up and say, 'You know what this is?' and he would hold up one finger and say, 'You know what this is?'"

"What was it, his tickle finger?"

"How'd you know?"

"My dad had one of those."

It was darker now, but the evening lingered, the usual prolonged surrender of summer twilight. The sidewalk puddles were harder to see, and earthworms sprawled like dark scribblings on the path. They took to the street. Lights shone through the windows now; after-dinner voices drifted through the screens. You could hear the clatter of dishes on the table, pans being scraped, faucets running. Televisions blared dissonant sound tracks house to house. From one kitchen wafted the smell of fried chicken. From another, something garlicky and burned.

Chapter 10

On the streets and sidewalks of Lockers Creek, the shredded remains of firecrackers lay like red and white confetti. Here and there, the telltale ash smudge of a Black Snake. Empty hulls of Roman candles and fountains stuck in the soft dirt of a yard. Smoke-clouded soda bottles cluttering a ditch, evidence of a late-night bottle-rocket war. All was still. The sun beat down like a reminder of death to come. In the dusty trees even the vireos were quiet. It was too hot to move.

"We probably shouldn't go on a day like this," Abe said. In spite of his calluses he had trouble holding the steering wheel. He alternated hands as he drove. The air conditioner dripped cold water onto Marie's feet but failed to cool the cab. She didn't answer.

He looked at her sunburned face, slack in the heat. Stray hairs frizzed over her brow. "Do you want to skip it?"

"No, I want to go. But don't make me talk anymore. I'm too sleepy and it's too hot."

It was almost noon. When he'd picked her up at Laine's house, Marie had come to the front door on tiptoe, a jug of ice water in hand. Apparently Laine and her parents were still in bed, with hangovers or hiding from the heat, or both. Marie hadn't said a word, only pulled the door quietly shut and walked out with him to his truck.

They'd been together until late the night before, at the holiday barbecue at Laine's house—a long, torpid, pleasant affair. Laine's mother was feeling better than usual and had spent most of the evening in a plastic pool in the shade, drinking the icy sweet salty dogs Mr. Sanders brought her. She sat spraying the water hose out into the sunlight, thumbing the nozzle to make a rainbowed mist for the children to run through. Mr. Sanders had manned the grill while Bill brought him steaks and chicken and hamburger meat. Neighbors drifted in and out of the yard, their children chasing one another with sparklers. It was terrifically hot; the children were the only ones moving around. The adults kept languidly to the carport and the tree shade, only shifting now and then with the breeze, to avoid the grill smoke.

"So I guess Repeat and Gay are through," Abe said. Repeat and Gay had both been at the barbecue, but Gay had kept the grill between them.

Marie looked at him askance.

"Oh, that's right. Sorry. No talking."

He wanted to talk. He had asked her to do this with him, and now he was nervous and wanted to make light of things. But she wasn't giving over to it. She was too serious, or too hot.

He parked on the shoulder just before they got to the new South Fork bridge. The unscarred cement gleamed white in the sun, and the bright metal flashed as they moved toward it. They looked down into the creek. The debris from the old bridge hadn't been entirely cleared away. It lay in the creekbed, clear water running just over it, looking as if it might always have been there, as if someone had made it that way. As if it had never been a bridge at all and should never have been mistaken for one.

Marie stood with her back to him. Abe quit looking at the bridge and looked at her instead. She was wearing hiking boots and cutoffs and a tank top. Dark sunglasses. Hair tied up in a knot to keep it off her neck. In the harsh sunlight her black hair shone with blue overtones. She held the cold water jug against her leg. He looked at the curve of her calves over the boots, her skin glowing with sweat. He wanted to hold her again, to breathe her in. He'd given up trying to figure why he loved her, why it was Marie and no one before her. You could name the reasons, but reasons didn't add up to love. It wasn't reasons; it was being afraid of what the other person could do to you and yet not caring to protect yourself. There wasn't much *why* to love; with love it was mostly *how*. In that way it was just like living.

Marie turned to him expectantly, and Abe quickly stepped past her and scrambled into the gully. At the bottom he waited as she picked her way down, wary of her footing. He was surprised at how slowly she moved, the way she threw out her arms for balance when she felt her foot slip an inch or two. He'd grown up playing in the woods and gave no thought to clambering down a rocky slope. If your foot skidded you went with it, trusting your next step would hold. But Marie fought it, asserting her balance with every step. He'd never seen her so careful. When she got down to him she was clearly relieved.

They followed the creek into the woods, where the air was sticky and smelled of decay. A bed of slick dead leaves carpeted the forest floor, and clumps of green fern spilled over the leaves. Occasionally cool air came off the creek and relieved them for a moment; then it would be insufferably hot again. They made their way through hanging screens of briar and dense, stubborn growths of scrub brush. Toadstools massed over rotting logs. Here and there lay the exposed yellow bones of a fish or bird. The mud marks were waist-high on the tree trunks.

He led the way along the creek. Nothing was as it had been that day. Except for the lingering signs of the flood, the mud marks and detritus, the woods were the same as always. Familiar and calm, the Ouachitas of his boyhood. He tried to imagine them dark and thundering and treacherous. It seemed unlikely even to him. He could picture those dark woods in his mind, but they were a different place entirely. The ditches and gullies, which during the flood had been fast-moving channels, were now damp and still, cluttered with sycamore balls, mucky with moldering brown leaves. He stepped over them almost without thinking.

At a fork in the creek he stopped. He looked down one branch, then the other.

"Which way?" Marie said. She popped open the spout to the water jug and took a long pull.

"I'm not sure yet."

She offered the jug, and he drank from it and poured some over the back of his neck. She jerked it out of his hands. "That's our drinking water. If you want a bath, get down in the creek."

He turned and studied the creek again. Heard her close the spout of the jug, heard the slosh of water and ice as the jug went to her side. After a moment she said, "I'm sorry. I'm just hot and cranky."

"You want to go back?"

She shook her head. "I'm sorry. I mean it."

"The creek water's pretty clean. We can refill the jug."

"It doesn't matter. Please let's drop it."

He nodded and studied the creek again. Along one branch he found a fledgling trail—trampled undergrowth and the prints of tennis shoes and boots in the rotting leaves. He spat into the creek.

"This way," he said.

They followed the trail along the winding creek. The ground was uneven, and Abe was imagining it underwater. Here it would have been shallow. Here too deep to stand. A knoll rising from the water like an island. Ridges like peninsulas of an unseen mainland.

Marie saw the car before he did. He was squinting at a ridge to the west, wondering if it was the one he'd crossed, when she said his name. He stiffened and looked downstream. To his surprise the car sat upright, its tires flattened and its rusting wheels partly buried in dirt that once was mud. With a nauseating snapshot of insight he saw a group of men pushing the car over to get Jackie out from behind it. The old oak towered above the car. Its creekside roots were exposed, gnarled and spidery tendrils trailing down over the mud where the creek had eaten away the bank.

The car had been vandalized. All of its windows had been broken, and glass sprinkled the ground about. Initials had been scratched into the paint with keys. He walked around the car reading them. He thought he recognized some. He had an ugly premonition and decided if he found Kylie's initials he would go to his house tonight. But he didn't, and he felt more disappointed than relieved. He had wanted someone to hit.

There were empty beer cans inside the car. Charred wood and stones on the ground from a campfire. Broken bottles among the ashes. The headlights had been shot out. The crumpled roof sagged like a collapsing tent, but it may have been that way before the vandals got at it. He stood near the front of the car and looked at the tree.

It was just a tree.

Marie walked slowly around the car, then went to the top of the creek bank and looked down at the water and waited. Abe moved downstream, wondering about the jack, whether the sheriff had taken it with him or left it where it lay. He lost his motivation almost as soon as he began and came back without looking for it. He found Marie bent forward at the waist, pulling up her shorts and peering at her legs. She pushed her sunglasses up on her head and bent forward to look again.

"What?" he said.

"Oh God," she said. She sounded sick.

For a moment he thought he'd misread the situation, that she was bending forward to vomit and gripping the hem of her shorts for support. But then she looked up at him with panicked eyes. He'd never seen that look on her face. Goosebumps rose on the back of his neck.

"What!" he said again.

She started swatting at her legs, letting out a frightened moan, and now he suspected a spider. In a sharp tone he told her to hold still. She stopped abruptly, obediently, and let him look. At first he saw nothing. He took his sunglasses off and saw hundreds of tiny dots swarming over her legs. He looked with a sort of amused dread at his own legs.

"Oh, man," he said. "Let's get into the creek."

Marie had already begun to move. "What are they?"

"Seed ticks," he said, leaping down the bank and splashing into the water. He didn't stop to remove his boots or clothes. He waded out into the middle of the creek and squatted until the water ran just beneath his chin. The water was gentle and cool. With some surprise he saw her once again carefully picking her way down the bank, in spite of her panic. He'd expected her to be right behind him. She was moaning, waving her arms for balance as she tried to hurry down the slope without slipping.

"They won't hurt you much," he reassured her. "You just want to get them off now or you'll be picking them off later."

"They're all over me!" she screamed. She reached the creek and plunged in.

Abe was scrubbing his legs under the water. He felt a tickling sensation on his neck and realized with disgust that they were swarming to high ground. He thrust his head under water and wiped frantically at his neck and face. When he came up for breath he said, "Get your head underwater!" But Marie was nowhere to be seen. Her head emerged a few feet away and went under again at once. He caught his breath and let himself down.

In the end they stripped their clothes off over their boots and sat in the creek with the water up to their necks. They were smiling now, laughing at themselves.

"But I'd never seen anything like it before," she said.

"You've never had a tick on you?"

"I've had *ticks* but not like that. Not—what did you call them?"

"Seed ticks."

"Is that the same as chiggers?"

"A chigger is just about any little thing that bites."

"Because I've had chigger bites."

"You can call these chiggers if you want to."

She shivered, thinking about them. "You think they're all drowned by now?"

"Hopefully. We'll know later, that's for sure."

"I hate chigger bites. They itch me for days."

"I've got some stuff to put on them at home."

"Don't look," she said. "I'm getting out."

"Don't look?"

"I'm embarrassed. Don't look."

He closed his eyes until he heard water dripping and then he looked. She stood out of the water, facing upstream, holding her wet clothes against her. He glimpsed white skin where her tan ended. She saw him looking and dropped back under the water. "You sucker!" she yelled, laughing. She splashed water at him.

He looked away. "Sorry. But I don't see why I'm not allowed."

"I feel funny out here like this. I don't know. Now you've got to promise this time."

"I promise."

Taking off her boots, she flung them up to the bank, then wrung out her clothes and waded into shallow water to put them on. Abe listened but didn't watch. Instead he looked up at Jackie's ruined car on the bank. He should be eaten up with shame, but he wasn't. He just gazed at the car and waited for Marie, and then he got out and dressed too.

They looked bedraggled and their wet socks and boots were uncomfortable, but in their damp clothes, at least, they were cooler. They crossed the creek by way of a fallen tree trunk and struck out again. It was easier to talk now. The worst part was behind them, and their moods had improved. They came to the clearing, the first broad and empty field. It was probably a crop field once, he said. They walked through knee-high patches of pale yellow St. Johnswort, and squat spires of mullein, and patches of sticktights that clung to their bootlaces and socks. Abe picked them from the hair on his legs. In some places the ground was bare and damp, but mostly the land was dry, the weeds sun-scorched. Along the western edge of the field a colony of late-blooming daylilies leaned sunward, a fringe of green and orange.

Beyond another stand of trees they found the farmhouse, bigger than Abe remembered it because he saw more of it. A dead building with buckled walls of gray weathered boards. The roof was still cluttered with flotsam, and barn swallows flew in and out through the gaping hole he'd left in it. They crossed the old dead garden, now thick with fleabane and butterflyweed. The doorframe was crooked and sagging. The house smelled of mildew. Abe walked into the room with the hole in the roof. The floor was spattered white and purple with bird droppings. Sunlight streamed in through the hole, swirling with dust motes. Pieces of rotten wood lay about the floor beneath it. He stood on his tiptoes and reached for the hole, could just touch it with his fingertips.

The torn, rotten curtain looked like a dead jellyfish on the floor. Behind it was the open window he could have swum through if he'd been in his right mind. He went into the other rooms. There was nothing in the house but rotted wood and animal scat. In what had once been the kitchen, a brown bat hung upside down against the far wall. Marie had seen it and quickly gone outside, her footsteps booming across the warped floorboards. Abe followed her out.

He found the old road, a lone rusted gatepost leaning precipitously where the gate had once stood. Chicory grew up around the post, the pale blue flowers withering in the sun. The road was overgrown with clover and dandelions. Bumblebees hummed and drifted flower to flower. They followed the old road up to rocky soil, then down again into the slough, a low stretch of marsh spiked with dead timber, the water teeming with skaters and backswimmers. A few minutes later they were at the highway.

The embankment was steep, and descending this time Marie placed a hand on his shoulder to steady herself. Abe felt an unexpected rush of pleasure, as if after all this he had only now been taken into her confidence. They hiked back down the highway. At the bridge they left the truck running to cool down and looked off into the trees while they waited. The jugwater had gone warm. Abe saved a last drink for Marie. She poured it over his head.

"How do you feel now?" she said.

"Wet."

"I mean after seeing the car."

He shook his head. "The same, I guess."

"I'm sorry I was cranky."

"Forget about it."

"I really am, though."

She kissed him, but it was too hot to last.

In Lockers Creek there was still no movement. A single car was parked outside Emma's Café, another outside the grocery. On Main Street something tiny scuttled crablike in front of the car and exploded with a flash and a pop. A gang of small boys appeared cackling and hooting from behind a parked car. Abe hit his brakes so they could see his brake lights flare. They scattered. He smiled and drove on.

At his trailer he brought out a bottle of medicine for their bites. Marie's ankles were already spotted with pink bumps. They sat in the truck with the air conditioner running. He applied the medicine with a dropper. "If there's still chiggers on you," he said, "this kills them. Either way it stops the itching."

"It burns like hell."

"Well, if it felt good, the chiggers would like it."

"What about seed ticks?"

"Seed ticks hate this stuff."

They sat there for a while, considering going inside to the couch. But it was too hot. It was too hot even in the truck. Eventually he drove them over to Laine's house. Laine sat on the front doorstep smoking, and Bill, wearing only shorts, lay snoring in a plastic lawn chair inside the carport. His great hairy chest rose and fell. As they pulled into the driveway Laine gave a little wave with her cigarette hand, then leaned forward again with her elbows on her knees. Bill didn't stir.

"I gotta be at work in twenty minutes," Laine said. Her hair was wet from the shower, but she wore no makeup. She had on an old torn tank top of Bill's, which all but revealed her heavy breasts as she leaned forward.

"How do you feel?" Marie asked.

"Sick. Hot." She stubbed out her cigarette on the cement step. "You kids have fun? I don't see how anyone could stand being out in this heat. What did y'all do, anyway?"

"Just went for a little hike and a swim."

"The swim part sounds okay. Lordy, I can't wait to get to Emma's and have me some coffee."

"I could make you some right now," Marie said.

"We're out."

"Well, why don't we go on in to Emma's and get you a cup? I could go for some iced tea."

"Because that would require her getting off her butt and moving," Bill said from the lawn chair. He didn't sit up or open his eyes.

"Oh great, we woke the beast. He came out here to keep me company and went straight to sleep."

"So do you want to go right now?" Marie asked.

Laine sighed and stood slowly. "I guess. Y'all are both coming?"

Marie looked at Abe.

He shrugged. "Sure. I'm pretty hungry."

"Me too," Bill said.

Laine's voice went shrill. "Well, if you're coming, Bill, you better get your lazy butt out of that chair and put some clothes on. I swear." Bill sat up, scratching his chest. He grinned at them with half-closed eyes.

He was ready before Laine. He went into the house and came out again with a shirt and shoes on, a baseball cap on his head. His eyes were bloodshot, his face puffy. Laine appeared ten minutes later in fresh clothes and makeup. She lit a cigarette on the way to Bill's El Camino and stood smoking it while Bill opened the doors to let the heat escape.

"Y'all riding with us?" he asked.

"Bill, don't be such a igmo. It's too hot."

"We'll come in the truck," Abe said.

"There's room. We could all squeeze in."

"Bill, would you shut up?" Laine said. "You're just trying to aggravate me and you know it." She checked her watch. "And now I'm going to be late."

"Whose fault is that?"

"Yours." She threw down the cigarette and ground it beneath her heel.

There were only two customers at the café, and one was settling his bill. Laine sent the morning waitress home and told the other customer to holler if he needed her. It was only Mr. Ridgeway, the grocer, looking sleepy over his newspaper and pie. She brought them drinks and told them they would have to wait to order their food; she needed her coffee first. Plus another cigarette.

Bill took the order pad from her apron and wrote down his order. She rolled her eyes, but she let him take Marie's and Abe's orders too, then gave him her own. He didn't write hers down.

"You're such an imp," Marie said.

He grinned and carried the orders back to the kitchen.

"He doesn't even know what a imp is. Do you, Bill?" Laine called after him.

"We'll see about that."

The cook was an old friend of Bill's. He sat dozing in front of a fan, listening to the radio. Bill gave him the orders, then washed his hands and stayed in the kitchen to help.

"I swear he can't keep his hands out of anybody's business. He used to work here, way back when. That's how we met, you know."

Marie looked at Abe and smiled. Sadly, he thought. He couldn't guess why. He frowned questioningly, but she turned to Laine again. "Y'all are so good together," she said.

Laine perked up. "You think so?"

"You're just right for each other."

"Well, he's just a big sweetie-pie," Laine said, beaming.

They lingered over their meals, all of them weary and reluctant to rise. Bill had trouble staying awake. A few customers came in, and Laine waited on them and returned to the table. It was wonderfully cool in the café. They drank a pot of coffee and a pitcher of iced tea. Abe and Bill each had two pieces of pie.

In the bathroom Abe studied himself in the mirror. Marie kept looking at him oddly, and he didn't know why. His hair was wild and his eyes bloodshot, but no more so than the others. He checked his teeth. When he came back out she was standing, preparing to leave. He pitched in more than his share to cover the bill. Laine argued briefly with him, then gave up. No one had the energy to figure the tab.

On the way back to Laine's house, Marie was quiet. Abe walked her to the front door. She was driving back to Hot Springs now and had to gather her things. Abe had thought he would come along with her, but she hadn't mentioned it yet.

"Well," he said, waiting to see.

She stood facing him on the low cement step. The added inches made them the same height. She was gazing at him just as she had in the café. A sad, searching look. His stomach tightened. She kissed him. Her arms went around his shoulders and pulled him to her. Her teeth hurt his lips. She was pressing hard—not a deep kiss, but a passionate, furious one. He held her tightly about the waist and felt his heart thumping.

Something had changed.

She pulled back, her hands trailing away from his shoulders. Reluctantly he let go of her. He half-expected her eyes to be wet with tears, but they were clear as ever. Unconsciously she lifted one foot and scratched at her other ankle with it, and he was reminded of the night he'd met her.

She said, "You'd better not call me anymore, Abe."

He blinked. "What?"

"You can't call me anymore. We have to stop."

"Am I missing something? I thought we— "

"No," she said, shaking her head.

"Is it something— "

She looked squarely at him. "It's nothing."

"I shouldn't have taken you out there," he said, with unexpected bitterness. He felt suddenly accused. He ought to have been more ashamed, he thought. It ought to have been different somehow.

"It's not that."

"Listen," he said, flustered. "Listen."

"I'm not arguing it with you. I can't."

"Damn it, Marie— "

She turned to go inside. He made a feckless attempt to catch her wrist, but his hand seemed disconnected from his body. He wasn't sure if he'd even touched her. The screen door groaned as she opened it. He was looking at her back.

"Marie, wait."

He heard her speak, but it wasn't to him. Laine's parents were in the kitchen, and she was greeting them as she went in. She closed the interior door behind her without looking back. Abe stood at the step, listening to the murmur of voices. He couldn't make out what they said, but he knew Marie's voice. It sounded cheerful and easy.

He walked to his truck, squinting in the terrible sunlight. Sweat stung his eyes; he wiped them with a sweaty hand. His hair felt like a wool scarf against the back of his neck. His T-shirt clung to him. He took his sunglasses from the dashboard and felt the plastic burn the bridge of his nose.

Later he read in the paper that this was the hottest day in years.

Chapter 11

Vincent was a chess player of the sort Marie imagined to belong to chess clubs: quiet, serious, and still, with hardly a change of expression as the game played its course. He wore a starched white shirt and a string tie, his gray hair impeccably styled, his red cheeks clean-shaven. In his aunt's antique chair he sat erect, unhurried, unperturbed by the goings-on around him, leaning forward only when his turn came. Otherwise he was absolutely still save for the occasional graceful sip of his sweet tea.

Marie's father, on the other hand, was of the country school. He whistled when Vincent made an unexpected move, rubbed his temple as he considered the board, looked distractedly about the room when his turn had passed. Marie brought a pitcher of tea and refilled the men's glasses. Without taking his eyes from the board, Vincent picked a sugar cube from the bowl at his elbow and stirred it into his glass.

She stood next to her father. "How are you doing?"

"I'm giving him trouble this time."

"Is that right, Vincent?"

Vincent's eyes rose from the board. He was a studious player but not one to be annoyed by interruption. He smiled. "To say the least. As you can see, he's hounding my queen, which rather arrogantly I brought out too early. And even when I move thus"—he interposed a knight—"I'm still in hot water."

Her father was nodding, puckering his lips. "That's what I'd have done, too."

"Well," she said, "may the best man win."

"Oh no," Vincent said, winking at her. "Don't say that."

In the kitchen Mrs. Baker was directing Angela what to pull from the cupboards. As soon as the sun set behind the trees across Lake Hamilton, taking the worst of the heat with it, they were heading out on a pontoon-boat picnic. Angela held up each item, debating with her mother whether it was worth bringing. Sardines? Of course sardines. Sweet pickles? Well, did Marie think she and her father might eat some? Yes? Okay, bring them. Vienna sausages? How on earth did those things even get into her cupboards? Vincent must have bought them; bring them along, then, he would eat them.

Marie had wanted to help, but the kitchen was tiny, and three people were too many. She stood in the doorway with the pitcher until Angela noticed and took it from her; then she drifted around Mrs. Baker's modest condominium—a comfortable, clean place with cluttered walls but empty rooms, and excellent views of the lake. The shelves and walls were covered with framed pictures of youthful Vincents and Angelas, as well as dozens of other nephews and nieces and grandchildren. Marie studied in particular the photos of Angela as a young woman. Her hair had been blond then, but she seemed otherwise unchanged. Her husband had been a stocky, belligerent-looking fellow who wouldn't smile for the camera.

Then she saw her mother. At first she was confused—she thought she was seeing her own face on Mrs. Baker's wall. But leaning closer, she saw who it was. An old photo, from the early seventies, the colors gone pinkish over the years. Her mother sat among other women in a trailer full of hay, with a smiling toddler—it must have been Marie herself—tucked between her knees. A church outing, a Halloween hayride. All the women had children in their laps with blankets tucked around them. She scanned the faces. Angela sat in the back, her face half-obscured by a woman next to her—Mrs. Baker, Marie realized after a moment. A woman in her early sixties then, cradling a grandchild. Marie's eyes returned to her mother. A pretty woman, though not strikingly so, not as she remembered her. Her hair windblown, her cheeks ruddy with cold. She wasn't smiling, but she seemed at ease, hands resting lightly on Marie's shoulders. The toddler could have been anyone's; at that age she looked like no one in particular. Round cheeks, eyes watery from the wind, bright red ear-muffs and scarf. Holding up one mittened fistful of hay. Marie had no memory of it.

Moving away from the photo—not wanting to be caught staring at it, not wanting to discuss it with anyone—she glanced back and was fooled, once again, into seeing not her mother's face but her own. She remembered meeting Angela on the day after the flood, how startled she'd been by Marie's appearance. Now Marie knew what had surprised her, the same shock of false recognition that had shaken her father when Marie arrived on his doorstep. Angela had thought Marie was her mother, stepping right out of the past, still in the full bloom of youth.

She went back into the living room and watched her father lose the chess game, a prolonged affair in which he tried unsuccessfully for a stalemate. They began another game. Before it was over the women had driven down to the pontoon boat—the party barge, as they called it—and loaded the deck with the ice chests and folding chairs. They came back sweating. Mrs. Baker said they would leave the ice chests for the men to carry, but Marie frowned and hauled the largest one out to the car.

Mrs. Baker said, "Honey, I didn't mean you weren't strong enough. I just wanted the men to think they were good for something."

Marie laughed, but she felt protective of her father. He had, after all, rented the boat—first making certain its carpeted floor would provide good footing for Mrs. Baker—and driven it over here from the marina in the heat of the day. And it would be her father who returned it after dark and paid for the gas and drove back by himself, while the others had only to mount the steps to the comfortable condo. She went in to watch the end of the chess game. Her father looked up good-naturedly and said, "You girls picking on us men again?" He'd heard them, of course, and of course he didn't care. He was enjoying himself immensely.

"Check," said Vincent.

"I figured as much," her father said.

It was a hot, windless evening, and the lake was calm, most of the boats having gone in for the day. They droned across the water in search of the perfect cove, her father at the wheel. The sun lay just behind the trees on the far shore; the high condominium windows on the near shore glowed blush-red with its reflection. Her father took them under the Highway 70 bridges toward a quieter part of the lake, where the shoreline was rocky and uninhabited and pine woods grew up on both sides. He knew the lake, had fished it for years, and he drove for some time, eschewing the popular ski coves. No one was in any hurry to stop. Cutting across the water there was just enough breeze to keep the heat off. They rode with lifted faces, like people who expected something.

Eventually they headed into a deep, open cove. They went around two bends, with the cove narrowing and pine and oak woods on either side. At the back of the cove three cows stood upon a grassy hill, looking toward their boat as it rounded the last bend, as if they'd been waiting for it. When her father killed the motor they went back to their grazing.

"Somebody better call those cows home," Mrs. Baker said.

"I doubt they need to be called, Aunt Catherine," said Vincent.

"Maybe they don't have a home," said Marie.

At this suggestion Vincent's eyes widened. He seemed delighted. "You think they're feral? Jimmy, what's your opinion? Are these cows feral?"

"They do have that wild cow look about them."

"Gracious, Jimmy," Mrs. Baker said, "don't let us drift too close."

Everyone was smiling now, including Marie, who realized her serious suggestion had been taken for a joke. At least it hadn't gone the other way. If they'd understood her, she would have been the joke herself.

Marie's father heaved the cinder-block anchor overboard; the nylon rope zipped over the pontoon as the anchor took it down; and then all was suddenly still. It seemed incongruous—the dramatic arrival of peacefulness—and for a moment no one moved or spoke, everyone reluctant to disturb the new silence. Crickets chirred in the woods and in the field beyond the hill, but around here cricketsong was taken for quiet. A lone pine warbler sent its lazy trill over the cove. You could hear the cows tearing up grass with their teeth.

Marie thought of Abe, of the Simmons cows he'd told her sometimes greeted him in the morning. It had been funny, the way he'd told it, though she couldn't remember why. She only remembered laughing.

She hadn't seen him for weeks. He'd called three nights in a row, from a pay phone somewhere, but after the first time she'd told her father she didn't want to talk to him, and after the third night he stopped trying. Which was of course what she'd told him to do but wished she hadn't. She felt it bitterly that he'd stopped trying.

There had been one night, though, very late, when she woke up thinking she'd heard a car door in the driveway. She lay in bed waiting for a knock. Her father was in the living room, watching a late-night monster movie with Angela, a more and more frequent occurrence these days. She could hear violins and an old man's frightened voice. There was no knock, so she went to the window and peered out. Abe's truck sat beneath the magnolia down at the end of the driveway. Abe was nowhere to be seen. He must be at the door, she thought, and she decided right then that if her father didn't turn him away, she would see him—let fate take it out of her hands. As she looked out the window she became aware of her uneven breathing, the flutter of anticipation in her chest.

He didn't knock. After a while she grew sleepy, and half-dozed at the window. She started awake when she realized she'd been dreaming. Abe had come in through the window. She hadn't tried to turn him away. They were together in her bed. Then they were arguing in the yard, and he was crying. She felt profoundly angry. When she came out of the dream her heart was hammering. She looked out at the truck. It sat as before in the dark, in the streetlight-shadow of the magnolia tree. A minute later the engine came to life and the headlights switched on, surprising her. She hadn't realized he was in the truck. The sound of the door closing must have come after he got back into it. How long had he been there, then? He'd stood at her window, and she'd not realized it. Or he'd gone to the door after all, trying to find the courage to knock. Or not to knock, to leave without shaming himself.

At any rate, he hadn't knocked. Maybe he'd never even stepped out of his truck, had only opened the door, considered, shut it again. Maybe he'd hoped she would hear it and would come out to find him. Maybe he'd seen her, after all, peering through the window at him as if at some lurking stranger.

She went back to bed and lay awake, imagining him there with her. It was good he'd gone. She fell asleep and dreamed again of him there with her—a lovely dream this time, the kind of dream in which nothing occurs to you, you simply inhabit it—and awoke in the morning resenting that it was only a dream. Since then, as far as she knew, he hadn't come back.

Dusk was growing heavier on the lake, the reflections of the trees dark and deep on the glassy water. A dragonfly buzzed by the boat, moving in a perfect lateral over the surface, disappearing lakeward. A fish splashed near the shore, and her father looked longingly in that direction, perhaps wishing he had a rod and reel.

"Well," he said at last, "how about some light?"

With the flip of a switch their faces were all illumined, pale and startled, by several large bulbs strung about the boat. They squinted in the sudden light and laughed at their own surprised expressions. Angela turned on the radio and opened the ice chests. The drinks were so cold they hurt your teeth. Marie's first sip brought a skim of ice to her lips.

Vincent had brought along his chess set, and he challenged Marie's father to another game. Her father deferred to Marie, claiming that his brain needed a rest.

"Do you play?" Vincent asked her.

"I know how, but I'm not real good."

"Set up the board, then, and we'll practice."

She set it up while Vincent drained the juice from his Vienna sausages into the lake and arranged them with crackers on a paper plate. The chess set was of a soft pink and gray marble. The figures, angular and simple, had blunt faces etched deeply into the stone. The queens were tall, ragged obelisks, easily tipped, and she noticed Vincent was always sure of his move before he reached, careful not to scatter the pieces. Despite his graceful figure, Vincent's hands, like those of his old aunt, were given to trembling. Marie wondered if perhaps his caution and not his manners was why he sat so still.

She liked Vincent, of whom she'd been seeing a good deal lately, along with the others. He had a wistfulness about him that left her reflective and slightly sad. He alluded occasionally, slyly, to his "iniquitous youth," but he wore no wedding ring, and no one ever spoke of any wife or girlfriend. She felt a certain affinity for him. He appeared to regard his life—not quite bitterly, but with bitter humor—as one that had developed in spite of something. Had he, like herself, made choices that seemed necessary one moment, random the next? Had he ever suffered from the inability to consistently pretend? If he had, there was scant indication of it now, and she envied his poise.

They played a long game, Vincent giving her several opportunities to retract her moves. He was complimentary, remarking more than once on what a quick study she was, but every few moves he would raise a finger and say, "Are you sure, honey?" and Marie would study the board again. It bothered her the game couldn't be fair that way, couldn't be real. Yet it pleased her to have all those second chances, and so she let Vincent let her have them. The Baker women were chatting with her father at the front of the boat, loading up on sandwiches and pickles and laughing lightly. From time to time she glanced over to see the way Angela patted her father's arm.

No one noticed when the cows went home. Darkness had fallen. A gibbous moon had come up over the trees, and a gentle breeze rose, rippling the moon's reflection on the water. They sat indolently about the boat, satiated and drowsy. Vincent moved to sit by his aunt. He'd said hardly a word all evening. Marie had seen him turn silently in his chair to watch the moon rise over the trees, ponderous and bright.

At Mrs. Baker's request, Angela had brought along her guitar, and she strummed it now with her thumb, forgoing a pick in favor of a softer sound. She was not a talented guitarist, but she played well enough, changing chords fluidly and surely, and she sang wonderfully. Her voice, so clear and bright, reminded Marie of silver bells. It wasn't the kind of voice that made you love music; it was the kind of voice that made you love the singer.

Somehow Marie managed both to resent Angela's power and to fall under its spell. As she sat politely listening, trying not to appear charmed, she had a sudden wry insight, and what was more, it came to her in Abe's voice. She heard him clearly: That's one of your special gifts. Not everyone can like a person and resent liking them at the same time.

Angela was choosing songs she thought they would all know, folk ballads and gospel songs, but nobody wanted to sing along. They only wanted to listen. After a while, though, Mrs. Baker roused Vincent from his reverie and persuaded him to sing a duet. Dutifully he agreed. They sang together with Vincent standing beside and just behind Angela, his hand resting lightly upon her shoulder. He sang exactly as Marie had thought he would, softly, but with a good deal of vibrato. His face was less composed than usual, his eyes unfocused and lost to the present. Their harmony was perfect. Occasionally Angela looked up at him and smiled. They were singing a slow gospel song:

Looking homeward, looking homeward
It's not far away
It's just the other side of the river

Her father listened with his eyes closed. Marie wanted to change seats and move closer to him, but it might be disrespectful to get up while they were singing. She looked away. Mrs. Baker was tapping her foot soundlessly, not quite in time with the music, but perhaps in perfect time as she heard it. It was a song to make you ache. It was a song to break your heart. When it was finished, Angela strummed the last chord slowly, almost reluctantly, and smiled up at Vincent. He squeezed her shoulder and nodded.

"That was just lovely," Mrs. Baker said after a pause.

"It sure was," said her father. "Wasn't that pretty, Marie?"

Marie's heart was throbbing. She said, "Yes, it was real pretty," and then, abruptly, she stood and said, "If y'all don't mind, I think I might take a little swim before we go back. The water looks so nice."

Her father's eyebrows came together, ever so slightly, and she knew she'd been rude. Too abrupt. Her throat tightened with embarrassment. Now she wanted off the boat even more.

"Oh, Marie! Aren't you afraid?" Angela cried. "It's dark. You couldn't pay me to get in that water."

"You better hope a snake doesn't get you," Mrs. Baker said. "Jimmy, don't you let her go swimming out in this."

Her father laughed. "If a snake got after Marie, it's the snake I'd be worried about."

She went to the back of the boat and stripped to her bathing suit, her stomach roiling with shame. What was wrong with her? Didn't she even know how to sit still when she was supposed to? Well, it didn't matter, she told herself. Who cared? No, really, who gave a flying shit? She lowered herself into the warm water.

"Don't sit down," Mrs. Baker was saying. "Sing it again."

"Oh no, Mother, not twice."

Marie's father said, "Yes, why don't y'all sing that again? It's beautiful."

"What do you think?" Angela said to Vincent.

"I believe I have my part down now."

Marie pulled away from the boat with a steady backstroke. She swam until she neared the first bend, oriented herself, and swam again. The sound of Vincent and Angela's voices drifted across the water, following her out.

Looking homeward, looking homeward
I've not long to stay
It's just the other side of the water

She swam a long way, coming out of the cove into the open lake, the moon shining directly above her. The stars seemed dim and tiny in comparison. She let her legs down, treading water. Far across the lake she saw the running lights of a single boat, green and red, bobbing over the water. She heard no motor, no sound but her own breathing and the indistinct strains of music from deep inside the cove.

The dark side of the moon was just visible. She imagined it cold as deep water. Quiet and cold and empty. She wondered how deep the water was beneath her now. Sixty feet? Seventy? The fish down there moving blindly about, living small and silent lives. The breeze passed over the water. If she turned her head a certain way she could hear it, a fluttering against her ear. A slight turn of her head and it was gone. She was out here in the deep water, pure black nothingness beneath her.

She might have seen it coming, but she didn't. She didn't see it and so couldn't stop it, and in a moment it all came up in her, rising like bile in her throat. The sudden and perfect despair. This isn't you, she thought. None of it is, and it never was. She let herself think it—it was such a relief just to let herself think it. Despair the unexpected comfort. No, there isn't any you, and there never was.

She exhaled, drew her feet together, and raised her arms above her head. She sank quickly, with her eyes open. Knifing down into utter blackness. The water went cold. Her ears popped. She swallowed instinctively against the pressure. She had no sense of movement but felt the pressure in her ears, the sharp cold of the deepening water. She must be very deep. She cast her eyes upward and saw nothing. There was no sound but her heartbeat and a keening in her ears.

She was excited only for a moment. Then she was afraid.

It's too late, she thought. She kicked, thought she felt her foot brush something, kicked wildly again, and brought her arms down, began to swim. She felt a burning deep at the back of her throat. It's too late, she thought again. She could feel her body through and through, her lungs flat and empty, the black cold water all around; and she was thin, insubstantial, a husk. She thought she must still be sinking despite her efforts.

Her pulse thundered in her ears. Her arms came down again, and she saw a shimmer of white, far away above her. That would be the moon. The water was getting warmer.

She broke the surface.

"Oh, Jesus," she gasped. "Oh God. Oh God."

She was lightheaded, but she knew where she was. She was up in the breeze again. She gulped it in, her eyes fixed on the moon as if it were the moon that had brought her up and kept her afloat. She gulped the breeze and the whole night sky too. The moon and the deep stars, she breathed it all in.

She lay back in the water and floated, letting her breath even out. Her ears were underwater, and she could hear her pounding heartbeat slow to a steady pulse. The moon hung in the sky just as brilliant as before, the stars around it just as dim. It seemed as if much time had passed, and the world should have changed. But nothing had changed. When she brought her head up, the breeze fluttered in her ears.

"Okay," she whispered to herself.

Her mind was clear of everything now, everything but the sweetness of air. The water was silky and warm. She swam back into the cove. She was all right. She had plenty of strength left. Her breath had returned. As she rounded the first bend, she cut close to the bank. If she wanted, she could even walk in the shallows, follow the shoreline until she reached the back of the cove. But she was feeling better now. She had only taken a swim, and the swim was fine. She imagined herself telling the others, It was a fine night to swim.

She heard singing again. A man's voice, but it wasn't Vincent's. Her father. The guitar sounded different too. So he was playing for himself. Strumming a bit clumsily, years out of practice. She paused and treaded water for a moment, listening. It was a song she recognized, a playful, waltzy tune he'd sung to her when she was very young, whenever she'd visited him.

The girl told the farmer that their love was a plum
The boy didn't follow, for the boy was quite . . . deaf
So the girl wrote it down, and the girl wrote it slow
How a plum needed hard ground and hot sun to . . . flourish
Hard ground and hot sun and a whole lot of rain

She swam again, as quietly as she could, trying to listen. She could hear the others chuckling. Maybe they'd never heard it. Her father pausing dramatically at all the right moments, before the unrealized rhymes. He didn't have a good voice, but he had the timing.

The boy didn't speak, for the boy was quite mute
But he wrote down, "I see now that our love is a . . . plum
Our love is a plum, ain't it sweet?"

The boat was unexpectedly bright as she rounded the final bend. She'd forgotten how strong the bulbs were. Moths thumping fuzzily against them. The people on the boat sitting about, laughing, tapping their hands against their legs. Her father half-standing, guitar propped on his thigh. He peered out in her direction as if he might have sensed her there, but he couldn't see her for the lights. He sang cheerfully:

Our love is a plum, good enough to grow
Our love is a plum, ain't it sweet?
Ain't it sweet, ain't it sweet, ain't it so?

Chapter 12

That evening, after he'd seen Marie at the bookstore and spent the drive back regretting it, Abe bought a tin of coffee at the Phillips 66 and asked for his change in quarters. For a long time he stood sweating, in the humid dusk, at the parking lot pay phone, trying to find the strength not to call her. It helped that he could think of no good excuse for calling. He considered dialing her and hanging up. In the end he swore at himself and dumped the quarters in his dashboard ash tray.

By the time he got home his resolve had disintegrated, and he went into the spare room, hugging the walls to avoid the sagging, rotten part of the floor, and retrieved his phone. Shortly after Jackie's funeral he had disconnected it in a fit of fury, or something like fury, and smashed it against the wall. Later he'd thrown it into this room, where he wouldn't trip over it and be reminded of his tantrum. Now he plugged it in, hopefully. There were pieces of plastic broken off, but maybe it would work.

It didn't. He took the receiver apart and put it back together again, the plastic growing slippery with his sweat. He hadn't turned on the fans yet. The phone was dead. He smashed it against the floor. It made a single muted ding, like a desk bell. He threw it back into the spare room and slammed the door.

He took his shower, baked his chicken pot pie in the microwave, brewed his coffee. Broke open the crust of the pot pie to let the steam escape and, while it was cooling, went to the new stack of books on the floor by his bookshelf. He'd gone into Hot Springs for cortisone shots in his knees and afterward had dropped by Hamilton Books. He'd had the idea for some time, but the act itself was impulsive; he hadn't meant to go. Now he wished he hadn't. Marie had looked distressed, even alarmed, when he came in. At the sight of her face, his hopes had soured. He'd made small talk—Hello, how are you, I'm fine, and you?—gathered up some books, and left. There were other customers in the store; she was talking to someone else even as she rang him up.

Now he read feverishly. He dug in. It was as it had always been. He retreated into his trailer and read. Only now he was even better at it. He was a machine, a muscle. When he glanced at the clock the hour hand seemed to jump. The heft of his books shifted smoothly from right to left, like water poured from a pitcher, and his mind filled up. In the early hours, he closed his eyes. He dreamed he stood up to turn off the light, but when he opened his eyes it was still bright in the room. He went back to his book, then back to sleep.

In the morning he woke himself shouting, jerking and flailing his arms, banging a hand on the coffee table and upsetting the cold coffee. It streamed across the table and over the edge. The empty cup lolled back and forth on the table. He gritted his teeth and got to his feet. His knees felt great now, almost like new, but his back was killing him. You lost one pain only to notice the other. Still, it was better to be awake than dreaming.

He let the shower run scalding hot on his back and placed his cheek against the cool plastic wall to help himself bear it, standing there until the hot water ran out. Steam swirled against the ceiling, the mirror fogged. At the sink he splashed cold water onto his face, bending forward carefully to test his back. It was relaxed, warm. He could tell where the pain came from, but the pain was gone.

Thirteen hours later he was reading again. He'd finished two books the night before and had started a third. At midnight he baked another pot pie, made fresh coffee. He stepped out onto the porch and called for Tabby. She didn't appear. Lucky had fallen asleep on the couch. A night wind rustled the poplar leaves, blowing his hair into his face. Through the screen of trees he saw the last light go off at Simmons's house. The clouds smoking across the moon. The whip-poor-will doing its number in the woods across the pasture.

The rain came soon after. It drummed on the roof, and he could smell it through the screen. He kept reading. After a while he heard Tabby yowl outside the door. He let her in, and she sat inside the door licking herself. She was dripping wet and looked like something just disgorged or birthed. When she was done cleaning herself she looked no better. She curled up under the coffee table and was soon snoring. Lucky jumped down from the couch and sniffed her. She didn't wake, and he lay down with his back pressed against hers and fell asleep. When thunder sounded in the distance their ears swiveled, but neither cat stirred.

It was after three when Abe finished the book. He fell asleep on the couch with the rain still pouring outside. Tabby wheezing in her sleep under the coffee table. Thunder grumbling in the hills. Barbed wire fence singing shrill notes in the wind.

The next day it was still coming down, so no roof work, and Abe went into Hot Springs again—berating himself all the way but not turning around—to roam the aisles of Hamilton Books. Literature, history, sociology. He carried a box with him. In the philosophy section he picked up several books and looked at them. If he could understand the first page, he bought the book. Plato he bought; Aristotle went back onto the shelf. Most of them went back onto the shelf. He moved on to the poetry section. When the box was full he toted the books to the register.

Marie was waiting for him, looking friendlier this time, but circumspect. He had nodded upon entering and said nothing. She'd been with a customer. Now they were alone.

"What have you been doing with yourself?" she said.

"Breaking things, mostly."

She frowned. "You look terrible."

"Thanks. I just want to buy these books."

"You look like you got left out in the rain overnight."

"I haven't been sleeping well."

She studied his face. "Well," she said, almost tenderly, "at least the scratches have all healed up."

"Yeah, I'm fit as a fiddle. Even got cortisone shots in my knees. Apparently my knees are twenty years older than the rest of me."

"Do they feel better? I mean after the shots."

"They feel pretty good, actually."

"That's good."

"I just want to buy these books."

"Okay," she said. She looked in the box. "All of them?"

"I'm doing a lot of reading these days."

She rang him up. She was drinking a cup of coffee, and Abe saw her eyes go to the coffee pot more than once. Considering offering him a cup. He watched her. She didn't look so good herself, her eyes puffy, no make-up, hair in a badly drawn ponytail. It might be one of her bad days.

"I'm giving you a discount," she said.

"You don't have to do that."

"You buy that many books, you get a discount."

"All righty."

She didn't offer him coffee. He waited a minute, then took the box with a nod and moved toward the door.

"Take care," she said after him.

"I'll see you."

He got home to a letter from Jim Townsend. It lay on his porch, along with his utility bill, in a plastic newspaper sleeve to keep the rain out. There was a note in the sleeve too, from Maggie Hearns, the old postmistress, that told him from now on he ought to stop by the post office and pick up his own mail, that these things had been there for three days and she shouldn't have to send her boy out delivering them over God's creation, he had his own work to do, but she figured he'd want these ones particularly and he could just stop by and thank her at his earliest convenience, it'd do him some good to see live people for a change.

Abe took the letter inside and sat down, turning it over two or three times without reading a word. It was written longhand in Jim's incomparably neat script. Finally he settled to read it:

Abe—

Thanks for your long letters. I'm well enough. You know I don't like being worried about, though, so you can stop it. Don't even hint it as you do. I'm well enough. Though you know I don't believe this kind of thing, in a way it has all seemed fated. I was there to lend some backbone to my mother when she lost my father, and now I'm here to do the same for him. As it turns out, he needs it worse. I do nothing but sit around with him, but he seems to need that. It's over for him with the girlfriend, by the way. I don't suppose she cottoned to his grieving so much for my mother. She was a *chica plastica*, anyway, as Roberto would say, and I, at least, won't miss seeing her. So we're living like a couple of desperate bachelors in Florida, sad bastards the both of us, and despite all the bad reasons for it, it's not so bad.

Not much to tell otherwise. The job is a sinecure as expected. I have met a guy here with a guitar and a ginger voice and I've been accompanying him late nights at a local club called New Blues. All I do is sit on the stool and play. When I leave, I'm sweating gin and breathing smoke and I don't know where the night went, and that has suited me fine. It's not quite a life, but it's living.

As for you, in your letters you have written at great length about very little. This is how I know you're worrying. You used to be reckless and that was better. Don't be careful with me. I've been glad to hear from you, but I don't want letters from someone I don't know.

That was an irritable thing to say; I'm sorry.

Now that I've been irritable I guess I owe you something, so I will say just this: I have bad days but I don't want to talk about them. Seems like it would cheapen them somehow. And if I talked about them and then felt better I would just be disgusted with myself. So now you know how I'm going about it. Probably I'm wrong about this, but I've been satisfied being wrong all these years, and why would I want to change?

Anyway, you should see me now; I have what might almost pass for a tan. My father takes me golfing with him. This is mostly what he pays me for, Abe—you can see the kind of pressure I'm under. I mean, golf: it's hard for me to say the word and keep a straight face. I just hack away like a mad butcher, much to his alarm, but really I've been getting a hell of a lot out of it. We're really just a couple of sad bastards, golfing away.

Jim

Later that week, Repeat and Roberto came out to the trailer. Abe heard the Camaro's engine and stepped outside to meet them. As they walked to the porch, grasshoppers arced away from their feet, buzzing. It was not quite dark. Repeat finished an apple and pitched the core over the barbed wire fence into the pasture. Abe watched it go. Grasshoppers flew up where it hit.

"Pitt," Repeat called, in his usual warble, "we came to check on you."

"Well, here I am."

They mounted the steps and stood with him on the porch.

"How you doing, man?" Roberto said.

"In the hour since I saw you?"

"He means in general," Repeat said. "Nobody's seen you around much. If you weren't going to work every day, people'd think you got killed or something."

"But I do go to work every day. So what do people think?"

"They don't know *what* to think."

"I've just been reading, is all."

"Reading?"

"You know—books?"

"Hey, you need a haircut," Roberto said.

Abe laughed until his eyes watered. His friends were looking at each other. He got control of himself and said, "That's one sentence I never thought I'd hear you say, Roberto."

"Well, it's true, man. You looking raggy."

"Why didn't you tell me sooner?"

"Point is," Repeat said, "you haven't been the same since your accident. We thought you were getting better, but then you backslid or something. You've turned into a social brown recluse."

"I've turned into a spider?"

"A spider. What the hell you talking about?"

"Maybe you meant to say I'm a social recluse. Or just a recluse."

"Whatever the hell it is. You know what I mean. Anyway, I think what the trouble is—"

"There's trouble?"

"Hell, yeah, there's trouble, Pitt. And what I think it is, is all this reading. You spend too much time *thinking* about things. You know? Life isn't about thinking, it's about doing. You got to be *doing* shit, not thinking about it."

"Thinking is doing something."

"No, it isn't. Not the same."

"Are you sure?"

"Pitt, do you see me laying around thinking when I could be out doing something? No. You don't. That's what I'm talking about."

"I get what you're saying. You run track, you go to school, you go to parties, you have a girlfriend. Next year you're going to finish up and get a coaching job."

"Exactly," Repeat said. "I'm *doing* something."

"So what do you think I should do? Other than get a haircut," he added, looking at Roberto.

"I mean it, man," Roberto said. "You need one."

"But other than that?"

"Other than that," Repeat said, "just anything. Anything except laying around on your butt. You need like a hobby. Or maybe you ought to go back to college."

"I wasn't very good at college."

Repeat looked disgusted. "Are you even listening? You think you got to be good at a thing to do it? If you like something, Pitt, *do* it. And do your best, for crying out loud, but you don't have to be perfect at it. Just do something."

"Just do something."

"Damn straight," Repeat said, and Roberto nodded.

"What's your something?" Abe asked Roberto. "I mean, what is it you're doing?"

"That ain't the point."

"I'm just wondering."

"Well, I ain't laying around in a hot trailer reading."

"Fair enough. Listen, guys, I appreciate y'all coming out here. I know you're just worried, is all."

"That's all it is, Pitt."

"Yeah, man, we just worrying about you."

"Well, I'll think about what you said."

"You do that," Repeat said.

"I will. I'll give it some thought. Now can I offer y'all a Coke or something?"

"No, man," Roberto said. "We going to a party in Hot Springs. You want to come?"

"Not tonight, thanks."

"You sure?" Repeat said, but Abe sensed he really didn't want him to come. Which was strange, considering the speech.

"Next time."

"Okay," Roberto said, clapping him on the shoulder and heading down the steps.

"I'll be there in a minute," Repeat said. "I need to discuss something with Pitt."

They watched Roberto walk through the grasshoppers.

"You have something to discuss with me?"

Repeat sighed, crossing his arms. His biceps twitched. He looked as reluctant as he ever looked. "Yeah. Listen. It's no big deal, but I wanted you to hear it from me and not somebody else."

"Okay."

"Me and Marie's started going out."

"You and who?"

"Marie Hamil—whoa, buddy!" He dodged Abe's swing and shoved him back against the screen door. Abe whirled, but Repeat jumped the railing and stood in the yard. He held his hands out soothingly.

"Calm down, bud. You got no right to be mad. I just wanted you to know."

Abe was coming down the steps. "No right?"

"Y'all had already quit going out. Now, just hold off, Pitt. I don't want to fight you."

Abe charged him. Repeat danced aside and clipped him in the jaw. He went sprawling. Grasshoppers came up in a little cloud around him. One of them got crushed under the palm of his hand, and it stuck to his skin, bloody and mangled and twitching. He wiped it off in the grass and climbed to his feet, feeling a twinge in his back.

Roberto, leaning casually against the car, said, "What's going on? You guys playing around?"

"I'm sorry I hit you, bud," Repeat said, nursing his fist. "Let's just cool off, okay?" He stood warily, poised, ready for another charge.

Abe walked past him toward his truck.

"Where you going? Listen, don't run off mad. Come on. We're friends. You think this shit is important? It isn't important. I just wanted—"

Abe got the tire iron from his truck and turned around.

"*Shit*, man," Repeat said, taking a few steps back. "You don't want to hit me with that."

"What you doing with that, Pitt?" Roberto asked.

Abe walked toward the Camaro. Roberto, puzzled but unflappable, watched him approach. Abe heard Repeat coming up from behind. He spun, wielding the tire iron, and Repeat backed away.

"Pitt," he said. "You don't want to hurt anybody."

He gave Repeat a matter-of-fact look as he smashed out the right headlight.

"Damn, Pitt!" Repeat cried, his voice splitting. "Stop that!"

"That ain't right, man," Roberto said, shaking his head. "You ain't hitting the car, are you?"

Abe held Repeat at bay with the tire iron and went to the other headlight and smashed it too. They kept up a little dance, Repeat charging and retreating, charging and retreating. Abe went around to the back.

"At least he's just doing the lights," Roberto said. "He ain't touching the paint. What's a matter, Pitt? Why you breaking his car?"

Abe smashed out the first taillight and heard Repeat running up again. He turned, bracing himself, but Repeat had jumped into the driver's seat. The engine fired and the wheels spewed gravel. Abe leaped away. On the other side of the car Roberto did the same. The car tore down the driveway in reverse.

"How am I supposed to get home?" Roberto said, looking after him. "You giving me a ride or what? What the hell?"

"I'll give you a ride," Abe said.

The car stopped fifty yards down the drive. They watched Repeat get out to inspect the damage, leaving the engine idling. He circled the car, shaking his head. "I can't believe this shit," he yelled. "I can't believe you did this, Pitt."

"He's right," Roberto said. "You can't go breaking a guy's car, man. He come right back and do the same to you."

"You think I give a shit?"

Roberto looked at Abe's truck, then at the trailer. He smiled. "Good point. Still, you know, it ain't right."

"You want that ride?"

"I think he's waiting for me there. I see you tomorrow."

"See you tomorrow."

Roberto walked out to the car and got in. Repeat was looking toward the trailer, shaking his head. Then he got in and backed away out of sight.

They had poured black oil on the dirt road to keep down the dust, and Abe drove slowly, breathing fumes. He turned off when he could, but the new asphalt on Fork Road was sticky from the August heat and wasn't much of an improvement for driving. He drove over a dead copperhead half-buried in the melting asphalt as if swimming a black river. There was the stink of a dead animal in the air and no breeze to carry it off. He looked roadside for the body of a possum or armadillo but saw nothing. The ditches were thick with weeds and dusty clover and clumps of balding gray thistle.

He turned onto Merrill Road and saw Gem Ridgeway, the grocer's old mother, puttering about her garden. It was too hot for her to be gardening. He got out of his truck and hopped across the ditch—he used to stop by here all the time—and rested his hands on the top strand of the barbed wire fence. The metal was scorching hot. He jerked them back.

Mrs. Ridgeway had always been a savvy gardener, and despite this year's late start, she had a bountiful garden. Okra, corn, squash, beans, tomatoes, peppers—all in perfect rows leading out from her back step. Where the garden ended the pasture began, several acres of it. She used to keep horses there—it was from Mrs. Ridgeway he'd bought his quarter horse and pinto, years ago—but the pasture was empty now, just heat-withered grass and patches of dirt, a dried-up pond, a few post oaks. Abe missed seeing horses running the fence. The barbed wire was a relic of those days. Now the fence seemed incongruous, nothing to keep in but a friendly old lady in her garden.

"Mrs. Ridgeway," he called. "Hey, Mrs. Ridgeway."

He saw her white bun of hair move south among the tomato plants—as tall as any he'd seen this year—until she appeared at the near end of the garden. She wore a faded yellow housecoat and no shoes on her blue-veined feet, and carried a wicker basket under one arm. Her glasses were the kind that tinted in the sun, but it was so bright she still squinted when she stepped out; he could see the plait of wrinkles gather.

"Who's that?"

"It's Abe Pittenger, ma'am. I was just driving by and thought I'd say hello."

"Well, howdy there, Abe." She took a polite step forward, shaded her eyes with her free hand. "How you been?"

"Fair to middling. How about yourself? You out gardening in this heat?"

"Oh, heavens no. I just needed to get me some tomatoes and peppers. I'm making up a salsa for Lainey Sanders's wedding. You know little Lainey, don't you? She's getting married today to a boy from Jessieville."

"Yes, ma'am. I'm headed home right now to get ready."

"Oh, you're going? Well, I am so glad to hear it. You knew Lainey's grandmother and I was cousins, didn't you?"

"Is that right?"

"Oh, yes. We come up through school together. Lainey's mama was like one of my own children. She's doing poorly these days, you know, bless her heart."

"Yes, ma'am."

"It is such a blessing that she can be here to see Lainey's wedding. The last of her girls. Isn't it just a blessing, though?"

"Yes, ma'am. I know Laine's glad."

"Oh, yes, you know she is. Now, how's your mother, Abe? I hear your father has started taking her to church."

"It's true. I think they're liking it."

"Well, praise the Lord. You know some people can't say nothing good about holy rollers, but I say church is church, and let the Lord take care of what kind. Better to be in church a-rolling around then setting at home watching the TV, ain't that right?"

"I know it's doing my father some good."

"Well, praise the Lord. Your mother's got to be so glad."

"I believe she is."

"She coming to the wedding?"

"No, ma'am, she had to work."

"Sam made her work? He couldn't have got one of them high school girls to work today?"

"Well, they're all friends with Laine, I guess."

"I guess that's true. Well, Sam says he don't know what he'd do without your mother. He just thinks she's the gravy. Couldn't do without her. You tell her I said not to take no grief from him. Don't let him get too big for his britches."

"I'll sure tell her," he said. "Now, I ought to let you go back in. I've kept you standing out in this heat too long."

"It is a scorcher, ain't it? You want to come in for some lemonade?"

"I better be getting on. But I'll see you at the wedding here in a bit. I'll be sure and try that salsa."

"Well, it ain't much," she said.

When he got back into his truck he was soaked. He blew sweat from the tip of his nose. The air conditioner blasted tepid air; only so much it could do with this heat. And here he'd kept the poor old woman out in it. He waited, chagrined, until he saw her disappear through her screen door.

At home he took a cold shower, just as he'd done at this time of day for the past several weeks. It was too hot to work on the roof during the middle of the day. Not for the men's sake—Pierce didn't give a rat's ass about that, by his own account—but for the shingles, which were easily scarred in this kind of heat. They went melty and soft; if you stepped on them the gravel skidded right off the tar. So the crew knocked off when the sun went high and returned in the late afternoon. The roofing boom had finally slowed, anyway. Pierce could pace the work. By late fall he'd be scrounging other jobs for them, everything from laying insulation to pulling up septic tanks. By winter he'd have too little work to keep them busy, and most would find other jobs.

Before Abe left the trailer, he cast about for Tabby. She hadn't been home for a few nights. Lucky lay curled in the bathroom sink, his favorite place in hot weather. Abe circled the trailer, buttoning his shirt and calling out. She wasn't in the shade beneath the trailer. He scanned the pasture. Sometimes she came home from the direction of the hills. It was hard to say how far she wandered. He hefted the food barrel and shook it loudly. Lucky came running out of the bathroom, but Tabby didn't show.

He finished dressing, watching the clock, not wanting to show up early. Marie would be there, of course. She'd given their separation plenty of reinforcement, and he thought it better to spare himself the discomfort of pre-ceremony small talk. If he arrived right on time, maybe he could slide into a back pew without her seeing him. Though he would probably have to speak to her at the reception, regardless.

He was embarrassed by his suit, the same he'd worn for years, the same he'd worn to his disastrous interview. His tie was long out of fashion too, but he had no other. He'd meant to borrow one of Roberto's or Kylie's or even one of his father's, who was more approachable these days, but now it was too late. Well, it didn't matter. No one cared how he looked. In two hours he would be out of the suit again, and then he would throw it away. It would feel good. He would cast it off like a molted skin and never put it on again.

Lockers Creek Baptist Church lay at the end of a winding gravel road, a small building with a steeply pitched roof Abe and the others had just reshingled the week before. The windows were basic house windows, made of clear glass, because the church elders considered stained glass a vanity of man. There was no steeple, for the same reason, and the pews were simple wooden benches. The church stood against a backdrop of pine woods, its back yard a narrow strip of grass studded with crawdad mounds. The parking lot, all gravel and crabgrass, was packed with cars. Little boys in their Easter suits were climbing atop the wellhouse at the rear. People milled nervously about the front steps. He hadn't come quite late enough.

Abe squeezed into a spot alongside the road, half in the ditch, and was just killing the engine when he saw Marie on the steps talking to Roberto and Julie Ann. She wore a pale orange dress, and her black hair, iridescent in the sunlight, was pulled back in an elaborate weave that seemed unlike her. He sat in his truck, pretending to fiddle with something in the seat. Surely they wouldn't stand out in the heat for long. He waited, feeling a strange prickling of awareness. He was becoming not just a person who hid himself away but one who pretended things. He would have to watch this. Or would the watching be part of the pretense? Like driving half-asleep, trying not to fall asleep, too far gone to realize you should already have pulled over. Abe lost himself thinking about this, and thus passed the time. Another trick.

You should just sit in the truck and do nothing, he thought, but by this time they were going inside. He looked around the parking lot for the Camaro and didn't see it. Maybe this wouldn't be as hard as he'd expected. When he got out he heard organ music.

A pimple-faced teenager in a tuxedo greeted him just inside the door. The pews were packed. Folding chairs had been set up against the back wall. As he came in, dozens of faces turned to look toward him. It was time for the ceremony—they were expecting the bride. He saw the organist craning her neck to see him, appearing disappointed when she did.

"Bride or groom?" the usher asked.

"What?"

"Are you here for the bride or groom?"

Abe frowned, unsure. "Both."

This upset the usher, who was just a kid and was feeling the pressure. He didn't seem to know what to do. He glanced around. "Well, where the hell do you want to sit?" he whispered fiercely. Disapproving faces turned toward them.

"Here," Abe said, taking the nearest folding chair. The usher scowled and turned away.

It was hot in the church. He remembered that now: no matter the season, weddings were always hot. And this was full summer. People were fanning themselves with their wedding programs. Trying to be discreet about it, Abe looked around for Marie, finally saw her sitting in the very same row, on a folding chair in the back corner. There were half a dozen people between them, and she sat next to Roberto, who all but obscured her from sight. Leaning slightly forward, he saw her muscular calves, the hem of her orange dress. She bent forward suddenly and smiled at him. He almost jerked back out of sight. He felt as if he'd been caught. She gave him a friendly wave.

Throughout the ceremony he went over this single interaction many times. Marie leaning forward to smile and wave at him, one hand going to her chest to hold her dress against her, a lacy scoop neckline. Her bare arms shining with perspiration. The quirk of her eyebrow. He would picture this—then he would picture her with Repeat, and his stomach would drop.

He paid little attention to the proceedings. Laine's friends Darla and Gay sang "Love Lift Us Up" to canned music. The preacher spoke at great length and with some heat, as if delivering a Sunday sermon. The vows were mostly unintelligible, Bill's voice coming across as a rumbling murmur, like elephant talk. The groomsmen were sweating profusely and trying not to fidget. Kylie, standing as best man, looked surprisingly good. In his tuxedo he seemed tall and slender but not gangly. He wore new glasses that downplayed his skewed eyes, and since Abe had seen him last, he'd grown a short, neat goatee.

The reception was held in the fellowship hall at the rear of the church. The greeting line extended through the doorway into the church proper, and the line for punch and wedding cake passed through an outside door into the yard. Abe wanted something to drink but was unwilling to wait in line for it. He went outside to stand in the shade of the wellhouse. He'd promised himself he would stay at least through the rice.

Marie and Julie Ann appeared around the corner of the church. Marie seemed to be looking for something. When she saw him and brightened, he realized it was him.

"Hi, ladies," he said. "Where's Roberto?"

"Getting us some punch," Julie Ann said.

Marie had put on dark sunglasses. It made her seem sly, somehow, perhaps because he couldn't see her eyes. But her smile disarmed him completely. She looked beautiful. She and Julie Ann were fanning themselves with wedding programs.

"How've you been?" she said.

"Not bad," he said. "Hot."

"Hot is right."

"I've never seen your hair like that."

"Laine did it. She did everybody's hair this morning."

"Who's everybody?"

"Everybody she could get her hands on. She called us all up and asked us to come over. She was a nervous wreck. She wanted to be doing something while Darla fixed her hair. So we took turns sitting in front of her and letting her do ours. It was kind of fun. She even wanted to do her mom's wig, but her mom wouldn't let her touch it. See, she did Julie Ann's too."

Julie Ann turned her head slightly so he could see the braid in back.

She was a pretty woman, with delicate features and sea-green eyes. She rarely laughed or smiled, though, and Abe had never been comfortable around her. He always got the feeling she didn't like him.

"Looks nice."

"Darla says we look like hookers," Julie Ann said.

"Well, some hookers are pretty."

Julie Ann gave him a bored expression, but Marie smiled. She seemed downright cheerful. Maybe she found it easier now that she'd put him off for good. Maybe she was happier now. They talked about the wedding, Laine's plans for the honeymoon in Eureka Springs, the house Bill was building them. While they talked, he glimpsed his distorted reflection in Marie's sunglasses and remembered his tie. He took it off and stuffed it into his pants pocket, unfastening the top button of his shirt. Eventually Roberto showed up with the punch. He'd brought a cup for Abe too. His tie was loosened, his shirt sleeves rolled. There were sweat circles under his arms.

"You about ready to go back to work, Pitt?"

"You're kidding me," Marie said. "Y'all are going to work today?"

"*Going* to work?" Roberto said. "We *been* working. The whole damn morning we been working."

"But it's so hot."

"Well, we ain't girls," Roberto said.

"No, of course not. You're too tough to get heat stroke."

"You damn right," Roberto said.

A sweaty boy of about five came running up. "They need all the single ladies," he said breathlessly. "She's about to throw the croquet." Roberto made a swipe at tousling the boy's hair, but he ducked and ran off, shouting his announcement to another group.

"Marie?" Julie Ann said.

"Not me," she said. "I'll just watch."

They moved toward the front of the church again, Roberto and Julie Ann in front. Abe and Marie fell behind. They watched Julie Ann shoulder into a knot of women at the bottom of the steps. Laine stood at the top with Bill, preparing to toss the bouquet. She was waiting for the photographer to get in position, a plainly irritated look on her face.

Marie kept walking, so Abe went with her to the rear of the crowd. They stopped under a pine tree to watch the proceedings at a distance. There was a shout as Laine cast the flowers back over her shoulder, then laughter and cheering. It was impossible to see who'd made the catch. Marie stood with her shoulder almost touching his. A stream of black ants arced around their shoes in the dirt.

"Abe," she said, turning to him. "I've been wanting to say—I'm sorry I was so . . . I don't know what to call it. I didn't give you much warning."

"Abrupt?"

"That's it. I'm sorry I was abrupt. I really am. You don't know how glad I am to see you. I mean it's really so good to see you—but I know you're mad at me. You surprised me each time you came into the bookstore, you know, or I'd have said something then. It's just—you know I can't be nice under pressure," she said, smiling, trying to make him laugh.

He nodded, keeping his eyes forward. "It's all right."

Her smile faded. "It's just that I didn't know what else to do."

"Well, Marie," he said, not harshly, but keeping it together, "I don't know what you were trying to do, but I'd say it worked."

She turned away again. Now the men were gathering at the bottom of the steps. Laine hiked up her wedding dress with a sleazy flourish. The men hooted and clapped. Even from this distance you could see the frown of disapproval on the preacher's face. Bill slid her garter off and held it for the crowd to see. He tried shooting it like a rubber band, but it fell at his feet, so he picked it up again and flung it out among the men. There was a tussle, the crowd backing away as two of the men went down in the dirt, and a moment of uneasiness as the onlookers tried to decide whether the fighters were serious. Then came a swell of laughter and applause as the men got to their feet, one of them with the torn garter in his hand. It was Kylie.

"What I don't understand," Abe said, "is why you chose that particular moment to brush me off. Just out of the blue."

"I didn't brush—"

"Whatever you want to call it. What I'd like to know is why that moment? I thought we were doing okay. In fact, from the moment we met, I thought—well, I guess that had just never happened to me before. I thought we were doing all right."

"We were doing all right."

"So why then? Why right then?"

"It was a gut decision."

"I wish you'd tell me the truth."

"I *am* telling—"

"Forget it. Forget I asked."

He considered getting in his truck and tearing out of there, but he stayed, thinking, This is the last time you'll see her. She was stooping now, removing a pebble from her shoe. He watched her out of the corner of his eye. She balanced on one foot, one hand holding her empty punch cup, her bare heel braced just below the knee as she shook out the shoe.

Striations of muscle standing out on her calf as it supported her weight. He could see down the neck of her dress. Her breasts pendulous in a lacy white brassiere. Her chest freckled from the sun. He looked for a long moment, then looked away.

She straightened but made no move to leave him. The crowd around the steps was dispersing. He was afraid Roberto and Julie Ann would join them again. If they did, he would just leave. No point in standing around saying nothing.

"The honest truth," she said after a minute.

"Yes, please," he said. "The honest truth." He wiped sweat out of his eyes and waited. She had tilted her head in the way she did when searching for the right words. He'd seen her do it often enough to recognize the gesture.

"This just makes me look stupid," she said finally. "I think what happened was that I thought for a minute that day that maybe I loved you. I felt close to you. Out in the woods I was thinking about what all you've been through and yet how good you treat me. And then at the café, I was watching Laine and Bill together, and I was thinking how easy it would be to be like that with you. Just casual and easy together. Me picking on you some, the way Laine does Bill. It sounded nice."

"So you decided to end it?"

"I let it go too far. I told you up front I wasn't getting serious."

"Not with me, at any rate."

"Not with anybody."

"So what you're doing with Repeat, I guess that isn't serious."

She was quiet for a while. He didn't look at her. He felt mean and couldn't have said why, except that he knew from her tone she'd been sincere. Whatever it was with Repeat, he didn't know, but Marie was being sincere. He finished his punch and watched people clapping Bill on the back. He saw Laine's father helping her mother down the steps.

"Who told you about that?" she said at last.

"Repeat did."

"That little shit."

"He thought he owed it to me."

"Abe, it wasn't serious. That's the only reason it happened."

"Okay."

"No, don't be like that. Listen. I don't even like Repeat very much. I just missed you. That's why I . . ." She couldn't finish.

"You missed me so you started sleeping with Repeat? If you missed *me*, why not come to *me*? I mean, if I missed *you*, I wouldn't run off with Laine, for God's sake. That doesn't make any sense, Marie."

"Well, it made sense to me at the time. I was confused. I was—I was miserable. I'm sorry."

"Don't be."

"Well, I am. It was a shitty thing to do. But Abe, I mean it, the only reason it happened at all was because I could never be serious with him. There's no way I could. Do you understand? It's just that right now I need to be able to choose—not to feel like, I don't know, like I'm just being swept along. Do you—?" She raised her eyebrows hopefully, but Abe said nothing. She tried again. "With you . . . well, I missed you, but I couldn't be with you, so I settled for that jackass. And now I'm sorry. Anyway, it's over."

"Don't do anything on my account."

"I'm not. It's already over."

"If you say so."

"I do say so."

"Okay," he said, and though the news didn't do him any good, he did feel better, which surprised him. Before he'd met Marie, he'd never been vindictive. Maybe that's what love did for you; it let you be vindictive.

"You know I don't understand you one bit," he said.

"I know. It's not your fault."

"Did you just say a minute ago you thought you might love me?"

"Yes."

"I just wanted to be sure I heard you right."

"You heard me right."

"But nothing's changed?"

She shook her head.

"But I don't under—Is it such a terrible thing to consider? Do I seem like such a complete and total loss that you'd never want to take a chance?"

"What are you talking about? You think this is about *you*?"

"Excuse me if I sound stupid, but yeah, I don't see anyone else here."

"I told you it was about me."

They watched the wedding crowd eddy around the corner of the church. A few people were heading across the grass toward their cars. He needed to get out of there before he said anything else he'd regret. It disturbed him that his stiffest resolve could fluctuate with the cadence of her sentences.

"I'm sorry," he said. "You've got your reasons."

"Don't be sorry."

"Okay, neither of us has to be sorry."

"You okay?"

"I think that punch made me a little sick, maybe."

"It wasn't very good, was it? I don't feel so good, either."

Julie Ann came across the yard, carrying the bouquet. They congratulated her. She told them Laine and Bill were getting ready to drive away. Roberto was behind the church with Kylie and the groomsmen, helping to trash the car with shaving cream and shoe polish.

Marie said, "I should go say good-bye."

Julie Ann put her nose into her flowers. "I'll come with you."

"You want to come, Abe?"

"Nah," he said, shaking his head. "I'll catch them later."

They stood awkwardly. Julie Ann had turned to go, but Marie didn't move, so she stopped and waited, looking puzzled. It never seemed to dawn on her they'd been speaking before she came up. Abe decided then that Julie Ann didn't dislike him—she was just oblivious. She had no idea other people saw her face and thus made no effort to adjust it for any occasion.

He also realized Marie was reluctant to leave him. It was good-bye all over again, and she'd hoped to do it better this time. She wasn't having much luck. Abe held out his hand and said, "Can I see your sunglasses a second?"

She cocked her head. "My sunglasses?"

"Yeah, can I take a look at them?"

She gave them to him. It was shady under the tree, so she didn't squint much. He turned them over in his hand, pretending to study them. "These the ones you always wear?"

"Yeah, why?"

"I don't know. They just looked different." He handed them back, taking her in. Her dark eyes. Face damp with sweat. Her hair done in a way he'd never seen. He could remember the feel of her hair, soft and fine beneath his hands. She wasn't smiling now, but he could see it, that half-savage grin that made you like her and made you worry too. That sense she had just got off at the wrong stop but wouldn't admit it. Your own spontaneous wish to get back on and go with her.

"They're fixing to leave," Julie Ann said plaintively.

Marie looked at him. "We'd better go catch her."

He nodded. "I'll see you."

They went off across the church yard. The sun shone off her hair. Her orange dress seemed paler in the bright sunlight than it did in the shade. She disappeared around the corner of the church.

Abe got into his truck.

In town he stopped at Ridgeway's Grocery. He bought a Coke at the vending machine and went inside to see his mother. She was ringing up the only customer in the store, Purdue the used-car dealer, who came in every day for bubble gum and chewing tobacco. She punched the register keys very deliberately, as if she were uncertain about the procedure, though she had worked at the store for twenty years. She was not uncertain. She had always been slow in her movements, perhaps to avoid calling attention to herself.

Not wanting to talk to Purdue, Abe went halfway down the first aisle and cooled off in the produce section. He came back when he heard him leave.

"Well, looky who's here," his mother said, grinning. She took out a pack of cigarettes from beneath the register.

"I thought Sam said y'all couldn't smoke in here anymore."

She took a long drag, turned her head to the side and blew it out. "He said we could if there wasn't anybody in the store."

"I saw Gem Ridgeway today. She said Sam thinks you're just the best thing in the world."

"That's nice. He ought to, anyway, with all I've done for this place," she said. She'd talk that way with Abe, though she'd be mortified if anyone else heard her. She sat on the tall stool and stretched her upper back, tucking her chin and gazing seriously at her feet as she did. Abe realized for the first time that he stretched his own back in just this way, and with the same expression.

"So how was the wedding?" she asked.

"Hot."

"To tell you the truth I was glad to miss it. At least I had an excuse. Times like this I wished I was like your dad. He won't go to weddings, period. He makes no bones about it. He just won't go. I could never do that. I'd feel too guilty."

"What's he up to today?"

"Blowing a ceiling in Benton. Can I have a drink of that?"

He handed her the Coke. She took a tiny sip, then passed the can across her forehead. It was warm in the store despite the air-conditioning. She had a flush in her cheeks.

"You ought to go stand in the freezer section."

"You don't know," she said. "I been standing there all morning."

"So what's this I hear about Dad? He quit entirely?"

"Quit cold turkey on Sunday. Right after church."

"I can't feature it."

She looked squarely at him. "Your dad isn't the same man, Abe. I swear it's like night and day. Honestly, I didn't think we could be this happy. Not in a million years."

"That's quite a thing to say."

"Well, it's true," she said. "The Lord has turned your dad's life around. He's happy, he's whistling all the time, and now he's stopped drinking. Doesn't even swear anymore. Plus you should see him in the mornings. He gets up early to study scripture."

"*Early*? He gets up at dawn."

"Gets up even earlier now. You haven't seen much of him lately, but I wished you could see the change in him. He's been talking about you a lot. He wants to see if we could help you out somehow."

"Help me out?"

"I don't know, honey. You ought to talk to him. Why don't you come over for supper tonight?"

"I've got to work."

"We can eat late, it's all right. Your dad won't care."

"Not tonight, okay?"

"Well, you ought to say when. Next week?"

He nodded. "Maybe so."

"If you got your phone fixed I could call you."

"I'll come by here again," he said. "We can talk about it."

"He'll be glad. He's been talking about you." She took another sip of the Coke.

"Why don't you drink the rest of it? I'll get another one."

"No," she said, handing him the can. "That's all I want."

She finished her cigarette and took out another one.

"What does the Lord say about cigarettes?" he asked.

"Don't get smart with me. If you want to know the truth, this is my last pack. Me and your dad are quitting together. No, it's the God's honest truth. But he's letting me go first so we don't irritate the fire out of each other. When I've got it licked, then he's going to quit."

"Isn't it hard enough on him giving up the liquor?"

"You know, that's the blessing. I mean, it *must* be hard, but he says the Lord's giving him strength to bear it. He says it's hardly a burden at all. He never complains about it."

"That's great. Seriously, it's great to hear. I'm happy for you."

"Thank you, sweetie. You know, you ought to come to church with us sometime."

"Well. I could do that."

"Why don't you come tomorrow?"

"I'll think about it. Probably not tomorrow."

A customer came in, and she hurried to stub out her cigarette. "I'll see you," Abe said, though he didn't really feel he would. He would, surely he would, but he didn't feel it. He was struck with affection for her that he couldn't rightly express, not without worrying her. She was one of those people who didn't know what to do with her worry. He kissed her on the cheek.

She beamed at him, exhaling smoke. "Okay, baby. You be thinking about what you want me to cook for supper."

"Just as long as there's fried okra."

"There will be," she said. "It's finally coming in."

He didn't know where he wanted to go. He drove along the dusty back roads for an hour, avoiding the oiled ones, and finally went home to change. At the work site, a ranch house on the highway near the Crows junction, he found Roberto already on the roof, alone, tearing up the old shingles with a potato fork. Abe packed up a bundle of new shingles and set to work. They nodded to each other without speaking. It was late in the afternoon and the heat had lost its murderous edge, but it was still sweltering. They'd been working half an hour before Lester and Mitch and Pierce showed up. They tore off old roofing until the sun was low, finished hammering down the last new shingles just as it grew too dark to find the nails. Abe went home hardly having spoken a word.

The cicadas were loud in the pasture. Sometimes he noticed them, sometimes they seemed part of a general silence. Tonight he noticed them. He mounted the porch steps and scooped cat food into the hubcap. The cats hadn't touched the food he'd poured that morning, but he emptied the scoop anyway, for the sound of it. Lucky appeared in the porchlight as if by magic; no telling where he'd come from.

He meowed and paced back and forth in front of the hubcap.

"Well, go ahead and eat," Abe said. He called Tabby.

Lucky kept meowing. Abe squatted to pet him, but Lucky didn't stop, only rubbed against his shins and meowed. Abe scratched between his ears. "What's wrong with you, crazy cat? Why didn't you guys eat anything today?"

Then he stopped petting the cat. He squatted with his arms crossed as Lucky went back and forth on the porch, occasionally sniffing the food, then leaving it again. He felt as if someone had just kicked him. When he stood up he was light-headed. He went inside for a flashlight.

There was nothing under the trailer. He slipped through the barbed wire fence and set out across the pasture toward the hills. Halfway across, his flashlight beam caught a garter snake in the grass. He stepped over it and went on, following the path he'd seen Tabby use a few nights before, as well as he could remember it. He reached the other fence without finding a trace of her. He thought back to the afternoon, trying to remember if he'd seen buzzards in the area. The image of Gem Ridgeway in her garden came into his mind. He'd thought she shouldn't be out in such heat.

He recrossed the pasture, taking a different route. A fat garden spider appeared in his flashlight beam like a jewel magically suspended, the web strands barely visible. Even as he saw it, a katydid stirred up by his footsteps leaped through the spiderweb, demolishing it, and escaped. He went on. Near the fence he saw a brown mound in the grass and tasted bile in the back of his throat. But it was only a dried heap of cow manure.

Again he thought of Gem Ridgeway, then realized why. He drove back out Merrill Road, past her house. Her lights were already out. She probably went to bed at sundown. He turned onto Fork Road and rolled down his window, pulling over when the stink hit him. He walked the ditch for a hundred yards in both directions, then crossed and walked the other ditch. A sliver of moon had risen. Scarcely a sound but for insects and gravel. Back in the direction of Merrill Road he startled two crows out of the darkness. They hopped away from him, cawing and flapping their wings, but they didn't fly off. He kicked at them and they fluttered up into the trees.

It was hard to say if she'd been struck by a car or if the sun had killed her. Hard even to tell it was Tabby. There wasn't much to her. There hadn't been much when she was alive. Now the heat and the birds had been at her, and the flies. The smell was terrible. He sat in the gravel a few yards away, figuring the days since he had seen her last. Three or four. A crow hopped tentatively out of the tree shadows. He flung a fistful of gravel. It flew off over the field across the road.

Half an hour later a truck passed by. It slowed when the driver saw him sitting in the ditch. He recognized Simmons's truck and waved him on. The truck went fifty yards down the road, turned around, and came back. He stood up, brushing the dirt from his legs. Simmons pulled over and looked at him through the open window.

"Having trouble?" He was a grizzled man, with a perpetual shadow on his cheeks and a double chin. His brow and neck were burned a deep ruddy brown.

Abe shook his head. "No, sir. Just lost one of my cats."

Simmons looked past him toward the ditch. "I thought maybe that was it, what with the smell. He come a long way to get killed by a car, didn't he?"

"The heat might have got her. She was pretty old."

"Nah, he'd be laying up under something. Animals know better than to stay out in the sun if there's shade around. I bet he got run over. Chasing a damn rabbit across the road or some such thing."

"I guess so."

"They know to hide from the sun but they ain't got cars figured out quite yet."

Abe said nothing. A faint breeze carried Simmons's truck exhaust up from the tailpipe. Abe felt its heat across his legs. The fumes helped obscure the smell.

"Well," Simmons said, "I got a shovel in the back, under that tool chest. You want to borrow it?"

"I've got one back at the trailer."

"Oh, hell. Take mine. You can bring it by tomorrow."

"Well, I appreciate it." He got the shovel from the truck bed.

"All set?"

"Yes, sir."

"I'll see you later, then."

The waning moon was high when he finally got around to digging. He'd considered moving her off into the field, but he had no good way to move her, and he was afraid of what would happen if he tried. Instead of digging a hole, he scooped earth from around her and covered her with it. He made a high mound and packed it firmly with the blade of the shovel. Weeds and grass stuck out of the mound and made it look whiskery in the dim light of the moon. Drenched with sweat, he took off his shirt and mopped his brow.

He waited to see if the crows would return. He thought he would try to hit one with the shovel. Off across the field a dog was barking. It stirred up a dog down the road, and they both barked until someone shut up the one across the field. Then the one down the road fell silent too. Abe stood still, holding his shirt over his nose and his mouth, waiting for the crows to appear. He was sick from exhaustion and from the smell. He waited a long time for the crows, but they never came. They were smart enough to wait until he was gone. He patted the mound one last time with the shovel, just for the feel of the blade smacking something. Then he took the shovel and the flashlight to his truck and went home.

Chapter 13

It should have been the perfect time to be out. There was the first tinge of autumn in the air, dry and with the promise of a cool night; the maple leaves were changing; and the sky was a whitewashed blue, with a few high, thin, peach-colored cirrus clouds stippled against it like strokes from a paintbrush. Despite the weather, though, and despite the almost daunting good humor Marie's father had displayed since the news of his engagement to Angela, the two of them were gloomy when they pulled into Emma's Café. They'd been out to visit Dr. Hodgkins. Marie wished she hadn't gone. And she didn't want to stop at the café now, not even to see Laine, whom she hadn't seen since the wedding. She wanted her father to keep driving, to put miles and miles between her and the nursing home. But she could tell he wanted to stop.

Inside the crowded café they had to wait for a table. Eventually a teenage girl they didn't know came over with menus. A loud voice from the kitchen said, "Huh-uh," and Laine appeared and explained to the waitress that no matter where they sat, these were her customers. The girl fled, plainly confused but too harried to ask questions.

Laine's arms were loaded with plates. "She's new," she explained. "She doesn't know I run the show yet. Now y'all set tight, and I'll be right back." As she stepped away she must have realized she'd been talking only to Marie, because she looked back with a smile and said in a girlish tone, "Hi, Mr. Jimmy."

"Hey, girl," he said. He and Marie looked at each other.

"She's a pistol," they said at the same time, then raised their eyebrows in exactly the same look of surprise. They laughed—and that did it, their bad moods burned off a little.

"Well, that was weird," Marie said.

"You must've learned that from me."

They ordered, and since neither was in a talking frame of mind, her father pulled out his newspaper. Marie skimmed the sections he passed her, but mostly she watched Laine bustling about the café and helping out the new waitress, and let her thoughts drift.

Coming out to Lockers Creek had brought Abe to mind. She'd been trying not to think of him. Since the wedding she'd wondered if she would ever see him again. Part of her had hoped so, but there'd been some change in him, she thought, and she figured it wouldn't be long before he'd forgotten her and moved on. At certain moments she despised him for it. Not just for forgetting her, but for being capable of that kind of change. She herself seemed wholly incapable of it. The more she thought of him, the more convinced she was of her own ineptitude: Abe, more than anything else, represented her disintegrating, foolish hope that you could choose which parts of your past to carry forward and which to erase. That you could change your life at all and not just your name for it. It's still running, she thought, you're still a runner.

"You all right?" her father asked.

"What?"

"You look a little peaked."

"I guess I'm just thinking too much."

"What about?"

"I probably couldn't explain it."

"You want to try?"

"I don't think so."

"Someday," her father said, "you're going to figure out you can tell me some of these things and it won't kill you."

"Well. I'll let you know if you're right."

He winked at her and returned to his newspaper.

The café was so busy Laine never managed to sit with them, but she lingered at their table when she brought their check. "I didn't want to tell you on the phone, Marie," she said in a low voice, "but can you tell?" She turned to show her profile. She seemed considerably pudgier than the last time Marie had seen her.

"You've lost some weight, haven't you?"

Laine cackled. "Marie Hamilton, you crazy nut! You say exactly what I want to hear. Oh, Lordy." She bent forward and whispered gravely, "I'm with child."

"What!"

"Congratulations," Marie's father said.

"You're pregnant?"

"Damn straight! Pardon the French. No, I mean it this time, I really am. Don't look at me like that, I am, I promise. And guess what else? It isn't just one."

"No! Twins?"

"Looks like. Apparently I'm just chock full of the little boogers."

"Well, for crying out loud, Lainey, I can't believe you didn't tell me right off. But congratulations, I'm happy for you."

Laine patted her hair as if posing. "Thank you, thank you."

"I'm just so surprised. I can't believe you kept it quiet this long."

"Marie Hamilton, you saying I can't keep a secret? Anyway it's not exactly something you announce at your wedding. Sorry, Mr. Jimmy, you can pretend you didn't hear that."

"But your mother didn't even mention it on the phone."

"I made her swear not to tell. I like to do the telling myself, you know, in person. But she's having a hard time not talking about her double grandbabies on the way, I can tell you. I just hope— " She caught herself, and her face hardened. "Well, you know, I'm not gonna talk about that right now. I'll just fall apart, and nobody wants to see that. Ask me something else."

"Like what?"

"Ask me what Bill thinks about all this."

"What does Bill think?"

"Oh, he doesn't know," Laine said, making her scandalous face. "Actually, he ought to have the house built for us just in time. When I told him the news I said, 'Go ahead and build a extra bedroom, Bill, cause it looks like we're getting a houseful.' And you know what that dumb ape said? I like to slapped him upside the head. He didn't even blink, said, 'I done planned it in, Laine. I figured the odds were for it.' Just standing there like he already knew, not the least bit surprised. Really ticked me off. But anyway y'all have got to come out and see the place. He's really doing it up right, with bay windows and a big deck to look out over the valley."

"It sounds beautiful," Marie said, though she couldn't imagine any of it. Knowing a place was yours from the ground up. Having someone know you from the ground up. Neither seemed likely or even possible.

Laine hustled off, but when they rose to leave, she reappeared from the kitchen and took Marie aside. She carried a platter in each hand. Her cheeks were flushed and a line of sweat shone over her lip. "Listen, have you heard about Abe?"

Marie's stomach turned. She saw Abe lying dead in an empty yard. It couldn't be true—the news would never have come to her like this—but the image hit her hard. She saw him there, alone in the yard, as if he'd fallen from a great height. Later she would realize it was the taxidermist's lot she'd pictured—who could say why? She stared at Laine and shook her head, unable to speak.

"Oh, honey, you all right?"

"What happened to him?" Marie said faintly.

"Oh, for God's sake, I ought to be shot. Me and my stupid mouth. He's okay, honey. I mean he's not hurt or anything."

"Oh," Marie said. She ran a hand through her hair. "Oh, okay."

"No, he's all right," Laine said, flustered now. "I mean he's—I'm sorry. Are you all right?"

"Just tell me what's wrong."

"I'm sorry. I'm such a nitwit. He's fine, he's just, well, he's just been acting funny. I thought you might want to visit him, or—Lordy, I wished I'd have kept my mouth shut. It's nothing. I'm sorry."

"It's okay. I'm fine. Really, if you'll just tell me."

"Well, it's not much, when you think about it by comparison. Bill just says that his buds are worried about him, is all. Like he's not talking to people, really, and is holed up—listen, I'm sorry. It's nothing, really."

"I thought he was always holed up."

"Well, sure, he has been. They think he's got worse, is all. Honey, can you just forget about it and forgive me for being stupid? I didn't know if maybe you'd want to visit him or something. I was being a busybody. It's none of my business if y'all aren't together. Fact Bill'd wring my neck if he knew I was talking to you about it. I don't know why I think I've got to sort out everybody's problems."

Suddenly Marie saw Laine clearly, more clearly than before. Waiting tables with twins in her belly. Barking orders at the other waitress. Fussing about Bill and Bill's friends as her mother dies a lingering death in the bedroom. Furiously ordering the world.

"It's okay, Lainey," she said. "Really."

"It is? Cause I can be just such a twit. I only—Oh shoot, Emma's giving me eyes from the kitchen. Can you just forget about it?"

"It's fine, Lainey. Now you ought to set those plates down. Your arms are trembling."

"I will here in a second. I don't have the stamina I used to. So you're not upset with me, though? Maybe you'll call me later?"

"I'm not upset with you."

"Will you call me?"

"Of course. I want to hear about things."

Laine flashed a relieved smile. "Well, good," she said, her tone changing. "When you've got twins you've got twice as much talking to do. You need twice as many people to listen to—Oh all right," she said, rolling her eyes. "Emma's getting aggravated."

"Go."

"Right. I'm going. Don't be mad at your old Lainey, now."

"How could I ever be mad at you?"

"Well, then, give me a kiss. That's better. Oh, your lips are so dry. Marie Hamilton. Don't you have some gloss?"

The car still smelled of fresh-baked cookies and cloying peppermint candy. Marie felt almost suffocated in it, and as they drove back to Hot Springs her image of Abe in the taxidermist's yard yielded to that of Dr. Hodgkins, the pall of their visit with him settling upon her again. Her father seemed to be keeping his cheer up—his chin dipped in time to the radio—but Marie kept seeing her grandfather, pale and pasty like some bloated lake creature dying on the bed. He'd looked much worse than before. Her father, who'd been visiting him regularly although Marie had not, said that he'd deteriorated noticeably even since last weekend.

Dr. Hodgkins hadn't wanted to put on his shirt, and Mrs. Garner had stood in their presence berating him for his immodesty. He lay on his bed with an afghan drawn over his bulk, unable to make up his mind if he was hot or cold. The afghan kept slipping to reveal the hairless white skin of his chest. He wouldn't speak to either of them directly, though he made general statements that seemed to include them, statements about the illegitimacy of the world—about the great big bastard world and its bitter, bastard children. The only one to whom he spoke directly was Mrs. Garner, who told him to watch his language and that he ought to be ashamed.

"Do you think Grandpa's going to die soon?" Marie asked. They were on Park Avenue, on the outskirts of Hot Springs, where grand old houses lay disintegrating behind roadside trees. A few stood fronted by scaffolding, undergoing renovations that would save the ruin for another generation.

"I don't think it'll be long," her father said, after a pause.

"Don't you think Mom would want to know?"

He glanced at her. "I don't know if she would, honey. Even when . . . well, even back then, she couldn't really stand to see him. I don't think he ever treated her well, you know. She had a hard time loving him the way she thought she was supposed to. One thing about your mother, she could lie up a storm to most anybody—I'm sorry if that hurts your feelings, but I guess you know it's true—she could tell lies left and right, but she couldn't lie to her father. He scared her too much, or threw her off balance, I don't know. She'd make me go out there, she'd raise a fuss if I didn't, but she hardly ever went herself."

"I still think she might want to know."

"Well. Maybe you're right."

"Have you heard from her?"

"Have I—," he faltered, caught off guard. "No, honey, I haven't heard from her in years."

"Since when?"

"Since the last time y'all left. I figured you'd know that."

"Not even a phone call?"

"Never."

"So then she could be dead."

"What? No, honey," he said consolingly. "Are you worried about that? No, she isn't dead."

"How do you know?"

"Why are you—," he began, but he broke off and began again, patiently, as if she were a child. "Okay. For one thing, I'm sure I would have been notified. And, for that matter, so would you. But I'm surprised you even ask. How long has it been since you talked to her?"

"A long time."

"What's a long time? Couple months?"

"A lot longer than that."

"You mean to tell me it's been more than a couple months since you saw your mother?"

"I haven't seen her since I was ten."

"Not since—?"

He squeezed the wheel, his knuckles whitening. She was looking at him askance, almost nonchalant. It was the only way she could talk about it. Her father stared straight ahead, gripping the wheel. After a minute he ducked his head quickly side to side, wiping at his eyes with his upper arms. "You mean," he said, his voice quavering, "you mean you've been alone since you were ten?"

"I didn't mean to upset you."

"But Marie, what happened? Why didn't you come to me? Oh, Jesus, when I think . . . I can't hardly stand to think—"

"It's okay," she said evenly. "I'm all right."

He pulled over onto the shoulder and put his face into his hands. Cars shushed past, swerving to avoid his bumper, which stuck out into the lane. Somebody honked. Marie saw the driver looking back in his rearview mirror as he passed. If not for her father she would have flipped him off.

"I just wanted to know," she said. "Sorry."

"I don't understand," he said, still covering his face, "I just don't understand why you didn't come to me. All those years. I was just waiting. I'd have been so glad for the chance."

Marie felt accused, and she almost lashed at him. She got hold of herself enough to explain calmly, in a dead tone: "I didn't know what else to do. I thought she'd get arrested or something, so I never told anybody."

He dropped his hands. His eyes were red, and his nose had a single teardrop trembling from the tip, but he was gazing at her now with a strange, admiring, wistful look. It baffled her that he could be so grieved and still show such fondness. "Oh, Marie," he said, shaking his head. He didn't seem to mind the suspicious, almost haughty expression on her face, the coldness with which she froze herself together. Maybe he'd look at her the same way if she slapped his cheek. She couldn't fathom it, had never been able to fathom it, the way he acted. "Oh, Marie, what a job your mother did on us. I was doing the same thing as you. The very same damn thing."

She handed him a tissue from her purse, in a peremptory way, like Mrs. Garner passing pills to her addlepated grandfather. Her father smiled gratefully, unaffected by her manner. He blew his nose, looking out through the windshield now almost as if the crying never happened and he was content to just gaze out on the world again. He took sadness in stride, her father, let it come and go as it pleased. He understood that running from it was like running from the sky. And in this way, she thought, he was wiser than she might ever be.

He folded the tissue and blew again. "Your mother, Marie. Lord bless her, she's fixed us all good."

Chapter 14

The car parked outside Jim Townsend's house was a sporty affair, metallic gray with custom wheels, tinted windows, gleaming chrome, a spoiler. And Florida plates: it was Mr. Townsend's. In the yard a white miniature poodle set to yapping when Abe drove up, its fur clipped in a typical poodle clownsuit. About the size of a squirrel, Abe thought. Lucky a hawk hadn't seen it. He sat in his truck assessing the poodle, which had taken up position just outside his door, poised to fight. He couldn't kick this dog away; he might kill it. He decided to wait a minute and see if someone would hear the barking.

It was the first he'd been here since the morning Jackie died. The yard was weedy and overgrown, with junk tree saplings here and there on the fringes, woods creeping in to reclaim the place. The house gutters looked in bad shape too, but they had been before. He had intended to take care of that for her.

The screen door opened, and Jim stepped out onto the porch, squinting in the noon sunlight. He shielded his eyes and smiled to see Abe's truck.

"Chrissy!" he yelled. "Chrissy, you little shit, come here!"

The poodle snarled and held ground. Jim came and took her by the collar. "She likes you," he said, yanking her around and sending her off toward the house.

"What the hell kind of name is Chrissy for a dog?" Abe said, getting out.

"Ask my dad's girlfriend. She named the damn thing."

"The one that left?"

"Yeah, he got Chrissy because her new place didn't take pets. It's ridiculous."

They faced each other. Jim was tan—something Abe had never seen—and wore different clothes: linen pants, an untucked golf shirt, dusty deck shoes. After a moment Abe realized his moustache was gone. He looked like someone Abe knew but not well.

"Look at you," Abe said.

"I was about to say the same thing. You're starting to look like a prophet."

"Yeah, well."

"I'm surprised to see you, actually. I figured I was going to have to come out there. I tried to call last week to let you know I was heading up. Come to find out you had your phone disconnected."

"It's broken. I just haven't replaced it yet."

"Well, you know the way people talk; they've got you standing on the porch with a shotgun, scaring away trespassers. Like maybe you're growing a pot crop out back. Kylie says you attacked Repeat's car. I'd love to have seen that."

"That wasn't about trespassing. Or not exactly."

"Well, I want to hear all about it. You coming in?"

They headed up to the house, Jim fending off Chrissy, who'd been skulking a few yards off, waiting for an opportunity. He stomped his foot to scare her back, laughing at her growls. He was being casual, so much at ease that Abe felt suspicious. Almost resentful, even, as if Jim weren't taking things seriously enough. A stupid feeling—he tried to suppress it. As if you know what you're supposed to feel in his shoes, he thought. As if you know what you're supposed to do.

Jim's father was on the living room floor, going through boxes. This was why they had come, to sort through a few last things. The house was sold, Mr. Townsend having arranged a quick deal with his local real estate buddies. In a few weeks a new family would be living here. There would be a swing set in the yard, a station wagon in the driveway. The house would resound with television and children.

Mr. Townsend half-rose to greet Abe and settled back down to his boxes. His cologne was sharp in the musty living room. A slender man, brown as a coconut, with salt-and-pepper hair and cheekbones so prominent his face seemed to cave inward below them. He was opening a set of cookie tins. "She used to keep stuff in these things," he said. "Most of it's junk, you know, needles and thread, buttons and whatnot. One of them still has cookies in it, no telling how many years old. But every now and then you find one with pictures in it, so I got to go through them all. Here's one of Jim. Take a look at this."

He handed Abe a snapshot from a stack of photos on the floor. A skinny child with arms flexed like a bodybuilder.

"You can see her in the mirror in that one," Mr. Townsend said.

Abe looked closer, and sure enough, there was Jackie, twice as tall as Jim, face obscured by the camera and its aura of reflected flash. She was wearing a short skirt and a stacked wig, one of those crazy getups of the early seventies. Abe looked closer for the makeup—he remembered how his own mother used to powder her face so pale back then—but you couldn't see her face at all.

Jim had left the room, was going through the house throwing open windows. "The whole damn house smells like a basement," he called.

Mr. Townsend took the picture back from Abe with a slightly trembling hand. He was wearing his wedding ring, Abe noticed. His eyes had gone red; he wiped them with the back of his wrist. Abe looked around the room.

"I don't think I said so at the funeral, Abe, but I'm glad it was you who found her. Jackie was always so fond of you. She used to call you her boy, her Pittenger boy."

"I remember that."

"She'd say, 'How's my Pittenger boy doing?' She was—well, we were both thankful for you. You were a good friend to Jim. He was a shy kid."

"Well, Jim was a good friend to me."

"Oh, he's a good one. No question."

They were quiet, Abe nodding as if still listening, Mr. Townsend idly flapping the old photograph as if it were in need of developing, as if Jackie's face might yet appear. They were waiting for Jim to come back in, but Jim was working at something in a back room; they could hear him grunting and swearing. A stuck window.

"I'll go see if he needs a hand," Abe said.

"Listen, Abe," Mr. Townsend said, raising a hand to check him. His voice lowered. "Listen. Listen. I been wanting to ask you. I don't know how to . . . I guess I'll just—Well. Was she peaceful, Abe? Did she seem at peace at all?"

"Did she seem at peace?" Abe repeated, to give himself a moment.

"Yes," Mr. Townsend said eagerly, as if he'd known his question would be hard to comprehend and was heartened Abe understood him. "Yes, was she at—? Because I wonder, Abe. I think about it. Lord knows how I treated her. I mean it wasn't entirely me, son. Though I don't want to get into that. She doesn't deserve that. But looking back I can see it much clearer, much clearer. I can see how I treated her. And she loved me. She loved me despite everything I'd done. I can't hardly stand to think of it."

He flapped the photograph again, breathing heavily. Abe hesitated.

"I know it was dark in those woods," Mr. Townsend said quickly, and everything that followed became a question, half-hopeful, half-despairing: "I know you can't have seen much? Or if you did, you couldn't have told one thing from another? I mean about how she was?"

"It was pretty dark."

Mr. Townsend nodded. "I figured as much. Yeah, I figured. I figured. But, you couldn't tell anything at all? Because you know I had spoken with her the night y'all left. And I wasn't cruel, Abe. You understand I wasn't cruel."

"No, sir. I'm sure you weren't."

"No, but I was cold. I was cold to her. I just asked to speak with Jim. He'd called for me, y'all were fixing to leave. And I could tell how she felt, me on the phone with her again. All those years living with her, you think I couldn't tell how upset she got? And on a night like that, saying good-bye to her boy. And I was just as cold as ever. But see we'd been through so much. I mean, three years of fighting a divorce. It was routine, you know. I just had to get through it. I'd level my voice and just plow through. Usually I had to do that. Not mean, just cold. But that night, when she was saying good-bye to Jim, I was cold to her, just matter-of-fact, 'Give Jim the phone, Jackie.' I was used to having to sort of direct her that way. Otherwise she'd just hang on the line sometimes, not saying anything. Or just waiting to say something again. I don't know. But it was the last time I spoke to her, Abe. And I was cruel to her. It was cruel to be cold to her; I can't say it wasn't, not on a night like that. It was cruel."

Jim came into the room. Mr. Townsend dropped his eyes, as if caught at something. Jim looked at him with a mixture of wariness and concern. "Everything all right in here?"

Mr. Townsend dipped his chin, a tight little nod. "Just talking about your mother."

"I can see that. You need a minute? I was going to ask Abe for a lift into town. We don't have any packing tape."

"No, that's fine. You boys go on. I'm fine here."

"You sure?"

Mr. Townsend frowned, nodded, waved them toward the door. "You boys go on."

Jim looked at Abe. "You on your lunch hour or what? Can you give me a lift?"

"I've got time."

"Abe, it was good to see you, son."

Abe leaned and shook hands.

The poodle was under the porch steps, waiting to nip at their ankles. Abe felt her tug at his pant leg, the sharp teeth just pinching his skin. He'd been amused before, but now he hated the dog. He kicked free and stomped the wood. Jim yelled at her. She retreated to somewhere in the recesses under the house.

"She's like the goddamn troll under the bridge," Jim said. "Does the same thing at home. Sometimes it's all I can do not to wring her skinny neck."

They climbed into the truck. Abe sat for a moment before starting the engine. The house had a sunny, open look now, with its windows flung up, curtains shifting in a faint breeze. Only Jim's old window was still closed.

"You didn't see my room," Jim said. "She painted it. I wasn't out of the house two days and she painted it yellow. Had her ironing board and her exercise bike in there. I couldn't get the window open, finally realized she'd painted it shut."

"How was it, seeing that?"

"My room changed? It was all right. Not my room anymore, anyway. Why shouldn't she do it?"

Abe nodded. He cranked the ignition, turned on the air conditioner.

"What," Jim said.

"What?"

"Why aren't we moving?"

"We're moving," Abe said, shifting out of park. He backed a few feet and stopped. Shifted back into park. "Can you hold on? I need to go back in for a minute."

"Just leave the air running," Jim said, casual as ever.

Mr. Townsend was exactly where they'd left him, on the floor with his legs spread out, leaning over a box. He wasn't looking in it, though, but had his forehead resting against its edge, the cardboard bent under the weight. He was staring at the carpet, the same photograph still in his hand, of his wife half-seen in a background mirror.

"I couldn't say she looked peaceful," Abe said.

Mr. Townsend looked up.

"I could say it, but later you'd wonder if I was telling the truth. How likely it was that she really seemed at peace."

"All right," Mr. Townsend said after a moment. His eyes lost their concentration. That unfocused look of the resigned. "I suppose you're right."

"She seemed tired, is all. I imagine it's how most people look. It's the shock. Like they just need some rest."

"Tired. All right. She looked tired."

"Mr. Townsend?"

The man was tired himself. He seemed unable to fix his gaze directly on Abe. Only looked in Abe's direction.

Abe said his name again.

Mr. Townsend's eyebrows went up. Eyes flickered. "Yes, Abe. I'm here. What is it?"

"She got up early that morning, you know, just like she always did. She was driving into Hot Springs to work, just like always."

"Just like always," the man repeated dully.

Abe wouldn't press him. Let him think about it. No one could be convinced of anything. He had to think it himself. He was in this house; he had seen the painted room, the exercise bike. He knew she was going to work that morning. Let him think for himself.

"I'll see you, Mr. Townsend."

Jim had got tools from the bed of Abe's truck and was under the dashboard, his legs stretched out the open door. "Your radio wasn't working," he said. "Don't tell me it's been this way since the flood."

"All right, I won't."

"You realize it's just some wires came loose? Five-minute job. I don't know how you stand it without a radio."

"I'm not in the truck much."

Jim hauled himself up and turned the knob. Static ripped through the speakers. He lowered the volume and tuned the dial up and down, searching for a clear signal. "The reception's never good up here in the summer."

"Any good stations down there?"

"One or two. There, you're all set. Five minutes."

Abe drove down the rutted woods road to the highway. "How are classes?"

"Dull. Easy. Pointless."

"That's good."

"Yeah, I couldn't ask for more."

"So what do you think?"

"What's there to think about? I knew it'd be two parts bullshit. I'll just plug through. It'll get better or it won't."

"I guess you have to stop playing your gigs at night."

"Actually that's going great guns. Club owner loves us—it's much more crowded there when we play. It's not me, it's mostly Clyde, but I do my part. He's even doing some of my songs now."

They had reached the new South Fork bridge. Abe wondered if Jim had passed through here much yet, what he must feel. But Jim was talking, not paying the road any attention. The bridge hummed beneath and was behind them.

"Clyde's the singer?" Abe said.

"You should hear him. He's the real deal. The owner's talking about setting up some night, recording a live session. Says people keep asking if we have any records, so he figures why not make one, sell it at the door?"

"You serious?"

"What he said."

"So what do you need school for? Damn."

"Well, I've got to have something to fall back on, you know. Case my career as a blues legend doesn't pan out."

"All this, and you're working for your dad. I don't see how you do it."

"How I do it is I'm only in the office two afternoons a week, maybe a few hours on Sunday if things get backed up. Lick some stamps, answer the phone, return any calls that get left on the machine. Stuff that has to get done, but it takes no time. So I get most of my studying in while I'm there, then for dinner I walk down to this crazy little noodle joint—a family of Cubans runs the place, it's called the Asian Café, swear to God—go meet Dad at the golf course, then head on down to the club. I finagled it so all my classes are in the afternoon on my off days, so I never have to get up early. Works out great."

Abe forced a smile. In the span of two minutes he'd gone from feeling hopelessly inferior (what had he been thinking? He hadn't been able to manage classes and a job, much less a musician's nightlife) to bitterly disadvantaged: Jim with his perfect schedule, his unearned paychecks, his real-deal musician friend. He was disgusted with himself. Say it out loud, he thought. Jim, it's not fair, you're leading a charmed life. Bridge not two minutes behind you. Say it out loud, show yourself.

"I'm glad," he said. "It's about time you caught some breaks."

"Damn right," Jim said. "Why don't you pull in at the 66? I think they have tape."

Abe parked at a pump while Jim went inside. "Get a hold of yourself," he said. Sucking salt from the neck of his sweaty T-shirt, he checked his tires, checked the oil. He'd tried to prepare himself for this but hadn't anticipated such a range of emotion; he hadn't expected resentment.

Jim came out with a gnarled strip of beef jerky he'd bought from the counter jar. "No tape. Let's try Ridgeway's."

At the grocery Abe's mother was working the register, ringing up bottles of ketchup for Emma Norman, who had unexpectedly run out at the café. Her quicksilver smile flashed and disappeared when they walked in.

"Looky who's here," she said. "I knew you two'd find each other."

"Mom's who told me you were in town," Abe said.

"Well, that explains how you found out. I guess even a hermit has to buy groceries. Hi, Miss Pittenger. Hello, Miss Norman."

Emma Norman, sixty years old and wiry of build and hair, was the most brusque of women, but she left her ketchup bottles for a moment and came to place a hand on Jim's arm. "Jim, honey. I missed talking to you at the funeral, but I wanted to say I was so sorry about your mother."

"Thank you, ma'am," he said, straightening his shoulders, immediately sober.

"She was one of the best. We all thought it."

"I appreciate your saying so."

"Well," she said, patting his arm and turning away. "We're glad to have you back in town for a few days."

A line had formed behind her. It was lunch hour, people coming in for deli sandwiches and box lunches. Abe's mother was ringing up the next customer. As Emma scooped up her sack, Abe felt Jim brush past him, disappearing down the first aisle. He had to hustle to catch up.

"You think we can slip out the back?" Jim said under his breath.

"What?"

"Every one of those people will feel like they have to say something. I mean, good God, if Emma Norman offers her sympathies, you can see what I'm in for. I'm not up to it, Abe."

"All right, follow me."

He led Jim through swinging doors into the storage area. The room smelled of produce and old wood and was empty—no one took breaks during the rush. Abe pointed to a table with a half-full ashtray and a hunting magazine on it. "Have a seat. I'll be right back."

But when he returned with the tape, Jim was pacing. His face appeared leaden, his features drawn. Abe took him out a back door, had him wait at the rear of the building while he pulled the truck around.

"Thanks," Jim said as they pulled onto Main Street. Someone was waving. They both pretended not to see.

"Am I taking you straight back, or what?"

"You have anything cold to drink at your place? There's nothing at the house."

"Sure." He turned onto Merrill Road.

"One at a time, I can take it," Jim said. "But a crowd like that? No, thank you. It'd be every other person."

Abe nodded. The ordeal, brief though it was, had made him feel as if he should say something pertinent—which was exactly the trouble, he realized. He kept his mouth shut. There was an unfamiliar, bubbly feeling in his gut, like excitement or possibly pleasure, though there was nothing to be excited or pleased about. He was trying to name it to himself when Jim spoke up again.

"You wouldn't believe the things people find to say. This one guy who works for my father, first time he meets me he starts going on about the healing power of loss. Loss, Abe. Without loss there can be no healing, he says. I said of course not, how could there be? Exactly, he says, and nods and sips his coffee like we've just had a meaningful conversation."

Jim's face had regained its color. He pulled out the beef jerky he'd bought and tore off a bite. After he'd chewed a while he rolled down the window and spat it out. Abe smiled to himself. This was the way Jim had always eaten jerky, as if it were tobacco.

"Still, it helps to be a quiet person," Jim said. "People generally leave me alone. Your problem is you're friendly by nature. That's why you're getting so much grief. When you get quiet, everybody notices."

"We're talking about my problem now?"

Jim shrugged. They were pulling up in front of the trailer. "I hope you intend to fix that window before winter."

"Well, I don't intend to freeze," Abe said, but the truth was he'd grown so used to the taped-up glass he might have forgotten about it until the cold set in.

Stopping in the front doorway, Jim looked around the living room with eyebrows raised. Abe tried to remember what it was like the last time Jim had seen it. The books, he realized. There hadn't been so many before. Now he had stacks of them spread out across the living room floor. He supposed it did look odd.

"If those were newspapers," Jim said, "and just a little higher, I'd have to call for help."

"I keep the newspapers in the back. You want a Coke or a beer or what?"

"Hell, give me a beer. Are these organized in any particular way?" He was weaving through the stacks, looking at the top book of each one, trying to find the pattern.

"In order of stackability," Abe said, bringing him a bottle.

"I see. And have you read all of them?"

"Most. That stack there is what I haven't read yet."

"Damn, son. You've got your own little library here. I mean without the organization."

"You're welcome to borrow anything you want."

"I might," Jim said, sitting on the couch. He propped his feet on the coffee table. "So now, tell me about this attack on Repeat's car. What grave offense had it given you?"

Abe leaned against a wall. "That was about Marie."

"Kylie told me that much. What gives? I'm gone a few months and suddenly you're in fist fights about some girl I never heard of."

"I loved her, that's what gives."

"And she threw you over, and so now you're in hiding?"

"Is this where I get a lecture? Because I didn't know I'd signed up for a lecture."

"I'm just trying to figure out who got to you so much that you scrap the Camaro and start playing the anchorite. From the looks of this place you're headed for total shutdown here."

"You wouldn't say that if you understood," Abe said, straightening. He grimaced and went to the taped window, looked out at his scorched yard. He'd sounded like a sulky school kid.

"Fine," Jim said. "Make me understand."

Abe opened his mouth to speak but closed it when he realized his mind was filled with rain and thunder and Jackie's frightened eyes. He blinked, wishing away the image. It was sunny outside the window. In the distance an owl that shouldn't have been awake was flapping low to the ground, beleaguered by angry crows. They arced over the fence and flew off over Simmons's pasture.

"You of all people shouldn't be out here trying to cheer me up," Abe said. "With what you've been through. It's ridiculous."

"Goddamnit, you're pissing me off with that stuff."

Abe turned. "Excuse me?"

"Everything you say is just dripping with self-pity. Surely you realize that."

"Are you not listening? I was talking about you. Not me, Jim. You."

"Of course. You can't do anything simple. With you it's got to be much more complicated. First you feel sorry for yourself, then you feel guilty because you think I have more reason than you to feel bad. But that's still about you, isn't it? It's not about me or anybody else."

"You're upset. I don't want to argue with you."

"You don't want to argue with me because there's something you're not telling me."

Abe felt an electric jolt down his spine, his skin suddenly on fire. "What?"

"Jesus, Abe. We've been friends our whole lives."

"I know that."

"So I don't know when you decided to start keeping things from me, but fine, keep them to yourself. Just don't pretend that nothing's different. Or that other things are different but you're the same."

"Am I pretending?" Abe asked, trying to regain composure.

"I don't see how else you can keep up this hideout routine."

"For God's sake, it's not a—"

"Don't try to tell me it's not a hideout routine."

"Will you let me speak?"

"Fine. Speak."

"First of all, I don't see why it matters to you whether I'm hiding out or not. What difference does it make to you?"

"It matters because I've lost my mother and my friend both. You think I don't care about that? This is what I'm talking about."

"I'm right here."

"Are you? I'm not so sure."

"No idea what that's supposed to mean."

Jim shook his head. His eyes lost their intensity; his shoulders sagged. "I don't know. Hell if I know, Abe." He took a swig of his beer. "Maybe I'm just talking to myself."

"I'm listening to you."

"I know. I mean I'm just as pissed off at myself as I am at you."

"You've got no reason to be pissed off at yourself."

"And now you're talking to *your* self."

"Fine. Let's agree that you're right, that I'm full of shit, and be done with it."

"Fine. Agreed." Jim put the beer bottle to his forehead, closed his eyes. "It doesn't matter, anyway. I don't know when I got so full of answers."

"It's all that sunshine. Vitamin D."

"Forgive me if I don't laugh right now."

"Sorry. You're right."

"Don't be sorry, I'm just not laughing."

"All right."

"Jesus Christ," Jim said, not angrily, but wearily. "It's just that I don't know how to do any of this. I don't know what's right, what's right to do. It's like I always expected there was some right way, and now that I'm on the spot, I have no idea; I just keep feeling like I'm not doing it right, like there's some other way that's right."

"I know," Abe said quietly. "That's exactly it."

"But there's no right way. However you do it, it's wrong."

"Well, there's no wrong way with something like this, is there? There's just how you do it, and that's all."

"It's the same damn thing," Jim said. "It's all wrong, no matter what."

They were quiet for a while. Abe stood at the window. The bubbly feeling in his gut had returned, and he was certain now what it was. He was happy, strangely happy, happier than he had been in ages. And though partly the feeling came from Jim's being here again, Abe understood now that partly it came, too, from Jim's panicked behavior at the grocery store, from this last admission of grief. You will have to live with this, he thought. Live the rest of your life knowing that you felt better because your friend suffered. And yet Abe was happy, if only for the moment, and it was such a welcome, unexpected feeling that he let it stay. Despite the guilt. Let it stay while it would, no matter the reason.

Jim had come to stand with him at the window. Both of them squinting out at the dry yard.

"It's funny how so many things look exactly the same," Jim said.

Chapter 15

It was strange to walk into the house and smell food in the oven she hadn't put there herself; strange to see the place bustling, people gathered in front of the television, people talking in the kitchen, Angela checking timers and washing dishes and pouring drinks and slapping hands away from the platters of food; strange to watch her father entertaining the guests, teasing the children, asking who wanted tea and who wanted Coke and did the kids want Kool-Aid; strange to see him place his hand lightly on Angela's back as they spoke in the kitchen. To be welcomed by a small crowd of people in what she had begun to think of as her own home. To be clucked and cooed over by Angela and Mrs. Baker and Mrs. Baker's niece Becka, a glass of punch pressed into her hands as though she were the guest, women stroking her hair, women saying, Why, don't you look cute.

Marie escaped to the bathroom with the odd sensation of her world having changed again without her seeing it happen. She wanted to laugh at herself for thinking it would last.

She put on more makeup than usual, dressed slowly, brushed her hair slowly, put on a touch of perfume. Changed her earrings a few times. She dropped one of them by accident, watched it slip down the drain in the bathroom sink. Threw the other one away, no point in having one earring. She heard the men shouting at the game on television, and Becka too, a great football fan. She heard the creaking hinge of the oven door in the kitchen. Angela and Mrs. Baker arguing matter-of-factly the way they did. Out of the corner of her eye she saw two tiny children peering at her from the doorway of her room. Kids she hadn't met—a girl, and a child who might be boy or girl, with delicate features and hair an ambiguous length—spying on the grownups from the safety of Marie's bedroom. Or whoever's bedroom it was.

She turned on them suddenly, stomping her foot and saying, "Boo!" They squealed and jerked their heads back out of sight. She could hear them giggling in her room. She left them there and went down the hall. Let them peek hopefully out again and find her gone.

"So if you go into the water up to your knees, are you baptized then?" Angela asked Joe. Joe was Becka's husband, a square-built man in his forties with a bowl haircut, florid cheeks, and a mustache. He and Becka looked very much alike, though her mustache was less obvious. They were Baptists.

"No," Joe said good-naturedly. He had already proven himself a jokester, was willing to go along.

"I think I've heard this one," said Becka.

"If you go in up to your bellybutton, are you baptized then?"

"We wouldn't be a family if we didn't argue about religion or politics," Vincent said, with a wink for Marie. Though he'd recently undergone prostate surgery, he seemed in good health. She had watched him carve the turkey at her father's insistence, and he was all grace and aplomb, no sign of weakness aside from his usual slight trembling. But she wondered how he felt, whether he was counting the turkeys now, whether he studied his old aunt like a country on a map, a place he'd read about but was unlikely to visit. Was he afraid? Half-relieved? No more watching the moon rise alone while the family women chattered and fussed?

"No," Joe said, "Belly-button baptism doesn't count, but I'd count it for a bath."

"He would, too," Becka said.

"Up to your eyes, then? Are you baptized yet?"

"Not quite."

"But if you go in until the water covers your head, are you baptized then?"

"Yep. Then you're good and baptized."

"So it's only the top of the head that counts, after all."

Joe guffawed. There were chuckles and smiles all around the dining table. "That's a good one," he said, nodding. "Top of the head. Okay. I gotcha."

"But you know," Becka said, "nowhere in the Bible do you see the apostles sprinkling water on people's heads. They took them to the river and down they went. Total immersion. That's the way the Bible shows us how to do it." She blushed. "I don't mean to preach."

Marie noticed Angela's son Eric squinting at her from the end of the table. Eric had come down from Missouri for the weekend. A short man, well-proportioned, with green eyes and shining spritzed brown hair, he was good-looking and knew it. And he was impish, in a facile, irritating way. When she met him for the first time—just before dinner—he'd said, "Hey, sis," and hugged her. She'd hugged him stiffly back, not missing the downward sweep of his eyes as he pulled away, the quick appraisal. She'd wanted to rabbit-punch him.

Too late she realized why he was squinting at her. He was getting ready to put her on the spot. One of those who thinks he's showing camaraderie by making you uncomfortable. He said, "What do you think, Marie? Who's right?"

There was a slight shifting of faces and chairs toward her.

"Well, I think I'll say Joe and Becka are right because they're outnumbered."

"Amen, sister," Joe said, giving her a thumbs-up.

"That's true Christianity, isn't it?" said Angela. "Jesus always sides with the low and downtrodden."

Marie noticed that her father and Mrs. Baker followed the conversation with the same expression of pleased confusion on their faces. It occurred to her he might be losing his hearing. He did tend to keep the television loud. She wondered if Angela would have the sense and stubbornness to force him into a doctor's appointment. But of course she would, and the delicacy too. It was Marie who didn't know heads from tails in such matters.

She had stopped listening to the conversation, as had Mrs. Baker, apparently, who tapped her glass loudly and said, "Will one of you Baptists pass the gravy?"

Later Vincent taught them a card game called Chattanooga Rummy that involved two decks of cards and the jokers. He was masterful with the cards, gracefully spreading and folding them in his hand like a paper fan, nimbly flicking them across the table as he dealt. Marie couldn't see how he managed it, with that slight quavering of his. Years, she thought. Years and years and years. Between hands she went into the living room to check on the children. They had eaten at the coffee table, and now the two youngest ones, the spies, were asleep on the floor, side by side in front of the television. The third, Joey, a boy of about ten, was tucked into a corner of the couch reading a comic book.

"Can I get you anything, Joey?"

He shook his head. A shy boy, overweight. He had his shoes on the couch. She knelt by the sleeping children. Their faces were damp, their fine hair sticking to their foreheads. The girl wore the earring Marie had thrown away, had salvaged it from the bathroom trash. Marie placed a hand on the girl's warm back, felt her ribs rising and sinking as she breathed. Like any sleeping animal. She brushed back the girl's hair.

Joey was watching her over the top of his comic book.

"Were you ever this young?" she asked him.

He cocked his head suspiciously, gave a hint of a smile.

"I know for sure I wasn't," she said.

"Yes, you were."

She gave him a quizzical look. "I don't think so."

He laughed. "Yes, you were, dummy. Everybody was."

She thought about this. "Well. Maybe."

He rolled his eyes. "You were!"

"I'm going to think about it."

"You were."

She looked away from him, stroked the children's hair. It was so soft. She glanced back at him with a doubtful look on her face.

He tittered. "You were."

"If you say so."

Through the open doorway of the dining room Eric called out: "Marie, you're losing in here. Vincent's giving you nothing but discards."

She stood up. "You don't want to play cards, Joey?"

"I hate that game. It's too hard to hold everything in your hand."

"Do you know how to play Speed?"

He shook his head.

"Well, if you've finished your comic book by the time we're done with our game, I'll teach you how to play Speed."

"I might could be finished by then," he said coyly.

Speed involved no thought and a good deal of slapping hands down on cards. At the youth home in Little Rock she had played a thousand games of it. She let Joey beat her the first few games to get his confidence up, then beat him once to get him riled. The other children woke and wanted to play too. It was a good excuse to stay away from Eric, who kept urging her to return to the adult game and for whom her hatred was ripening by the moment, so she taught the children how, and they played a tournament until Joe and Becka said it was time to go home. Joey whined. He didn't want to go. He wanted to stay and play cards with Marie.

"Nope," Joe said, "it's time to go, Junior. Put your shoes back on and get your jacket."

"Don't worry," Marie told him. "Next time we get together I'll play you again, and I'll beat you every game."

"No, you won't!" he said, with more of a whine than a laugh.

"We'll see about that."

He stuck out his tongue. He was mad at everybody now.

"Joe Junior, get your shoes on," Becka said.

After they'd left and Marie was cleaning up the children's mess in the living room, Eric came in to hover around her as she worked. "You didn't miss much," he said. "Vincent and Grandma just took turns winning."

"I'm glad," Marie said, meaning it. To get away from him, she went into the kitchen. He followed her.

"Don't you have a girlfriend, Eric?"

"Not here," he said, and she really wanted to slap him.

"She still in prison?"

He laughed. "Hey, you crack me up."

"I was just trying to figure out how many stepnieces and nephews I could count on in the future."

"Well, let's see," he said, opening the refrigerator. He got out a beer, opened it, and handed it to her without asking if she wanted one. He took one for himself. "Mom has two older brothers, and they both have kids."

"Those would be cousins."

"Right. Just testing you. You know I got a sister. She's coming down tomorrow. Maybe y'all can talk girl talk. You probably have sex secrets and whatnot you could share. Like where you lost it or how you like to do it."

He was leaning casually against the counter, but she could feel the excitement in him. She could smell that sort of thing. She started drinking the beer. It was finished here, she thought. This was going to be her brother-in-law. She took long pulls, thinking of hitting him with the bottle when it was empty. Just a glancing blow, enough to hurt, to give her the memory of having almost done worse.

"Whoa, you just trying to get drunk?"

She didn't answer.

"You handle that bottle like you've had a lot of practice."

How Angela could have raised this man was a mystery. He was nothing like her. Perhaps he was like his father. Perhaps that's why Angela was divorced and about to marry Jimmy Hamilton. You couldn't divorce your children. You could take them in or close the door on them, raise them or leave them, beat them or baby them, but they were your children, no changing that. Angela would never leave her horrid son. Marie's mother abandoned her little girl on a fall afternoon at the Burger Chef. Both of them tethered to their children, by different kinds of love and regret.

"You not gonna say anything?" Eric said.

Marie was finishing the beer. She would talk to him with the bottle. This was all going to be over anyway. She felt it boiling up in her.

The phone rang. She heard her father answer in the living room. He came in. "For you," he said.

She set the bottle on the counter next to Eric, clapping it down hard, but he didn't know what it meant and only smiled gamely after her. Vincent and Mrs. Baker and Angela were still sitting around the dining room table with her father and could see her through the open doorway. She took the phone and turned her back to them. When she heard the voice on the other end, she really did want to laugh. It was too perfect. This was the perfect night to get a call from Little Rock. She should have seen it coming.

The others grew quieter, out of politeness or curiosity. They heard her say, "Okay. Okay. No, that's—No. All right."

"Everything all right?" her father asked, when she hung up.

"I need to go meet someone."

"Right now?"

She went into the bedroom for her purse. The kids had gone through her closet and scattered her things about the room, but that didn't matter. It was a five-minute pickup, and she might not even bother. She might not even be back. She went down the hall again. Everybody was quiet, wondering.

Eric came out of the kitchen and stood before her. "You're not rushing off, are you?"

"Get the hell out of my way, asshole," she snapped, and he leaped back, shocked.

"Somebody's in a nasty mood," he said.

She slammed the door behind her.

Chapter 16

He could tell it was Kylie's car by the way it skidded to a stop in the gravel. Kylie always braked as though he were driving an automatic and using both feet. Dust hung in the headlight beams. Abe watched from the screen door, a finger marking his place in his book. He turned on the porch light. It was cool outside now. An early fall night.

"Pitt," Kylie said, hurrying up the steps, "I got something important to tell you. I tried to call, but you still haven't got your phone hooked up."

"I know I haven't." He wasn't getting worked up. Kylie always had something important to tell. "Come on in. Can I get you something?"

"No. We need to talk."

"Okay, then, let's talk."

Kylie picked his way across the living room, stepping around the neat stacks of books, and sat on the couch. He still wore the glasses and the goatee, and Abe had the vague feeling it was a stranger on his couch. Almost a handsome stranger, in fact, and that was an odd thing to consider.

"I think you ought to set down too," Kylie said.

"All right," he said, sitting on the arm of the couch. "What's this about?"

"Marie Hamilton."

"Are you going out with her now?"

"Am I what? No."

"Well, that's a relief."

"No, listen. Do you remember when we first met her, at Charleton? I said I thought I'd met her before, but she says, 'No, I don't think so'? Well, turns out I had met her before. Last year. Course I didn't remember how I knew her, so I thought maybe she was right."

Abe was alert now—alert and uncomfortable. At the mention of Marie, he had woken as if from a dream, as if someone had turned on the light. Like Kylie, he had begun, strangely, to think of Marie as someone he thought he'd met but hadn't. Someone he'd dreamed about, someone whose significance you couldn't explain with your waking mind.

"Okay," he said. "So you met her before."

"So, okay. So today I run into this guy Roy Hildreth—all right, let me back up. You remember when she and Repeat were going out a while back?"

"I think I remember that."

"Well, that all started at this party we went to in Little Rock. A huge party at this house on the river. Tons of people there. And at one point this big redneck-looking guy come up to Marie and says, 'Marie?' says, 'What are you doing here?' And she goes all white and says, 'Roy?' And he says, 'I can't believe it. We thought you was gone for good.' And she kind of laughs and says, 'I am gone for good,' or something weird like that. And so he says he's got to talk to her, and she says okay, but not right then, let her get a drink first.

"So then she and Repeat go into the back, and she tells Repeat she doesn't want to talk to that guy, can they just leave? And you know Repeat, he says, 'You damn right we can leave. You don't have to talk to anybody you don't want to.' So they head out the back. But this guy Roy sees them go out, and he follows them to the car. Meanwhile me and Roberto's watching all this, cause it looks like trouble. And sure enough the guy starts yelling at her, saying he wants to talk to her and she can't just take off again, and she keeps saying to Repeat, 'Let's go, let's go, let's go.'

"But you know Repeat, he gets out to tell the guy to back off, and for a minute I mean it looked like it was gonna get nasty. This guy was big and, I don't know, kind of greasy-looking mean, like he tortured cats when he was a kid, that kind of guy, but then there's Repeat, who nobody in their right mind wants to mess with— "

"Kylie, get to it, who is this guy?"

"So, okay, me and Roberto come up, and the guy backed off, and that was the end of it. He left right after they did, maybe trying to follow them, I don't know— "

"Did Marie say how she knew him?"

"She told Repeat he was a friend of a friend but she never liked him and didn't want to talk to him. And then just a little bit after that she told Repeat to kiss off, so nobody heard anything else about it till today."

"What happened today?"

"Today I'm working at the Photo Stop, and this guy comes in to pick up some pictures for his grandma. When he gets up to the counter we recognize each other at the same time, and it's this Roy guy, and I'm thinking, 'Oh, shit.' But we talk a while and he's not so mean as he seemed like at the party, so it's cool. But then he tells me this about Marie, and then I'm like, Now I remember where I knew her from— "

"What did he tell you?"

"Well, see, how I knew her was because last summer she brought in some pictures to develop. That's where I'd seen her. Course I'd seen all her pictures too. And the reason I didn't remember her was— "

"For God's sake, will you tell me—"

"The reason I couldn't remember her was because she was alone when we saw her at Charleton, Pitt, but when she came in last summer she was married."

Abe looked at him as if at a stranger. The same slightly good-looking stranger who had come and sat on his couch. It was Kylie, though, giving him that Kylie-look, triumphant but not quite smug, because he couldn't master smugness. It was more like hope—it was Kylie looking arrogant and hoping he'd done the right thing.

Abe looked away. "Marie was married."

"I thought you'd want to know."

"To this guy Roy?"

"Hell, no, not to Roy. To his friend. But that guy's dead now. Got killed by a burglar in his own kitchen, just a few months ago."

There were several people in the house Abe hadn't met, but Marie wasn't there. An old couple sat at the table drinking coffee, looking at him with a sort of bemused friendliness. And he heard a woman's voice in the kitchen, but not Marie's. Mr. Hamilton asked him to sit down, have a bite of cake, have something to drink.

"Do you know where she went?"

"She left a while ago," Mr. Hamilton said cautiously. "Was that you that called and got her so upset?"

"No, sir. We haven't spoken in a while."

"Didn't think it sounded like you. This guy wasn't so polite. Listen, if you need to run off, I can have her call you when she gets in."

"I don't have a phone."

"Well, then," Mr. Hamilton said, as if he didn't know what to do with him, "like I said, why don't you set down for a minute? I'd tell you where she was headed, but she didn't say."

Abe hesitated.

"Let me introduce you to everyone," said Mr. Hamilton.

So he met them all, the older man and the very old woman, and Mr. Hamilton's new fiancée, Angela, and her son, who came in from the kitchen. He accepted a piece of cake and coffee and sat with them at the table. And for fifteen minutes they sat there making small talk, trying to include him. But Abe couldn't concentrate. He kept thinking: It wasn't about you, you dumb shit. And thinking: Look what she did, what she tried to do. Marie.

"You really don't have any idea when she'll be back?" he said aloud. From the expressions on their faces he realized he had interrupted somebody. They all turned expectantly to Mr. Hamilton, all but the son, Eric, who was smirking at Abe as if at a curiosity.

"No, son, I sure don't. But you're welcome to wait as long as you like."

"It is getting late," Angela said, rising. "We ought to be heading home."

They made their good-byes, Angela lingering at the door to talk privately with Mr. Hamilton. Not knowing what else to do, Abe waited at the table. He heard a car start up, the front door close. Mr. Hamilton came back and sat at the table with him.

"Is there something I should know about, Abe? Is Marie in some kind of trouble?"

"I don't know, sir. I don't think so. I just wanted to talk to her."

"You thinking y'all might get back together?"

"No, sir," he said, somewhat taken aback. "No, sir, I doubt it."

"But you want to talk to her. Tonight. At—" He checked his watch. "—At ten o'clock at night."

"I think it might be a hard night for her. I wanted to be here in case she needs me."

"In case she needs you," Mr. Hamilton said, an edge coming into his voice. A pink streak appeared on his bald head. "What, is she pregnant?"

"Is she—? No, sir, not that I'm aware of."

"Then what?"

Abe shifted uncomfortably in his seat. "I mean no disrespect, Mr. Hamilton. But I don't know whether I should talk about Marie's business, even with you."

Mr. Hamilton frowned for a while. Then his face relaxed. He leaned back from the table and regarded him, tapping his fingers absently on the wood. Finally he nodded. "Fair enough, no disrespect taken. I wouldn't have suspected it of you, anyway, Abe. I appreciate your concern about my daughter."

"Well, it comes natural."

"You mean to say you love her."

"Yes, sir."

"But you don't think she loves you?"

Abe considered. "I'm not sure that matters."

Mr. Hamilton nodded again. "I'm poking my nose right back in where I meant to take it out. All right. One last thing, and then I'll let it go. I want to hear one more time from you that I don't have anything to worry about here. She said she had to go meet somebody. Should I be calling the police?"

"Not as far as I know."

"If you were her father, would you be calling the police?"

He thought about it. "No, sir. I guess not."

"So you're not worried about her safety. You're just afraid she's upset about something. Is that it?"

"Pretty much."

"Well, I can verify that for you. She's upset," said Mr. Hamilton. He rubbed his face as if trying to come awake. Then he placed his palms flat on the table and sighed a deep sigh, as if he had settled something in his mind. "You want some more coffee?"

"That's okay."

"You sure? Cause I'm thinking of having some."

"Well. Are you having some?"

"I'll make a fresh pot."

They went into the kitchen together. Mr. Hamilton looked around at the bright counters, the scrubbed sink, the mopped floor. He shook his head, amused. "I don't think it's been this clean since I moved in. That woman is a miracle."

"Congratulations, by the way. I don't think I said so earlier."

Mr. Hamilton had taken out a tin of coffee, and he paused now with his hand on the lid, as if he'd forgotten how to open it. "You know, each time someone mentions it, it kind of catches me off guard, like I'm hearing about it for the first time." He grinned. "You'd think I'd be old enough not to get nervous about such things. Course we got some technicalities to work out. It's never just as easy as stepping up to the altar and saying the words. You like it strong?"

"However you like it."

"Strong it is. No, it's never so easy as all that. Got to figure out where we'll live, what to get rid of, what kind of wedding, who to invite, who you don't want to invite but have to anyway, all that razzmatazz. I didn't like it the first time, either. But the fact is it doesn't matter whether you like it or not. You want to get married, you got to pay the piper. You take cream?"

"If you have any."

Mr. Hamilton opened his refrigerator and seemed surprised. He shook his head and began digging around, trying to find the milk.

"Have you decided where you're going to live?" Abe asked.

"Thinking about selling both houses—Angela's and this one—and moving into a condo out near Mrs. Baker, on the lake. It's a nice place. We don't need much space just for the two of us."

"What about Marie?"

"I said she could live with us if she wanted, or else I'd set her up in an apartment. She said she'd have to think about it, but I figure she'll want her own place. Rent for a while, save up to buy a little house. Hey, how do you like that trailer of yours?"

"It's been fine for me. Wouldn't do for anybody else, I don't think."

"I was thinking about a new one. I mean buying one for Marie and her living there till she figures out what she wants. I hear you can resell those things sometimes for about as much as you put into them."

"Some of them are nice."

"You think she'd like it, though?"

Abe thought about it. "I have no idea," he said finally.

"Well, it's just something I'm thinking about," Mr. Hamilton said. He poured their coffee. "I take it you don't think you know Marie too well."

"Well. It changes minute to minute."

Mr. Hamilton smiled. "That's one lesson you learn the hard way. At least I did. Some people you can't really know. You can almost know them, and that's about as close as it gets."

"I think you're right."

"My opinion," said Mr. Hamilton with a shrug. "And sometimes it's good enough—almost knowing somebody, I mean. And sometimes it isn't. But it's all we've got."

"Sounds like you've thought about this."

"Twenty years setting alone in a bookstore, Abe, you think about things. Plus fifteen years of coming home to an empty house, wondering why it's empty. Wondering do you go on like it didn't happen, or wait, or try to get it back . . . What was my point? Oh, yeah: thinking. No, if I haven't been thinking, I don't know what you'd call it."

"What did you decide?"

"About what?"

"Going on, waiting, or trying to get it back."

"I didn't decide. Which, for a long time, that amounted to waiting. And then at some point it turned into going on. I let that be my decision, kind of ex post facto."

"Seems to have worked out all right."

"It's true. Suddenly I've got more women in my life than I can even account for. Not that I pretend to know what I'm doing. But you can't let that stop you." He sipped his coffee. "Marie ever tell you about her mother, Abe? I mean all that happened?"

"Yes, sir. Some of it, at least."

"Well, what Marie could not have told you is how her mother used to be when I met her. Beautiful, crazy, smart, and for the most part, together. That's what Marie couldn't have known, how together her mother used to be. Course she had a few problems, we all do, but they didn't seem big at the time. She had them in her hip pocket. And then—well, eventually I watched them just eat her away. That's what I was thinking when I said you can almost know a person. I knew Marie—I mean my wife—but I didn't know who it was that was letting all that happen to her. If it'd been somebody else doing that to her I'd have hated them, I'd have beat the hell out of them, something. But it was just her, falling apart all by herself, and me just a dumb country boy not knowing what to do."

He was talking to his coffee, only glancing at Abe from time to time, his expression troubled, maybe regretting this line of talk, maybe just deep in memory. He sipped his coffee again, not taking the cup handle but holding the rim with his fingers like a Japanese teacup.

"Marie never told me she was named for her mother," Abe said.

"She didn't? Well, strange to say, it was her mother's idea. She liked the idea of Marie having her first name and my last name. You don't see that done too much. I was so in love with her I thought it was a great idea. Thought it'd be just great to name someone after her."

"I can't imagine Marie with any other name."

"No. It's just that sometimes I can't say one without saying the other—I'm saying two names at once. It isn't always easy, is I guess what I'm saying. But then would I want it any other way? I guess I wouldn't."

"No?"

"Well, I'd take it easier, but I wouldn't take it different."

"We'd all take it easier if we could get it that way."

Mr. Hamilton smiled. "We can have some more coffee. That much is easy."

When they had finished the pot, Marie still hadn't returned. Their talk had finally dropped off. It was close to midnight, and despite his share of the coffee, Mr. Hamilton was noticeably flagging.

Abe said, "I should go. I'm keeping you up."

"You're welcome to stay. But let's go set in the living room, where it's more comfortable."

They watched television until very late, an old black-and-white movie. Finally "The Star Spangled Banner" played, the screen went blank, and a flat-line tone began to sound like a warning note. Abe turned the volume down. Mr. Hamilton had fallen asleep in his recliner and was snoring fitfully. Abe lay back on the couch and stared at the ceiling. Hearing the mosquito whine of the television with its volume off. The dim room suffused with the pale, steady blue from the screen.

Outside, the roads were quiet.

He had had many dreams this summer. The worst of them, and the most common, was the one in which the reality of his colossal mistake struck him. It had come to him the night after Jackie died and had recurred many times since. He was pressing back against that flood, trying to get the jack in place. But in the dream, it occurred to him he should work the wrench a while first. Get the jack almost ready, and only then—not before—try to set it in place. That way you weren't fighting the current the whole time, you weren't holding the jack underwater the whole time you were turning the wrench. You were less likely to drop it that way. In the dream, there was always this moment of profound relief: This is the way to do the thing, Abe; it's going to work this time. It was always for just a moment. Then he would know he was dreaming. Then he would wake, gut-sick and alone, to the truth.

But when he dreamed this time, it was different. The revelation was not as it had always been. What struck him now was unreal yet true, the strangest and simplest of realizations: She was already dead. Her eyes were gazing at him, just as he remembered them, and she spoke to him as any living person might. It was Jackie as he had always known her. But she was dead. What he was doing was performing a ritual. He was not trying to save her. No. There were some things you could not control, and some things you could. He could not save Jackie, but he could do something—something, by God, that mattered.

He dreamed that she was already dead, and he was praying for her with his hands.

Chapter 17

The Roof Fell Inn was just what you'd expect: a broken-down shack of a place with a carefully painted sign and carelessly swept floors. A savvy black bartender-bouncer who probably owned the place but wouldn't admit it. The beer came in cans and everything else was bottles and shot glasses. Eight tiny tables and ten chairs, so that some tables were crowded and some people had to stand. The place lay almost hidden on a back street off a run-down stretch of West Ninth in Little Rock. It was just the kind of place Roy would want to meet. A place where, given his personality, he was as likely to get killed as get drunk. He was the only white person in the bar until Marie showed up, and then she was the only woman.

"You came," he said, rising from his table. He seemed to keep rising. He was a big man. He'd spent his boyhood hauling hay and his adulthood jerking carcasses from the kill floor. A big man who had the jaundiced, loose-boned look of having once been even bigger. Wearing a baseball cap and a torn T-shirt. His bottom lip with its telltale swell of dipping tobacco.

Marie hugged him, stiffly. Roy had saved her a chair by propping his boots on it. She swiped a clod of dried mud from it and sat down.

"How you been?" he said. "You looking good."

"I'm okay. How about you?"

"I'm terrible."

She nodded.

"Hey, you want something to drink?"

"I think I need something, yeah."

He got the drink and came back. She was smoking a cigarette now. "Thought you was gonna quit them things," he said.

"I did."

They sat for a minute getting used to each other again. From time to time Roy leaned and picked up a soda can he kept by his chair and spat tobacco into it. He did it almost surreptitiously; it was a kind of politeness. Marie stubbed out her cigarette and lit another one.

"Who was that guy you left the party with?" he said.

"Just a friend."

"I sure as hell hope so. I hate to think you'd already be hooked up with somebody."

"Well, that's my business, Roy, not yours. Anyway, I'm not 'hooked up' with him. I'm not 'hooked up' with anybody."

"I hope not, Marie. I sure as hell hope not."

"Like I said, Roy," she said coldly.

He nodded, took a drink. "Okay. Well."

Marie waited.

"I was surprised to see you," he said. "We all thought you left town for good."

"I did. I've been in Hot Springs."

"I know that now. I never even knew you had family there. You never said nothing about it. In fact Tom never said nothing about it."

Marie took a drag on her cigarette and held it.

"Why is that, Marie?"

"Why is what?"

"Why didn't Tom ever say nothing about that?"

"Tom wasn't much of a talker, Roy," she said, exhaling smoke. "You know that."

"He'd have told me that much. I don't think he even knew, did he?"

"I'm not much of a talker, either, Roy."

"You got that right. Shit. You want to tell me why you just picked up and left like that? Without saying a word to no one?"

She shook her head. There was no use trying to explain to Roy what she hardly understood herself. It would be like trying to describe a highway map to someone who couldn't see it and didn't much care. After the funeral she had packed her things into Tom's car and driven away. Just driven away, before the day got dark. There was still food on her table some of her friends had brought over from the halfway house. There were dishes in the cupboards. She left Tom's clothes in the closet for his parents to go through. She left everything that had belonged to him or to his parents, except his car, which she needed. The front door of the house, which had never locked, she left wide open.

She'd driven to Hot Springs with a plan to start over. The idea had just come to her, had washed over her like relief. Now, with the summer behind her, she was ashamed for thinking you could do something like that. It didn't matter where you went, you could never drive far enough to start over, and she should have known that. Hot Springs was hardly an hour's drive from Little Rock, yet Marie had convinced herself that was enough.

Though she'd been determined not to think about him, there had been nights she'd lain awake wondering about Tom. It had seemed sometimes as if he hadn't really lived. She hadn't known him long. He'd worked at the cookie factory across the river with her halfway-house roommate, Shenisa, who introduced them. A steady type, hard-working, easy to amuse, with yellowish, catlike eyes and a slow voice. He had strong arms but skinny legs. He tended to smell sweet and lemony from the factory. Marie made him laugh. She had never thought of herself as a funny person, but she made Tom laugh. He always wanted to be touching her. He liked putting his arm over her shoulder, as if they were schoolkids. She could see him and hear him in her mind now, not as in life, but as in a filmstrip. A little shy, a little slow. She was much smarter than he was—she could always guess what he was about to say. And yet she hadn't known him. She didn't think she ever knew him. As she remembered him, he was hardly more substantial than a memory itself, a memory of a memory. She'd been a girl who married a memory.

After two months of late nights in Tom's car, Marie turned eighteen, and they eloped. She'd always wondered what she would do when she became an adult and was no longer at risk of the various juvenile institutions. She'd always thought she would drive off into a new life. As it turned out, when she came of age she was sleeping every night with an earnest man who wanted her to marry him, so that's what she did. They eloped because his parents, poor but with an acute sense of what was respectable, hadn't wanted them to marry. They were too young, his parents said, but Marie knew that she was the real reason for their disapproval. They didn't want their boy marrying this strange girl. She wasn't as polite as you'd expect. She had a filthy mouth, a shifty manner. She had no history. Was living in a halfway house, for God's sake.

But they got married anyway, and they moved into a rotting set of rooms that were part of an old, once-stately house. It was in an area of town that used to be lovely—and abutted a part of town that still was—but now housed the cast-offs and hard-ups, people like Marie, mixed in with a handful of hardworking, hopeful doomed, and a few elderly poor who were afraid of the blacks and the drunks and the would-be teenage hookers but hadn't the wherewithal to move away, and so kept their yards tidy and stayed in their houses after dark. Marie and Tom's own yard was lush with white-blooming dogwoods and yellow forsythia, but the sidewalk was crumbling and honeysuckle had completely overtaken their steps, even climbing halfway up the screen door. The windows were skewed. The front door had no lock. Tom insisted the lock parts were too complicated and he would buy an entirely new door once they had saved some money, so Marie rigged a broken padlock on a nail to make it look secure from a distance. Inside the house the wooden floorboards were warped and buckled; she had once set a rubber ball down by the sink, and they had watched it roll through the living room and out the front door. Tom had laughed and laughed.

Marie had laughed too—it was funny, after all, those pathetic floors—but even then, even alone in the house with Tom, she was embarrassed. She had married a fool—a good man, but a fool. She had leaped at the first option that appeared to her, had chosen simply because she was able to choose, and now she would regret it for the rest of her life, because she would never leave him. She wouldn't be like her mother. About that much, at least, she was determined. So she was embarrassed, and she was angry, but she didn't feel guilty. Not then. You couldn't feel guilty for not loving your husband if you stayed with him in spite of it. Or somebody could, she supposed, but not her. No, she didn't feel guilty until he died, when suddenly it was no longer acceptable not to have loved him. He was a good man who had deserved to be loved, and she hadn't loved him, and when she sat in front of someone who knew him, even someone like Roy, she was ashamed.

She smoked her cigarette, not looking at Roy. She'd abandoned a dead man, and his friends, quite rightly, had come back to haunt her.

Roy said, "Well, like I said, I been doing terrible."

"What's wrong?"

"Some of us has had to stick around and deal with this shit, Marie. Couldn't all of us just go running off to who knows where. To Hot Springs."

"Sorry, Roy."

"Look, I ain't blaming you. Let me get you another drink."

Men stared at her while Roy was away at the bar. Most of them turned away when he came back with the drink. He was a big, mean-looking son of a bitch. Marie didn't like him, but she was glad when he sat down with her again.

"You'll have to start helping me if we buy any more," Roy said. "Cost a whole paycheck for a damn rum and Coke."

"This is my last one. How much was it? I'll pay for it."

He shook his head and sipped his own, drinking from the side of his mouth opposite the tobacco. "What I want to know is, don't you even want to know if they caught the guy?"

"No."

"No?"

"I don't want to think about it, Roy."

"Well some of us has had to think about it."

"I know. You told me."

"Well?"

"Well what?"

"Ain't you gonna ask if they caught him?"

"If you want to tell me, why don't you just tell me."

He scowled. "Goddamnit, I don't understand what's wrong with you. He was your husband. Looks like you'd give a shit if the guy that killed him is walking around free as a jaybird."

"I don't see what difference it makes."

"You don't—I can't believe I'm hearing this."

"Roy, do you have something to say to me or not?"

"Hell, yes, I have something to say to you. The answer to the question is no, they ain't caught the guy yet. They ain't even looking for him."

She nodded and finished her drink. It was mostly Coke. It only smelled of rum.

"So that's it?" Roy asked. "You don't want to know the rest?"

"There's more?"

"You damn right there's more. They ain't caught the guy, but I found him."

The hair rose on the back of Marie's neck. It was as if she'd been shaken awake from a nightmare only to be told it was real. The world was real and familiar, but there was terror in it now. Roy had brought her back at last.

"You found him?"

"Me and Shawn and Philip found him. We started doing some investigating as soon as it happened, okay? Asking the neighbors what they seen and didn't see. Turns out there's some dope addict lives just a few doors down in his dead grandma's house."

"How do you know it's him?"

"That's just it. We don't know for sure. But we think it's him. The guy's a junkie, and he's got a rap. Sells shit at the pawns all the time, shit you know he couldn't afford to buy."

"Maybe it's his dead grandmother's stuff."

"Or it's stuff which he broke into and stole, Marie. What I want you to do is come with me tonight and take a look at the guy. You tell me if it's him or not."

"Roy, there's no way I'd recognize him."

"But you seen him."

"I saw him climbing out my window when I came in through the front door. I was scared to death."

"But you told the police what he looked like."

"Roy. They asked was he black; I said no, he's white. They said was his hair dark or light; I said dark. They said was I sure he wasn't black; I said yeah, I was sure. That was it. That was all I told them, that was all I knew."

"I still want you to take a look at him. Maybe it'll jog your memory."

"Roy, did you hear me? I don't want to go. I don't want to think about it. I—"

"Well, some of us has got to, Marie," he said angrily. "This is about justice, all right? Justice. And I ain't taking excuses. Now finish your drink and let's go."

"I'm finished."

"Then let's go."

She rode in silence as Roy drove. He wouldn't let her take her car. He said he didn't understand her mood and didn't trust her to follow him. He was right—she wouldn't have come. But he made her get into his truck, and so she sat in silence and listened to him rant. She had never liked Roy. She suspected Tom never liked him much, either. But they had grown up together, Tom said, and he was probably Roy's only friend. Shawn and Philip didn't count—they were not so much friends as trouble buddies. Tom had never trusted any of them alone with her.

Now she found herself riding in a truck with a stranger. She lit another cigarette and watched the city go by. She had lived in Little Rock a long time, but she didn't know the city. She'd never felt as if she lived here. She'd grown up here as if she'd been dropped off and was only waiting to be picked up again.

She'd been waiting a long time.

Roy drove them through several blocks of modest homes, well-kept yards and unbroken streetlights, to where the houses became shabbier and trash accumulated in the ditches. He turned onto the street where she used to live. The potholes jolted so badly her cigarette ash broke off and fell into her lap. She'd almost forgotten about the potholes. It had been springtime and raining every few days when she and Tom had moved out here, and the neighborhood kids were always skimming the potholes for tadpoles. She remembered that. It was springtime when she left, too, when she drove up this street in the relentless rain, swerving out of habit to avoid the potholes, headed the other way.

There was the house. A light was on inside, in the bedroom. Someone else was living there. There had been no blood to clean up. No mess. Tom had surprised the man, and the man had struck him with a baseball bat—Tom's own bat, a pocked and splintery old thing, which the man had just found in the closet. One swing and it was over, the police said. Tom had looked perfectly normal on the kitchen floor, his head and shoulders pressed against the bottom cabinet doors, as if he'd just lain down there, maybe to check the trap under the sink. Marie took one look and never looked again. Now someone else was living in the house. She could walk in there and go straight to the bedroom, to the bathroom, to the closet.

She knew the warped floorboards. She knew the house better than these people did. But they were living there now. Someone else was cooking dinners in the kitchen.

That was one thing she had liked. She had liked cooking dinner for him. It was one of those things you're supposed to do that she had actually done, that she did and did well, without feeling as though she were pretending. There had not been many of those things.

Roy went past the house and parked on the street. He pointed out the drug addict's house a few doors down. She remembered it—a breadbox of a place, a shotgun shack with a porch. There were lights on there too. She could see someone moving around in the front room.

"What are we going to do?"

"We're gonna look in the window, and you'll see if you recognize him."

"What if I do?"

He spat tobacco out his window and looked at her matter-of-factly. "Then me and Shawn and Philip is gonna tie him to this truck and drag the son of a bitch till you can't recognize him no more."

Marie's breath started coming short and uneven. "We can't just go up to his window."

"Yes, we can. Get out."

"Roy—"

"Get out of the truck. Right now, Marie. Get out of the goddamn truck."

She got out. It was cool outside. She hugged herself. She wasn't wearing a jacket. Her nose was running. She stayed close to the truck until Roy came around and took her arm. His fingers went all the way around.

"Now just stay calm," he said. "It's gonna be all right."

They walked through front yards to avoid walking in gravel. Under a mimosa tree, under a maple. There were no streetlights here. She looked fearfully at the houses. These people had been her neighbors. Most of the windows were black. It was getting very late. Roy tightened his grip and led her across the last yard to a side window in the man's house. She could hear music playing from somewhere inside. The curtains on the window were lacy and diaphanous, a grandmother's curtains. She could see through them into the living room.

"Can you see?" Roy whispered. "You need me to lift you up?"

She shook her head.

They waited for a long time. She could hear the music. Also a television. Her breath rose in wisps of vapor. In a few minutes she had the absurd feeling she had spent her entire life standing at this window, looking in. An absurd feeling, but familiar. Roy had let go her arm and stood crouched beside her. So long as she stood there, he was patient. He didn't keep asking if she saw the man. He simply waited.

Marie's mind wandered. She was stiff with tension and the cold, she was afraid to be here, and her mind went away. It couldn't stay at that window. It drifted, backward through the night, back to the squalid bar, talking to Roy there about the police, then back out Central Avenue in Hot Springs, past her father's bookstore, where she worked—where she once worked, she thought, where she once worked in a different life—the building quiet and empty now on a quiet and empty street, and back, back into her father's house, where it was warm, and there was a card game going, and coffee and cake, and children.

Then it came forward again. She thought about the police. Roy had said they couldn't find the man. She thought surely if they hadn't caught him yet, someday they would. Probably they had already arrested him for something else; they just didn't know what all he'd done. In her experience the police were more thorough, and criminals more reckless, than anyone gave either of them credit for. Her mother had always behaved as if you needn't worry about the police, but Marie had seen right through that. Her mother had been afraid of the police—it was just that she'd been more afraid of the Morton Wests. And here was Marie, despite all attempts, here she was, thinking the same things, preoccupied with the same things that had so concerned her mother. And where is your mother now? she asked herself derisively. Where is she now? Either dead or in jail.

She gave a startled gasp.

"You see him?" Roy whispered.

Dead or in jail. One or the other. Almost certainly one or the other. But your father said he'd have been notified. But he was never notified. But you never thought . . . It was one or the other. One or the other, and you might find her again, if you looked. If you wanted to look—actually cared, actually dared to look, you might find her.

"You see him?"

Marie shook her head, and just then the man walked past the window and all her nerves fired, all over her body. She ducked away instinctively, then peeked in again. He'd gone into the kitchen. She moved to the other side of the window and strained her neck. He was in the kitchen looking inside his refrigerator. Just living his life. He stood up with a pizza box and set it on the counter. It might have been him. He looked familiar. It could be she recognized him because he'd lived on her street. Maybe she had seen him go past her house, walking to the liquor store. He only lived a few doors down. He had been her neighbor. He turned toward her again. He did seem familiar. It might be him. She tried to picture him going out her window, a terrified look on his face. Marie had felt just what she saw on the man's face. Somewhere in the back of her mind she was thinking the look on the man's face was the look on her own. She tried to picture this man terrified. Scared out of his mind, scared of his entire life. It might be him. He walked past her with cold pizza in his hand, into his living room. Watching television at one in the morning.

She felt the certainty come over her at last. She had never felt such certainty.

"Well?" Roy whispered.

She put her hand gently on Roy's shoulder. It was solid, meaty. The T-shirt was thin with age, too thin for such a cool night. Roy crouched low, shorter now than Marie, and stared up at her with huge eyes in the scant light from the window. He looked like a boy who wanted everything in the world, good and bad alike. And he was only going to get half. He crouched there, hopeful and cold. He almost looked as if he were scared of her.

She shook her head and said, "It's not him."

Chapter 18

Before supper Abe's father offered a prayer that constituted more words in one sitting than he used to utter in a day. He gave thanks for this meal, for his wife, who had prepared it, for this opportunity to sit down together as a family, and for their guest, and he asked that the Lord bless this food to the nourishment of their bodies, and for strength to do His will. When he finished, he smiled and said, "And everybody says amen."

They all said amen, Abe and his mother and Marie, and his father passed the plates around. The last of the garden vegetables were finally in—everything was late this year—and so they had fried okra and thick slices of tomatoes, fried potatoes with mayonnaise, skillet corn and black-eyed peas and fresh-baked bread and butter. His father had gone fishing with the preacher and caught some big black bass and a beautiful walleye pike. He'd brought them home in a tub of lake water and cleaned them in the back yard, whistling in the cool evening air. He was red in the cheeks and had lost that gut-punched look of sickness about him. In fact, he'd begun to grow stout.

"Marie, we sure are glad to have you," he said, buttering his bread.

Marie smiled shyly.

"It's such a nice surprise," Abe's mother said, not for the first time. "We've heard so much about you."

"Well, I appreciate y'all letting me barge in on your supper."

"Now you just hush. Don't keep saying that. We are so pleased you could come."

"You're gonna have to listen to me spout a little, Marie," his father said. "No help for it. God's been good to us, and I've got to give Him the glory. I've got to make up for lost time."

"Speaking of which," Abe said, "Mom tells me you've quit smoking."

"Quit smoking, quit drinking, quit swearing, quit badmouthing, quit my bad attituding, quit skipping church, quit missing out on God's blessings. Quit everything but quitting, I guess, but only the good kind. One thing I'm not quitting on though is Jesus, son, because after all these years he's never quit on me."

Abe was shocked by this speech.

"He's turning into a preacher himself," his mother said.

"I noticed," Abe said, smiling a little. He was still careful around the man. He kept feeling the curtain would be yanked back, and he would find himself fixed in a gaze of contempt.

His father gave no sign of darkening, though. "Every one of us has got to say the good things, or they won't get said. If we don't do it ourselves, the scripture says the rocks will cry out for us. And I don't know about y'all, but I prefer to speak for myself and not let rocks do my speaking for me."

He laughed, showing his full spread of yellowed teeth, and Abe was so surprised that he laughed too. Beside him, Marie seemed frightened. She gulped her iced tea, and under the table Abe felt her hand tighten ever so slightly on his knee. He felt sorry for her, unprepared for this as she must be, but the pressure of her hand made him giddy nonetheless.

His mother said, "Will, you're gonna have to quit preaching long enough to put some food in your mouth." But she was clearly happy. She kept sneaking pleased looks at Abe.

"It's hard to quit talking, because my cup runneth over. But I know my mouth runneth over too. I'll shut up for a minute and let y'all talk. Marie, Abe says you're heading out of town for a while."

"Yes," she said. She brought both hands above the table. "Yes, sir."

"Where you headed?"

"Memphis."

"Is that a fact? What's in Memphis?"

"Dad," Abe said.

"I'm sorry. Am I being nosy? You don't have to tell me nothing you don't want to, girl."

"It's okay. I'm going to see my mother."

"Well, that's nice," his mother said.

"When you heading out?"

"I was actually on my way out of town tonight."

"Tonight! So we just caught you, then. Well, we'll be praying that the Lord will keep his hand on you as you travel."

At this, Marie brightened. "Thank you. I'd sure appreciate it."

"That's a long way to be driving," Abe's mother said. "I hate to think of you on the road by yourself at night."

"I'll be careful," Marie said.

"She'll be careful," Abe's father said. "And the Lord's gonna take care of the rest."

After supper Abe's father said, "Now Marie, I know you probably want to get started, but if you can just excuse me and Abe for a few short minutes before you go, I'd appreciate it. We've got something important to discuss."

"We do?" Abe said.

"Yes, indeed we do. But I'll keep it short and sweet."

"Take your time," Marie said. "I'll help with the dishes."

"You'll do no such thing," Abe's mother said. "But you can keep me company. Now put them down. Abe, tell her to put the plates down."

"Marie, put the plates down," he said. He went into the living room with his father, who turned and drew himself up and crossed his arms to speak seriously. Abe felt the old dread come over him.

"Abe, I don't want to keep your friend waiting, but I wanted to talk to you."

"All right."

"How you been, son?"

"I've been pretty good."

"Why don't you set down here with me? Let's set on the couch."

They sat down. Abe's dread lingered, though he could no longer guess what for. The television, he noticed, was blank and silent, the room comfortably lit by a bright new floor lamp in the corner. His father crossed his legs and looked at him.

"Now, your mother and I've been talking, and we want to help you out. We think you ought to go back to school, if you want to, or else do whatever it is your heart desires. The Lord has blessed us over the years, and I believe we can afford to help you a little if you'll just let us."

"I appreciate it, Dad. I don't think I really need any help."

"Well, I want you to think about it. I don't believe I ever felt I was in a position to help you before, son. But I was wrong. I was always in a position to help, and I just didn't know it. That was the devil keeping a cloud before my eyes, but the Lord has finally pulled it away."

"It's okay. I appreciate it."

"What I want you to think about is not so much us helping you but the fact that you got to accept some help now and then. We all need some help, every one of us. If Jesus didn't help me I don't know what I'd do. Well, I tell you what I'd do, I'd still be a miserable man, that's what. Married to a wonderful woman, with a good son, and just as miserable as miserable. What I'm saying is that if you aren't ready to accept help, what you're doing is denying someone else the blessing of giving."

"I don't want to deny anybody anything, Dad. I just don't think I need any help."

"Well, do you hear what I'm saying?"

"Yes, sir. I hear you and I appreciate it."

"You hear me saying that there's help here if you need it. And I don't mean you got to ask for it. It's right here. You just come and get it. What

God has given me to offer is yours to accept. You hear me? You need to just come to me and say, 'Give it up.' It's not a question of asking."

"Yes, sir. Thank you."

"All right?"

"I appreciate it. It means a lot."

"Well," his father said. He cleared his throat. "Well. I wanted to tell you something else too."

He waited.

"I'll make this quick, else I doubt I can get it out."

"All right."

"I want to tell you . . . well, you want to know how the Lord showed me I was on the wrong path? I'm gonna tell you. It was watching you walk away from this house after—well, after you'd been laid up here, after Jackie's funeral. That morning. I stood there thinking, There goes your only son, and you never got to know him at all, and now he's a man, and you might not ever will. Standing right there in the doorway. I won't ever forget it. Your mother was in the shower. She hadn't slept in three nights for worrying about you. It was still cool outside, and there was dew on the grass, and you were walking out to your truck. I'd just realized you weren't coming back to work with me. Not then or ever. And I was thinking how bad, how bad I must have disappointed you—"

"Jesus, Dad," Abe said, covering his eyes with his hand. He had braced himself, but not for this.

"Now be careful what you say, son," his father said gently.

"I'm sorry," he said. The reprimand helped to set him. He took a deep breath and lowered his hand. "Sorry."

"Well, you're right," his father said, sounding grateful, "I don't need to make a speech about it. I'm just telling you. If it wasn't for you I don't know if I'd ever have seen the difference. Between God's way and my way. But I did see it. Standing right there in the doorway watching you go. I did see it."

Abe nodded, his stomach churning. He thought he ought to say something; instead he only nodded. It was better than saying the wrong thing, which considering this unfamiliar territory would be easy to do. He nodded again, dumbly.

"Well. All right? I just felt like God wanted me to tell you that."

"Yes, sir. Okay."

"All right. Now I want you to think about what I said, about there being help here for you."

"I will."

"Do you know what you want to do?"

"I'm working on it."

"Well, I'm all ears. What's the plan?"

"Let me tell you next time. I don't want to keep Marie waiting."

"You're right. Good enough." They stood up. "Now don't you forget what I told you. Cause I meant every word."

"No, sir, I won't. I'm happy y'all are doing so well."

His father grinned and clapped a hand onto Abe's shoulder, shaking his head in pure wonder. "Thank you, son. I tell you what, it's nobody's doing but the Lord's." Then he hugged him, patting his back, and said, "God bless you, son. We're praying for you."

They drove out to his trailer, where Marie had left her car. She had shown up just as he was leaving and told him she was on her way out of town. It shook him to think he'd almost missed her. But he had finally promised his mother he'd come for supper, so he asked Marie to come along, and she seemed glad to be asked. Now, pulling up the long drive, he asked her if she might stay a few minutes. Laying her hand on his, she told him she'd never had any intention of leaving before morning.

A huge harvest moon, yellow and fat, had risen over the trees, and Abe made hot chocolate with cinnamon and brought out some blankets, and they sat on the porch looking up at it. They leaned against the trailer wall with their legs outstretched. Marie crossed her ankles over his. Lucky climbed into her lap, kneaded her belly for a minute, and settled down to sleep. It was quiet out, no birds or insects or even a breeze to scuttle the leaves. They sipped their hot chocolate.

She had come home that morning, almost a week ago now, and found him and her father asleep in the living room. She was prepared—she'd seen his truck in the driveway and had got herself together before she came inside. It seemed fateful to her that he would be here on this of all mornings. She'd already washed up in the bathroom and got out some eggs for breakfast before Abe heard her and woke up. He came to the kitchen and watched her from the doorway. In the living room her father snored. It was bright in the kitchen and dark outside—their reflections showed in the window over the sink.

"Good morning," she said.

"I'm glad you're home. Are you all right?"

"I'm fine. What are you doing here?"

"I came to apologize."

She faced him but didn't move from the stove. She stood with two eggs in her hand, reluctant to crack them. Finally she did. She turned from him and cracked them into a bowl and said, "What in the world would you be apologizing for?"

"Just everything. Anything that matters."

"You're a weird individual."

"What did Roy have to say?"

She turned to him again. "Okay, now I get it. Kylie told you. He got it from Roy and came running straight to you with the gossip."

"Don't be angry, Marie."

"With him or with you?"

He smiled. "I don't care if you're mad at Kylie or not."

"Well, I'm not. I'm not mad at anybody. I'm just tired and cranky. The whole damn world caught up with me last night."

He had wanted to take her in his arms. Not try to kiss her, not ask for anything, but just hold her. Instead he stood there in the doorway, put off by her manner. She was whipping up the eggs. Very brisk. Very matter-of-fact. She reached into the cabinet for a pan. Then he did what he had meant to do. He crossed the kitchen and stood behind her and put his hands on her shoulders. She froze.

"I'm sorry," he said.

"You don't have anything to be—"

"I'm just sorry, Marie," he said, turning her around. Her eyes were red and swollen from lack of sleep. She had washed off all her makeup, and her face was splotchy and dry. Her hair was tied back in a haphazard ponytail. He pulled her to him, and she didn't resist.

She laid her head against his chest and sighed. "I'm very, very cranky," she said. "I'm just warning you."

"Rough night?" he said, rubbing her back.

"You wouldn't believe."

She let him hold her, and after a while she pulled away, brushing staticky strands of hair back from her face. She retied her ponytail. "Plus I'm starved," she said. She turned back to the stove, but not before he saw the grateful look in her eyes. "I've got to eat."

She finished cooking and left Abe to dish up the food while she went to wake her father. Mr. Hamilton came in rubbing his eyes and walking with a slight stoop.

"What's wrong with your back?" Marie was asking him, following him into the kitchen.

"Just getting too old to sleep in chairs. I'll feel better once I get some food in me."

"Food won't help your back."

"Oh, you'd be surprised what food'll do. Morning, Abe. Whoa doggy, does that coffee smell good."

They had eaten breakfast together and Abe had left for work, and that evening he'd called her from a pay phone. She was all right, she said. She would come see him on Sunday. But it was only Saturday and he was leaving for supper at his parents' house when her Corolla came up the drive. And he had walked out to meet her and seen the suitcase in her back seat.

Now he said, "How did you find your mother?"

"I thought I told you."

"You said you called someone and got her address. Who did you call?"

"An old boyfriend of hers."

"Have you spoken to her yet?"

"No phone. Just the address."

He was thinking about that morning in the kitchen. How she had fixed breakfast, how she had let him hold her. Tying her ponytail again. He said, "Have you ever just broken down, Marie? I don't mean get angry—God knows I've seen you get angry. I mean have you ever just cried your eyes out to see if it made you feel any better?"

She took the question calmly. Somehow he'd known she would. "I got that out of my system way ahead of time," she said, "when I was real little. I got all cried out, I guess."

"I think your tear ducts are supposed to keep working your whole life."

"Anyway, I've found that smoking cigarettes does the job just as well."

"Plus it's better for you," he said, and she smiled. He wanted to ask when she was coming back, but he didn't know how to ask her the right way. He waited for her to tell him, but she didn't come to it. Finally he said, "When's your dad's wedding?"

"December. Christmas wedding."

"You going?"

"Maybe. Course he wants me to. They want me to be in it, even, but I don't know about that. He sure didn't want me to leave today. Said he wanted to fix me up in a trailer or an apartment or something."

"You're not going to let him?"

"Not quite yet," she said.

The moon had gone from creamy yellow to bright white. It gave off so much light Abe could see the tree trunks over by Simmons's house. He could see the tractor parked by the new barn, moonlight gleaming off the metal. Beside him, Marie's face showed clearly as if in lamplight. Her eyes shone with it.

"You want to know something funny?" she asked. "I just thought of it on the way out here. Maybe because I was thinking about my mom, or because I was headed out of the city. What it is, is, when I was real little, people sometimes used to ask my mom where we were from. And her answer to that was always, 'Oh, we're from out of town.' I heard that I don't know how many times. What I just remembered coming out here was that for a long time I thought out of town was a place. Like an actual place where my home was."

"Like a place in itself."

"Yes, like a country or something. Isn't it funny how you can do something like that?"

"Like thinking nowhere is somewhere?"

"Like . . . Yes," she said, and he could tell from her eyes that the way he'd said it had somehow robbed the thought of its pleasure.

"Maybe not funny, exactly," he said. "Maybe just interesting."

"Sometimes you irritate me for no good reason," she said.

"I didn't mean to."

"That's what I'm saying," she said. But she reached under the blanket and took his hand.

After a while they got too cold and went inside. Abe made more hot chocolate. When he came back from the kitchen he found Marie standing in the middle of the room where he had left her. Her arms hung at her sides.

"Didn't you want to sit down?" he said, nodding at the couch.

"Abe, I don't know when I'll come back."

He stood with the cups in his hand. "Okay."

"I may need to be gone for a while."

He nodded.

"I mean I want to come back, but I don't know when."

"Okay," he said. "I understand."

Now she was irritated. "What I want to say is will you be here, or what? When I come back."

"Will I be here?"

"Yes."

"As opposed to what?"

"As opposed to, I don't know, being gone. Being with somebody, or off doing something . . . I don't know as opposed to what. How am I supposed to know?"

"Whoa, take it easy. Yes, I'll be here."

"Then why didn't you just say so?"

He had to consider this. "Because I didn't know until just now," he said at last.

In the morning he watched her go. It was just getting gray outside. One of her taillights was out, but it was too late to tell her now. She disappeared down the long gravel drive. He watched until she was gone. Then he ducked through the barbed wire fence and crossed the pasture to Simmons's house. A thin white mist hung over the cattle pond, and the grass was wet. By the time he reached the barn his shoes were squeaking. Light showed through the crack beneath the barn door, and he heard Simmons in there with his cows. He went inside and told Simmons if he made a good enough offer, he would sell him the land.

Simmons didn't blink. He made a good offer.

"Sold," Abe said.

"One condition. You got to get that trailer off yourself."

When he came back from Hot Springs that evening he drove out to Repeat's place. Repeat had gone back to Fayetteville for his last semester, but Abe had heard he was in town for the weekend. The Owensville road wound past cow pastures and bottomland farms and heavy pine woods. The sky was deep blue above the deep green pines. He came over a hill and passed Kylie's place. Kylie was in the front yard bending over a length of white PVC pipe. After they offered him a full-fledged manager position at the Photo Stop in Little Rock, Kylie had decided not to go back to the university. He recognized Abe's truck on the road and waved. Abe waved and drove over a rise and up the cement drive to Repeat's house. It was his parents' house, but his parents had gotten into time-sharing and were always taking trips. Repeat tended to come home when they were gone.

There were potatoes scattered in the yard and lying here and there on the driveway. At first Abe thought they were crawdad mounds and the yard had gone to hell. But they were potatoes, all right. He drove over one and felt it give beneath his tire. Repeat was sitting inside the carport on a kitchen chair next to his Camaro. He'd replaced the lights on it. When he saw Abe pull up he disappeared into the house. He came back out a second later with a pellet gun and laid it on the ground by him and sat down again. He was fooling with a length of PVC pipe, poking down into it with a broken broom handle. A sack of potatoes lay behind his chair.

"Hey," Abe said, coming up. "You won't need the pellet gun."

"Good."

"What's that you're working on?"

"Kylie called this morning and said, 'Go outside, I got something to show you.' So I go outside and hear this thump from over the hill, and a couple seconds later this potato hits the ground not ten feet from where I'm standing."

"So that's what he was messing with."

"Is he out there right now? It's been every half hour or so, all day long. Good thing I pulled the car inside. He keeps calling me up to say, 'Did I hit you? Did I hit you?' Says it's called a spud gun. So I said, 'How the hell you doing that?' and you know Kylie, he told me every little thing about it. So I went into town and got all the shit I need to build one. I think I about got it figured out. It's basically just a cannon."

"Somebody could get killed."

"Maybe. I guess. You know what I think he did? I think he practiced at night, getting the angle right. Probably snuck over here to find where the potatoes hit and went back to adjust the angle and powder and whatnot. Otherwise I don't think he could have got so close on his first shot. You can't be accurate with these things."

There was a muffled poomp from the direction of Kylie's house, like the sound of a wine bottle uncorking. Repeat stood up. "Here comes another one, the son of a bitch." They looked out over the yard. Abe didn't see the potato fall, but he heard the thud and looked to see it bouncing high off the grass down by the ditch.

"That was a bad shot," Repeat said. "Most have been closer than that." He stepped out of the carport and licked a finger. "Maybe the wind caught that one." He went back to his pipe.

"Listen, I wanted to tell you that I forgive you."

Repeat gave him a look. "I didn't apologize."

"I know. I forgive you anyway."

"I don't want your damn forgiveness. I got nothing to be forgiven for."

"I think you do. Anyway, it's out there. You don't have to take it if you don't want it."

"Good, cause I don't want it. You can keep it. Is that all you came out here for?"

"No. I need you to help me do some stuff."

"What kind of stuff?"

"You think you can come back down here next weekend?"

"What kind of stuff?"

"Will you help me or not?"

"Shit, you know I'll help you do any damn thing you want. What kind of stuff?"

"Moving some boxes and hauling that trailer off and a few other things."

Inside the house, the phone rang.

"Let it ring, the son of a bitch." Repeat bit a length of string off a spool, then spat, picking fibers from his tongue. "So you're finally getting the hell out of there. That's smart. But I don't think you can get that trailer to go anywhere. Best just burn that thing to the ground and call it a day."

"It'll haul."

"I doubt it."

"It will."

"And are you getting anybody else to help out, or is it just gonna be me doing all this shit?"

"There'll be plenty of help. I'm fixing to go ask Kylie."

"Yeah? Do me a favor when you go over there. Tell him his shots are way off target. Tell him he's shooting way too short. That ought to buy me a little time. I know he's gonna try and keep me awake all night with potatoes on my roof."

"So can you come down next weekend?"

"I'll come down Friday night. Now I got something to ask you. You gonna pay for the lights on my car?"

"No, those lights were your apology."

"Wrong. I told you I'm not apologizing."

"That's fine. I did it for you."

"That's bullshit. You're gonna pay for them."

"Repeat, I accept your apology."

"Goddamnit, Pitt, you better shut the hell up."

"Or you'll turn your fritter gun on me."

"Spud gun. And I will, as soon as I get the goddamn thing to work. The powder keeps spilling out of the little fuse hole."

"Put a little caulk or something right there."

"Caulk."

"Or pipe dope or something."

Repeat went over to a shelf and rummaged around. They heard another poomp from over the hill. "Damn," he said, "that was a fast reload. He must be trying to impress you."

This time Abe saw it drop. It streaked into view right in front of them and went through the windshield of his truck. It sounded just like a car wreck. They leaped back, covering their heads. When they looked again they saw a web of cracks radiating from the potato hole.

"Whoa!" Repeat said.

"Good God."

Repeat bent over in a sort of soundless laugh, slapping his hip. They went to the truck and looked inside. There were shivers of glass everywhere. The potato had split over the steering wheel. One half was in the floor, and the other sat neatly in the driver's seat. Abe turned and scowled at the hill.

"Good luck getting him to pay for that," Repeat said.

Chapter 19

It was Joe she'd called, and that itself was a gamble. She'd thought he would be gone—dead or gone or in jail. In fact he was still living in Mena and had his number listed. She'd called him late at night after her father had gone to bed.

"Marie?" he'd said. He sounded hopeful, even penitent, until she explained who she was. Then he sounded amazed. "Oh—Little Marie? For Christ's sake, girl, what happened to you? I can't believe this shit. Is it really you? After all th—"

"I'm looking for my mother, Joe."

"Honey, that makes two of us. That makes—Hey, you ought to come out here and visit me, girl. We can have a few drinks and maybe think of something together."

"Then you don't know where she is."

"Well, I ain't saying that, I ain't saying that. But me and her kind of had a falling out a while back. Some years back. Kind of a argument. She ain't called me in a long, long time."

"What about Uncle Brady? Would he know?"

"Old Brady the bootlegger? Shit, honey, he's been dead for years. Started going deaf so he shot hisself. He was blind as a bat, you know. Now, listen—"

"You don't have any idea?"

"Well, let me think," he said. "Let me think. But hell, Marie, how the hell are you? I can't believe it's you. You're a grown-up woman now. Christ. Christ, I can't believe it. You don't know how good it is to hear from you, honey. I can't tell you how bad things—"

"Joe. I'm not looking for you. I'm looking for my mother."

"Well, don't get pissed, girl. Don't get pissed. Let me think." She could picture him standing in a dark, cluttered room, circling confusedly about, entwining himself in the phone cord. He was alone, she knew that by the way he was talking. After a moment he said, "I'm just so excited to hear from you, you know? I mean, it's so goddamn weird, after all this time—"

She continued to push him, in a way that, as a girl, she would never have guessed she would be able to push him—though even then she'd known he could be pushed, not by her mother, perhaps, but by the right person, in the right way. Now she happened to be that person; she knew the right way. Eventually he came up with the Memphis address. He read it to her from the back of an old envelope he'd saved. "But I doubt she's still there, honey. That just used to be a place she'd go, you know? One of her stopover places. Listen here, though, what you ought to do is come out here and visit me, girl. We could—"

She hung up and began to pack. That was Friday, after days of arguing with her father, who did not want to see her go, especially not alone. He'd even offered to help her. She'd insisted no decent soul would ask that of him, and if he pressed her on it he must be implying her indecency. In the end she worried him down, took advantage of his obliging nature, garnered his anxious blessing. She'd hated to argue with him—she could have just left. But it was the least she could do, giving him this opportunity to bless her departure. It was his first such opportunity.

The sun had been up for hours when Marie found the dilapidated apartment complex in Memphis—a derelict and time-struck place, with buildings from the thirties and cars from the sixties and a fenced-in satellite dish behind the office. Erase any two parts of the picture and you had a different era. The sun had been up for hours, yet the day was darkly overcast and so chilly it hurt her knuckles to knock on the door. You could tell the apartment numbers quite plainly by the discolorations on the doors where fiberglass numerals had once been glued.

"Number fifteen," she murmured as she knocked, and checked her watch to know the time. "Number fifteen, at nine-twenty in the morning."

An old man, rib-skinny and drunk, answered the door wearing only his pants. He was carrying a portable television around the dark apartment with him, trailing cord. He said he couldn't remember if her mother had lived there or not. He wouldn't know, he said. He'd only been living there himself since his grandson got married. He wanted to show her pictures. Instead she talked him out of some change for the pay phone and left him standing in the doorway with the television under his arm. It was cold enough to see your breath, and he stood there, shirtless and hunkered, watching her go.

She found a cafeteria before she found a pay phone, and she stopped for a cup of coffee, toast and eggs. Abe had offered her breakfast, but she'd wanted to get moving. That was hours ago. Hours had seemed to matter then. Borrowing a phone book from the manager—who gave it to her reluctantly, worried about getting it back—she went through it as she ate her breakfast, marking all the likely government numbers, then ripped out the pertinent pages and took them with her.

After she'd exhausted her change at the pay phone, she could see this might take a while. That in fact, in the end, it might not be possible. But she had always suspected this. She'd never had much faith in the apartment address. If she had, she doubted she could have knocked on the door so casually, without bracing herself for the sight of her mother's face. She had braced herself for disappointment, not for her mother. How could you brace for your mother? Still, she'd hoped for some hint of her real whereabouts—what city, what prison, what cemetery or newspaper account. There hadn't been any such thing. It didn't matter. Here she was, in Memphis—out here in her own life, looking. Maybe normal people didn't have to go looking for their mothers. It didn't matter. Here she was.

Her father had given her money and made her promise to call if she needed more, but when she called him she didn't want it to be for money, so to keep solvent she found a job as a waitress and took a motel room for sixteen dollars a night. She could eat for free at the diner where she worked. She had no interest in entertainments. The can of roach poison with which she nightly sprayed down the legs of her bed she swiped from the motel's utility closet. Her only expenses were long-distance charges and gas.

During the day she worked, and made her phone calls, and went through newspapers at the public library. In her motel room at night she listened to the wind shaking the window in its frame, thinking maybe the shoddy walls would fold up and blow away. As a girl she had always fancied that the wind was caused by the turning of the earth—like the air on your face when you ride with the windows down. Now as she drifted to sleep she sometimes imagined the wind blowing away everything in the city, even the lights. They would blur, then streak, then snuff themselves into oblivion. In the morning the world would be swept clean.

When she awoke it was usually quiet outside, the early morning still and gray, with its chill air seeping in around the window frame. She would be hungry and have sleep residue crusted in her eyelashes; the toilet seat would be shockingly cold; her back and feet would be sore. Still it was early enough to get coffee from the pot in the lobby before it was burned. She could drink a cup, bathe, brush her teeth, and be sitting wide awake at the phone with her revised list of numbers when the government finally opened for business.

Every county official, she learned, has a different way of answering the question. Sometimes they make a point of correcting you when you tell them you believe your mother is in prison. It's called a correctional facility, they'll tell you, as if that will be better; you'll mind it less if your mother's in a correctional facility. Mostly, though, the answer is a telephone number—even the helpful ones answer with a telephone number, and the number is not the one you need. You can sense the helpful ones right away; these are the ones you have to push. You can have clerks in three states digging through files and calling you back if you know how to ask them right.

Marie would learn how to ask them right.

But when she had finished her day shift at the diner, and when the library and all the government offices had closed, there was nothing to do. She hadn't met anyone here. She hadn't wanted to. This was her life, but it was not where she lived. It was her life, and an inexpert and inefficient life besides, and she knew it and didn't care. But when she had finished her day shift and the clerks and officials had all gone home, Marie's motel was dreary and she had nowhere to go. So she would get into her car and go nowhere, at least nowhere in particular.

She quickly discovered that outside Memphis, just over the state line, you can drive out the Hosea Highway in the bottomland and see the rice and the late-blooming white cotton and the picked-over bean fields gone rusty and leafless. You can take the highway out till it's nothing but back roads and the long, flat horizon still blushed from the sunset, and sometimes come upon a flock of snow geese in a wet fallow field, watch them lift from the mud like a fog, clamorous and hovering, see them settle again in the rearview when you've passed. There are broken-down barns there and gutted frame houses and abandoned shanties overcome with kudzu and creeper. And even in the yards of the living, old tire swings hang from swamp oak boughs, cradling mosquito water, the rubber rotting out. You can drive down the cypress swamp cutoff and see the herons stalking the ruddy cypress knees and the dead tupelo leaves on the skin of dead water. Then you can take another back road and hit the Hosea Highway again, and what looked like nightfall under the cypress is just flat evening on the empty highway.

Marie spent hours behind the wheel driving the highways. You're young, her father had told her. Don't forget, you're still young. Sometimes when she was driving she did feel young. Sometimes it was the wrong way to feel. Nevertheless she would drive, watching the highway lines strip past until the day went dark and the evening wind picked up. Even when it turned cold, she kept her windows rolled down—she would crank up the heater and roll down the windows for that highway breeze, and the dotted lines would slide past. And there were days, but only some days, when it felt like home.

Chapter 20

The shower was a small one, nothing fancy, but brand new. The water pressure was terrific. He let it drum on his back a long time. Red-skinned and clammy, he got out and toweled off and shaved and brushed his teeth. Steam hung about the ceiling like an indoor weather system, but his feet were cold on the tile floor, and the old porcelain sink was cold to the touch too. The bathroom smelled of fresh paint.

Back in his room he folded up the cot and stood it against the wall next to the antique safe. His notebook lay on the floor where he'd left it under the cot the night before. He read over what he'd written, found a few lines worth keeping, and put the notebook away. Opened his wardrobe, a good-sized piece of oak furniture he'd bought at a secondhand store. He'd found space for it in the room by moving the filing cabinets around. He dressed in jeans and boots and a flannel shirt and jacket, closed the door to the room and locked it. The building wasn't zoned for residential use. It wouldn't do to have customers peek in and guess he was living there.

He put on some coffee and made himself a cheese sandwich, heating it in the microwave. The store was chilly and dim. He held the sandwich against his nose for warmth, took a bite, and went down the aisle to the display window. It was early on a clear autumn morning. Central Avenue was deserted. In the gray light the buildings had a grainy look. He watched the chimney swifts flitting about the eaves of a building across the street. The way they moved en masse, they seemed to bloom from the eaves only to collapse inward again, like a filmstrip run forward then reversed. Bloom and collapse, bloom and collapse, a shifting cloud of birds. Lucky came padding down the aisle from no telling where and leaped onto the window ledge to watch. He made a chittering meow, wanting to get at them.

Abe poured his coffee into a thermos and went back to his truck, parked in the tiny warehouse among the stacked boxes of books. Mr. Hamilton had gone with him to a book fair in Little Rock to help him fill some gaps in the stock, and now several new boxes waited on the pallets. He was slowly going through them. A few hours a day, off and on, adding books to the inventory, pricing them, shelving them. It was slow going because he was always stopping to read passages or write something down. It didn't matter. The days seemed spectacularly long—even when there were customers, even when he was busy. Sometimes he lost hours in conversation with the people who came in, offering them coffee, pulling up the reading chairs. On days when Mr. Hamilton came to visit, bringing lunch for the two of them, they might spend the better part of the afternoon talking. There were all these things to make a day short, yet the days were never short.

One of the stacks had a precarious lean to it. He put down his coffee and shifted a few of the boxes. Mr. Hamilton had insisted on scouting books with him at the book fair, saying he wanted the business to be in good shape when Abe took over. He'd seemed almost embarrassed about the place. It wasn't exactly a cash cow, he apologized. He'd done well enough over the years, but then again he was just one man, and maybe it wasn't quite enough to raise a family on. Abe said he'd cross that bridge when he came to it. For now it was free rent and a split of the meager profits. In time he might save enough money to buy the place, if he wanted it. Then he would see.

As he drove along the empty morning street, he regarded with interest the renovations being made on Bathhouse Row. Many of the once-forsaken storefronts and bathhouses were being restored. New roofs, new windows, new paint on the brick. Slight changes appeared almost every morning; he liked to look for them. Today it was the simplest thing—they'd stripped off an old awning on the Fordyce—but it was the grandest effect yet. Take away a patch of rotted fabric and a few aluminum struts, and suddenly the whole building looms larger. Open-faced and somehow sturdier, a new thing entirely. Abe hoped they wouldn't put up another awning, though probably they would. This town was crazy for awnings.

He took Park Avenue out to Highway 5, was just rolling into Lockers Creek when the sun broke over the trees and made him squint. He drove out Merrill Road to Simmons's land, went up the old drive, and parked his truck in the spot where his trailer once had stood. The ground still bore the marks of its years on the property.

In spite of everyone's doubts, the trailer had, in fact, hauled. He'd had a good deal of help: Roberto, Kylie, Repeat, and also Bill Smith, who had secured the truck to haul it and did the hauling himself. Laine, heavy with her twins, brought pink lemonade and sugar cookies. For her own snack she'd brought plums, but she finished the plums and had some of the cookies as well. Bill kept calling her "Big Mama," and Laine would lose her breath scolding him. When Abe asked after her mother, Laine thanked him and said they would just have to see. They were counting the days till the babies came, she said, and hoping for a pardon from God. But thank you for asking, she repeated; said he couldn't know how many people didn't care to ask. And in the next breath said now why didn't he get started on those cookies so she wouldn't be tempted to finish them all by herself?

The men ate all of Laine's cookies and downed several cups of lemonade before they started. Once they did, it took them no time. In half an hour they'd cleared out the bedroom and the kitchen. Bill, poking his head into the other bedroom, saw the phone on the floor against the wall, but Abe caught him before he went in, told him to leave it and help with the couch instead. As they came down off the porch with the couch, Abe sent Repeat inside for the phone. Then they set the couch down and waited.

He had expected the floor, if it gave at all, to split in the middle like a wet paper bag. Instead it ripped along the seam of the far wall, one side falling to the ground with a metallic groan and bang, like an unhitched tailgate. They heard Repeat yelp from inside, and suddenly he was outside, tumbling down the canted floor and spilling into the yard. He came up quickly, with grass in his hair and grass stains on the knees of his jeans, and one of his forearms scraped. He saw the phone beside him and kicked it out into the yard.

"Good God Almighty!" Laine cried, shrieking with laughter and losing her breath again.

"Man, it looked like the house just spit you out," Kylie said. "Like something out of 'The Amityville Horror' or something."

"You all right?" Abe asked.

Repeat inspected his forearm and said, "I thought it was a goddamn earthquake or something."

"You should've seen it," Kylie said. "You should've seen the look on your face. Did you see the look on his face?" he asked Roberto, who only nodded carelessly and smiled a little. He had sat down to rest on the couch and looked as if he might be falling asleep.

"You're not hurt or anything?" Abe asked.

"Scraped up is all."

"You sure?"

"Like you give two hoots in hell."

"Well, I'm just glad you're okay."

"Like you give two hoots."

They had ripped out the rest of the bedroom floor and shored up the remaining weak spots, and in two hours the lot was clear. Now it was just a bare patch of land. The utility poles along the gravel driveway seemed like a mistake, or else the product of some lunatic vision of powering an empty field. Eventually Simmons would take his fence out to the road, opening up another half-acre of pasture for his cows.

Abe got out of the truck. The air was sharp and had the tangy odor of distant smoke. Someone burning leaves or trash. A touch of frost lay on the grass. Slipping through the barbed-wire fence, he started across the pasture. The cows were standing around the cattle pond, and Dollar stood among them as though he were part of the herd. Abe called out to him as he headed for the barn. He was a dumb old horse, splashing across the pond shallows and nosing through the cows when he could have taken a much easier path along the fence. Abe grinned to see him come. Dollar quick-walked part of the way, then knickered and broke into a trot when Abe opened the barn door. He came in right behind Abe and poked his head into the empty feed bucket. His back was matted with dirt from rolling on the ground, his flanks dripping from the pond.

"You're filthy," Abe said, patting his neck. Dust flew out. Dollar nuzzled his boot and checked the feed bucket again. Abe scooped feed into it. He brushed and saddled him while he ate. As a young horse Dollar used to blow up when Abe saddled him. He was less trouble now. He still blew up a little, out of long habit, but Abe just waited until he gave out—he was too old to hold it for long—then tightened the straps. He was a bribeable horse, too, and Abe wasn't above bribing him. He gave him a handful of alfalfa, feeling the rubbery wet lips tickling his palm, and after the alfalfa Dollar took the bit without complaint.

He led him out through the pasture gate and hauled himself up into the saddle. He'd been riding a week now and had lost most of the soreness in his legs and groin. Since he'd come down from the roofs he didn't even notice his knees anymore. The saddle creaked comfortably beneath him as he settled. They walked out to the road. The sun was taking the edge off the morning cool. You could still see the moon like a wisp of cirrus in the brightening sky, and the breeze was almost imperceptible, carrying that sweet tang of smoke in it. He felt Dollar warming up against the inside of his legs as they crossed the ditch and moved along the gravel shoulder of the road. Mostly he just let him walk. He was getting to be a very old horse.

He'd had no luck finding the others. Enemy had been sold again, bought by a man who moved to Texas and left no trace. Bluebell, who had been old when Abe sold her, old and gentle, had been carted off to a glue factory. The man who bought her had told Abe she was for his young daughter, who was crazy for horses, but in less than a year he had sold her to the factory. Abe found this out from the man himself. He didn't have a phone yet and had driven out to the man's house in Jessieville to ask about her. Caught off guard, the man hedged, lied, and finally told him. Abe turned and left him standing in the doorway.

"I don't have to explain myself to you," the man called after him. "You got no right taking that attitude with me."

He said nothing, only kept walking. The man got angry and followed him out into the driveway. "You come out here to my house, on my land, and give me that attitude—"

Abe turned then and came toward him, and the man hustled back to his doorway. By the time he started his truck the man was swearing at him from the yard again. This time he didn't look back.

He had found Dollar, though. He'd sold Dollar and Enemy together because they liked each other, but the man who bought Enemy again and then moved to Texas hadn't wanted Dollar, so he was still around, still with the people Abe had sold him to at the outset. Abe drove out to their place near Blowout Mountain, where they kept a wooded plot of land for their horses. A good place for roaming, but poor pasture. They were happy to sell Dollar back. They said horses were no way to make money anymore. They were trying to get into emus.

"You wouldn't want to buy any of the rest of them, would you?" the woman asked him, standing at the gate and holding Dollar by the halter. Her name was Jean Thomas, but she introduced herself as Thomas. She was rough-looking—lean and gray and fidgety—and matter-of-fact. She did all the talking while her husband stood around smoking and looking into the distance. Every now and then her husband would nod.

"If you're into horses," the woman continued, "you couldn't do better than some of these here." She jerked her thumb out over the near field, where a half dozen mulish animals nosed the dirt, looking for grass. A pretty sorry lot, a bunch of spavined and swaybacked old creatures. The dregs. Dollar, whose whinny of happy recognition had broken Abe's heart, had been one of them. Abe felt like buying them all out of pity.

"No, just this one," he said.

"We could make you a deal."

"I'm not looking to buy any more."

"Well, if you only want one, we got better horses than this one. I even got another quarter horse if that's what you're looking for. Now that's a good horse, isn't it, Larry?"

Her husband nodded.

"This one hasn't got much left," she said. "He kind of sagged out."

"Well, this is the one I want to buy."

"Tell you what, you buy the other one for a fair price, we'll throw this one in extra. You can't hardly refuse."

"I'm only buying this one."

She spat, not meanly, and shook her head. "Well, suit yourself. You're not gonna get much out of him, though."

"That's all right," Abe said.

"Well," she said, "suit yourself."

They walked out Fork Road. There were no cars, and the morning was quiet except for the clop of Dollar's hooves in the gravel. On a good flat stretch Abe prodded him into a trot, then a canter. The air was cold against his face. His eyes watered. Dollar puffed and snorted beneath him, heating up.

"Whoa," Abe said, reining him in. "Whoa now." He took him down to a walk again. Dollar snorted and tossed his head. He wanted to canter more, he was feeling lively, but Abe didn't want to press him.

"Don't be so ambitious," he said.

They turned onto Merrill Road, passing Gem Ridgeway's house. A row of pumpkins had fattened up along one side of her garden plot. In the high branches of a yellow-leafed hickory in the side yard, a squirrel was gnawing away at a nut, the shavings ticking down onto the roof. Abe took Dollar farther up the road and let him rest a minute at the top of the rise, where the road turned to gravel and you could see cleared farmland for half a mile before the trees took over and the hills rose up. He turned back. When they passed the house again, Gem Ridgeway was standing on her back step, squinting out at the day.

"Morning, Mrs. Ridgeway," he called out. He reined up.

"Hello?"

She peered toward him. Her glasses hung on a cord around her neck, and she lifted them now and put them on. She gave a cheerful smile. "Well, hello. That's a pretty horse you got there."

"I guess you ought to know. You recognize him?"

She moved carefully down the steps. She wore only her housecoat and slippers, but didn't seem to mind the cold. "Do I what?" she said, coming to the fence. Her slippers left faint tracks on the frosty grass.

"Do you recognize the horse?"

"No, I don't reckon I do. Should I know him?"

"It's Dollar. You sold him to me years ago."

"Well, I'm just as sorry—," she said apologetically. She shook her head. "I just don't rightly remember you. What's your name again, honey?"

It took him a moment. He sat the horse while she looked up at him. "Abe Pittenger, ma'am. You don't remember me?"

"Oh, goodness, Abe, you wouldn't believe what all I've forgot. My daughter says I had one of them brain things happen to me. Something happened to my brain? It might have been a stroke, I don't know. She keeps telling me, but I can't never remember."

"When was this?" He was surprised he hadn't heard.

"I don't rightly remember. Not too long ago."

"Well, are you all right?"

"I'm doing just fine, thank you. It's just that I don't remember some things. I had a stroke, you know."

"I'm sorry to hear it. You look good, though."

"Oh, I get taken good care of," she said. "My daughter Jana's staying with me and we're having us a fine time. She keeps me company, helps me with my garden . . ." She trailed off, turning to gaze at the garden.

"Your pumpkins have sure come along."

"Oh, yes," she said, turning back. "I got me a whole mess of them. You ought to take one with you when you go."

She bent and picked some grass and held it through the fence for Dollar. She didn't seem shaky or even much changed. Dollar sniffed the grass, then lipped it from her palm. Mrs. Ridgeway smiled. "I've always been partial to quarter horses."

"They're good horses."

Clapping her hands together to get the grass off, she said, "Now, why don't you come in and set down for a minute. I just took some muffins out of the oven. You like muffins, don't you?"

"Yes, ma'am."

"Well, come on in and get you some."

"I don't want to interrupt your morning."

"I sure wished you would."

He shifted in the saddle. The leather creaked satisfyingly beneath him. "All righty," he said. "I appreciate it."

The muffins were indeed hot. He slathered them with butter and let them dissolve sweetly in his mouth. They took tea with the muffins, putting honey in the tea. Mrs. Ridgeway spooned the honey from a mason jar that had a chunk of the comb in it. All of it spread on a checkerboard oilcloth on her kitchen table. They sat at the table with the light off, the room soft with sunlight from the sink window.

"These are good," he said. "I can't remember the last time I had such good muffins."

"Have you another one. I got too many."

"I better stop."

Mrs. Ridgeway rose and went to the refrigerator and stood looking in. "You don't want anything else?"

"I'm fine, thank you, ma'am."

She peered into the refrigerator for a long time. “I think I want me some cherries,” she said finally. She came to the table with a bowl of maraschino cherries and two spoons. Then she poured two glasses full of cold water from a jug in the refrigerator and brought them too.

“You like this kind of cherries?” she said. “I wished you’d have some with me.”

There was a stirring from elsewhere in the house. Mrs. Ridgeway’s daughter appeared in the kitchen doorway. She wore a housecoat and slippers, and except for her pudginess and black-dyed hair, she looked like her mother. Her hair was tied into a smart little bun the size and shape of a spool of string. She looked at Abe with surprise.

“Oh,” she said. “I didn’t know we had company. Y’all setting in here with the light off?”

“Morning, Mrs. Thompson,” Abe said.

Mrs. Ridgeway said, “Jana, this young man is—I’m sorry, honey, I forgot your name.”

“It’s all right, Mama, we know Abe Pittenger, remember? He bought some horses from you a long time ago. His mother works for Sam at the store.”

“Well, of course,” Mrs. Ridgeway said, uncertainly, and as if he had just walked into the room she said, “What have you been doing with yourself, Abe?”

“Those muffins smell good,” Mrs. Thompson said.

“I run a bookstore in Hot Springs.”

“Well, praise the Lord, that is just wonderful. Just wonderful. Did you hear that, Jana? This young man runs a bookstore in Hot Springs.”

Mrs. Thompson, buttering herself a muffin, smiled at him. “I *heard* about that, Abe. Good for you. You taking the day off? I guess if you’re running the show you can close up whenever you like.”

“No, I’ve got to be heading back here in a minute. I just came out to feed my horse and walk him around a little.”

“Your horse outside?”

“Yes, ma’am. Tied to your mailbox. I hope that’s all right.”

She went to the window. “Well, I’ll be.”

Mrs. Ridgeway said, “I wished you’d eat some cherries. Lord knows I can’t eat them all.”

He did. He finished his muffin and drank off his tea, and then he ate the cherries. They were very cold from the refrigerator, and the water was cold too. Soon his teeth hurt from the cold. Mrs. Thompson had gone to get dressed, and he and Gem Ridgeway sat at the table alone. She smiled at him and kept urging him to eat. It was bright in the kitchen now; Mrs.

Thompson had turned on the light when she came in. With a thoughtful look on her face, still chewing her cherries, Mrs. Ridgeway rose and switched off the light and came back to the table. Abe smiled and nodded. It tickled him the way she liked her cherries and just the sunlight coming in. The maraschino cherries and the cold, cold water. He had to give it a rest for a minute, that water, until his teeth stopped aching. Stretching out his legs, he sat back in his chair to listen. It was still early, and Mrs. Ridgeway was telling him again about her pumpkins—did he see them outside?—about her pumpkins, and her plans for pie.

About the Author

T. ROWETSEEL NOTNERT

A native of Hot Springs, Arkansas, Trenton Lee Stewart has worked as a residential counselor in a youth home for troubled girls, a residence assistant for men with mental disabilities, a lost and found clerk, a rural roustabout video deliveryman, a reference assistant in the art and music department of a public library, and a professor of writing and literature. He has had stories in many literary venues, including *The Georgia Review*, *Shenandoah*, *The Virginia Quarterly Review*, *New England Review*, and *The Chattahoochee Review*. He is the author of a forthcoming children's novel, *The Mysterious Benedict Society* (Little, Brown Books for Young Readers). He lives in Cincinnati, Ohio, with his wife and two sons.